SECRETLY PUCKING

ROSEMARY A JOHNS

BEING PUCKED © copyright 2024 Rosemary A Johns

www.rosemaryajohns.com

Copyright notice: All rights reserved under the International and Pan-American Copyright Conventions. No part of this book may be reproduced or transmitted in any form or by any means, electronic or mechanical, including photocopying, recording, or by any information storage and retrieval system, without permission in writing from the publisher.

This is a work of fiction. Names, places, characters and incidents are either the product of the author's imagination or are used fictitiously, and any resemblance to any actual persons, living or dead, organizations, events or locales is entirely coincidental.

Warning: the unauthorized reproduction or distribution of this copyrighted work is illegal. Criminal copyright infringement, including infringement without monetary gain, is investigated by the FBI and is punishable by up to 5 years in prison and a fine of $250,000.

Fantasy Rebel Limited

❦ Created with Vellum

BAY REBELS

I'm the coach's daughter and I'm in love with a gorgeous NHL player...well, three players.

Now, I'm PR Director to a whole team of ice hockey rebels. My hardest job? To manage three beautiful misfits.

The captain, D'Angelo, is intimidatingly hot, grumpy, and my first love from college.

The star player, Shay, has a smile like sunshine, mesmerizing gray eyes, and a body that makes my breath catch. Plus, he has a twin, the sweetly protective, tattooed Eden, who's hiding a heart-wrenching secret.

They're obsessed, and I'm falling just as hard.

Yet our new lives, rising careers, *everything*, depends on them winning this season.

If I'm caught secretly pucking these hockey players, will our hearts be broken?

BOOKS IN THE REBEL VERSE

ALL BOOKS ARE STANDALONE SERIES

<u>PACK BONDS OMEGAVERSE</u>

REBEL & HER KNIGHTS
EMBER & HER MARSHALS
ANGEL & HER CHAMPIONS
JEWEL & HER KINGS
PUCK & HER BLADES
MERCY & HER DEVILS
CANDY & HER SAINTS

<u>CONTEMPORARY STANDALONE</u>

DARLING MADNESS, LOST BOYS OF NEVER
ELITE
ONE SECRET RULE

BAY REBELS, ICE HOCKEY ROMANCE

BEING PUCKED
SECRETLY PUCKING
PUCKING ROAD TRIP

REBEL ACADEMY - WICKEDLY CHARMED COMPLETE SERIES

COMPLETE BOX SET
CRAVE
CRUSH
CURSE

REBEL WEREWOLVES - COMPLETE SERIES

COMPLETE BOX SET
ONLY PERFECT OMEGAS
ONLY PRETTY BETAS
ONLY PROTECTOR ALPHAS

REBEL: HOUSE OF FAE - COMPLETE

HOUSE OF FAE

REBEL GODS - COMPLETE SERIES

BAD LOKI
BAD HADES
BAD RA

REBEL DEMONS - COMPLETE SERIES

MY DEMON OF FIRE
MY DEMON OF AIR
MY DEMON OF EARTH
MY DEMON OF WATER

REBEL ANGELS - COMPLETE SERIES

COMPLETE SERIES BOX SET BOOKS 1-5
VAMPIRE HUNTRESS
VAMPIRE PRINCESS
VAMPIRE DEVIL
VAMPIRE MAGE
VAMPIRE GOD

REBEL VAMPIRES - COMPLETE SERIES

COMPLETE SERIES BOX SET BOOKS 1-3
BLOOD DRAGONS
BLOOD SHACKLES
BLOOD RENEGADES
STANDALONE: BLOOD GODS

THE SHADOWMATES SERIES - COMPLETE

WOLF TRIALS
WOLF FATES

AUDIO BOOKS

LISTEN HERE...

BOOKS IN THE OXFORD VERSE

RECOMMENDED READING ORDER

OXFORD MAGIC KITTEN MYSTERIES
COMPLETE SERIES

A FAMILIAR MURDER
A FAMILIAR CURSE
A FAMILIAR HEX
A FAMILIAR BREW
A FAMILIAR GHOST
A FAMILIAR SPELL
A FAMILIAR YULE
A FAMILIAR BRIDE

OXFORD PARANORMAL BOOK CLUB
COMPLETE SERIES

BITING MR. DARCY
HEXING MERLIN

MERCHANDISE, SIGNED BOOKS, AND LIMITED EDITIONS

A GUIDE TO DATING HOCKEY PLAYERS

Robyn's Number One Rule: Go on a date with a hockey player every week.

Top three reasons:

1. *They look gorgeous in suits, are creative with their sticks, and are mind-blowing at teamwork in bed.*
2. *They'll burn down the world to protect you against your stalker NHL ex-husband and press.*
3. *The Prince twins.*

But never forget that it all began with D'Angelo...

CHAPTER ONE

Captain's Hall, Freedom

obyn

"Are you writing a smut book along with those hockey stickmen drawings?" I struggle to sit up on the bed, pushing my tangled wavy, flame-red hair out of my emerald eyes.

The gorgeous man who's sprawling in the covers next to me, as if he's not doodling sexy stickmen on a blank page, shoots me a cocky smile.

Of course he does because he's Jude fucking D'Angelo.

Captain of the Bay Rebels NHL hockey team, my best

friend from college, and the man who I'm desperately in love with.

Also, a grumpy dick.

But you can't have everything.

D'Angelo's bedroom is large and overlooks the pasture at the back of Captain's Hall ranch. The drapes are open. The pale morning light streams over the stunning antique silver bed, which is lavish and elegant.

The floors are carpeted and white like the walls. The entire far wall is a mirrored walk-in closet.

"Are you judging my first attempt to write romance?" D'Angelo replies, coolly. "Being trolled to my face by my own girlfriend will at least thicken my skin to cope with such a tough industry. But still, harsh."

"More wondering why you're illustrating that romance with pictures of…is that doodle holding a tentacle dildo?" I blush.

D'Angelo looks like he's struggling not to laugh. "Can't you tell? I even drew on the suckers."

"How did you find out about my vibrator?" I splutter.

I curse that I was ever convinced into reading monster romance by my bestie, Neve.

It doesn't matter how interesting the double or even *triple* peens are in those books. Useful as they'd be (and they would, so it's a shame that evolution can't keep up), they're not worth the embarrassment factor that owning certain *items* has caused me.

"You're dating three men. We talk. And if you want to try that tentacle thing out for real," D'Angelo's lips twitch, "use it on our good boy Shay."

My mind short circuits at *that* image.

D'Angelo's six foot three with olive skin and piercing ice blue eyes that are so frosty they make me shiver. Raven curls frame his strong face, as he tips his head forward to concentrate on drawing boobs onto the stick person who's caught between three others like she's having a seriously good time.

With my vibrator.

Is it anatomically possible though?

I need to test it out, right?

Purely for science.

I'm a committed truth seeker.

D'Angelo's dressed in an immaculate designer navy suit and waistcoat with the sleeves rolled back to reveal his strong forearms, while I'm naked with sticky skin and puffy eyes.

Allergies suck.

"Isn't it problematic to represent the woman like that?" I glance significantly down at my breasts, or as I call them in my head, *my bouncy crumb catchers*. Don't judge. "She looks like she has two watermelons with cherries on the top stuck onto her."

"Don't insult your beautiful breasts that are, admittedly, fruit shaped." D'Angelo looks affronted. "Can't you see the drawing's curly hair? It's clearly meant to be you. I must be hungry because now I think about it, her hair also looks like spaghetti. But I never claimed to be Leonardo Da Vinci."

"More like Picasso."

"Or Leonardo DiCaprio. I do pull off a tuxedo well like

he does. It was rather hard, principessa, to subtly capture your klutzy charm and love for monster romance in a simple drawing."

"You made a good effort." I huff. "Klutzy charm, huh?"

"Have you counted how many times a day you fall over? Do you think that we should take out extra insurance?"

Damn, he knows me too well.

Plus, it's a good point. Especially with the Prince twins in the mix, who get into more accidents than I do.

When I reach over and trace the scruff of stubble on D'Angelo's chin, his gaze softens.

I know that it must be love, when he can look at me like I'm the most beautiful woman in the world, when I'm a hot mess with smudged mascara around my eyes like a panda.

One who's allergic to bamboo.

Of course, it's D'Angelo's fault that I look like this.

Although my other two boyfriends, Shay and Eden, must take an equal portion of the blame.

My brow furrows. "Where are Shay and Eden? I'm sure that our terrible twins collapsed in your bed with us last night."

"They did," D'Angelo replies. "Shay was wrapped around you like a limpet. I refuse to tell either of you how cute you looked."

Except, he just has.

I sniff the air, letting out a delighted sigh at the delicious smell of coffee. "Eden's cooking breakfast for us."

"He always gets up at the crack of dawn. He should

have been in the military, especially since he's a gym bunny. Can I help it, if I look better lazing in bed, draped over a piano, or with a cocktail in my hand? Shay's taking a shower, which means that he could be quite literally *minutes*. Do you think that he has a button that plays him at slow-motion?"

"I've already inspected him thoroughly, and if he does, then it's not on the outside."

"Internal search it is then, which sounded sexier and less prison strip search in my head."

I laugh. "Shay enjoys playing the sexy prisoner at my mercy. He'd probably love that roleplay."

I've woken up each morning for the last few weeks thankful for these three men, who each meet a different need in me, in the same way that I do for them.

I'm lucky to have found them on my return to my hometown of Freedom.

I never knew that I could experience this type of love, but after a marriage that trapped me and made me feel owned, it's liberating and empowering.

I've never felt so seen.

Adored.

The guys kept me up almost all night celebrating the news that D'Angelo and Shay had been selected for the NHL Bay Rebels team for the new season.

And by *celebrating*, I mean the type of fun that my illustrated self is having in D'Angelo's drawing.

Perhaps, you can have everything.

At least, I'm able to have this polyamorous relationship with three men, with whom I've been falling in love.

Shay Prince is the golden retriever new star of the team who brought me to life with his sunniness. Plus, he's loved equally by D'Angelo, fitting between us in a way that none of us knew that we needed but now can't live without.

And Eden is Shay's introverted and tattooed twin, who's lost his career through injury but spends his time caring for and protecting all of us. He's also going to be D'Angelo's PA.

After my divorce from the star NHL player, Talon Wilder, who abused and cheated on me, I never intended to be around hockey again.

I schemed never to date another hockey player.

Certainly, not to fall in love with one.

But here I am: PR Director in the Bay Rebels and secretly dating two players and their PA.

Robyn McKenna, twenty-seven.

Successful businesswoman.

Independent.

But serious player magnet.

Yet a bone-deep joy and contentment warms me. I'm exactly where I want to be in this found family, and shit, I've never experienced that before.

Except, D'Angelo is writing his *romance* in the book, which I created to try and strengthen my resolve *against* these gorgeous men.

My eyes narrow. I wriggle closer to D'Angelo, squinting against the light at the thin, pretty book that D'Angelo is balancing on his knee.

At first glance, it looks like a hockey strategy book in

arctic blue and white with lines, arrows, and arcs on the front.

There's also a crude puck and hockey stick.

I know because I drew those.

I also wrote the scrawled words, which are along the top:

A GUIDE TO AVOID DATING HOCKEY PLAYERS

The **AVOID** is scratched out.

During my yearlong nightmare divorce proceedings with Wilder, I created it as a guide, which explains the reasons that I should never, *ever* date a hockey player again.

It includes photographs and press clippings.

There's an entire chapter on D'Angelo, including photographs of him pole dancing.

My favorite is the one of him wearing a horse riding outfit like he's Darcy in *Pride and Prejudice* by Jane Austen. The outfit's so tight that my mouth becomes dry every time I see it, along with the way that his knuckles are white, as he clasps a riding crop against his thigh.

The Guide was more positive (according to my therapist), than cutting out the ass on all of Wilder's hockey pants or using his bank account to sponsor a dung beetle to be named after him at a local zoo for $25,000.

Wait, I did those too.

Yet I'm back in Freedom now.

This is my second chance with D'Angelo.

We were both played by the narcissistic Wilder. He kept us apart for years.

All that time, D'Angelo never stopped loving me.

"The stickmen who *you* drew of *me*," D'Angelo drawls, "weren't having such fun."

I blush, remembering that I'd drawn them having hockey sticks used in creative but painful ways on them.

And their asses.

Okay, valid.

"What are they doing with *those* hockey sticks?" I point at the page.

D'Angelo gives a wicked grin. "They're not sticks."

Oh, hell.

I snatch back my hand.

My blush deepens. "So, this is meant to represent all of us then. Are they secretly pucking too?"

I take a deep breath of D'Angelo's masculine scent, as I tangle my legs over his.

D'Angelo arches his brow. "Are you questioning my artistic ability? The one with the big, puppy like smile is Shay. The serious one with the big dick vibes is Eden. You're obvious because you're the one being worshiped in the middle. And I'm the one in charge with my hands on my hips."

"Impressive." I tap the page. "You have high hopes about my flexibility. Can non gymnasts really bend like this?"

D'Angelo's eyes flash. "Let's see, principessa."

He drops the book onto my lap, which protects my modesty.

It's actually a shock to realize that I have any modesty left, after the wild and earth shattering night that I've just spent with my three lovers.

D'Angelo twists to me.

He wraps his hand in my hair, dragging my head back and exposing my throat.

I swallow.

My breath hitches. Anticipation thrums through me.

When D'Angelo tugs my hair, it sends delicious tingles through my scalp.

D'Angelo skirts the Guide with his free hand, along the sensitive skin of my bare thigh.

"Stay still," he commands.

I whine.

I bite my lip, struggling not to move.

Then D'Angelo edges his hand underneath the book, and I moan. His fingers explore between my thighs, teasing and featherlight.

He draws me into a kiss, which is passionate and drugging.

I lose myself in it.

D'Angelo is possessive, stealing these moments alone with me, even though we're in a relationship with two other men.

He pulls back with a final, lingering kiss. My eyes flutter open.

D'Angelo's gaze is intense as it meets mine. "We agreed that today would be a fresh start. In a week, the hockey season begins. This is a new relationship for us all. So, why not add tips and positions to your dating Guide?"

"Like the Hockey Kamasutra."

He chuckles. "Was that a compliment, cara mia? I

remember everything that you say, you know. I hoard compliments, since our love language appears to be…"

"Banter?"

"It works for us. Anyway, I may be an asshole but I'm also a trained dom. We've negotiated contracts, limits, and safe words. Repeat them."

"Green, yellow, and red. And I'm so, *so* green"

"Talon was a selfish, useless lover. He made you feel like your desires and fantasies didn't matter. He didn't respect your consent, hard and soft limits, or boundaries. That's never going to happen to you again. I intend to take this week before the season starts to show you that your needs will always be met from now on. You'll never be made to feel anything but pleasure, as long as you're mine." D'Angelo loosens his hold on my hair, tucking a strand behind my ear. "It will never be a case of *if* you come but how many times."

I draw in a sharp breath.

Wilder took his pleasure but never bothered about making me feel good. I spent years thinking that if I didn't come in a certain way or time, then it was my body that was faulty or broken.

Yet my time with these men has allowed me to take back the sensations and power over my own body.

There's nothing wrong with me.

There never was.

Wilder was the problem.

D'Angelo pushes my head down by the back of my neck to face the Guide on my lap.

I can't forget for a second what's happening beneath

that book with his caressing fingers, even though D'Angelo's acting calm like he's not even touching me.

I struggle not to hump my hips.

My breathing is ragged.

"Read," D'Angelo whispers.

Is he serious?

"Eden's the bookworm," I protest. "Shall we call him in? He can read, while you and I concentrate on what your wicked fingers—"

"Now," D'Angelo commands, frostily.

I swallow, struggling to focus on the words that he's written above the naughty drawings.

Robyn's Number One Rule: Go on a date with a hockey player every week.

Top three reasons:

1. *They look gorgeous in suits, are creative with their sticks, and are mind-blowing at teamwork in bed.*
2. *They'll burn down the world to protect you against your stalker NHL ex-husband and press.*
3. *The Prince twins.*

But never forget that it all began with D'Angelo...

"You used my glitter pens to write this," I say in shock.

"You like glitter pens." D'Angelo smirks. "What section in this book did you use them on again…? I remember now. The one where you numbered and bullet pointed my negative characteristics."

I knew that he wouldn't let that go so easily.

Damn.

"I could list some right now," I pant.

"Don't worry. I memorized that part."

"Your name is underlined."

"Yes."

"With a wavy line. Three times."

D'Angelo's thumb ventures lower. I'm so fucking wet.

Pleasure winds through me but at a lazy pace.

D'Angelo is deliberately edging me.

Still, if this is revenge served kinky, then I'm tempted to get in trouble more often.

"You rewrote my original wording. Is it satire?" I demand.

D'Angelo runs his hand through his silky curls. "Hmm, let me think…"

He looks like a sinful fallen angel.

I can never tell whether he's a devil pretending to be an angel, or an angel pretending to be a devil.

That's a fun PR image problem for me to deal with this season.

Suddenly, my eyes widen. "Is this your way of adding a rule that we need to go on dates? A way of asking me out?"

"Is the answer yes? We need to get to know each other. I feel like I've been married to you, since I met you nine years ago, principessa. I know that with our arrangement, I can't legally marry you. It wouldn't be fair for one of us to get a public and legal recognition like that, while the others are left on the outside in the shadows. But it's how it feels in my heart." How can D'Angelo say such sweetly romantic things, when he's doing such dirty things under the cover of the Guide? "Yet I want to treat Shay and you to a date. We should catch up on the stages of this relationship that we missed out on. Eden deserves the same. This is his first relationship, and he needs the time to experience the wonderful sides of that."

Now I'm thinking that D'Angelo's definitely an angel.

I smile. "I may be a rebel, but this is one rule that I'll follow. Three men and three dates. Although, you've set the bar high. *Creative with your stick? Mind-blowing at teamwork in bed?*"

D'Angelo growls.

Whoops, I've poked the bear.

"Is that a challenge? Because I can call the twins in here…"

"Is that meant to be a threat or a reward?"

I don't even question the *burn down the world to protect me* part.

I know that it's true.

All three men would give up their hockey, careers, and reputations to protect each other as well.

"I love you, principessa." D'Angelo presses his lips to mine, and I melt against him. "Okay?"

He's checking in with me.

When I nod, he assesses me carefully for a moment, giving me time to process the overwhelming pleasure that's coiling through me.

Then he presses his cheek to mine in an achingly intimate way. His silky curls brush my skin.

I reach to run my hands up and down his back, wrinkling the soft fabric of his suit.

His muscles are corded and hard, however, beneath the material.

Then he noses down to my ear, licking across its shell, before pressing a kiss to the skin behind it.

It's the most sensitive place on my body.

That's cheating.

When I almost levitate off the bed, D'Angelo chuckles.

I'm close.

"I'm going to…" I warn.

Casually, D'Angelo pulls his hand out from under the book and rests it on my thigh.

My eyes widen in outrage. "What are you doing?"

"Take your time." D'Angelo sits back, stopping touching me altogether. "There's no rush. Trust me, if you want mind-blowing, then this is how we get you there."

In shock, his words startle me out of the pleasurable haze.

Shit, I'm in trouble. Because there *is* a rush.

How could I have forgotten the meeting this morning?

"Dad!" I blurt in panic.

D'Angelo reels back from me, bristling like a disgruntled cat. "*Yellow.* Don't call me dad or daddy, especially not in bed. With my past, it has too many bad associations. We talked about honorifics. Now, you're always welcome to call me *Sir…*"

I redden.

My pussy is still throbbing. I'm pushing my thighs

together, feeling like I have one foot over a cliff, I'm so close to coming.

And I've just called out my dad's name in bed.

Ouch.

Cringing, I wave my hands around like somehow I can erase D'Angelo's memory of the last few minutes. "I didn't mean—"

D'Angelo crosses his arms. "There's no need to be defensive. These things slip out in the heat of passion. It's not surprising with your daddy issues."

Daddy issues...?

I sit up onto my knees. "This is not about my — alleged — daddy issues. I wasn't trying to call *you* my daddy."

D'Angelo wrinkles his nose. "Principessa, are you telling me it's better that when you're in my arms, you called out your *real* dad's name?"

Ehm, no...?

My cheeks flame. "Okay, so it's worse. But only because I suddenly thought of him."

Dad, Austin McKenna, was a pro hockey player who won the Stanley Cup. Then he was caught in a scandal that tore apart his life and haunted my brother, Cody, and me all our lives.

Dad took up coaching the Bay Rebel's new team to redeem himself and offer the same chance to his team of misfits.

D'Angelo's gaze is icy, as he adjusts his cuff links ritualistically three times. "Uh-huh. I think that this has highlighted how much we really do need to practice dating. I suppose that it's not surprising since we spent so much time over the last month being stalked, at the ice rink, or simply fighting to be together. I didn't think that the problem was as dire as this."

"I mean," I scramble to explain, "your words about us not being in a rush made me think of Dad. Look, I'd be better at explaining this, maybe, if you hadn't driven me into a frustrated puddle of…"

"Desire?"

I nod, clenching my hands on my lap and with great self-discipline not inching them to push myself flying over the cliff to ecstasy. "There is a rush. I'm late. I forgot in the midst of the celebrations and then…you…this morning…that I have a last minute meeting with Dad about Bay Rebels' PR."

D'Angelo's expression suddenly becomes serious. "And our secret relationship, I suppose."

My pleasure simmers down, reduced by worry about the upcoming meeting.

My expression becomes grim. "The twins and you. Dad wants me to continue to manage you twenty-four seven isolated here in Captain's Hall to ensure that your careers are protected against press scrutiny. The next week will be intense and dangerous. And Dad's pet peeve is tardiness. If I'm late, we'll all be in trouble."

CHAPTER TWO

Captain's Hall, Freedom

obyn

"WE'RE GOING to be in trouble, and you're only remembering it now?" D'Angelo taps his thigh three times, before stopping himself with a grimace. "When's this meeting with coach? He hates people being late. I know because he normally blames *me*. Also, because I'm normally the one who's late."

"He summoned me last night." I frantically glance around D'Angelo's bedroom for my iPhone.

The light is brighter now through the drapes. It's like an accusation against my lazy ass.

I know that D'Angelo carried my phone up here last night. He's organized like that and hates leaving mess around the rest of the house.

To be fair, it's normally my empty chocolate wrappers, Eden's tea cups, or Shay's...everything else.

Where's my phone?

I scramble off the bed. Goosebumps chill my skin.

"*Summoned?*" D'Angelo snorts. "You sound like a demon. A forgetful one. It's not like you. You're normally on top of this stuff."

Is that how he sees me?

So, this is what being blinded by love means.

"Have we met? Hello, I'm Robyn, Hot Mess Queen." Frustrated with myself, I huff out a breath. "Unfortunately, being human, when my lovers keep me up all night with kinky sex, I oversleep the next morning."

I didn't know that until I met these three men.

"Then it seems that this time I am to blame." D'Angelo rests his hands behind his head smugly, and his shirt tightens in a distracting way over his muscled chest. "As someone who's used to pulling all-nighters at bars and clubs and functioning the next day on no sleep, we'll have to practice this to up your tolerance for debauchery."

"Are you corrupting me?"

"I already have, cara mia."

I shiver. "Stop using your sinful Lucifer voice on me, or I'll never get out of your bed. Then we will be fucked and not in a good way. What time is it?"

D'Angelo looks at his elegant Rolex watch with a flourish. "It's only seven thirty."

Shit.

"*Only...?*" I clench my hands. "The meeting's at the arena at nine thirty."

"That gives us time. An entire two hours."

I stop my panicked glancing around. "What do you mean *us?*"

D'Angelo swivels around on the bed, slinging his long legs over the side. "You didn't think that I'd let you go into a meeting with coach by yourself, did you? We're in this together. I'm the team's captain. If coach wants you to continue to handle us and kick our asses—"

"*Manage* you," I correct.

"Then I want to be in on that. I'm mentoring Shay and becoming Eden's boss. This is our family. I'm going to be in control of that."

D'Angelo always needs to be in control. If Dad let him, he'd be bossing around the staff at Bay Rebels too, including its billionaire owner.

"My phone...?" I ask.

"Bedside table, top drawer. You abandoned it, and it slipped down the side of the couch. But there's no panic. Shay should be out of the shower." D'Angelo flashes a seductive grin. "Why don't you take a shower, then I can join you?"

I drag open the bedside table and pull out my phone.

Everyone else feels like their lost kid has been found, when they find their lost iPhone, right?

The panic is real.

"It's okay for you because you simply shrug yourself

into a suit like it's a glove. But it takes me time to, well, still look like a hot mess. A power dressed one."

D'Angelo's arctic blue gaze is piercing. "You're always beautiful to me, principessa."

"Sweet but also, not helpful."

Unlocking the phone, I steel myself, before glancing down at the messages.

Two missed already from **THE GRILL SERGEANT**.

I decided to change his name from **DAD** in my contacts.

With our position increasingly in the spotlight and heightened security awareness, it means that if someone finds or steals my phone, they won't be able to pretend to him that I've been kidnapped.

They also won't know who he is under my contacts.

THE GRILL SERGEANT sums up both Dad's BBQ and interrogation skills.

He actually uses both skill sets as a coach. Sometimes at the same time in his infamous team cookouts at his lake house.

D'Angelo pales. "How bad is it?"

I sink onto the bed. "Bad."

THE GRILL SERGEANT (05:47): Are you up? Don't forget this morning. Do NOT be late

I wince, clenching my jaw.

I force myself to look at the second message.

THE GRILL SERGEANT (06:01): Reply, unless you're dead. Reply, EVEN IF YOU'RE DEAD. Zombies can text too

Then the third.

THE GRILL SERGEANT (06:16): If J, S, and E screw up this season, their asses are on the line

Horrified, I stare at the last two messages.

Dad sent them over an hour ago.

How can I pull off that I haven't forgotten the meeting now?

Plus, how is Dad so certain that zombies can text?

When the phone vibrates, I throw it onto the pillow like it's a snake, which is about to bite me.

D'Angelo raises an unimpressed eyebrow. "Unless he messaged to say that we're being executed before practice today, then you should read that."

I gingerly pick up the phone and glance at it.

THE GRILL SERGEANT (07:37): You better not still be in bed *unamused face emoji*

I eep.

Parental third eye.

Terrifying.

I jump up from the bed, clutching the phone to my chest, just to be careful.

I truly hope that Dad doesn't develop the all-seeing parental third eye because if he ever saw the way that I writhed with the twins' tongues on my pussy, while D'Angelo dirty talked and commanded us all like a devil master of ceremonies, then I don't think that any of us would recover from the trauma.

I hurriedly type a response.

RH (07:38): I'm up. I'll be at the meeting *thumbs up*

I groan.

Did I really just add a thumbs up? The most passive aggressive of emojis?

Now my message has a sarcastic edge to it.

Too late.

"I'm getting dressed." I start toward the door. "I sent Dad a thumbs up. What the hell is wrong with me? We truly had better not be late now."

"We won't." D'Angelo fluidly rises to his feet, smoothing down his jacket. "Remember that as intense as the next few weeks will be, nothing matters more than you to me, principessa. This love that we're exploring with Shay is too important to me to risk. I won't let coach bully us into a panic. This meeting was meant to keep us on our toes. It wasn't prearranged beyond coach's out of the blue text. He knew that we'd be celebrating getting into the team and likely up all night."

I hesitate with my fingers around the cool handle; my feet sink into the plush carpeting. "Huh, you're right. Dad's ruthless. You know, with a gruff heart of gold underneath. It's exactly the sort of dickish move that he'd pull."

D'Angelo runs his hands through his curls, pushing them into place. "I can be a dick as well. I fight to protect those who I love. I'll do that to give our relationship time to breathe."

I understand what he's saying. But it's going to be hard.

"Breathe in secret," I say, "at least for the time being. Press interest is at an all-time high on the Bay Rebels, and we're trying to hide that the coach's daughter is sleeping with both the Captain, the star player, and his recently injured twin."

"You were always a high achiever. Although, I'm sleeping with the star player as well." D'Angelo strolls to me, grasping my hand. "One of the reasons that I suggested these dates is because we're at different stages. I've known that I've loved you for years and I've been openly bisexual for a while. But our Shay's only just found his place between us both. He's started his journey, discovering about himself and his sexuality. The press could tear him apart, before he's ready." D'Angelo's gaze becomes fierce. "I won't allow that. And Eden's a virgin. He hasn't been in any relationship before."

"Then Eden and I will need to go slower. Eden hadn't kissed anyone before me. I want to explore things at his speed. He's introverted but he's so intense that I can feel as connected with him after an hour, as spending an entire day with his brother."

"But then, Shay's like a roller coaster, both thrilling and fun to ride." D'Angelo raises my hand and presses his cool lips to the back of my knuckles. "Do you think that we should get Eden a cat?"

"You can't put the image into my head of riding Shay and then innocently talk about gifting Eden a pet. By the way, he'd fucking love a cat."

D'Angelo hums. "I'll think about it. Now, you should at least eat some breakfast, before we go to the meeting. Eden's taken the time to prepare it, and *his* love language is taking care of us, especially by feeding us."

I fling open the door, preparing to march into the corridor.

My nose scrunches up at the heavenly scent of coffee, which is wafting through the house from the kitchen. "Fuck, I feel like I'm about to have my first coffeegasm of the day. Come on then, what are you waiting for?"

I peer impatiently over my shoulder at D'Angelo.

Doesn't he realize, even after everything that I've said, that we're in a rush?

D'Angelo's looking like he's trying hard not to laugh, as he leans in the doorway. "I love the idea of you eating breakfast naked each day, but you may want to put on some clothes first."

CHAPTER THREE

Captain's Hall, Freedom

den

My brother, Shay, shakes his wet tumble of golden hair like a dog, before grinning at me. "What's the problem, Dee? Jude's not here to spank me for spraying water over his marble floors."

The kitchen is flooded with warm light through the wide, bay window behind the oak table, which looks out over the forested mountains. The table is laid for a delicious breakfast that I was up at dawn to bake.

I've added bowls of chopped fruit because Robyn loves fresh fruit, as well as sweet muffins and pastries for Shay.

I'm not sure what D'Angelo will eat. He often skips breakfast.

He's too busy sleeping, drinking, or brooding.

He does a lot of brooding.

It's hard to bake with my arm in a sling.

But an obstacle is simply something to overcome.

The vast kitchen's counters are marble. The high ceilings are vaulted with beams.

The entire bottom floor of our adoptive parents' tiny house back home in England could fit into this single room.

I'm beginning to get used to this luxury. Shay isn't.

I don't think that he ever will.

It freaks him out more than he'll admit. We know each other, however, in a way that no one else can. He doesn't need to say it out loud.

I deliberately don't react to Shay getting water on the floor. It's always best with my twin.

I'm happy because Shay's in a good mood.

I'm always happy when he is.

If he needs to burn off some of his energy after the excitement of earning his place in the Bay Rebels, then I'll let him.

He's achieved his dream. He's made the NHL.

Without me.

I force that thought not to show on my face. I'm good at that — hiding my feelings.

I don't understand most of my tangled feelings anyway. Emotions are confusing.

My twin is identical to me, but our personalities are so different.

Shay's golden hair tumbles over his sharp cheekbones.

His eyes are winter gray. They're flecked with rich gold. His skin is ice-white, and his nails are painted black.

I frown, when I notice that Shay's nails are chipped. I'll paint them later for him. He can never do them properly for himself without smudging them because he jitters around like an excitable dog, whenever a thought pops into his head.

He says that I'm more like an inscrutable cat.

Of course, Shay also doesn't have tattoos, unlike me. I've taken ownership over my body. The ink helped me, when college became overwhelming.

I may be falling in love but I'll never be possessed by anyone again.

I'm not a thing.

I'm not.

I'm a man.

The ink helps to remind me of that, protecting me, every time that I run my fingers along it.

Black roses wind up both of my forearms with spiky thorns. A phoenix blazes across my back.

Yet I managed to tell Robyn some of the story behind the tattoos. I can talk to her more than I can any other woman.

I've been numb for as long as I can remember, but she makes me feel things that I never have before.

I can't lose that.

I want to feel more…and more…and fucking *everything* that I can.

I want to experience the same intensity of life that my twin does.

The thin red t-shirt that Shay threw on is clinging to his muscled chest because he's damp from his shower, and as always with my brother, his jeans are skin-tight.

But then, so's my black leather trousers and gray t-shirt.

Shay's athletic with broad shoulders but he's only six feet tall. Our college coach gave us both such shit, warning us that we'd never be tall enough to play in the NHL.

Joke's on him, huh?

I hope that Shay becomes the best player in the NHL. Then everyone who hurt and bullied him will see that he's worthy of their respect.

The best revenge is to move on and become successful.

Shay convinced me that it wasn't to burn down the college ice rink.

I still think my way would have worked.

Shay's sprawled on the bench, precariously fidgeting with the vase of orange roses.

I clench my jaw, trying not to rush to stop him.

It'd be the third broken vase this week. But sometimes, Shay needs to break things.

Perhaps, because we're broken.

Since we traveled from England to America, I'm struggling to learn that I can't protect him from everything.

Or himself.

Just like he hasn't been able to protect me. And I don't expect him to. Except, we have two more people in our corner, when it's always been us against the world.

Robyn and D'Angelo.

My shoulder aches. I adjust my arm in my sling. When a sharp pain shoots through my chest from my cracked ribs, I force my breathing to become shallow.

The pain eases.

I got my ass kicked out on the ice. But it's not like I haven't had worse.

I ignore the throbbing headache and the way that the light hurts my eyes.

I know how to deal with a fucking concussion.

I don't need to bother the people I love with my shit.

I learned early on not to show pain. It only lets people know your weak spots, where to hurt you better, whether with humiliation, physical, mental, or emotional pain.

Is love a weak spot?

Unfortunately, Shay knows me too well.

He stops nudging at the vase and narrows his eyes. "Are you okay, Dee?"

"Fine." I lean against the breakfast bar, which runs along the back of the room.

"And that means you *are* in pain." Shay bounces to his feet. "Shall I get the meds?"

I shake my head. "I need to hit the gym. It's making me on edge not to exercise."

Shay's smile is like sunshine. "You're in a sling with cracked ribs and look like a walking bruise but you *still* want to be in the gym from dawn to dusk. No one can say that you're not committed. How about I see if I can get more physio sessions booked for you? You know that I'm going to do whatever it takes to make you feel better. What about with Robyn's brother, Cody? He's a brilliant bloke. Plus, when you were in hospital, he kicked my ass on every game that we played on my phone. He has skills."

My eyes dance with amusement. "How hard was that for you to admit?"

Shay dramatically throws his hands over his heart. "My gamer ego may never recover."

Yet it's going to be a struggle not to be at Shay's side on the ice this season.

We played together throughout college and from the moment that our adopted parents took us in and discovered that it was the best therapy for me.

The ice is my voice.

How can I talk now?

Sometimes, it feels like the words are caught in my head. It burns my throat to force them out.

Being trapped in my head has always felt safest. When you're quiet and simply observe the world, you can learn about it. Sometimes, you can even control it.

Now, if I take the job as D'Angelo's PA, I'm going to have to risk talking to other people, having them watch and *judge* me.

My heart beats hard in my chest.

I grit my teeth, grabbing hold of the kitchen counter.

On the other hand, as a PA, I can continue to work for the Bay Rebels. I'll still be able to attend games, organize the schedules, and be part of the hockey scene.

Everything is worth it to become a staff member.

Everything is worth it to support my brother.

Shay deserves his moment to shoot for the stars.

Perhaps, I'll find something that I can shine at too.

I pull the **SORRY, I WAS THINKING ABOUT CATS** mug, which is on the counter, closer toward me by one shaking hand. I warm inside, and my heartbeat slows, when I remember that Robyn singled me out to buy me this gift.

It felt incredible that she only bought one for me.

Plus, *cats*.

I'd be happy if everything in this house could have cats on it.

Or squirrels.

Would D'Angelo throw a fit, if I told him that I wanted to get a pet?

Would he throw even more of a fit, if he found out that I've been sitting at my window each night and allowing a squirrel to visit me, sort of like a pet already?

But then, you should never have wild animals as pets. The squirrel's more like a nighttime colleague.

Perhaps, *he* adopted *me*.

Humans can be pets, I've recently discovered. Shay is Robyn and D'Angelo's.

I take a swig of my tea, which smells softly aromatic and fragrant.

Then I tap a second blue porcelain mug, which is on the counter. "Tea."

Shay ambles to the counter. "Thanks, Dee. You're the best." He takes a long drink. "Perfect. Are you running out of your emergency Earl Grey?"

I look affronted. "No, I carry emergency tea on me at all times. Would you forget to order me chocolate ice cream?"

Shay gives an easy smile. "Never. We have a pact."

See, the Circle of Twins.

Since we both love Robyn, can we add her?

I'd better check.

I clear my throat. "Do you love Robyn?"

Shay spits out his tea in surprise — wasteful. "If having my tongue in her pussy, moaning her name, and saying *I love you*, weren't clear enough clues, Robyn is my fucking world. What do you feel about her?"

I run my hand through my slicked back hair.

I can't put it into words. I've never felt like this before.

I struggle for a moment.

Shay gently nudges my shoulder; I mask my wince. "Don't worry. There's no rush. You can date her and work things out however you like. I've never had someone who wanted me like this either. I was just the hookup or the…" I don't miss how his hand tightens around the mug. My heart clenches. "Robyn and Jude want me as a *boyfriend*. I'm bloody obsessed with them both but I never saw that coming. The strange thing is that they seem obsessed with *me* too. Who knew that our lives would change this much by taking the risk to come out here to Freedom? We're so lucky…" Then he catches sight of my sling and blanches. "Fuck, I'm sorry, Dee."

It isn't my shoulder that hurts now. It feels like my soul is in flames.

It's not Shay's fault. I'll never let him think that.

He always blames himself. He believes that he deserves to be punished.

I straighten. "Drink your tea before it's cold."

Obediently, Shay takes a sip. "Does that mean I'm forgiven for being an insensitive bastard?"

"You're not. You're honest like we've always been with each other. And we *are* lucky. Here, I have Robyn. Family. *Your happiness.*"

Shay throws his arms around me, almost overbalancing. "Thanks, bro."

I pat him on the back. "Ribs, remember?"

Shay lets go, flushing. "Whoops. I blame the other two for spending so long in bed, rather than being down here kissing or otherwise touching me."

"They need their time alone as well."

Shay shrugs. "You're good at this. You know, giving people space and sharing in a relationship."

"People aren't property. I don't have a hold over Robyn."

Shay's expression gentles. "You're right. I wish her bastard ex had known that." He drains the rest of his tea, before cautiously asking, "Do you mind if I talk about hockey around you?"

I cross my arms. "I'm living in a house with two hockey players, one of whom is going to become my boss. I'm dating the PR Director of the team. I'm going to need to keep my shit together and deal with it. I can face this."

"But not alone." Shay brushes his damp hair back from his eyes. "I can't wait until the season starts. Training week was incredible. In some ways, bloody torture. But also, I loved pushing myself and having the chance to learn from the best. Coach is tough as fucking nails but incredible at getting the best out of the team. Did you read the list that was sent through this morning of who's been selected? Atlas, Lucas, Grayson, and Zach... I can't wait to work with these exceptional athletes. I'm going down to the rink today to fit in some extra practice. I'd live at the rink if I could."

He's vibrating with excitement.

"Mum always said that you'd never take off your skates and go to bed in them if you could."

Shay laughs. "Like a hockey Edward Scissorhands."

Shay has always been a god on the ice. He's going to become one of the best players in the NHL.

Deep down, I've always known it.

I've been playing catch up to his talent like his shadow all my life.

Now, I don't have to.

It's brutal. But life is brutal.

I'd allow myself to be hurt or killed, if it meant Shay succeeding.

Isn't that what brotherly love means?

Also, co-dependency.

But what do therapists know? They've never sacrificed everything since they were kids to protect their twin.

When Shay starts to talk about some drama between the players, before moving onto what I call his *geek talk* on astrophysics, I zone out.

He doesn't expect me to answer.

The good thing about being the quiet introvert is that people are fine with you listening and nodding occasionally.

My brother's genius level smart, although he hides it from most people like it's something to be ashamed about.

I don't understand his geek talk.

On the other hand, he wouldn't understand me, if I started talking about my English degree or pulled him into my book club discussions with Robyn.

Last week, Robyn and I chatted about omegaverse romance.

I love the stoic, stern Alphas.

I can relate.

"Don't you think the best thing about omegaverse is the Omegas' nests?" Robyn snuggled closer to me on the bed, which we'd turned into our own nest of blankets, books, and chocolates for the evening. "Well, that and the Alphas' huge knots? Who wouldn't want to be knotted through a heat for days of wild sex?"

I arched my brow. "Me."

Robyn looked cute, wearing a long, black t-shirt, which was embroidered on the front with a cat.

The cat peered out of a cup and saucer, above the striped gray words:

KIT- TEA.

It's a t-shirt that I used to sleep in, until my brother gave it to her. I never took it back because I love the feeling I get deep in my stomach, when I see her wearing it and smell my scent mingled with hers.

Robyn snorted. "I could tell an Omega joke right now but I better…knot."

I groaned, lowering my head to take a deep breath of her neck. "Do you want to know the best part for me? The way that Alphas love the scent of their fated Omega. The only one who's their soul mate. Especially, when the Omega is wearing their clothes."

My eyes darken at the memory. My dick hardens.

I stare across the kitchen, lost in the happy haze that has only one name: *Robyn*.

Nothing else makes me feel the way that she does.

No one else has the same connection like I've known her for years.

"...and then, he took his stick and rammed it right up my..." Shay finishes.

I slam back into my body with a jolt away from my happy place.

"What?" I grab Shay by the shoulders. I focus on him intently. "Who hurt you?"

Shay chuckles. "No one. But I figured that you weren't listening."

I flush. "I was..."

"Zoned out?"

I nod, letting my hand slide away from Shay's shoulder.

Shay hops onto the counter, swinging his legs. "Pay attention. Jude is going to come sweeping into the kitchen any minute to eat the breakfast that you've made, before he negotiates your PA contract. We need to talk about that."

"What's to talk about?"

"Tut, tut, Dee. You're as bad as Robyn who signed (without reading it all first), her novel length contract with the Bay Rebels. Look, Jude has been an incredible mentor to me. He's taken me under his wing, and it's his one-on-one work on the ice that helped me make the team. No one has made an effort to help me like that before. But you and I are *brothers*. We stick together. And that means, we're going to get the best contract for you."

"Jude looked after me in the hospital," I admit. "He's been caring for me and this house, when I couldn't."

"He's a good bloke. He simply likes to hide it."

"But why has he been helping us?"

Shay tips to the side, slapping his arse. "I have some assets."

I narrow my eyes. "You're worth more than your body."

Shay blushes, avoiding my eye.

"But why care about *me*? Because I'm your twin?" I persist.

Shay's gaze snaps to mine.

Why does he look bewildered?

"Because you're his friend," Shay answers, simply.

I don't have friends.

Why's Shay saying this?

Admittedly, what I have in Captain's Hall feels like *family*.

I understand D'Angelo. In some ways, I'm closer in character to him than I am to Shay.

Certainly, in bed.

But friendship...?

I'm not sure I know what that is.

"You and I are each other's friends," I say, sternly.

"Anyone else wants to break into that, then they need to earn it."

"Circle of Twins, huh?" Shay swings his legs. "I get it. But Jude already sees *you* as *his* friend."

"I don't understand."

"I know. I hope that you will soon. I wouldn't have laid myself bare (in more ways than one), if I didn't trust both Robyn and Jude. You know that I've told them things about our past that...well, we swore to each other that we'd always keep secret. If you allow yourself to trust them both, then we're going to find a new home here. Don't you want that?"

I swallow; my throat is dry. "More than fucking anything."

Shay nods, suddenly all business.

"So, we go into negotiation on your salary higher than you want or expect," Shay says like he's held a dozen CEO jobs, rather than a handful of crappy shop jobs in the weekends and holidays to help pay his way through college. I worked as a cleaner and in kitchen jobs because shop work triggered my social anxiety. The cleaning and kitchens did give me useful skills. "Jude is our friend but he's going to also become your boss. If he tries to pull rank on you, tell Robyn. Jude won't want to look bad in front of her. But business is still business. He'll knock us down, but then, you'll end up with a good salary anyway. Dad told me that tip."

"Have you told Mum and Dad yet about making the team?"

"Not yet with the bloody time zone differences. I'm

going to call them as soon as they finish their day jobs, you know, catch them before they start their night shifts. It's going to make their week. Dad was talking about breaking out the Prosecco that they've been saving."

I hate that my parents are still working two jobs.

They sacrificed a lot for both Shay and me: to pay for our time on the rink, our therapy, then to help us through college, even if Shay's scholarship helped.

Shay can send money back to them, as soon as his new pay comes through. Robyn promises to get him sponsorship deals too.

The dream is that they won't have to work two jobs anymore.

We'll buy them a car.

A house.

Except, *I* won't be able to.

And that's more painful than anything.

My weak spot.

Because it'll be Shay completing that dream alone.

It's always been Shay and me together, until now.

My gaze hardens because if I negotiate well enough, then I'll still be able to get a good enough salary as a staff member to send some money back home.

I know how to be frugal. I've had to be my entire life.

It's going to be tough for me to learn to be a PA. I'll be facing my fears.

Yet it'll be worth it to support Shay, not be separated, and earn money for my parents.

First, I must find a way to out negotiate D'Angelo.

I straighten my shoulders, tilting up my chin.

If this means going to war, then I'm ready.

I glance around the kitchen. I've already laid out everything for breakfast.

It looks perfect.

Why aren't Robyn and D'Angelo coming down?

CHAPTER FOUR

Captain's Hall, Freedom

*E*den

"You're going to burn a hole through the kitchen door in a moment," Shay points out.

He jumps off the marble counter.

I don't look away from the door.

Robyn and Jude will be here for breakfast at any moment.

Sometimes, they don't notice me in a room.

I like those times, when I'm in the shadows. I can watch them. Observe and listen.

But I *always* notice them.

Shay begins to hum the Arctic Monkey's "Baby I'm

Yours," dancing around the kitchen like he has Robyn held in his arms.

I roll my eyes.

My brother loves dancing, as much as I hate it. In fact, he loves going to parties, the pub, and live music gigs, also as much as I hate them.

Shay snatches up the empty mugs, dangling them from one hand, and dances toward the dishwasher next to the fridge at the back of the kitchen.

My gaze darts away from the door to watch him. "I wouldn't do that, if I were you."

"I know. But I would."

"You like to live dangerously."

"Guilty." Shay yanks open the dishwasher hard enough to make me wince.

D'Angelo loves that machine. He's the commander in this kitchen, as much as he is on the ice or in bed.

Is Shay testing him?

Shay stuffs the mugs — the wrong way up — messily into the incorrect section of the dishwasher.

He never can learn the right way to stack it.

"He likes it, when I tidy up." Shay's cheeks tint with pink. My expression gentles. I've misjudged my brother. "I promised that I'd be better about keeping this place clean and not making extra work for him. I am trying. I want to show that I care about... It was hard for him to admit about his OCD. You know that I don't create mess and chaos on purpose. You always did call me the most forgetful person in England."

"You'd lose your arse, if it wasn't attached to you."

"I wouldn't lose it; I'd simply need you to find it for me." Shay leaves the dishwasher open, leaning next to it. "We need our captain in a good mood, right? No hurt in earning some brownie points."

"Then why not wash up? You're banned from touching the dishwasher."

"Am I?" Shay gives me a pretend innocent look that we both know I'll never believe.

So, I didn't totally misjudge my brother.

When the kitchen door slams open, my breathing speeds up. I force myself to relax against the counter.

I cross my arms and watch D'Angelo swagger into the room looking elegant in his suit.

I'm growing to like his suits. I wouldn't mind dressing in one myself more often.

"Good morning." D'Angelo looks more harried than I'm expecting. "Robyn is just pulling on some clothes. She tried to come down here naked." I flush at the thought of her walking around the house naked, while the rest of us are dressed. My cock hardens. "You know, I may encourage that another day, but it turns out that coach has summoned her to a meeting. I'm crashing that party. We're in a rush."

I frown, looking at the food that I got up at dawn to prepare. "You're not going to eat."

D'Angelo studies the spread on the table. "We certainly are. Thank you, delicious as always, Eden. You could have been a baker or chef, you know."

I glow at his approval.

I respect D'Angelo, and I want him to respect me.

Is the easy way that he talks to me *friendship*?

D'Angelo cocks his head, and his hair falls into his eyes. "Cucciolo, is there any reason why you're looking like you can't work out whether you're about to be spanked or kissed?"

I'm not sure that my brother knows what he wants from D'Angelo.

I think that he may want both the scolding and the kissing.

Shay reddens, and his fingers edge, as if against his will toward the dishwasher. "Both sound like fun, darlin'."

Finally, D'Angelo notices Shay's guilty fingers. His expression clouds. He marches toward Shay, but I'm not flooded with my normal protectiveness.

This is their dynamic.

All's fair in love and war. And their relationship definitely contains both love *and* war.

D'Angelo grabs Shay by the scruff of the neck. When he squeezes, Shay melts like it's a caress.

D'Angelo pointedly drags Shay away from the side, then pulls open the dishwasher.

D'Angelo's eyes widen. "You stacked it."

Shay grins. "Surprise! I didn't leave out the dirty mugs."

D'Angelo lets out a long breath like he's trying to calm himself. "In every relationship, there's one person who knows how to correctly stack a dishwasher and one who does it like an over excited puppy. You're the puppy."

Shay looks like he's trying not to laugh. "I got that. I'm your *pet*."

D'Angelo turns the mugs the right way up with his free hand, before stacking them to his own precise system. "Are you ever going to follow my rules?"

Shay salutes. "Not a chance, oh my captain."

D'Angelo tightens his hold on Shay's neck, dragging him closer. "Still, you're a good boy for trying."

Then he kisses him, slow and tender.

I've always noticed my brother's soul deep connection to D'Angelo (the way that he leaned toward him subconsciously, seeking his validation), before Shay told me that he was attracted to D'Angelo.

It wasn't a surprise.

I hated the anxious way that Shay wrung his hands in his lap, ducking his head, as he told me about his bi-awakening.

Did he think for a moment that I wouldn't accept anything that he told me about himself?

I'm happy, if he's happy.

He's my twin.

I've already died and risen from the ashes for him.

Once, when we were kids, I was thrown against the wall so hard that I cracked my skull and passed out.

When I came round, all I could hear was a frantic voice whispering: *he's not breathing, he's not breathing, he's not...*

I don't think about that time, which I call only The Room.

I remember that I put my arms out, however, as I was thrown and imagined that instead, I was flying.

I was a phoenix: I died and I was reborn.

I drop my gaze, grabbing a cloth and wiping down the top of the counter.

D'Angelo reluctantly pulls out of the kiss. Shay's eyes look glassy, and his lips are kiss swollen.

D'Angelo is the only man who my brother wants to tame him.

I hope that D'Angelo knows that I'm watching, however, because if he ever hurts my brother, then I'll bust his fucking balls.

D'Angelo releases Shay with a final stroke to his neck, as if soothing him. "We have your PA contract to negotiate, Eden. I would have gone through it thoroughly this morning, but coach decided to mind fuck us with a meeting of his own."

I turn away from the counter and cross my arms. "We can delay it."

Shay pushes back from D'Angelo, shaking his head. "Hey, hold up. Eden matters too. You offer him this job and then—"

"Have already drawn up a contract and sent it to his email…?" D'Angelo replies, smoothly. "I thought that it'd be easier for you to deal with as a written document, than talking about it directly for hours. You can look over it and then get back to me in your own time with any questions or things that you want to change."

That's thoughtful.

It's like when D'Angelo realized that our contract negotiation and checklist with kinks and limits was too much for me. So, while the rest of them talked about it face to face, he sent it to me in a document to annotate by myself.

Shay rocks on his feet. "Are brilliant...?"

"Better, cucciolo." D'Angelo smirks.

I tilt up my chin. "I want to negotiate my pay."

"Done," D'Angelo drawls.

I blink. "What?"

D'Angelo adjusts his tie. "I'm rather wealthy, even if I'm stuck in this mountain prison with you. I haven't been able to show you my own mansion, or wine and dine you properly, which I promise that I will correct as soon as I can. I could afford twenty staff, however, if I wanted them. So, whatever figure is in that smart brain of yours, write it down on the blank space in the contract for pay, and it's yours. Scratch that, whatever figure you're thinking...double it."

I stare at him.

Is he serious?

He's serious.

A strange feeling soars through me.

Is this hope?

Trust?

"Best boss ever." Shay whoops. "You're a legend, darlin'. He's thinking *a million dollars a year.*"

I stare at Shay, horrified.

I'm not.

"He's not." D'Angelo's serious gaze meets mine. "Remind me never to write you a blank check, cucciolo."

D'Angelo and I exchange a nod.

We both understand each other.

I'm going to be the best PA that D'Angelo could ever have. He's saved both Shay and me with this offer, and he's paying me whatever I think is fair.

I won't let him down.

I love that I don't need to say it. He doesn't make me either.

He accepts my silence. He reads me well enough without forcing my voice from me.

"Who's being given a million dollars?" Robyn says from the doorway.

Instantly, I swing to her.

My cock twitches.

Robyn is dressed in an ivory suit, which looks crumpled and creased. Probably because she rolls her clothes up and sticks them at the back of her closet.

I'll offer to iron them.

Yet she still looks like the most beautiful woman who I've ever seen.

I love her curves, emerald eyes, and phoenix-red hair.

I love more that she's interested in my ink, shares her favorite books with me, and has never made me feel like I don't have a place that I fit in this relationship.

She's made me an equal.

Yet I feel out of control, spiraling with emotions that I don't understand but never want to stop.

My heart speeds up like it always does, when I'm with her.

My palms are sweating.

My expression, however, remains inscrutable.

Robyn smiles at me, and my stomach swoops.

Fuck, I love her.

"Eat," I say.

She glances at the bowls of fresh fruit and plates of pastries and muffins that are spread across the table. Her nose wrinkles in a way I love at their sweet, freshly baked scent.

"Wow, this looks amazing. Thanks, Eden." Robyn rushes to the table like the devil is after her and throws herself down on the bench.

She must be in a panic about this meeting.

Is it really that bad?

I frown.

Shay studies her. "It's good to see you, love. I'd have preferred the naked version…"

Robyn twists to look at him. "I should have known that D'Angelo would snitch on me. How about you guys serve me naked tomorrow."

D'Angelo snorts. "Only if it we wake up and there's a pig flying outside our window."

"How about if you win the three opening games?" She challenges.

"Why aren't we the ones rewarded?" D'Angelo demands.

"You will be." Robyn scans the breakfast, selecting a couple of rolls and a handful of fruit onto her plate hurriedly. "If you serve me well naked."

D'Angelo looks like he's about to protest, but Shay silences him by clapping his hands together, as if it's an auction.

"Deal," Shay exclaims.

"What just happened?" D'Angelo catches my gaze.

"We got played," I reply.

Robyn looks amused. I watch her for a moment, as she snatches a blueberry muffin. She doesn't hesitate, stuffing it into her mouth.

Then chokes.

All three of us rush to her, patting her on the back.

She coughs and splutters, red faced. "Stop beating me like a rug."

Then she chokes again, gasping for breath.

"I'm going in for the Heimlich maneuver. Stand back," D'Angelo orders.

I drag Shay back by his arm.

"Fuck," Shay mutters, concerned.

I hold onto him tightly in case he thinks that he's a Disney prince and a kiss of life will work better than first aid.

D'Angelo wraps his arms around Robyn's waist, beginning to wrench her out of her seat.

I'm glad that he's strong and can manhandle all of us, although I'd kick him in the balls if he ever tries that with me.

Well, apart from if he's saving my life.

Maybe.

Robyn coughs, beginning to gasp in breaths all by herself again. "Get off me, white knight. I can breathe. I may die of embarrassment but not of choking on a blueberry muffin."

D'Angelo clings onto her for another long moment

like he doesn't entirely believe her, before he lowers her onto the bench again.

D'Angelo's arms are clutched around her middle like he still fears losing her. "Can you imagine the headlines? **Bay Rebels Team Members Murder Coach's Daughter with breakfast pastries?**"

Shay shrugs. "It could be worse: **Coach's Daughter Chokes Rather Than Swallows**."

D'Angelo lets go of Robyn to cast Shay a quelling look. "You're worse than the hacks. Are you looking for a job with that snake, Melanie, at Peninsula Daily News? She loved coming up with puns like **Pucking the Playboy**, which was me, of course. Being in the public eye is strangely like having people punch you in the dick, then ask you for an interview an hour later. I need to warn you that you're signing up to a team that's jeered at as both the Misfits and the Losers. Expect strangers to insult you to your face and haters to feel entitled to troll you online. Welcome to a world of being punched in the dick professionally."

Shay blinks. "So, what you're saying is that celebrities must sign up for cock and ball torture. Harsh."

D'Angelo kisses Robyn's head. "That's why we need to stand together against CBT."

"Plus, you have me," Robyn declares. "I'm your PR Director. I'm here to shield and protect you. I promise, I will."

She bravely reaches for the muffin again.

"Slow down." I pin Robyn with a stern stare. "Be careful."

"I got the memo from the near death breakfast experience." Now, Robyn edges her plate away. "I'm just worried."

Shay perches next to her on the table. "I'd better hand-feed you, love. It's safer that way and kinkier. Two birds with one stone."

He picks up a large, plump strawberry and hovers it in front of her lips.

Robyn blushes, adorably. "We don't have time."

D'Angelo leans against the wall. "We do. Relax. I promise, we'll get to the arena with time to spare. Well, probably not. But we won't miss the meeting."

I snag an apple off the table and toss it to D'Angelo. He catches it.

When he thinks of other's needs, he forgets his own.

It could be a dom thing. On the other hand, all of us in this new found family do it.

We need to look out for each other.

D'Angelo gives me an inquiring look, before crunching into the apple.

I'm mesmerized by the way Robyn nibbles and sucks on the tip of the strawberry like it's a cock.

I shift from one foot to the other, hoping that it's not too obvious that it's because my own cock is now uncomfortably hard in my leather trousers.

Perhaps, I should stop wearing such tight ones around Robyn.

Plus, if I wear joggers, then they're loose enough for her small hand to slip in the front and...

I bite my lip.

Not helping with my problem.

"Like that do you, love?" Shay leans closer to Robyn, as his voice becomes deeper and like caramel.

She doesn't respond with words but laps the remaining strawberry into her mouth with her tongue. Then she licks and sucks the juice off Shay's fingers.

Shay shivers. "I didn't know that I was into food play but I am now. I'm adding that to my list. Hmm, this gives me an idea."

D'Angelo looks amused. "Sounds dangerous."

"It's how you like me, darlin'."

D'Angelo doesn't reply but takes a crisp bite of his apple.

I force my gaze away with Robyn, as Shay breaks off a bite size piece of muffin that hopefully won't make D'Angelo repeat his attempted Heimlich maneuver and feeds it to Robyn.

Robyn chews and then swallows, before twisting on the bench to face the rest of us. "I meant what I said about my PR role. Now the season is starting, it's more important than ever. We played the David and Goliath card, beating some of the biggest teams in the NHL in a scandalous game. This season will be the most pressured of your careers, along with the added difficulty of keeping our relationship secret from the press."

D'Angelo fiddles with his cuff links three times. "Are we still sure that we want to keep our relationship secret?"

He looks to Shay.

I like that.

Shay bites his lip. "I'm not ready…"

"I'm not talking about announcing your sexuality," D'Angelo says with a flash of steel. "You don't owe that to anyone. The public's not entitled to know that. We could even keep the poly part private. I know that some in the traditional press and sports world may not be understanding about it, and I won't damage Shay's sponsorship chances. He's just starting out; it's too important. You could cover for us by telling those sharks that you and I are dating."

My hand balls into a fist.

Am I the dirty secret?

If it's what needs to happen to protect the others, then I'll accept it. It's enough to know that Robyn wants me in her life.

But it's hard.

Robyn firmly shakes her head, however, and her gaze meets mine. "It's all or nothing. We're equals in this relationship. We can either get to a position that I'm able to announce you're all the men who I love, or we keep it secret and protect the most precious thing in the world to me. So, we'll need to keep on secretly pucking."

My hand relaxes, and I lean forward, tracing a finger down her cheek. "I don't want the world to break what we have."

I hope that she understands.

"I don't want them to break our hearts. I won't allow that to happen." Robyn's expression hardens, as she claps her hands. "So, that means I need to keep the press off our backs. As PR Director, I must spin PR disasters into successes, making sure that the Bay Rebels are not devoured by the world's new interest in the youngest team in the NHL."

Shay licks crumbs off his fingers. "You've got this, love."

Instantly, Robyn points a firm finger at him, and his eyes widen. "I do, if a certain Terrible Twin learns to control his temper on the ice and adapts to playing without his twin."

D'Angelo snorts. "Good luck."

"And you," Robyn's scary pointy finger turns on D'Angelo, and he freezes in place, "will have to continue to reform your wild child, cocky playboy image and captain this new team to the playoffs. Dad has made it clear that this is your final chance."

"I'll never be reformed." D'Angelo's eyes gleam. "But I will get the Bay Rebels to the playoffs."

Fuck, the finger is slowly turning in my direction.

Is it too late to run?

"And you…" Robyn's lips twitch. "Actually, you don't have to worry about anything but recovering from your injuries and learning your new role working for D'Angelo. Let us take care of you for once. I know that's hard for you to accept."

She has no idea.

"She didn't kick your ass, Dee." Shay mock pouts, but I know that he's teasing.

"She doesn't need to." I draw my thumb from Robyn's cheek to her jaw, pushing up her chin. "May I kiss you?"

"Yes, please."

I claim her lips in a chaste kiss that still sends chills through me.

Every time that I touch her, it lights me up.

When I draw back, I lick over her plush lips. She tastes sweetly of strawberries.

Her gaze meets mine, searchingly. "Okay?"

"Now that I'm with you."

When I straddle the bench next to her, she grabs my hand, entwining our fingers. It appears to calm her.

Robyn's expression becomes serious. "You know, I'm going to make good use of my PR knowledge to build my independence, career, and to protect our relationship. The only good thing that Wilder ever did for me was to pay for my Public Relations PhD. It's why I don't have that debt hanging over me. Did I say *do for me*? More like he couldn't stop me studying, and I only spent the money that other wives paid out on million dollar house redecorations. As long as I still went to events as his trophy wife and it didn't interfere with me supporting his hockey career, he didn't care."

My Robyn's ex was an abusive, narcissistic cheater.

I respect her strength so fucking much.

We understand each other because we've both survived in different ways.

"I'm sorry that you were treated like that." D'Angelo's shoulders are tight. "I wish that I could knee him in the balls again."

Shay's expression is fierce. "I wish that I could rip them off."

I wish that I could kill him.

Robyn's fingers tighten around mine. "You have. After his actions on the ice, he's been suspended. He's also being investigated for stalking, harassment, filming without consent and blackmail by his own coach. He's no longer the golden boy of hockey."

"But we're still the rebels," Shay says, proudly.

Robyn smiles. "And that's the narrative that we go with. Bay Rebels aren't the *losers*. They're the underdog rebels, here to take on the arrogant elites of the NHL. Privately, I've moved on from Wilder. I'm back in my home town with my family, friends, and new men who I love. I have a dream career. Whatever happens, I can face it."

D'Angelo taps his watch. "Talking of that, it's time to face the coach."

Robyn pales. "Can I take back my rallying speech?"

"Too late." Shay grins. "It was rousing. In more ways than one."

"Should I get my sword?" I keep my face straight. My sword is already hard as steel and ready for action. Robyn's glancing significantly at my pants and raises her eyebrow as if to say that she knows. "It's like Queen Elizabeth the First herself is here to lead us into battle. You even have the red hair."

"I'm not a queen. I'm the rebel, Robyn Hood," Robyn replies, defiantly.

"You're *my* Queen, love," Shay murmurs, low and seductive.

I know my twin. He means it.

"Okay, I can't put it off any longer. Dad hates people

being late." Robyn sighs, but then her eyes light up. "I did have one idea for social media this week, however, to start building some diehard fans. You know, fans who are invested in your journey this season, loving you as people, and truly being feral for the Bay Rebels. I'll work on this angle but I'll need someone to take some photos that aren't the stiff, dead-eyed official ones. Something relaxed, at home and the rink. They need to be taken on phones or iPads, so they look authentic."

To my surprise, Shay points at me. "Dee is brilliant at taking photos. I cut off people's heads, take them just when a stranger walks in front of the picture, or forget that I've left the Fleshlight on the bed in my college dorm. That was an interesting picture to accidentally show poor Mum…"

"Eden will do it," Robyn says, quickly.

"I'm not brilliant," I protest. "I just didn't own a Fleshlight to leave out."

"Don't minimize your talents." Shay tilts his head. "You're good at this like you're better than me at reading and in the gym. You can do this."

"Why don't you take the first photo now, before I have to leave to face Dad?" Robyn suggests.

It's the edge of hope and something else in her voice that has me standing up from the bench and backing across the kitchen, readying to take the photograph for her.

I wouldn't do anything for her, in the same way that I know Shay would.

It makes him emotionally more vulnerable to her.

The hold that D'Angelo and Robyn have over my twin is dangerous. It's why I'm keeping a close eye.

Shay's always been at risk.

When Robyn looks at me in that way with her beautiful eyes and asks for help, however, I know that I'd never say no.

I pull the phone out of my pocket, unlocking it.

I switch it to camera, then I point it at the kitchen, centering the photograph. Shay is perched on the table, smiling and relaxed. Not many people get to see this side to him.

Robyn's idea is smart.

Who will be able to see him like this and not fall in love with him?

Want to cheer for him to succeed on the ice and off it?

D'Angelo is posed, appearing typically cold and elegant against the wall. He arches his eyebrow at me.

"Perfect," I say.

He looks like the dominant captain as in charge at home as he is at the rink.

And Robyn…?

I crop her out of the photograph.

I'm going to take photographs of her though. But they'll only be for me to look at and print out to pin on the wall beside my bed.

When I look through the camera lens on my phone, taking this happy photograph in the warmth of the kitchen, my hand tightens around the casing.

For a long time, I didn't know what family meant. I felt constantly on high alert. I wore my silence as a thicket of roses with thorns around me like Sleeping Beauty to keep everybody out.

When I was twelve, I fell on the ice.

I hit my head and sprained my ankle. It wasn't a bad concussion, although I hurled and my temples throbbed.

What I cared about was the way that Shay cried, when he was forced to go to school without me for the first time.

Dad insisted.

I propped myself up in bed, listening to Mum's anxious voice on the phone outside my bedroom door.

"Sir, it's only one day. There's no one else to stay home with him, you see, and he's my son...yes, my adopted son, but that doesn't change anything... Please, don't fire me. I need this job. I'll work a double shift tomorrow."

I balled my fists. I hated it, when her boss made her beg. He did it a lot.

One day, I was going to be big and strong enough to stand up for Mum.

For all women.

When Mum appeared in the door, she looked exhausted. Her black hair hung in a messy pony tail. Strands fell around her fawn, heart shaped face.

Her brown eyes looked tired.

She gave me a strained smile. "Always so serious, Dee. It's not a problem for me to take time off to look after you, sweetheart, as I promised."

I shook my head, which made me woozier.

Concerned, Mum sat on the edge of the bed. When she

reached to stroke my hair, I couldn't stop myself flinching.

Carefully, she adjusted the covers over me. "You'll feel better soon. Shay and you matter more than anything and far more than some bloody cleaning job."

I perked up at Shay's name.

Was Shay coping at school without me?

He'd texted me six times already. I wasn't telling Mum that because he wasn't meant to be texting during class.

Shay was better at being sneaky than I was.

Mum arched her brow like she could already tell. "No worrying about your brother. He'll be fine. Just rest. Later, I'll read you another chapter of your new library book. Is it another one on myths? I don't know, you two are so smart. Sometimes, I think that you'll be professors someday. You'll be the first in the family to go to college, I can tell. I'm so proud."

The pain in my head and ankle meant nothing. I was used to pain.

There was a happiness surging through me, however, that I wasn't used to.

Mum thought that I was smart, as well as Shay...? That I'd go to college?

She intended to *keep* me, despite knowing where I'd come from and everything that was wrong with me? *Possibly forever?*

For the first time, I dared to believe it.

I started to shake.

These emotions were overwhelming. My mind was buzzing.

Alarmed, Mum grabbed hold of my hand. "What's wrong, sweetheart? Should I call the doctor? Is it your head?"

How could I explain?

Even within my mind, I didn't have the words.

I'd never spoken anything out loud.

My twin would understand. He must be feeling the same as me. Was that why he wept?

I needed Shay.

Shay. Shay. Shay.

"Shay," I whispered.

My first ever word: *My brother's name.*

Mum's eyes widened, before she whispered, "What did you just say?"

"Shay," I repeated.

Then Mum was pulling me up, dragging me to her chest and crying like she'd never stop. "Yes, sweetheart, you're so smart. What do you say we have a celebration, the three of us, once your brother's home from school? Cheer us all up and get us smiling again? I'm the luckiest mum in the world to have such incredible sons."

Now, I stare at the photograph in this warm kitchen with Shay looking like he's never been happier, and right here is what I've sacrificed for.

These men and women are precious.

My family here in America who think I'm smart and love and want both Shay and me.

I'll do anything to protect it.

Whatever it takes.

CHAPTER FIVE

Rebel Arena, Freedom

*R*obyn

WHEN I TIP BACK my head, sunshine washes across my face.

I allow myself this final moment of silent, sunbathed happiness, before facing the press pack who are swarming outside Rebel Arena.

Shay jitters from foot to foot next to me.

He's dressed in one of my favorite outfits of his because it reminds me of the night that I first met him in Merchant's Inn: A motorcycle jacket over a punky red shirt and black jeans

He doesn't look like a hockey player, which makes him a honeytrap for coaches' daughters.

Fuck, every time that I look at him, somehow it feels like it's the first time.

When Shay smiles, his large, winter gray eyes, which are framed by butterfly lashes, meet mine.

I feel suddenly lighter.

Braver.

He once told me that because life was short, he wasn't wasting a single heartbeat.

...If I can take joy in something, then I'm seizing it...

When I'm with him, I can believe that.

Shay's spun gold hair tumbles over his sharp cheekbones and jaw line.

Hot and cold flushes through me because hell, I've been around NHL players all my life, but *no one* has looked as much like a god as Shay does.

I nudge Shay with my elbow, wishing that I could take his hand.

I can't because we're in public, however, and that hurts.

I lick my lips, remembering the taste of sweet strawberries that Shay fed me, while I'd been imagining his cock sliding into my mouth.

Is there any chance that my near death by muffin will be forgotten?

I haven't quite got the hang of eating sexily yet.

Eden at least appeared distracted by taking the photographs.

I know that he has more hidden talents than he's able to admit but I was still surprised how good Eden's photograph was.

He captured a hidden truth to both his brother and D'Angelo, which was almost uncomfortable. It'll be a game changer, when I post it on the Bay Rebels' social media account.

I'll need to be careful, however, how much of our personal lives that I share.

It's a difficult balance.

When I studied the photograph, even though D'Angelo and Shay aren't touching in it, I could tell the sexual tension and dynamic between them, the same as if Shay was stripped naked with his face pushed into the bedding, while D'Angelo dominantly spread him open and roughly fucked him like a toy.

Yet is that only because I know the truth?

It also felt good to see how happy Eden was to see that he's always going to be included.

At least, I'm guessing that he was happy.

Reading Eden comes down to judging twitches of lips, long looks, and the length of silences.

Of course, he can make me wet, simply by crossing his arms or giving me one of those long looks.

D'Angelo stands at my other shoulder.

He's wearing a long, woolen coat, which is the same arctic blue as his cashmere scarf. It lies open over an elegant, designer navy suit and waistcoat.

With the icy gleam in his eyes, cruel twist to his

sensual lips, and hands clasped behind his back, he looks like a general who's about to go to war.

An impossibly hot general.

I'm screwed, aren't I?

Is there any chance that he won't give these journalists the exact type of reaction that they want for their clickbait and get this season off to the worst possible start?

He has form.

"Remember the silence and no comment rule," I whisper. I drilled both D'Angelo and Shay on this in the taxi that we took over here from Captain's Hall. "It's PR's most powerful tool."

D'Angelo hums noncommittally.

I grab his scarf and yank him to a stop.

I'm grateful that the paparazzi haven't noticed us yet or else the PR Director holding the team's captain, as if by a leash, would make an interesting photograph for the front page tomorrow. "We talked about this in the taxi."

"You did," D'Angelo agrees.

Shay chuckles. "You should be a lawyer."

"We're going to walk through those vultures, and you're not..." I wrench D'Angelo closer, until our noses are touching. His gorgeous blue eyes widen. "...repeat *not* going to say anything in your coolly dangerous voice like—"

"Keep sticking that camera in my face, then I'll see whether I can hit it as far as I can a puck...?"

"You truly said that?" Shay sounds impressed.

"Look what you've done," I tut. "You're being a bad influence on the man you're mentoring."

All of a sudden, D'Angelo's expression becomes serious.

I should have known that tactic would work. D'Angelo takes his role as captain seriously, especially his responsibility to Shay.

D'Angelo turns his cold gaze on Shay, who shrinks back. "Under no circumstance will any words cross your pretty lips, apart from *no comment*. Your PR Director has given you directions. You should learn to follow them. I'm the captain. My reputation has been damaged for many years. But you're a new and a rising star. I won't allow your reputation and career to be ripped to shreds like mine has been. So, respect Robyn."

Shay looks down. "Sorry, love."

"Hey, it's okay. You always respect me." I smooth D'Angelo's scarf down, before letting go. "It's your captain here who I'm worried about. What he just did is called deflection."

D'Angelo looks called out. "No comment."

"Come on, let's get this over with." I grit my teeth.

Why are there so many press here today? Did someone tip them off about the meeting with my dad or is it going to be like this from now on, until the season starts?

There's a reason that I call journalists glorified stalkers.

I straighten my shoulders and march through the morning sunshine toward the journalists and paparazzi who are huddled around Rebel Arena's entrance, blocking it.

Despite the stress, excitement still tingles through me

as it always does at the sight of the arena. It's the familiar anticipation for the thrill of the incredible game, which has always stolen my heart.

Like they have a hive mind, the journalists turn and swarm around us. Eden looks panicked but steadies with a glance at D'Angelo.

"Melanie from the Peninsula Daily News." A woman who's my age pushes herself in front of us.

Her eyes light up with a horrible excitement.

This isn't good.

Melanie was the chief Queen Bee and mean girl in my class at high school.

She's dressed in a flannel jacket and pink jeans. Her hair is streaked with silver.

D'Angelo opens his mouth either to tell her to *fuck off* or to reply that he knows *precisely* who she is, since she's been writing trash articles about him…but snaps it shut, when I glance significantly at him.

I start to push a route through the crush. I'm careful not to trip over the tripods. I blink at the flurry of camera flashes, as if I can't hear the shouts from the paparazzi of *D'Angelo, Prince,* or *loser, misfit, this way, this way, look over here…*

Kudos to both men.

They don't reply. Their faces are like masks, despite having insults hurled at them by a gang of strangers who are attempting to get them to lose their tempers.

Do they realize how close they are to getting their dicks punched with these two?

"Don't you want to know what my exclusive reveal will be next week?" Melanie calls, sidling next to D'Angelo. "It's a full spread on you."

I pale.

Is she serious?

But there aren't any new scandals. I've made certain of that.

I knew that Melanie would still be a mean girl.

Melanie sticks her microphone in D'Angelo's face, as he tries to walk away from her. "The headline will be: Secrets of a Puck Boy Captain. Any comment?"

Shit.

My heart aches for D'Angelo.

I hate that he's been unfairly represented and shamed in the press. I've been doing everything to reflect the truth about him.

The good man who's dedicated to his team like they're family.

The type of man who sets up and runs a sports charity and hockey scholarships anonymously and won't allow me to use his charity work in his PR.

It means something important to him. He won't cheapen it, even if the press don't care about cheapening his life.

D'Angelo becomes ashen. "Print that, and I'll sue."

So much for silence.

Melanie looks like the snake who's caught her prey.

She looks even more delighted, when D'Angelo bats the microphone out of his face.

"Then you'd have to prove that what I say isn't true." She grins. "You could go on the record with me about your side of the story first. You don't have any actual relationships recorded. Would you like to tell me now that you have a long term girlfriend or boyfriend?"

I snatch D'Angelo by the elbow, hauling him through the pack.

I don't care that I'm stepping (literally), on people's toes.

Shay's vibrating with fury.

"Don't say anything," I warn Shay.

Shay drags his phone out of his pocket. Confused, I watch as he fiddles with it.

I know that he enjoys his games on there and is working hard to beat Cody's highest score on Candy Crush, but now isn't the fucking time.

"What about Wilder Talon? Why don't you take a break from busting my balls and focus on his?" D'Angelo yells over his shoulder like he's unable to hold it in any longer. "He's suspended. Isn't that the real story right now in hockey?"

"Is that a quote?" Melanie asks, sweetly.

"No," I shoot back.

At the same time, D'Angelo snarls, "It's a fact."

Shay's expression hardens, as he glares at Melanie, at the same time as holding up his phone.

"No comment," blares from the phone in an automated voice, followed by the same phrase in every language that he's been able to program on repeat.

Shay and I march shoulder by shoulder with D'Angelo

to repeated *no comments* that sound exactly like the *fuck offs* that they're meant to be.

We escape through the high, steel doors of the arena.

My heart is hammering, as the doors clang shut behind me.

CHAPTER SIX

Rebel Arena, Freedom

*R*obyn

AT LAST, I'm alone with D'Angelo and Shay. The high steel doors protect us from the gang of journalists and paparazzi on the other side.

Or is it protecting them from D'Angelo's rage?

Studying the icy storm in his blue eyes, it's a close call.

D'Angelo breaks away from me, dragging his scarf out of my grip. He stalks down the arena corridor, which is painted white with low, blue lighting.

Shay and I exchange a glance, before following him.

D'Angelo fusses with his scarf, muttering to himself.

Shay's phone is still spewing *no comments*, this time in French.

"How about you turn that off?" I say. "Nice trick."

Shay grins, as he switches off his phone and then slips it into his pocket. "You could tell us a different phrase each time, and we'll all set it up on repeat."

It's not a bad idea.

"I'll find out what Melanie means." I meet D'Angelo's gaze. "I'll kill her story."

My heart speeds up, as he sweeps back to tower over us.

Sometimes, I forgot how tall he is. He's much taller than me…and Shay.

I need to tip back my head to meet his frosty gaze.

"Puck Boy," D'Angelo growls. "Fucking *Puck Boy*…?"

"If those bloody bastards are going to call anyone that, then it should be me," Shay says, sounding insulted. "I can be your puck boy if you want, darlin'."

D'Angelo's pupils dilate, and he sucks in a sharp breath.

He looks like he's struggling to control his anger, pushing his curls back from his face.

Wait, not control anger…

He growls, before shoving Shay against the wall with an arm across his neck. "You already are."

Shay's eyes widen and then become glassy with desire.

"Shit." I look around the empty corridor wildly in case someone comes around the corner.

Not knowing these two men the way that I do, they'd probably think that it was the hockey captain kicking the ass of the newbie star player in the typically physical way that my ex-Wilder was known to use on his teammates.

Whereas I know that D'Angelo and Shay love to play rough, and D'Angelo is only interested in *fucking* Shay's ass…

Right now, it's what D'Angelo needs.

"Guys," I hiss, "this is dangerous, risky, *forbidden*…"

Shay's long eyelashes flutter, and he moans, pushing his hips against D'Angelo's. "Fuck, keep talking, love. You're making me so bloody hard. Tell me again how *forbidden* this is. Am I being a bad boy?"

D'Angelo pushes his arm harder against Shay's throat. "Shut up and kiss me."

Shay groans, opening his lips obediently.

D'Angelo claims them hard, fast, and brutal. He doesn't let up his hold on Shay or the way that he steals his breath.

It's a thrill, watching them like this. It's even more of a thrill to snatch this moment together.

I know that both men are getting off on me watching them.

I used to be spontaneous.

As much as I'm vibrating with the terror of being caught, that fear is being transformed into excitement.

I wet my lips. My breathing is ragged.

When D'Angleo breaks off the kiss, then drags a dazed Shay around until both men are facing me, I'm flushed.

When they look at me like *I'm* the prey, I'm torn between running into the arms of these gorgeous men and running away.

"Hold up," I whisper. "It's 9:30. We'll be late, if you…"

D'Angelo taps Shay's shoulder, and he nods.

When both men stalk toward me, I back away down the corridor.

I tumble backward. I have a survival instinct. I'm not taking my eyes off these two.

Shay's kiss swollen lips quirk into a smile. "Where are you going, love?"

"Meeting," I blurt. "Dad."

D'Angelo raises his brow but he doesn't stop stalking me like a well-dressed wild cat. "She does that: shouts out her dad's name in bed."

"Kinky." Shay pushes his hands into the pockets of his leather jacket, cocking his head.

"Hey, I don't think about my dad during sex," I protest.

"I'm relieved to hear that, Robyn," Dad's gruff voice says from behind me.

I eep, losing my step and tripping over my feet in horror.

Dad reaches out to steady me by the elbow.

I close my eyes.

Is there any chance — any chance at all — that when I open them Dad will have disappeared?

Slowly, I crack open my eyes.

Nope, no luck.

Shay is grinning, looking far too amused.

D'Angelo, however, appears pale and tense. He struggles around authority figures, especially parental ones because of his troubled past.

Now that Dad is essentially his father-in-law, as well as his coach, it puts him in a double position of authority.

Dad holds D'Angelo's career, which means everything to him, as well as his relationship with Shay and me, in his hands. I'll do everything that I can not to allow Dad to wreck either.

On the other hand, Dad holds the control within the Bay Rebels.

During my childhood with Cody, I long realized that no matter how much I tried, I couldn't change Dad or his mind once it was made up.

He hurt my brother by not loving him unconditionally, and I don't know if he's accepted how much damage he did to him.

At the same time, he lost his wife to cancer, as much as we lost our mom. But he left Cody and me to grieve alone.

I'm as fiercely protective of Cody, as he is of me.

Yet I love Dad.

He's the only parent that I have. And he loves me in his dickish way.

Parents, huh?

Dad's warm hand is still firmly on my elbow, as he turns me to face him.

"Morning, Dad." I blush.

Dad once had the same red hair as me but now, looks like a silver fox. He's tall with a neat beard and twinkling, emerald eyes, which means that there's still no missing that he's my dad.

He's dressed in a sharp charcoal suit with a green shirt and tie.

He lets go of my elbow. "You're late, Robyn."

D'Angelo makes a show of checking his Rolex. "Actually, she's precisely on time, coach."

I love his courage that he always speaks up for me, even though I can see how anxious he's feeling by the way that he taps the watch's face three times.

Dad doesn't look impressed. "My cheap piece of crap watch tells me that you're two minutes late. So much for your flashy waste of money. I can only assume that you're the reason that my daughter didn't reply to my first messages, as well as being late. At least you're dressed smartly and don't smell like you bathed in whiskey this morning. It's an improvement. My daughter's rubbing off on you."

"No, that's Shay," D'Angelo replies, deadpan. "At least, he was last night."

Shay splutters with laughter, before trying to smother it behind his palm. "Sorry, coach."

Dad narrows his eyes. "Get out of here, I have a meeting with my daughter."

He turns on his heel and marches to his office.

I trot after him. "Just so you know, Dad, I'm the reason that I didn't reply and am late. I can screw up without help from anyone else."

Shay continues on down the corridor. "Have fun, love. Come get me at the rink, when you're done. I'm going to get in some laps on the ice."

I smile and wave.

D'Angelo's eyes dance with amusement, as he swaggers after me, rather than following Shay to the rink.

If Dad thinks that's he going to keep D'Angelo kicking his heels out in the corridor like he did in my first ever meeting here, then he's going to learn that the power dynamics have changed.

D'Angelo and I are partners now.

D'Angelo puts me first above his hockey. It makes my heart warm.

Wilder didn't.

Dad didn't.

I never believed that anyone would truly put me first.

I follow Dad into his office.

Flat screen monitors hang on the walls of his office. Dad uses them to watch back the games with his team, analyzing their plays to improve them.

On the far wall is a white touchscreen that's scrawled with red and blue lines of strategy like the front of my Guide.

I throw myself down into one of the chairs, which is opposite the large, mahogany desk. I wriggle around for a moment, trying to make it look like I'm not adjusting the way that my lacy thong has gone up my ass.

It serves me right for being in such a rush this morning that I grabbed the first pair of panties that I could find and ended up with the one that I've christened *the wedgie*.

Seriously, I'm thinking of taking up Shay's suggestion and going commando from now on.

When the chair creaks from my squirming, Dad turns around. "Robyn, do you have ants in your pants or...?"

Then he sees D'Angelo strolling into the room as well

and shutting the door with a bang, his eyes widen in surprise.

Saved by the alpha male showdown.

"What are you doing following my daughter like a lost puppy, D'Angelo?" Dad demands. "Have you forgotten the way to the rink? Do I need to get the Colton down here to escort you there and put you through some drills for the next hour?"

"Pass, coach." D'Angelo slouches to the chair next to me and folds his long legs into it. He adjusts his cuffs, casually. "Can we start the meeting now?"

He has big balls. And I should know. I've struggled to suck them into my mouth.

Seriously, it's impossible.

I struggle to keep the thought off my face.

By the way that D'Angelo is side-eying me, I have zero idea what expression I'm wearing right now.

Dad studies D'Angelo for a long, heart-stopping moment. "Don't get cocky. You've made the team, but the season hasn't started yet. This is your chance to redeem yourself in my eyes, as well as the fans' eyes, Freedom's, and the whole fucking world's. Bay Rebels are the underdogs who are battling to show everybody that they can compete with the big boys. This is legacy time — for me and you. We can't screw this up, Jude."

Dad's use of D'Angelo's first name hits him harder than his talk about redemption or legacy.

D'Angelo sits straighter in his chair. "Of course, coach. We...*I*...won't."

Dad is fond of D'Angelo. He's seen more of him over

the last few years than he has of me. After all, I only returned to Freedom last month, but Dad has been working with D'Angelo closely on the team since it was founded.

He's the only one on the team apart from the twins who knows about his charity work.

Of course, that was before he found out about D'Angelo dating me.

I don't know whether Dad will be able to separate that from how he works with D'Angelo here at the rink.

I hope so.

Without realizing it, I've stiffened.

D'Angelo glances at me. His hand twitches like he's aborted reaching to grasp mine.

Dad pretends not to notice.

Only, he has.

"So, red eyes and crumpled suit." Dad gestures at me. "It *is* Zombie Robyn who decided to turn up."

Damn my allergies.

I rub at my puffy eyes.

Life's too short to iron, right?

I think I have that on a t-shirt.

"Laugh it up, Dad," I grumble. "You're the one who insisted on a morning meeting on the night after you announce team selections. What's so important?"

Nervously, I watch as Dad leans against the wall next to the window. The arctic blue drapes are open, and sunshine streams through, making his silver hair gleam.

"I'm sure that you expect me to kick your ass now," he

says, gruffly. "Did you think that this was an ambush? Is that why you brought your white knight?"

D'Angelo looks startled like he's never been called that before. "I'm more like the wicked dragon shifter who helps the damsel flame the knight because he's trying to force her into marriage, then hoards her with my treasure."

"That's sweet, sort of," I say.

In a typically possessive D'Angelo way.

When Dad marches to the desk, before throwing himself down heavily into his chair, I jump. "Well, here's what I wanted to tell you."

My pulse speeds up. My mouth is dry.

Why does he look so troubled?

What the hell is he going to say?

I wring my hands in my lap, hardly daring to breathe, as he leans on his desk.

Dad's gaze darts to D'Angelo like he wishes that he wasn't here. He looks like he's struggling to make up his mind about something.

Finally, he ignores D'Angelo and focuses on me.

"Robyn," Dad's eyes meet mine, "I know that I haven't always been the best Dad. That's not easy for me to admit. I want to try and repair our relationship. I've screwed up, so many times. I get that. But what's happened with your bastard ex-husband has shaken me. Hell, what happened on my watch…how he stalked you…"

"I don't blame you," I reply. "It's on my abusive ex and not you."

This is not how I expected this conversation to go.

Not at all.

"I know, but as your dad, it's my duty to protect you. It's bullshit, if you tell me that it's not because that's how I feel. And now, you have this relationship with these three men. I thought that I'd hate it. I know that I gave you a hard time about it, when you first told me. But I needed time to think."

My expression hardens. "And have you?"

He nods. "You're a grown-ass woman. I wouldn't dare my worst enemy to suggest to you that you were anything less than an independent woman who knew her own mind. So, if you tell me that being with these three men is what you need…"

Next to me, I can tell how still D'Angelo has become.

Does he think even now that I'll reject him? Ghost him again?

I guess those wounds run deep.

"It is. It really is, Dad."

I glance at D'Angelo, as he relaxes into his seat at my words. He tries to cover it by flicking non-existent lint off his jacket.

"Then I'm going to support you." Dad's gaze darts between D'Angelo and me. "I've made sure that your therapy is booked, Jude. Now, we need to keep a lid on Shay's temper. He's a golden retriever off the ice but can turn into a pit bull on it. Only time will tell, if it's different now that he's playing without his twin."

I wince. "That may be good for Shay's career, but it ended Eden's."

Dad's expression softens. "I know that Eden lost his

career, while he was injured playing for me. Anything that he needs, just ask. I lost my career too, even if it was because I was an asshole and not because I was concussed. I get that he'll be devastated and grieving right now. Don't underestimate the mental impact, simply because Eden doesn't talk about it. I never told your mom what it was doing to me."

"How did you cope?" D'Angelo asks.

"I took up boating. Boxing. And lots of barbecues."

"So, I tell him to take up something beginning with 'B,'" D'Angelo drawls.

"He loves baking. So, we're okay." I bump my knee against D'Angelo's.

I don't add that he doesn't do bottoming, so that's out.

"What about supporting Cody?" I've wanted to say this to Dad for weeks. "Will you call him in and talk to him like this too?"

Dad clasps his hands together on the desk. "Why?"

"Because you need to repair your relationship with him, even more than you do with me. You owe him a one-to-one conversation at least to apologize. I'm seeing him for brunch tomorrow. We can work on this as a family."

"It's not the same," Dad grumbles. "He doesn't have a crazy ex. He has a husband who coddles and overindulges him."

"He doesn't." My lips thin. "He has a husband who loves him like he deserves, unconditionally. Think about it."

To my relief, Dad nods.

"Are we done?" D'Angelo begins to push himself out of his chair, relieved.

"Sit your ass back down," Dad barks.

Reluctantly, D'Angelo sinks back into his chair. "Yes, coach."

I should have known that there would be an ass kicking somewhere.

Here it comes.

The stealth ass kicking.

As kids, Cody and I used to joke about Dad's hidden attack modes.

If you *thought* that you'd got away with not finishing your punishment chores, he'd act friendly like you didn't have anything to worry about…until bedtime. Then you'd discover him scowling and waiting in your room ready with a scolding and a list of additional punishments that you'd earned for the next week.

Never let your guard down around a wily silver fox.

"Did you think that the hard work was getting through the training camp and retaining your captaincy?" Dad's gaze is sharp. "The hard work starts now."

D'Angelo swallows. "Yes, coach."

D'Angelo's tapping out a rhythm of threes on his thigh. I hate to see him under pressure, and the season hasn't even started yet.

"We get it," I promise.

"Do you?" Dad leans further over the desk. "As PR Director, I hope that you do. You'll have meetings with other senior staff, including Felix, who's the operations manager, as well as Jon who works in marketing. Do you know what Silas, the finance manager, won't tell you?"

"My fortune?" I venture.

D'Angelo's lips twitch.

Dad is stony faced. "He won't tell you that the Bay Rebels are likely to still be here next year. At least with me and the rest of us staff at the helm. The Bay Rebels are in financial difficulty and need to radically turn around both gate and merchandise sales. They'll do that by winning over the fans. This season is our best and possibly only chance to prove ourselves to them and the world. At the same time, the board have made it clear that they're only going to let me run the team my way with those who don't fit into other teams or need a second chance, if I get them to the playoffs. If *we* do. Press scandals could derail this. Robyn, you're still needed to manage my two most valuable but volatile players. This season will either save us or fuck us in the ass."

CHAPTER SEVEN

Tide Cottage, Freedom

Robyn

"We're fucked, Cody." I bang my head back against the striped, window seat in Tide Cottage.

"Dad actually said *save us or fuck us in the ass*?" Cody scrunches up his nose. "I don't want anyone but my husband in my ass. He's possessive. You don't deserve this pressure, Ryn. You're doing an awesome job. Plus, I've only just been appointed the Director of Physical Therapy. I'm excited about starting properly with the guys. I've worked years for this chance to prove myself."

Prove himself to Dad he means but doesn't say.

But we both hear it.

Cody is two years younger than me, although he's so athletic and sun blushed by his time spent surfing that he could still be a college student.

He's handsome with neat brunette hair, freckles across the bridge of his nose, and russet eyes. He's dressed in a pastel blue t-shirt and matching boardshorts.

I've always been close to my brother, and he's spent his life being fiercely protective of me.

But then, I'm equally protective of him.

Until he married his husband, Michael, he had no one else in his corner.

David Bowie's glam rock "The Rise and Fall of Ziggy Stardust and the Spiders from Mars" is playing on repeat.

It's my brother's favorite album.

I glance out of the window.

The beach is remote and wild with sea stacks, which rise from the swelling waves. Above, in the sapphire sky, bald eagles soar.

It's breezy today and cold.

After the stress of the last few days and the meeting with Dad (and admittedly, forgetting to stick on my laundry), I'm bundled in an old, faded One Direction sweater over green leggings.

Cody's eyes lit up when he saw the sweater. He asked if he could borrow it for the sake of *nostalgia*.

Yep, definitely for no other reason.

"It'll work out," Cody says. "Your guys are dedicated. You know that I'll do whatever the team needs to make it succeed. How about we hold brainstorming meetings at Merchant's Inn? Neve's got freaky business skills."

"You choosing that venue has nothing to do with being able to drink beer at the same time, huh?"

"It's got everything to do with that."

I laugh. "Sounds good to me, Code."

"Do you want one of these while we wait?" Cody slices open a crusty roll on the butcher block countertop and butters it.

My stomach growls. "You read my mind."

"I've been practicing mentalism." He waggles his eyebrows.

Cody's brunches are famous. He bakes everything from scratch, and I've never tasted *anything* as delicious as his fresh bread and pastries.

That gives me an idea.

"Why don't you send some of your recipes to Eden?" I suggest.

"Hmm, they're based on secrets passed down from generation to generation…"

"You got most of them from Ina Garten, didn't you?"

Cody looks sheepish. "Busted."

"Anyway, Eden's family now. So, the secret recipe stuff is bullshit. You could start some kind of Bakers of Bay Rebels online WhatsApp chat. He's isolated right now. But that would be a way to…"

"Get to know him as a friend." Cody smiles. "No problem."

"Is Mike going to be here soon?"

Cody drops his gaze. "He's late. You know how it is.

He's had an all-night shift at the hospital. I never know when he'll get back."

That's not a surprise.

Michael works in ER at Freedom Heart hospital.

Darling, I'm saving lives is a pretty good excuse for canceling plans.

Cody's used to never knowing when his husband will be home. As the husband of a doctor, it's something that you need to be supportive about.

Yet it can be hard.

"He loves you," I say. "Your marriage is everything that I wish mine had been. I bet that Mike's thinking of you, even while he's elbow deep in blood and guts."

Cody shoots me a grateful smile. "Romantic."

I understand what he can't say because my ex was a hockey player who canceled because of training or games.

He wouldn't call to let me know. Instead, he sent me a text with an emoji: Stick and puck.

It took me years to realize it was often these times that he was cheating on me with other women and hockey fans.

Can you be triggered by an emoji?

Cody strolls across the kitchen and passes me the plate. The scent of fresh bread wraps around me like a hug.

The tension seeps from me like it always does, when I visit my brother's cottage by the sea.

The kitchen is cozy with exposed beams and wide-planked wooden floors. The walls and open shelves are painted sky blue. Cody's surfboards are stacked against the far wall, and the tangy brine smell wars with the sweet scent of fresh bread.

I take the plate from Cody and balance it on my knee. He sits on the window seat next to me.

My mouth waters, as I pick up the bread. "You are about to make my mouth very happy."

I take a large bite and then moan.

Fuck, this is a mouthgasm.

Incredible.

The bread melts, delicious and buttery. I swallow, licking my lips.

"Funny, I said the same to Mike this morning but I was kneeling at the time..." Cody's eyes twinkle with amusement.

I shove him, laughing. "TMI, Code. What would Mike say? I don't want to hear about your adventures with Doctor Kink."

"Why not? And Mike would become stern and take me gently in hand like he always does. Anyway, I have to hear about your adventures with the three hockey musketeers. Do their swords cross, or is it like *Ghostbusters*, disaster if the streams cross?"

I flush, thinking of Shay and D'Angelo's streams crossing.

It's definitely explosive every time that they do.

I almost had an explosive moment myself, when D'Angelo and I went to watch Shay at the rink after the meeting.

The lights were dim, apart from the spotlights that were directed onto the vast rink.

D'Angelo and I strolled close to the boards. D'Angelo leaned on the glass like he was trying subconsciously to get as close to Shay as possible.

I didn't blame him.

Shay is mesmerizing on the ice.

"He truly could be the best," D'Angelo murmured.

My heart sped up. My pulse was loud in my ears.

It's always thrilling to watch Shay: My English hockey god.

He's fast on the ice.

Faster than D'Angelo.

Faster than anyone in the NHL.

He's going to burst onto the NHL season, and it's going to shock everyone. Even after the exhibition games, when Shay comes into his full potential over this season and shines in the light, it's going to blow everyone away.

The world isn't going to know what hit them.

Are any of us ready for what that'll mean?

Is Shay? *Eden?*

Thoughtfully, I take another bite of the delicious bread.

I mumble around my mouthful, "Fuck, I needed this. The last few weeks have been brutal."

Cody's expression softens. "You can visit or even stay here whenever you like, Ryn. Mike and I have agreed that our home will always be open to you. Was Dad that much of an asshole?"

"Not only Dad."

Cody jumps up like he's ready to fight some invisible opponent. "Who's giving you a hard time? Is it one of the other hockey players? It better not be D'Angelo; he still hasn't got a full pass from me. I'll punch all of them in the dick."

My lips quirk. "They're twice as large as you and could break you in half with one hand tied behind them. But nope, it's no one in Bay Rebels. Plus, it'd be hard for you to punch them in the dick, since they don't have one."

Cody crosses his arms. "Who is it then?"

"Melanie Helt."

Cody pales. "*The* Melanie? Melanie the leader of the Mean Girls? The girl who called you *fat fox*?"

I wince. It's all coming back now. I'd forgotten that creative insult.

"Yep, the one and only." I take another bite of the bread to stop myself calling her what I really want to.

It doesn't stop Cody. "Melanie the fucking *body-shaming bully*? Don't you remember how many fights I got into at high school, trying to protect you from her?"

I do.

And that's the problem.

I place the plate down and stand. Gently, I draw Cody into a hug.

"Thanks, Code," I whisper. "I hope that you know how much it's always meant to me. She had that gang of jocks hanging off her every bitchy word, willing to do her bullying for her. It was a manipulative trick, so that she wasn't the one who could get in trouble for what was said or the times that they fought you."

"They were her dumb jock flock of flying monkeys."

I shudder, when I think of all the times that I had to

help Cody limp home and clean up bloodied noses and viciously bruised ribs. I shudder worse that those fights are why Dad marked my brother as the screw-up, keeping him on punishment chores for years that cut him out of family life and isolated him from his friends.

I hug Cody tighter. "She's still a pink haired witch. Only, this time, instead of me and you, the McKenna siblings, she's going after the entire Bay Rebels. Actually, she seems to have it in specifically for D'Angelo. She seems to scent blood and then that's it, feeding frenzy."

Cody pulls back from me. "So, she's a shark witch…? As a surfer, you've given me nightmares about going back into the water, Ryn. Still, we should have known with her love for gossip and spreading false rumors that Melanie would have become a journalist. What's she doing now that's so bad?"

I drop back onto the window seat with a sigh. "Threatening an exclusive against D'Angelo. I don't know what's in it. Plus, with D'Angelo's past, there could be a lot."

Cody's expression becomes fierce. "We may be adults, but I'm still going to defend you. Words can hurt as much as blows. She'll be doing this for a reason."

I nod, thoughtfully.

Then Cody's eyes light with wonder, and he whistles.

He points out of the front window of the cottage. "Shit, a classic car that looks like it's worth more than my entire cottage has just driven down my lane. It appears to be lurking at the bottom. It's only a guess…but is it waiting for you? Not many people apart from the hockey players in Freedom can afford something like that."

My mouth drops open.

"Ehm, that may be the carriage for my first date." I grin. This is going to be interesting. "He's early but D'Angelo's not good at following rules. They each agreed that they could take me on a date. It'll distract them from the pressure of this start to the season. It's intense because we're like the little David, the newest team, taking on every other Goliath in the rest of the NHL."

D'Angelo has responded to the pressure by prowling around Captain's Hall and playing Gothic music on the grand piano like something out of *Phantom of the Opera*.

Eden's been going on long hikes into the woods and communing with squirrels.

And Shay has simply been breaking things accidentally. My last count is two vases, a picture frame, and the mirror in the bathroom, which he cracked with a reckless high kick.

All of a sudden, Cody rubs his hands together.

I don't trust the gleam in his eye.

Sometimes, my brother is scary.

"This sounds like bet territory," he declares. "Three dates, and I bet that you don't—"

I leap up, slamming my hand over his mouth. "Nope, not this time. Once ice burned, twice shy. I'm not taking a bet with you and ending up wearing a tutu, standing on a table, and singing ABBA's "Dancing Queen"."

Tentatively, I remove my hand from Cody's mouth.

His lips twitch. "Shame because I love watching you do those things and I'm the King of Bets."

"Anyway, I already have a bet going. Can I be the Queen of Bets?"

Cody looks like a proud parent. "I feel like I'm passing on the torch. What is it?"

"If my guys win the three opening games, then they serve me breakfast naked."

Cody groans. "Here's some betting tips, since you're in serious need of them. Firstly, don't make a bet that they *want* to win. Secondly, don't make one that you *don't want* them to fail. Thirdly, and this is the important one, don't make a bet, where the outcome is ruled by chance or outside your control."

"But you made a bet about whether I'd kiss a hockey player by the end of the season."

Cody laughs. "The easiest dollar I ever made. It was guaranteed, before the words were even out of my mouth. I know you, Ryn. Funnily, it appears better than you know yourself."

Rude, but since he won the bet in less than a week, also fair.

I stand and wander to the front window.

My eyes widen, when I see the car that's idling at the bottom of the drive.

It's a gorgeous, sexy as hell red (of course it's red), vintage racing car.

Is it an Alfa Romeo?

"Boys and their toys," I mutter.

Normally, sex toys.

This may simply be a penis extension.

I don't know why D'Angelo thinks that he needs one.

Perhaps, guys would even if they had an eighteen inch dick swinging between their legs like a pendulum.

"Have fun with the new toy then." Cody winks, conspiratorially. "When Mike and I bought our SUV, we decided that the back seat needed thorough testing."

CHAPTER EIGHT

Freedom

D'Angelo

I LEAN against my new car with my hands in the pocket of my suit.

I'm precisely two and a half minutes early for my date now. I spent a further thirteen minutes lurking at the bottom of the drive.

Will Robyn be impressed that I'm beating my reputation for always being late?

I'd never be late for a date with my principessa. I spend every minute wishing that I could be with her.

Obsessive. Possessive. But also a millionaire.

Isn't that the crucial difference between a man being a keeper or one step away from a restraining order?

My expression darkens, when I think about the person who I wish I could take out a restraining order against: Melanie Helt.

Fucking journalists.

Secrets of a Puck Boy Captain.

Will it be another tell-all story from one of my one night stands? *A submissive?*

I party with a lot of people but I don't tell them anything private about myself. My true friends are a small, close group and loyal.

What secrets?

I run my hands through my curls, taking a deep breath of the tangy sea breeze.

Eden would love it out here.

Whereas I think that it'd be improved by a development of luxury seafront apartments with all-night clubs and bars.

I'd never tell Cody that because I value my balls.

I glance out at Ember Beach, which lies down a long, sandy path beyond Cody's ramshackle, seafoam green cottage.

The light sparkles on the waves. The air shimmers.

I tap my fingers on the bonnet of the car in patterns of three, thoughtfully. When it's the right month for it, I'll take Eden and Shay out on a boat to see the whales and seals.

I'll hate it but I'm prepared to sacrifice for the way that Shay's face will light up like the sun. Every time that I manage to get him to look that way, I feel less of an asshole and more like he's mine.

Coaxing a smile from Eden is just as rewarding. I know that I've been treating him like a brother and I haven't had one of those for a long time.

Eden would probably want to adopt a seal.

I shift from foot to foot.

That does it.

I feel like I've been waiting all my life for these dates with Robyn.

No more waiting.

I twist to snatch the bouquet of orange roses, which are elaborately wrapped in ribbon (Robyn would look even more beautiful tied up in these silky, golden lengths), off the bonnet of the Alfa Romeo.

Then I hiss out a sharp breath at the scratch of the thorns along the vintage paintwork.

Fuck, that's sacrilege.

Robyn's worth it.

I run my thumb along the scratch with a wince.

Forgive me, baby.

I remember the first time at college that I found out that Robyn loved orange roses. She missed them because they reminded her of a rosebush that her mom had lovingly tended.

Robyn was homesick for her first semester.

The next night, I raided an elite fraternity across campus to steal a bunch of roses from their gardens, getting my ass beat — literally — when I was caught.

I bargained six extra strokes of their frat paddle to keep the roses though.

I sprayed the roses orange with graffiti paint and spread them in front of the door to Robyn's room.

I don't know if I realized that I was falling in love with Robyn from the way that she fell over on her ass in surprise the next morning, smiling in pure joy at the sight, or whether I'd already been well on the way there.

I only know that I always wanted her to keep on smiling.

But Wilder fucked that up for both us, didn't he?

He's not here now, however, and these are real roses clutched in my hand.

I adjust my tie, raising my hand to knock on the door.

Just at that moment, the door swings open, and I'm left mid-motion, staring into Robyn's amused face.

"Smooth," Cody calls from inside.

Robyn's wearing stained jeggings and...*fuck, is that a One Direction sweater?*

Shoot me now.

I feel overdressed. This is my best navy suit, along with diamond cuff links.

I took hours getting ready for this date. Although, I'd never admit that.

I made sure that my new car would be perfect as well.

I suppose that I'm going to need to accept that messy is Robyn's natural state.

She looks beautiful even with smudged lipstick. Does she put it on without a mirror?

Would it be justification for a smack for me to ask

that? What if I managed to correct the lipstick in a seductive way, for example, by kissing the smudge away?

I force myself to flick my gaze up to Robyn's eyes, trying to not let it bother me in the same way that I attempt not to let it make me want to spank Shay until his ass is red and hot, whenever Shay sticks his fingers in the jam or trails mud over the marble floors after his runs.

I cough. "These are for you."

When Robyn's eyes light up at the sight of the roses, I forget all about the smudged lipstick and questionable sweater.

I even forget the image of Shay's gorgeous, scarlet spanked ass over my lap.

Robyn takes away my breath.

"Thanks." She cradles the roses. "They're beautiful."

"You are, principessa," I murmur.

"Come on. Show me this new toy of yours."

"Toy...?" I retort. "Remind me how old you need to be to drive."

Robyn takes my hand, allowing me to lead her to the car.

"Backseat, remember." Cody waves with a wink, before slamming shut the door.

I blink. "Your brother doesn't know much about cars, does he? This is a two-seater sports car. It doesn't have a backseat."

Why is she looking disappointed?

"Oh, well. We can still have fun."

When I open the passenger door for Robyn, she struggles to swing herself into the low seat elegantly. She rests the flowers on her knee.

"Okay?" I check.

She nods.

I close the door, before bounding around to the driver's side. I open my door and slide onto the leather seat, shutting the door.

I turn on the car, listening with satisfaction to the growl of the engine.

Robyn's lips twitch. "You're in heaven already, right? Shall I leave you two alone for this private moment?"

I ease the car down the drive and onto the winding road that leads away from the beach and up into the mountains. "Don't tell me that the car's growling doesn't do something for you."

"It'd do something if *you* growled."

I indulge her with a deep, rumbling growl.

She shivers.

Interesting.

Primal kink is one of my favorites. Plus, there's a forest behind Captain's Hall…

That idea is going in the Guide.

I'm being won over by the whole idea of a book dedicated to our relationship, even if it started as a *these are the reasons that I hate hockey players and especially D'Angelo* rant book.

A journal on our explorations, kinks, and fantasies, however, sounds like exactly the type of thing that I'd invent.

"Yeah, just like that." Robyn's pink tongue darts out and licks across her lips.

I smirk. She's already primed for this date.

Foreplay shouldn't begin ten minutes or even an hour before an orgasm. It should begin within moments of the *last* orgasm.

It's why I've built the tension since yesterday morning with Robyn, when I drove her within a second of tipping over the edge, before stopping.

I know that she must have been throbbing with need ever since, which is why I've been teasing and denying her. It's one of my favorite games: a brush of a hand against her lower back here, an intense eye fucking there.

Frustration makes her look even more beautiful.

This morning, I sent her a text.

JUDE (9:48): Be ready at 11 a.m. I can't wait to have fun with you on our date

I didn't have long to wait for her reply.

MY FOREVER (9:49): What type of fun?

I smiled. She took the bait.

JUDE (9:52): The type that means I can't concentrate on anything bc I'm so hard

This time, it took longer for her to reply. But she did.

This was the best type of foreplay.

MY FOREVER (10:01): What are you doing rn?

JUDE(10:02): Stroking my hard cock and thinking about how incredible it's going to feel inside you...

After that, I didn't reply to any of her texts, even the begging ones.

See, tease.

"So, how far are you taking me?" Robyn looks at me out of the corner of her eye. I hope that she's thinking about either my texts or hard cock. "This is exciting."

"How far do you want to go?"

"I meant in the car…as in, are we riding…?" She puffs out a frustrated breath as she babbles. It's adorable. "How long is the journey?"

I try to keep my expression shuttered. "A really, *really* long way. Get comfortable."

"Comfortable? This is…"

"Thrilling?"

I slip my hands around the wheel, loving the rush of racing up the mountain roads.

Excitement surges through me. It's the same sensation, as when I push myself on the ice like flying…or falling.

Except, unlike in dreams, sometimes you do hit the ground.

"This is a 1960's Alfa Romeo Stradale," I say, quietly. "I've dreamed of driving this car all my life. I don't know why I never bought one. Except, I do. I didn't think that I deserved it. Making the team this season, I finally feel like if I don't buy one now, then I never will."

"You do deserve this car," Robyn replies. "Why wouldn't you think that you did?"

"Because it was the car that my brother and I always talked about growing up." I swallow. Fuck, it hurts to talk about Bruno. "Being raised in an Italian American family, Bruno and I were close. Family meant everything. He was older than me but he still took the time to chat to me about things like cars, sport, and religion. The three most important things to him."

I smile, bitterly.

I hadn't meant to say any of this.

Yet Robyn has a way of making me feel safe enough to share vulnerable sides to myself that I keep shielded from everyone else.

She's the only person who I trust not to use them against me.

Once, Bruno meant the older brother who'd ruffle my hair, swap a joke, and always protect me.

He'd been strict, but there was a type of safety with knowing the rules.

But then, everything changed.

He caught me kissing a boy and transformed into someone who I didn't even know.

I didn't fight back against the type of stranger who could look at me with such hate.

Shock, I guess.

I'd never been beaten like that before. Beaten, until I passed out. Beaten, until I tasted my own blood.

After that, at the private boarding college for troubled teens that my parents sent me to, I almost forgot that there'd been a time that I didn't know the taste of my own blood or a time that I respected the meaning of family.

Trusted them.

Can I really trust that my new, found family love me? Or do they only love me in the same, conditional way that my parents and brother did?

"I'm sorry." Robyn rests her hand on my knee. "I'm

glad that you bought this car. I know how close I am with Cody. I wish that you hadn't lost your brother."

"I didn't lose Bruno." I clench my jaw. "He was always the best looking guy in the room. A jock. And he's back in my home town with my parents still, married with kids. I didn't *lose* him. They chose to throw *me* away like trash because I kissed a boy. That's why I'll do anything to prove to Shay, Eden, and you that none of you will be thrown away…for any reason. This family that we're creating will last as long as you want it. I'm fucking obsessed with all of you. You're my forever family, and this car is like my…"

"Fuck you?" Robyn offers.

I snort. "Precisely. It's my *fuck you* car to Bruno."

I begin to slow the Alfa Romeo, pulling off to a cliff point. A small, blue canvas ice cream stall perches on the edge.

Robyn glances around her, confused. "We've only been driving for a couple of minutes. This is still in Freedom."

My lips quirk. "Strange."

"Did you seriously buy this car so quickly to impress me for a *five minute* drive?"

I struggle not to laugh. "My principessa deserves to ride in style."

I switch off the car, as excitement vibrates through me.

When I climb out, I gesture to the man who owns the stall. He's a silver haired man in his fifties with twinkling eyes. He nods at me, before disappearing on his long trek down the mountain, as arranged.

Then I open the door for Robyn, who abandons the roses in the car.

Robyn looks around. "It's beautiful up here."

Noticing her shivering, I wrap my arm around her. "When I needed time to think about the season or game strategy, I'd come up here."

I stroll with Robyn across the grass closer to the cliff edge.

The view over the Atlantic ocean, which extends in the distance, is breath-taking.

"This ice cream stall is the best in Freedom. I also know the owner personally. They're discrete. These secret dates aren't easy to pull off." I kiss the top of Robyn's head.

"They can't be that good, there's nobody around." Robyn burrows closer against my chest, as if seeking body warmth. "Plus, I've never heard of this stall."

"You've been away from town. Anyway, they're normally closed today. They opened especially for us."

Robyn glances up at me in wonder, as if she's not the most precious thing in the world to me. "Did you pay them to open just for us?"

"I bought out the entire stall for the day. So, I hope you're hungry."

Robyn makes a cute meeping sound, which I'm interpreting as delight.

"Can we take the chocolate ice cream back for Eden?" She claps her hands.

"On my vintage leather seats?" I demand.

She nods. "Plus, the vanilla one for Shay. It's ironic that vanilla is his favorite flavor."

I sigh.

This makes me a good man. It must.

"If you promise to keep them on your knee." I hold up a warning finger. "And not to drop them, or I'll enforce page four, clause two of the contract."

Robyn's cheeks flush, as I hoped that they would. She always looks best like this, flustered but caught on the knife edge of arousal.

I love this moment — the thrill of power.

What truly makes me feel connected to someone, however, is that the person I'm with is *choosing* to submit to me.

Robyn can tell me to fuck off. But she's making the decision not to.

I'm in control, pushing at her secret, hidden desires like the devil on her shoulder. It's innate, a part of me, which is intimate and meaningful. I've trained and learned about myself in ways that I haven't yet shared with Robyn.

She hasn't visited my mansion. She doesn't know about the other secret business that I own either.

I'll tell her once the season is properly underway.

She isn't ready yet.

I'm also a mod on an online BDSM chatroom, which supports my community because they've supported me in the past.

My online user name is MasterFireandIce22.

22 is my hockey jersey number.

I chose it because '22' is Robyn's lucky number. So, even though we were apart for six years, I could still feel close to her during every game.

I see the same natural dominance in Eden as I have in me, although he's more of a caregiver than I am.

All I know is that I was born dominant in the same way that I was born bisexual.

Figuring this stuff out about myself and learning about communication and trust has helped me. My kinks and power exchange relationships have been the most healthy and positive part of my life.

Also, the most fun.

What's beautiful to me is how a sub gives over their body, mind, and will within the boundaries of consent. Then I use all of that to bring us both pleasure.

I grip Robyn's chin, forcing eye contact. "Tell me what that would mean."

She doesn't want to say it but she still obeys.

"Discipline," she whispers.

My dick is pressing against my trousers now.

"Good girl." I reward her with a kiss.

Robyn's lips search out mine to deepen the kiss, but I draw back, loosening the hold. "Come on, we have over one hundred ice creams to try."

I slip my hand from Robyn's chin, trailing it down her throat. Her eyes become glassy, as I trace the hollow of her neck, where the gold pendant of a jersey lies, which I gave her.

Then I slide my hand to the collar of her hideous sweater and tug more firmly, pulling her after me.

Robyn stumbles along, unable to look away from the bright stall, which has trays of multi-colored blocks of ice-cream in its front and a cut-out sign hanging down of an overflowing ice cream cone with sprinkles.

Robyn smiles up at me. "I should have known that you'd have chosen something cold."

"Like my heart, you mean?"

"Frosty, but when your lips lick it just right..." She takes me off guard, twisting in my grip to lick down my neck, hot and needy. It's my turn to shiver. "...you melt."

"We'll see about that."

She's right, but I'm not letting her know that.

She doesn't realize how much power she has over me.

She could destroy me with a word.

She could kill me by abandoning me again.

"Are you looking forward to your date with Shay on Friday as well?" She asks.

"He's never had a date with a man before. He's under the false impression that men don't get nice things like dates. I'm going to show him how wrong he is. How much he deserves to be treated well. How worthy he is. I don't know what truly happened in his past, but someone made him feel like trash, and I don't only mean his asshole biological parents who literally sold him. He'll tell us when he's ready. I won't push. For now, I'll endure..."

"A horror movie night with homemade curry...?"

My lips pinch. "It's what he wants. It's probably what he's been dreaming about. I know how that is. How can I tell him that I have no tolerance for scary movies? That I'd rather be fine dining on an Italian, before taking him home, tying him to the bed and then fucking him, until he doesn't remember his own name?"

"There's always the second date."

I chuckle. "Then I'll get the rope ready for *both* your second dates."

I love how she flushes.

"I half expected you to turn up with a carriage or on horseback today." Robyn allows herself to be manhandled toward the stall. Shay and her both love that I can give this to them. Together, these two are trouble. "After all, you're my *white knight*."

"You forget," I reply, deep and dangerous, "I told you that I'm actually your wicked dragon."

I tighten my arm around her, as my eyes blaze in demonstration.

"Dragon or not, you do still own that horse riding outfit, right?" She asks, looking hopeful. "The one from the photograph in the Guide that makes you look like Darcy, if they ever did a mash up of *Pride and Prejudice* and *50 Shades of Gray. 50 Shades of Darcy...?* I'd watch that."

"Christ, I wouldn't." I stare at her, horrified.

What has she just dreamed up?

She scrunches up her nose. "Now you even sound like Darcy."

My eyes darken. "Careful, cara mia. I don't have the outfit but I do have the riding crop."

In fact, it's one of my favorite implements. The supple leather fits into my hand by now, comfortable and familiar.

It'd make beautiful marks on Robyn's skin.

I shake my head, trying to clear my mind of the vision of Robyn stretched out and writhing in ecstasy under my crop.

"Will you show me some time?" She asks, tentatively.

As if she's still unsure whether she has a right to her own needs being met.

I took great delight in kneeing her ex in the balls. I want to do it again.

"I'd love to introduce you to the kiss of my crop," I murmur. "You'd love to please me, wouldn't you?"

Her breathing picks up like I knew it would.

She nods.

"Words," I say, more sharply.

"Yes, Sir."

"Good, girl." I let go of her, swaggering the final few steps toward the stall. "Come here."

She bites her lip, before obeying me.

She's falling into the right headspace now.

We've both been under a lot of pressure this week. We need this. And we're alone up here on the top of the mountain with the crashing ocean beneath and the deep blue sky above.

"Do you remember our ice cream breaks at college?" Robyn asks dreamily, wandering to join me in front of the tubs of ice-cream. I take a deep breath of the delicious sweet and fruity smells. My mouth waters. "You never stopped working, outside hockey practice. I'd find you late at night still hunched over your desk. Some nights, the only way that I could coax you away was by promising to buy you an ice cream from that incredible all night parlor off campus."

I couldn't afford to eat in that parlor as a poor scholarship student. Robyn didn't know that. It would have hurt my pride to tell her.

I knew even then that I was competing both for her friendship and heart against wealthy, elite students like Wilder, whose parents owned half the county.

I was a dumbass but I didn't feel like I'd have a chance to move out of the friendzone, if she discovered that the best I could offer her were stolen roses covered in spray paint.

Yet Robyn was so kind that she'd drag me out of my dorm coffee induced work haze to that luxury parlor and pay simply to get me away from my essays.

She also didn't know the rigorous demands of my scholarship meant I had to work that hard.

"And now," I gesture at the stall, "I'm returning the favor."

I steel myself, before swiping two fingers through the strawberry ice cream.

I shudder at the cold, slimy sensation. I hate it. But this is romantic. It's what people do who don't have my struggles with OCD and touch.

I can do this.

I hold my fingers up to Robyn's lips, deliberately smearing it around her lips. Then she opens her mouth eagerly, sucking in my fingers and licking around them.

I growl at the sensation, fellating my fingers in and out of her mouth, deeper and harder.

I entwine my other hand in her hair at the back of her neck. "You're taking my fingers so well. Let's see what else you can handle."

I withdraw my fingers, resisting the temptation to wipe them dry. Instead, I run them through the melted chocolate ice cream now on the edges of the tub.

Robyn opens her mouth, eagerly.

Naïve.

I smirk, deliberately smearing the ice cream all around her lips. "Whoops." Her eyes widen. "Don't close your mouth. Don't lick."

When I yank her head back by her hair, her pupils dilate. Then I trail my cold fingers down her exposed throat.

She shivers, and I avidly watch the way that her neck bobs, as she swallows.

The ice cream melts, dripping down to pool in the hollow of her throat.

"Look, I made a mess." I press even closer to her, teasing her open mouth with my fingers, before sucking them into my own mouth. She watches me, breathing raggedly. Delicious — both the ice cream and my gorgeous lover. "I'd better clean you up."

I dip my head to catch the melted ice cream with my warm tongue, before it stains her sweater. Then I swirl my tongue in teasing circles, where the liquid has pooled at the hot base of her throat.

Her chest is rapidly rising and falling.

I take my time, as I lick up her neck in long swipes, before nuzzling underneath her jaw.

I'm driving her wild. It's how I want her.

Because it's what she needs.

After Robyn's meeting with her dad and knowing what this season means to all of us, we need a moment of connection that's beyond words.

She needs to be wrecked, and I need to be the one to wreck her.

To push her down into a place where there's only sensation, feeling, and pleasure.

It's a fucking rush.

Then I'll bring her up again, reborn and refreshed.

At last, Robyn can't restrain herself any longer. She clutches me by the front of my shirt, pulling me impossibly closer.

I allow myself to finally kiss the ice cream off her lips.

And this is how you seductively sort out smudged lipstick without getting smacked.

"Kiss me, cara mia," I whisper.

Robyn eagerly kisses me back now like I taste as delicious as the ice cream that we can taste on each other's lips.

I slide my hands to her waist, clutching tightly. Then I walk her backward toward the car.

She doesn't notice.

She's lost in our frantic kissing.

Fuck, these lips should be mine alone.

She tastes so sweet.

Her lips are soft, but her hands are hard, as she twists at my shirt desperately like she wishes that she could rip it off me.

I kiss her harder, hungry.

She sucks on my lower lip in answer, before catching it between her teeth.

I arch my brow, welcoming the flash of brat in her that's always attracted me.

Of course, Shay could give her lessons.

If my two pets don't think that I know how to handle two brats then they're in for a shock.

I love the challenge.

Fuck, I love them both.

I gentle the kiss, and in response, Robyn releases my lip and kisses over it, soothingly.

When I draw back, Robyn's gaze softens in surprise. "Okay?"

"Just thinking about how much I love you."

"I never stop thinking about how much I love *you*." Her eyes are large and vulnerable.

She fucking means it.

I lower my head to place a searing kiss on her jaw, as the back of her knees hit the bonnet of the Alfa Romeo.

I circle my thumbs teasingly along her hips, holding her in place. She needs to tip back her head because she's so much smaller than me.

She's so strong and has such a big personality that I forget how much taller I am than her.

I'm not going to let her forget it now.

I tower over her, pinning her in place with a stern stare. "Don't move. I want to see if you can come just with me touching you...like this."

I graze my fingers up her hips and over her curves that I've always loved.

I tease my fingers higher, mapping out every moan and quiver.

I memorize each point that makes her breath hitch or hands clench. I'm going to learn everything that there is about her responses, until I can play her and draw pleasure or pain with the same strategizing that I'd plan a hockey game.

She struggles to come with vaginal penetration alone and she's used to an ex who never cared. I'm going to show her, however, just how many other creative options there are.

I push my hand underneath her sweater. She holds my gaze, as my nail grazes over her nipple through her bra. She stiffens, sucking in her breath.

She's so sensitive.

Her eyes become glassy. "Again."

"You're playing a dangerous game. Beg me."

"Please."

"You can do better than that."

"Please, Sir, I want your hands on my breasts. They feel so fucking good."

"*You* want? This isn't about what you want. It's about what *I* want."

Robyn opens her mouth and then closes it. Then she tries again.

My good girl. She's smart.

"Please, please Sir, I'm wet for you. I'm desperate to

feel your hands on me, making me come...but only if that'd bring you pleasure."

I flick across her nipple in reward. She whimpers, before pushing out her chest, hoping for more.

I take her cue.

Then I drag up her sweater, exposing her bra.

She reddens. "What if someone sees?"

"Are you safe wording?" I check.

Hurriedly, she shakes her head.

"Then what if they do?" I ease my fingers into her bra, rolling one of her nipples between my thumb and forefinger. She moans and begins to hump against me. "Poor, principessa. Out here in the open, being such a naughty girl. What if someone comes up the mountain and sees you? How does it feel? What if they're hiding and jerking off to the pretty picture that you're making?"

They're not because I'd fucking rip off their dick if they tried to.

Also, I'm facing the road. I can see all the way down it. It's why I chose this location. There's nothing up this drive, apart from the stall, which is meant to be closed. There's nothing on the other side of us but the wide ocean.

We're alone.

If anyone *did* somehow creep up without me seeing, then I'm shielding Robyn. All they'd see was her back.

But she doesn't need to know that because the fantasy is driving her right to the edge.

She's about to tip over...

"What if they're watching you right now, humping my

leg?" I rub over her nipple again, and she whines. I know how much she loves this from our negotiations. "Are you going to come from this…alone…?"

Then, she does.

Fast, hard, and perfect.

She screams, hiding her face against my shoulder.

"Fucking beautiful." I ease her bra and sweater back into place.

She's shaking but she looks blissed out.

That was only orgasm number one, however, and I'm determined to give her a second one. This time, fulfilling my own long term fantasy.

I don't wait for her to pull herself together. I need her like this, relaxed and wrecked.

I turn her, bending her over the bonnet of the car. It's so low that when she catches herself by her hands, splaying them, it pushes her ass up in a way that frames it perfectly.

I drag down her jeggings. Her ass in her thong looks gorgeous.

"I'm going to fuck my toy now," I'm unable to hide the amusement in my voice, "over my toy."

Robyn has the strength left to shoot me a challenging grin over her shoulder. "So, you admit that this car *is* a toy."

Challenge accepted.

I spank her ass.

Fucking. Satisfying.

My hand leaves a crisp red imprint on her pale skin.

Robyn doesn't flinch away but pushes into my touch, as if she's asking for more.

I can't wait to have her over my lap for a proper erotic spanking. I bet that she could come from that alone.

Shay definitely will.

I trace over the hot skin.

Another time.

Robyn wiggles her ass, and I smile, fondly.

"So, despite the fact that it looked like you rummaged through your old laundry to find something to throw on for our date, you actually wore your best underwear." I tease the skin around the edge of her thong.

"Wedgie," she mutters.

My brow furrows. "It's not my kink but it's not one of my hard limits. So, if we talk about it more, maybe next time…"

She looks round at me, wildly. "I meant that the thong feels like a wedgie. Step away from the evil thong."

"But they're so good for easy access."

I simply push the thong to the side, slipping two fingers into her folds.

She's already dripping wet.

I work my fingers in and out of her pussy, and she relaxes, resettling herself over the car.

While I keep her distracted, I undo my trousers with one hand. I've been so hard that it's painful ever since the drive up here with the woman who drives me wild.

The only woman who I've ever loved.

I pull myself out of my trousers, indulging myself with

one long, twisting stroke up my shaft. I bite my lip as I rub over the head just how I like it.

Touching myself is no longer satisfying, however, since Robyn touched me.

Now, I get to bury myself in her hot, tight heat.

I don't care whether my cock is buried between her thighs, ass, deep in her throat, rubbing between her thighs, or worked between her clever hands... I only know that I crave her touch.

I pull a condom out of my pocket.

Reluctantly, I stop fingering Robyn and rip open the condom, before sheathing my cock.

Then I can't hold myself back any longer.

I need to lose myself in Robyn.

I stroke my hands down her spine, before gripping onto her hair like reins. Then I fuck into her wetness in one, long hard thrust.

Robyn and I moan at the same time.

Fuck, it feels incredible.

"Robyn," I murmur.

I snap my hips, faster and faster.

My pulse is roaring in my ears. I can't tell if the loud breaths that I can hear are Robyn's or mine.

"Please, please, please." Robyn scrabbles on the bonnet. "Harder."

Instead, I pull out, flipping her over onto her back. She lands with a whoosh of breath.

Immediately, I thrust back into her, fucking her harder like she begged for.

But this time, I can press my body against hers.

I needed to see her face.

I want to gaze into her eyes, as she falls apart. I want her to see mine, as I do.

I lean down, and my curls cover her face. It's like we're in our own world, as my cock spears her, and my lips claim hers.

Then we're kissing, fucking, and loving.

Out here, under the sky by the ocean with the innocent sweetness of ice cream on our lips, it feels almost like the last nine years didn't happen.

Almost like we're back in college with those bright hopes and dreams.

Like this second chance between us is real.

I slip my hand down to her clit, rubbing circles over it just as fast as I pound into her. I'm working her up to crashing her over the edge at the same time as me.

"I'm close." I rest my forehead against hers, as my thumb grazes across her clit. "Come when I do."

My hips stutter. My back arches.

"Jude," Robyn gasps, "I love you."

Robyn is staring up into my eyes — beautiful and the only woman who I'll ever love — as we both come together.

Yet even as I'm still lying over Robyn with my cock buried in her pussy in the glow of our joint orgasms, I know that it's *not* the same as nine years ago.

We've both grown up and changed.

I'm not innocent. I have secrets.

CHAPTER NINE

Merchant's Inn, Freedom

Robyn

It's Friday night, and I'm still buzzing from my date with D'Angelo. I'm never going to be able to look at ice cream in the same way…or his car.

I'll also never make a joke about his Alfa Romeo again.

Maybe.

It may be a penis extension, but D'Angelo definitely doesn't need one.

On our date, it filled my heart with warmth to remember our friendship at college but also, made me realize that he's truly a different man now.

I need to learn to see D'Angelo as he truly is — love him for it.

He's complex.

It's been incredible, finding out about and supporting him, just as he's supporting all of us.

I'm going to hold tight onto this second chance with him.

Anxious, I shift from foot to foot on the sticky floor of Merchant's Inn. I run my hand through my hair, which is damp with sweat in the heat. I'm dressed in a simple, cotton green dress and black heels.

D'Angelo is on his date tonight at home in Captain's Hall with Shay. So, I'm giving them space. They need their time alone as well.

Plus, it's an excuse to take a break myself from managing my beautiful PR nightmares.

I'm leaving them alone.

Can I trust them?

I'm meant to be with them twenty-four seven, but they still have the security team at the end of the road, and my phone is in my pocket.

How much trouble can they get into without me for a couple of hours?

Don't answer that.

I force the image of Eden lost on a trail in the forest, or D'Angelo and Shay burning down the house as they cook the curry together, out of my head.

I need a drink.

My nose scrunches at the scent of smoke and stale beer. Sweat trickles between my shoulder blades.

Friday nights are always crowded. Merchant's Inn is a rare safe space in Freedom with the added bonus of cheap beer, loud rock music, and a couple of rooms for travelers.

The locals love this old, grungy slice of town with its tacky floors, dance floor, and stained wooden walls that are covered with paintings of Neve's favorite Emo bands like a shrine.

Neve owns Merchant's Inn.

We were best friends in high school. She still wears the emerald and silver friendship bracelet that I made for her. I know how much it means to her because she doesn't wear jewelery but she's never taken that thing off.

This town once treated her like an outcast. Yet she didn't leave or quit. Instead, she worked harder than fucking anybody and beat the haters through her success.

Freedom is a town with two sides: the wealthy, including the tourists, and those who are struggling but working hard.

Merchant's Inn is at the heart of the working side of town.

I hope that one day I can achieve half as much as Neve has.

Tom, the tiny but feisty bartender at Merchant's Inn, with hair that's even redder than mine and beautiful jade eyes, pushes the beer across the counter to me. "It's on the house."

Always be friendly to the local bartender.

That's a pro tip.

I grab the glass, sloshing the liquid over my fingers. "Thanks, Tom."

"It's not from me," Tom replies, hurriedly. "I have strict instructions to never hit on customers. I mean, you're beautiful, if klutzy. The number of glasses that you broke here was a record. Neve made a whole plaque with your name on it and put it up in the staff bathroom to commemorate it and everything. But I need this job and—"

I put him out of his misery. "I get it. A plaque, huh? You're not breaking the rules, and I suck at serving. So, who's the drink from?"

Tom lets out a relieved sigh. "Neve. She's setting up the karaoke right now but said she'll be joining you as soon as she can."

My eyes widen in shock. "K-k-karaoke…?"

Tom's smile is mischievous. "Didn't she tell you? Friday nights are going to be our regular karaoke nights."

Oh, fuck.

I take a deep swig of beer to fortify myself.

My number one nightmare, apart from sitting an exam that I haven't prepared for…naked…is being in front of a room of people and singing karaoke.

My throat is dry. I swallow.

I used to be more spontaneous, before my marriage to Wilder. I'm trying to be again.

I'm taking baby steps, however for example, singing with Shay, while D'Angelo plays the piano, in the privacy of our own lounge.

Karaoke in front of all these people is a method of torture.

If I'm ever captured by an enemy army, they'd only have to put me in front a drunken crowd, stick a microphone in front of my face, and insist that I sing "I Touch Myself" by the Divinyls to break me.

What's wrong with keeping singing to the shower?

When my phone rings, I hurriedly snatch it out of my pocket.

I bet it's one of the guys. They promised to only call me tonight, however, if it's an emergency.

Still, gorgeous disasters that they are, they've still saved me from Neve's torture.

As long as they haven't burned down the house, anything that they've done is forgiven.

I glance at the number.

Yep, it's D'Angelo.

Or, as I still have him in my contacts, **GRUMPY**.

I answer **GRUMPY**, grinning as I hold the phone to my ear.

D'Angelo's date with Shay can't have gone wrong already, right?

"Hey, what's up?" I hold the phone close to my ear against the chatter and music.

I can barely hear.

"Help," D'Angelo hisses.

Suddenly on the alert, I stand up. "What the fuck? Are you okay?"

"Do I sound okay? Why didn't you warn me?" He sounds terrified.

My pulse speeds up. My hand tightens around the phone.

What the hell's happened?

"Stay calm." I try to sound calm myself, when I'm not. "I'll come straight home. Is anyone hurt?"

Silence.

Finally D'Angelo replies, "What are you talking about? You don't need to cut your evening short. You're having fun, and one of us should be. I'm talking about our little horror fanatic. He's out in the lounge now, having the time of his life, while I'm—"

"Why does your voice sound echoey? Are you calling me from the bathroom?"

At last, it's beginning to make sense. I try…hard…not to laugh.

"Yes, yes." D'Angelo sounds embarrassed. "All right, I admit that I may be hiding out in the bathroom to make this call."

I narrow my eyes. "Is this an emergency?"

"I'm trapped in the bathroom, hiding from a horror movie because I can't bear watching them, while my date is in the other room unaware and excitedly munching popcorn. I'd call that an emergency."

I settle back on the stool, placing my beer on the counter. "You can't even watch *Labyrinth* without freaking out over the creepy goblin puppets. What the fuck has Shay got you watching?"

"Shay said that it was an English classic. I thought that I'd be safe. He tricked me."

Shit, these two need me as a permanent mediator or possibly, a referee.

"What film is it?" I ask.

D'Angelo takes a deep breath like he can barely bring himself to answer. "*Hellraiser.*"

I choke. "You're scared of the Goblin King. What in the hell, pun intended, made you think that you'd cope with Pinhead?"

"Shay swore that it was a love story. I thought that it'd be romantic for our date."

I can't help it. I burst out laughing.

I wish that I was back with them. But they need to figure this out together.

Plus, it kind of says something about Shay, filled with sunshine as he appears to be, that he sees *Hellraiser* primarily as a *love story*.

My expression steels. "Jude D'Angelo, as soon as I stop speaking, put down your phone, get out of that bathroom and back into the lounge with your date. Be honest with Shay. He won't judge you for not liking horror movies. Both you and I enjoy comedies. Shay will have to join Mike for horror movie nights because he's into them too, probably because as a doctor, he's desensitized to gore."

"But this is Shay's night. His first ever date with a man. I need it to be perfect. And he loves them."

D'Angelo may act like a cold asshole. Deep down, however, he's allowed me to see his vulnerable side. I understand why this is important to him.

"Shay only cares that you're with him," I reply, softly.

"Trust me, your needs matter too. He'll be happy that you're showing the real you, beneath the mask. Try it."

There's a slight hesitation.

Then D'Angelo says, quietly, "Thanks, principessa."

I swipe off the phone, resting it on the counter.

Someone's kicked off the karaoke evening now with one of the most uncomfortable and awkward sounding duets that I've ever heard.

It's meant to be David Bowie and Queen's "Under Pressure."

It's an apt title.

I peer through the crowds and then chuckle, when I glimpse Cody next to Michael, his husband, at the front of the inn.

I should have guessed that Cody would choose Bowie to sing. It's testimony to his friendship to Neve that he's singing first. It's also testimony to Michael's love for his husband that he's agreed to duet with him.

The stern doctor is even less likely to enjoy performing than I am.

I whoop encouragement, as Michael tries to make a particularly high note with his deep, rumbling voice.

And fails.

I wince, when I realize that I'm the only person whooping and clapping.

Neve winds through the crowd toward me, looking like an Emo Queen of Friday night.

Neve's my age. She has chestnut eyes and spiky midnight hair. Large horn-rimmed glasses are pushed firmly on her nose. Her rich brown skin glows bronze on her cheeks.

She's dressed in a Jimmy Eat World black t-shirt and skinny jeans with a studded belt.

She snatches a bottle from Tom's waiting hand, before pointing it at me. "You fucking made it."

I pick up my bottle and clink it with hers. "Cheers to your official karaoke opening night."

"Did it feel like spitting glass to get out those words, RH?"

I give her the finger.

She laughs. "Your turn will come. I've chosen a song already."

"Shut up." I hide my smile behind my bottle. "We both know rules dictate that I get to choose, or you'll have me singing "Welcome to the Black Parade". Do you want the mood to become funereal?"

"I wouldn't mind. It'd be a vibe."

She'd do it too.

"How's business?" I relax back. "It looks to be booming."

Neve slouches against the bar. "People — all people — no matter who they are or love need somewhere that they can go to drink, dance their asses off, and feel safe. You know, it's getting harder here every year for folks. You haven't seen it because you left town. But I have. At least once a week, they need to forget about their sucky job, rising rents, or shitty neighbors. In this rundown inn with cheap beer, they can be themselves and just fucking…"

"Sing?" I wince.

Neve grins, wickedly. "Yep."

I nudge her with my shoulder. "So, tell me about that blonde nurse who you were having a wild time with, while I was having one with Shay. Are you dating her?"

To my surprise, Neve blushes.

She never blushes.

Intrigued, I study her closer.

Neve twirls her bottle between her hands. "The pretty blonde with the badass smoky make-up who was eye fucking me that evening is called Lucy. It turns out that she works at the hospital with Mike. He's given his Michael Seal of Approval. I also give my Tonguing Seal of Approval because fuck, she knows what to do. It's like poetry."

"Pussy poetry." I tilt my head. "I like it. Are you seeing her again?"

Neve pulls a face. "She's all athletic and shit. She's into these thrill-seeking, risk your life sports because things aren't hard enough already, right? So, she wants to share them with me. She's taking me skydiving next week."

"What?" I splutter, spitting my beer out and needing to wipe my mouth. "You've never even been in a plane. There's no way that you'd jump out of one."

I can't imagine Neve in skydiving gear.

Can you skydive in all black?

"The things you do for…" Neve's mouth twists. Is she going to say *love*? I hold my breath. "…hot blondes."

I chuckle. "D'Angelo's finding that out tonight on his date with Shay."

When there's a sudden smattering of applause, I realize that Cody and Michael have stopped singing.

I leap up and down, clapping wildly.

I ignore the disbelieving stares of the people around me.

Neve snorts.

"Here they come," I mutter, as Cody and Michael weave toward us, "insincere praise at the ready."

"Yeah, not my style." Neve collapses onto a stool, resting back on her elbow on the counter.

Neve doesn't sugarcoat. Actually, it's my favorite thing about my bestie.

Michael looks worn down by the ordeal, or it may be that he's simply exhausted from the twelve hour shift at the hospital, which he finished before coming out tonight.

He's an awesome partner, however, because whenever he can, he takes Cody out to have fun, no matter how tired he is.

Cody and Michael are both lucky to have each other.

Michael is in his late thirties. He's hot but stern with ebony skin and salt and pepper hair. He's dressed in a casual tan suit that's open at the neck.

Michael's arm is slung possessively around Cody's shoulders. As always, Cody is relaxed against Michael's chest, happy and secure.

My heart clenches to see it.

"Here come the rock stars." I raise my beer. "The next big thing."

"If the next big thing is two awkward men who sound like cats fighting," Neve agrees.

Cody only grins. "Eden would have liked it then."

"I don't think anyone's heard someone singing Freddy Mercury and hitting such low notes before." Neve arches her brow.

"And they never will again. Thank you for the backhanded compliment on my deep voice," Michael says, dryly. "That was my first and last performance. You're honored to have witnessed it."

"Well," I meet Cody's eye and wink, "unless you lose a bet with my brother. Then we'll be hearing you sing ABBA."

"In a tutu," Cody adds, smugly.

Michael freezes. "This is one of the many reasons that I respect my husband...and no longer make bets with him."

Cody pouts.

Michael looks like he wants to kiss the pout off Cody, but since he's not one for PDA, settles for giving him a stern stare.

"Cody," he says, warningly.

And that works just as effectively on my brother.

"Come on." I tap my beer bottle. "We're together now. Okay, we're a little pissed but that's a good thing. I did my best work at college, when I was tipsy. Don't tell my dad that. What I'm trying to say in a rambling way is that we need to brainstorm about how to improve Bay Rebels' finances. They're fucked."

Neve looks confused. "Are they? Even after the successful exhibition games and all the attention in the news?"

"I guess that helped…"

It should have done. The arena was packed.

Why didn't it?

"What do you need me to do?" Michael tightens his hold around Cody. "Isn't it up to the players to win their games? I can't put their skates on for them and trust me, if you'd seen me do any kind of sport in my college days, you wouldn't want me to."

"The pressure is already on the players," I reply. "It's been messing with their heads. It's a mind fuck to have done as well as they have but *still* be on the chopping block, especially after what happened to Eden. I can handle the PR side. What I need is help with out of the box ideas to improve the finances."

"You're awesome at business, Neve." Cody gestures around the room. "Just look at this place. There's hardly space to move. I'm better at spending money than earning it."

Michael snorts. "That's certainly true."

Cody tilts his head, and his hair falls over his eyes. "So, how'd you manage it?"

Neve becomes very still; her expression is serious. "I could tell you the boring business shit. It takes years of twenty hour days and not taking a salary. Years of putting the business above everything, which wasn't hard to do, since my asshole family threw me out, and I was alone apart from you guys. But the real answer, the one that helps you, is this business is built on this town itself. The people here fucking love the place. I respect them, and they respect me. There's no bullshit. And that goodwill —

truth — is what connects me to our community. It's about authenticity."

I furrow my brow. "How do we copy that at Bay Rebels?"

When Neve taps my nose, I yelp.

"Dumbass." She taps my nose again for good measure. "Freedom already loves the Bay Rebels The team is part of the town. They may be misfits, but they're *our* misfits. You can't buy that type of loyalty."

"I'm willing to bet that gate receipts, merchandise, and concessions are already up," I say, slowly. "Shit, you're right. I don't understand this sudden pressure. Why's the team in financial trouble?"

"What if they're not?" Cody ducks his head, biting his lip. "The fans love the team. You're turning around the players' images. But what if it's still not enough for the board and higher up management? They're the ones who don't love screw-ups like us. They're elitist. They don't love how Dad's supporting players with difficult pasts. What if this is an excuse for those entitled assholes to get rid of us?"

My stomach swoops, and my skin goosebumps.

He could be right. But why does he sound so sure?

I slip off my stool and lay my hand on Cody's arm. "Has someone been giving you a hard time?"

Instantly, Michael's eyes darken. "Have they, Code?"

Cody raises his head, and our gazes meet.

They have been.

Fuck.

"The players have been amazing." Cody leans even

closer against Michael for support but still without looking away from me. "The coaches are hardasses, but I'm used to that, having grown up with Dad. The equipment manager is great like most of the medical side. But it's some of the senior staff…"

"Code…" Michael twists Cody now in his arms, holding him firmly by his shoulders. "You know that you can tell me anything. That includes, surprisingly enough, when your colleagues are giving you a hard time. I bitch about the Senior Consultants at the hospital. It's normal."

"It's my first serious job," Cody replies. "You were so proud of me for getting it."

Michael gently tips up Cody's chin to make him meet his eye. "It doesn't matter what happens. I will still be proud of you."

"They're just always around the arena, and I don't know why, assessing things and sneering," Cody admits. "The way that they talk to me…it seems petty when I say it out loud but…it's small things like they call everyone else by their first names but they call me *the coach's son.*"

"Assholes," I exclaim.

Cody worked for years for that job. He earned it.

He was appointed *despite* being Dad's son and not because of it.

If these management guys knew anything about our relationship with Dad, then they'd know that we're not given handouts.

We're not even written into his will.

Neve shoves herself off her stool. "I'm getting my shovel."

I blink. "What?"

"To bury the bodies," she clarifies, pushing her glasses more firmly onto her nose with frightening determination.

"I have a more realistic suggestion." Michael hugs Cody but he looks as close to murder as Neve is. "We work out how to beat the board and management. If they think that they can humiliate and degrade any of the people who I love and care about, taking away the heart of our town as they do it, then they don't know us at all."

My heart soars. "The players have the ice covered. I have the PR angle."

Neve gestures across the throngs on the dance floor. "Plus, we have the people of Freedom to bring the love."

Unexpectedly, my phone rings again.

I grin.

That'll be D'Angelo hiding from Pinhead in the bathroom again, unless he's escaped up to his bedroom this time.

I guess that could work out, as long as he's carried Shay with him.

I answer the phone with a deep, English accent, ready to tease D'Angelo. "Your suffering will—"

"Excuse me?" Melanie's sneering voice cuts me off. "Threats aren't professional. Was that on the record? I don't know why I was expecting anything better from you, Robyn."

Shit, shit, shit.

Can I switch off my phone and pretend that this call never happened?

Why do I have to be a PR, when she's the journalist?

"It's Ms. McKenna," I say, stiffly. "It was off the record, and I apologize. I thought that you were someone else."

"Do you have a long list of people who you threaten then?" She sounds delighted like she's sniffed out a story. "Do tell."

"What do you want?" I snap.

"A full, live interview with the captain of the Bay Rebels. You can make up for your rudeness that way."

"I'll send you a muffin basket."

"It would be in D'Angelo's best interests to put his side of the story."

I freeze. "What side of which story? If you tell me what exclusive you're running on him next week, then I'll talk to him about the interview."

Melanie's laugh is nasty and holds an edge to it that makes me shudder. "Do the interview and he'll find out. I have a secret…"

Then she's the one to cut off the call mid-sentence.

CHAPTER TEN

Captain's Hall, Freedom

*S*hay

"Hellraiser is a bloody brilliant love story," I say, brightly. "Okay, it's a toxic romance, but that only shows love can be dangerous sometimes. I like the thought that love can last, even after death."

Even more bloody brilliant is the way that I'm sprawled on the crushed velvet couch with my head resting on D'Angelo's hard chest. My arm is slung across his middle.

I hope that I haven't drooled on his expensive looking silk shirt.

"You're a strange puppy," D'Angelo drawls.

"I thought that I was your cucciolo."

I'm staring avidly at the flat screen television that hangs on the wall in the lounge in Captain's Hall. It's a thing of beauty. Eden and I would have killed for a television this size, when we were teenagers.

Moonlight streams through the windows over the room, which is so grand that I always feel like I'll get in trouble even for sitting down on the heavy, purple and black furniture.

A gilt mirror gleams above a fireplace, which reflects back the in-built bookcases that are Eden's favorite part of the room.

I know that they're his favorite because he hovers around them every evening like he's in heaven.

I hover around the black Steinway grand piano.

I never thought that I'd love a piano most. But it's like an extension of D'Angelo.

When D'Angelo can't express how he's feeling in words, he plays the piano. Sometimes, he composes.

I like to go for a run or kick some football with Eden on the lawn, but D'Angelo plays some beautiful shit that makes me feel things that I never have before.

I always wanted to learn guitar but I knew that Dad didn't have the cash for shit like that. I couldn't ask him. It would have been unfair.

It felt like learning music wasn't for people like me.

D'Angelo says, however, that he's going to teach me. He thinks that I can. So, maybe I'm wrong.

Plus, sitting on the piano stool is where I told D'Angelo and Robyn that I wanted to be with *both* of them.

It's where I kissed them for the first time.

I was so fucking scared.

Terrified like I haven't been in years.

It was like jumping out of a plane without a parachute, only neither of them let me hit the ground.

They caught me with their acceptance and love.

Fuck, I love them both.

I wrinkle my nose at the smoky, sweet scent of the fire, and my eyes sting. I wish that it wasn't masking D'Angelo's masculine, whiskey scent.

Since we started the film, D'Angelo's been clutching onto a glass of whiskey.

Is that a sign of how much the movie is scaring him?

This is our first date though. It's special. And he looks fucking gorgeous in a crisp, navy pinstriped suit.

I've even dressed up for this date myself. I'm wearing my favorite punky red shirt (the one with strategic rips in it over the nipples and stomach), and tightest black jeans that I own.

Eden repainted my nails for me in silence but with an intense concentration that told me it was important to him.

I hope that D'Angelo appreciates the adventure I had in the shower cleaning myself out in case this date goes as well as I hope that it will.

The madras curry that we cooked together was perfection. It was just like the curry that I'd get in England with Eden.

I don't know why D'Angelo only managed a few bites, before diving to the fridge and downing all the milk that we possessed.

Is it toxic masculinity to feel proud that I can eat a hotter curry than him?

Still, it was hard to feel dominant in any way, when I was squirming on my chair to the unfamiliar feeling of the small plug in my arse.

D'Angelo dropped the plug off earlier with a wicked smile. "Just something to loosen your sweet, tight hole."

I didn't know that I could both flush so red…or get hard that quickly.

Still, only D'Angelo could say things like that to me and not get punched in the dick.

I'm fucking obsessed.

When the credits roll on the movie, I sneak a kiss onto D'Angelo's chest.

Scary movies are the best excuse to get close to someone, even someone as bristly as D'Angelo.

He's been playing with my hair, and I'm not even sure that he's noticed.

I fucking love it.

I peer up at him and then laugh, when I realize that his eyes are closed.

I discretely cough. "You can look now, darlin'. It's finished."

"Thank Christ." D'Angelo's beautiful eyes snap open.

When he takes a deep swig of whiskey, I can't look away from the way that he swallows and his throat bobs.

"You could have told me that horror movies weren't your thing," I say, casually.

"Why would I have missed out on using you as a plushie, while giving myself nightmares for the next…forever?"

"I did think for a moment there that you'd had second thoughts about *us*." I push myself up to sit straighter.

D'Angelo arches his brow. "What could have given you that idea?"

"I don't know. Possibly, your mad dash to hide in the bathroom and…wild guess here…call Robyn for urgent advice."

D'Angelo moves his hand to the back of my neck, squeezing just on the edge of too hard.

I melt.

It's the casual possessiveness of the gesture that I bloody love.

"Where would any of us be without her?" D'Angelo admits without any shame. "She's the reason that I came back in here and negotiated to watch the rest of the film but with a drink in my hand and on subtitles only. The only thing that I have experience with is negotiations. I get to choose the movie for the second date. It's going to be a comedy."

Called it.

And *second date*? So, this must be going well then.

I glow, as happiness surges through me. "Don't worry, darlin', I'll protect you from the things that go bump in the night or want to drag you to hell."

D'Angelo tightens his hand on my neck; the wicked

look in his eyes makes me feel like I could come untouched. "You forget, I'm a fallen angel, which means that you should be scared of *me*."

"Sorry," I shrug, "sort of hard, when horror villains were like my babysitters. Mum and Dad had to work night shifts. Eden always had his nose in a book. So, I was left watching late night TV."

D'Angelo gentles his hold, running his hand up into my hair. "There's a lot that we still need to find out about each other, huh?"

I nod. "I figure that curry isn't your style, either. I wanted to share that meal with you, however, because Eden and I would save up each term, so we'd have enough to eat out at this Indian place in Guildford in the final week. Money was bloody tight, but we'd worked hard in both our college courses and on the ice; we deserved to have something good, right?"

How can D'Angelo understand?

He's wealthy. He has everything. I must sound like trash to him.

Without meaning to, I wrench away from D'Angelo, wincing as a couple of my golden hairs are pulled out in his grasp.

I edge away from him on the sofa to put some distance between us.

Normally, it's Eden who has difficulty with talking, not me.

Yet this is different.

I'm trying not to hide behind my sunny mask.

Eden, who's up in our room right now giving D'Angelo and me some time alone, advised me to allow D'Angelo to see beneath that.

It's hard.

I've managed it with Robyn but it's more difficult with another guy to let down my defenses. It's even worse with the man who I fucking idolize.

A man who I've respected, looked up to, and watched playing in the NHL, throughout college.

I had D'Angelo's picture as my screensaver. I'm not telling him that.

Perhaps, I always had a crush on him, in the same way that I have one on Tom Hiddleston and Idris Elba, and simply hadn't worked out that side of my sexuality yet.

D'Angelo is watching me warily. "You deserve everything, cucciolo."

Is that how life has worked for him? You get what you *deserve*?

I wish.

If that was true, then Eden wouldn't have been beaten so hard and repeatedly as a kid, while I was locked in the room next door banging and screaming until I lost my voice trying to get to him, that he can't skate now because one more concussion could kill him.

But then, Eden was the one who never spoke. The bastards who had us locked up liked that about him. They had a contest going to see who could get him to speak first.

Neither of them won that bet.

I have a sick satisfaction about that.

If we got what we *deserve*, then they'd be dead, and

Eden would have a place on the Bay Rebels team and a mansion filled with books and cats.

One day, I'm going to buy him that.

I need D'Angelo to understand.

Why is he even trying to date me? He already has Robyn, and she's bloody perfect.

She's beautiful and smart.

She doesn't have the type of baggage that I do. D'Angelo and her come from the same background. They've known and loved each other since college.

How can I compete?

If D'Angelo wants to fuck me, then I'm fine with that. He doesn't need to pretend that this is an actual relationship.

No one has wanted that from me. I'm still pinching myself that Robyn does.

"I know what I deserve." I cross my arms. "You shouldn't have to deal with… The guys on my college hockey team weren't keen on having me around. I know that I'm an adorable ball of sunshine, but back then, they didn't like two odd twins with poor clothes who could never pay for their round at the bar being their teammates."

D'Angelo's eyes flash with anger. "Assholes. I wish that I could kick them in the balls for you. But you know that I had the same problems. Talon took delight in telling you about the way that I was hazed for being a scholarship student, as if it would shame me. But it didn't. The shame is all on those bastards. You and I aren't so different. Come on, scoot back here."

When he holds out his hand to me, I take it and edge closer to him on the couch again.

My eyes light up because he's right.

"The scholarship brothers." I clink an imaginary whiskey glass with D'Angelo's. "We can reclaim that and make it cool, right?"

"I'll let you believe that," D'Angelo takes a long drink of his whiskey, effortlessly elegant, "along with the fact that *cool* is in any way a *cool* word to use."

I laugh, relaxing.

Is it a good thing that we're bonding over our shitty pasts?

Definitely.

It's like being on a date with your best friend who also makes you want to rip off their clothes.

On instinct, I lean closer to him.

Our gazes meet, and his becomes heated.

My heart hammers.

Before D'Angelo, I'd never kissed a man. I didn't think that I wanted to.

But it's not *any* man who I want to kiss.

It's him, D'Angelo.

Jude.

I let out a shuddering breath, before I clutch onto the front of his silky shirt, needing something to anchor myself.

D'Angelo angles his lips toward mine. I brush my lips against his.

It's not enough.

He rests his strong hand against my neck, where I'm so sensitive, and I relax against him.

I can feel that he's letting me lead.

I kiss him again and again, drinking in his breath, scent, and taste. I'm greedy for everything that he can give me, as he grows impatient, taking over and deepening the kiss.

I slide my hands up to his shoulders.

Then I pull back, before I won't be able to stop myself unbuttoning his shirt like I've been desperate to do all evening.

D'Angelo's pupils are dark and dilated. "You have no idea what kissing you like this…being on a date with you…means to me." Unexpectedly, a cloud crosses his expression, which I don't understand. He reaches to touch my face like I'm a ghost and he's already lost me. "I couldn't bear the thought of anyone hurting you, simply for wanting to kiss me."

My heart speeds up.

He's tapping the side of the glass in patterns of three. He does that when he's anxious.

It looks like he's remembering something, and it's not a good memory. I should know.

Eden gets the same look sometimes.

My brow furrows. "No one's going to. Jude, are you with me? Are you okay, darlin'? Is this about my parents? Because even though I haven't told them about my bisexuality yet, I'm sure that they wouldn't hurt me. They've never raised their hand to me."

There's a look in his eye, when I say that, which makes my stomach twist.

Someone in D'Angelo's family has raised *their* hand to *him*.

Was it his parents?

Is this why he never mentions them? Why they don't call?

Rage slams through me.

It shakes me how powerful it is. I've only felt this protective toward two people before: Eden and Robyn.

"Good." D'Angelo looks like he's battling with whether to tell me something, before he forces himself to continue, "But it's hard because mine did. They caught me kissing a boy. So, they sent me to this school for troubled teens. It was hell being trained and conditioned like a dog. I haven't told Robyn everything that happened there. I was tortured with ice and heat to make me averse to images of men kissing."

"Shit." I tighten my hold on his hand.

I don't ever want to let go.

I don't know if he's shaking or I am.

"As you can see," D'Angelo kisses me, slow and tender, "it didn't fucking work."

"You're an incredible man," I murmur against his lips, "strong and brave."

"This is why you're my favorite player on the team; you know how to compliment fellow players." He looks down, and his curls brush my cheek. "I'd give anything to allow you the chance to experiment, explore, and have fun without shame or fear."

"You are."

He puffs out a breath in relief. "Excellent. Will you move in with me?"

He appears mildly startled that he's blurted the words.

"Ehm, aren't we living together now?"

D'Angelo's cheeks are tinted pink. "I meant after the season ends. You could move into my actual house in Freedom. I do have one, you know. I'd like to take you all there and show you. I think that you'll like it. I need you. As a friend, boyfriend, and lover. I want us to be a family — Robyn, Eden, me…and you."

He holds his breath like there's a chance that I'd say no.

He's shared something painful from his past about what went on at the school that he'd been sent away to, and by the look in his eyes, he's never told anyone else.

Eden and I have held onto our own secrets for long enough for me to know that.

Then he's opened his home to my twin and me, asking us to become his family.

I'm lost now.

This is deeper than love.

I feel safe and secure with this man in a way that can't be undone.

Have you ever fallen in trust?

My eyes are burning with happy tears. My heart swells.

"We'll have to talk to the others, but you're already my family." I grin. My mouth aches, but I can't stop grinning. "You do know that I'll probably break all your expensive shit within a week."

D'Angelo smiles, genuine and relaxed. "Don't worry, that'll give me an excuse to spank your adorable ass."

I mock gasp. "Monster."

"I thought that you liked monsters." D'Angelo's expression suddenly becomes dangerous. *Fuck.* "And this demon wants to carry you to hell."

"And I want to be carried. Only..." I lick my dry lips. "I've never..."

"I know."

This is my first time.

I'm suddenly very aware of the plug in my arse.

D'Angelo's expression becomes darkly dominant. "Let me show you how this can work. How I can wreck you with pleasure."

And doesn't that just shoot straight to my crotch?

I shift, trying to hide how hard I am in my tight trousers. Of course, D'Angelo smirks, glancing significantly downward.

Bastard.

He lets go of my hand, sprawling on the couch like he's a king.

He crosses his legs. "Strip."

Now, this I do know how to do.

I leap up eagerly. "I thought that you'd never ask, darlin'."

I pull off my t-shirt with one hand as seductively as I can manage, before shimmying down my jeans.

I can't smother my grin, when D'Angelo's breath catches.

I decided to go commando tonight.

There's something about standing here naked in front of D'Angelo for his inspection, while he sits comfortably in his suit sipping whiskey, which is seriously turning me on.

"Do I pass?" I grin, cheekily.

"Put your hands at your side," D'Angelo replies. "Don't cover yourself." I flush but obey him. "Good boy."

Those two words.

They make me feel warm and fuzzy inside in a way that nothing else can.

I'd do almost anything to make him — or Robyn — say them.

I struggle to stand still and earn his praise again.

I search D'Angelo's expression to see if I'm doing the right thing. He appears cold, but his eyes are warm.

"Look at you, standing still and letting me see how hard you are merely at the thought of me fucking your tight, virgin hole." D'Angelo doesn't let me flinch away from his piercing gaze.

I redden.

But he's not wrong.

My cock is already curved against my stomach and dripping precum.

D'Angelo lazily twirls his finger. "Turn around for me, pet. Show me that you obeyed my instructions and are wearing my gift."

"Fuck," I breathe.

I take a steadying breath.

Then I turn around with as much of a sway of my hips

as I can because I know that my arse looks good but I don't expect D'Angelo's next command.

"Now, bend over, spread your legs, and let me see."

I hesitate.

This isn't any different to his commands as my captain on the ice.

I lick my wet lips, bending at the waist and spreading my legs. "Yes, Sir."

D'Angelo growls, surging up from the sofa.

I have power too.

I know that *Sir* has as much of an impact on him as *good boy* does on me.

I feel smug for about three seconds, before D'Angelo grabs me by the arm and is dragging me around the couch.

I stumble after him.

Then he's pushing me down over the back of the couch.

Perhaps, I'm in for that spanking after all.

I steady myself with my arms on the couch cushions.

D'Angelo's fingers tease around the edges of the plug.

Even the light touch is intense.

To my shock, I feel a trickle of whiskey and the last of the ice in D'Angelo's glass fall onto my lower back. It pools, before trailing down my ass crack.

"Shit," I hiss.

"That's what you get for teasing me, pet," D'Angelo murmurs.

He ducks behind me, licking a hot stripe down my back along the path of the ice.

I shake. My skin is tingling. I'm breathing rapidly.

"And this is what you get for obeying me, cucciolo." His voice is rich with promise.

He swirls his tongue over the whiskey that's pooled on my lower back. Then my eyes widen in shock, when his tongue continues to chase the alcohol that's trailed around the plug and over my balls.

The sensation is enough to make me jolt with pleasure.

If that's what I get, then I'm going to be really fucking obedient.

I can feel D'Angelo's hot breath against my balls.

When his cool fingers nudge at the plug, I can feel that he's lubed them up. I bet that the sneaky bastard had lube in his pocket all along.

At last, he moves to ease out the plug but then hesitates. Instead, he toys with it. The movement sends sparks through me. He's deliberately pressing it against my prostate.

D'Angelo pushes the plug in and out of me for a couple of minutes, until I'm curling my toes in a blissed out state.

"If you don't want me to come yet," I pant, "then you'd better stop teasing me."

D'Angelo smacks me crisply on the hip. "Don't come, until I tell you."

"Then don't make me."

To my relief, he eases the plug fully out of me.

I hear a *thunk*, which I think is him throwing the plug to the floor. Then the rip of a condom packet being opened.

I knew that I could piss him off enough to fuck me.

Only, he replaces the plug with his finger and he's back to slowly stretching me out again.

One finger, two, then three.

I raise my head to glare over my shoulder at him.

Then I wish that I hadn't because the sight of D'Angelo standing looking so elegant and in control in his suit almost makes me come on the fucking spot.

"You don't have to be gentle with me," I say. "I won't break."

He arches his brow. "This is your first time with a guy. You may. And I want to be gentle." He leans over me, whispering low and dangerous, "Just don't get used to it."

Hot and cold flushes through me.

I twist, trying to raise my body over the couch. I'm desperate for D'Angelo to kiss me…fuck me…something.

He takes mercy on me, capturing my lips with his.

D'Angelo's kiss is controlled and like he's staking his claim.

He slips his hand under my throat, pulling me up toward his chest, just as he thrusts into me.

It punches the breath from me.

He holds me in place, not moving for a long moment.

It doesn't hurt, but I feel fuller than I ever have. Despite all the preparation, there's a burning stretch.

But I want this.

I need to feel him.

"Okay?" He turns my head, tightening his grip on my throat and kissing me again.

I don't think that I can talk but I nod.

"Words," D'Angelo says sharply, thrusting into me again.

It's too much and not enough at the same time.

This is the missing piece of the jigsaw. I was scared that it wouldn't feel right. But it does.

It bloody does.

"Brilliant." I smile, kissing D'Angelo back. "Harder, darlin.'"

He appears to take this as permission to break me because he fucks into me harder and deeper and faster.

I'm trapped against the back of the couch and by D'Angelo's arm across my throat, holding me to his chest.

Yet I feel safe held like this.

His cock's deep inside me and it's sending sparks through me, which is making intense waves of pleasure wash through me deep inside.

"Please…" I'm begging. I've never felt anything like this before. I can't tip over into coming. "Please, Jude…"

"I've got you." D'Angelo's voice is so bloody tender. He pulls me back from the couch to slip his hand to my cock, then he's wanking me off at the same that he fucks into me, slower now and deep. *Perfect.* "Come for me, my good boy."

And on his command, I do.

Jude D'Angelo.

My captain. My boyfriend. My sex god.

I know then, as I'm still shaking with the aftershocks, that I'm fucking screwed because I'm in love with both Robyn and D'Angelo.

The type of love that you never fall out of.

CHAPTER ELEVEN

Captain's Hall, Freedom

*R*obyn

I STUMBLE into the hallway of Captain's Hall, slamming the door shut behind me.

"Honey, I'm home," I call with a grin.

I kick off my black heels and massage my bare calves. They're aching from the wild dancing that always happens, whenever Cody and I get together.

It's Michael's fault. He hates dancing, although he loves to watch his husband shaking his ass.

How could I say no to my brother, even when he

wanted us to do our high school routine to Shakira's "Hips Don't Lie"?

Hell, I'm a good sister.

I look around at the silent, shadowy hallway.

"Huh, no Shay." I push my tangled hair out of my eyes.

Normally, he'd have bounded up to meet me like a dog does their owner by now.

I stayed out as long as I could to give Shay and D'Angelo the best chance on their first date. Eventually, however, even Neve kicked me out at the point that she was putting stools up on tables and turning off the lights.

If Shay's not here, then the date must have gone well, right?

Silently, I pad toward the lounge.

Part of me wishes that I was drunk. But after the phone call from Melanie earlier, where she decided to go full on villain vibes with her whispered threats of knowing *secrets*, I haven't been drinking.

In fact, it sobered me right the fuck up.

Who knew if she'd call back?

Is she blackmailing us?

Anxiety spikes through me. My mouth is dry.

Melanie is playing a dangerous game. And she plays dirty.

I'll never forgive her for the way that she wrecked Cody at high school. She body shamed me at a time that was already tough, when I was grieving for my mom.

It was the way that she manipulated the gang of jocks and mean girls around her, however, to beat the shit out of my younger brother for sticking up for me, destroying his relationship with Dad in the process, that truly shows me the type of girl she was.

Now, how she's hounding the man I love.

I don't think that she's changed at all.

Yet I have.

It's her mistake not to realize that.

I'll ask D'Angelo if he'll do the interview but I can tell what his answer to her will be already.

It starts with *fuck* and ends with *off*.

Luckily, as his personal PR Director, I'll turn it into something more diplomatic like he can't fit Melanie into his busy schedule, since the season begins on Tuesday.

Then I'll work with Eden to find out what's really going on.

I peer into the lounge but stop myself calling out for Shay just in time.

I smile.

D'Angelo is lying on the couch. He's still dressed in his suit, but his eyes are closed, and he's sleeping.

Shay is naked, although a soft blanket is wrapped around his shoulders. He's lying with his head resting on D'Angelo's shoulder. His legs are tangled with D'Angelo's, and fuck, his ass looks incredible at this angle.

Is that a handprint?

I lick my lips.

This is the hottest aftercare turned exhausted nap that I've ever seen.

I'm definitely getting all the details tomorrow.

For now, I tiptoe back into the hall, smiling to myself. Then I climb the stairs with a groan.

Shakira's hips may not lie but mine are fucking sore.

This is what happens when you forget that you're not still eighteen.

Cody didn't appear to have the same problem. I think that he'll be dancing on tables when he's ninety.

When I reach the top of the stairs, I'm surprised to see that there's light coming from the open doorway of the twins' bedroom.

The twins are sharing the smallest bedroom in the mansion. I hope that it's Dad being thoughtful, which he can manage sometimes, because he installed metal framed bunk beds, so that the twins could share the room.

They've never been separated before. They need to be close to function and feel safe. Knowing their troubled past, I understand why.

I hope that I can help them to begin to feel secure enough to spend increasing amounts of time apart.

There's a closet and mirrored chest of drawers and wardrobe against one wall. On the far side is a large, arched window with gray drapes.

"Not able to sleep, huh?" I call out.

Then I stop in surprise.

Eden is sitting balanced on the open window ledge, precariously. His hand is outstretched toward the branch of the old oak that grows outside.

He's as still as a statue, and as beautiful as a Greek one.

One with silver piercings through their nipples, which glint in the light.

My eyes widen in shock.

Fuck, what's he doing? What if he falls?

Is he trying to climb out?

He isn't going to jump, right?

My eyes widen.

"Eden, don't…" I rush into the room.

Startled, Eden looks around.

He's only dressed in gray joggers. The silver moonlight through the window glimmers across the pale skin of his bare chest and makes him look ethereal. It lights the flames of the phoenix on his back.

For a heart stopping moment, I think that he's going to fall out, unable to stabilize himself with one of his arms still in a sling.

I dive to him, throwing my arms around his neck.

"I've got you," I gasp. "What are you thinking? You can't climb trees with busted ribs and your shoulder injury."

Eden's body is still purple and black with bruises. It makes my heart ache. I want to kiss each of them in turn.

Eden arches his pierced eyebrow. "You scared away Puck."

"Who?"

"My squirrel."

He glances at me out of the corner of his eye like he expects me to make fun of him or take away his right to his new pet.

"Good name." I peer out of the window at the tiny red squirrel with tufted ears and a pointed face that's scampering away down the tree. I can't hold back the laugh. "Would you mind moving back from the window, before I have a heart attack? I've had enough nasty surprises tonight. Puck will have to go to sleep."

"He should be in his nest sleeping anyway. He likes to say goodnight."

"You really do like animals, huh?"

Eden glances down. "They don't make demands. They're easier to understand than humans. When I was a kid, I wanted to be a vet."

"What changed?"

Eden's expression tightens, although he allows me to tug him away from the open window. He's cold, and I run my hands up and down his arms to warm him up.

"Nothing changed. Ice hockey happened." Eden's serious stormy gray eyes meet mine.

My chest tightens. "So, are you waiting up for your brother?"

He nods. "It's a big night for him."

He looks as anxious as a parent on prom night.

It's not only Shay's first date with D'Angelo, of course. It's also Shay's first time bottoming with a man. I trust D'Angelo to be both careful and make it good for him.

But still, for both men, their pasts mean that that it's more complicated than normal.

I trace down the strong muscles of Eden's chest. "I peeked into the lounge. They've fallen asleep together on the couch. Let's just say that it looks like they had a very good date."

Eden's expression is inscrutable. "Jude had better have made sure that it was the best first date, or I'll cut off his balls."

I laugh and then realize that Eden's not joking. "Shay's fine."

Eden scrunches up his nose. "I can't tell these things. He sent me a whole string of emojis, including egg plants and peaches. I still don't have the heart to tell him that I don't know what they mean."

I chuckle, pulling him to sit on the bottom bunk, which has scarlet bedding. "I think they mean that he had a *really* good time."

"This is Shay's bed," Eden protests.

"I'm not clambering onto the top bunk," I reply. "Who got to claim which bed? Did you arm wrestle or something for it?"

Eden cards his fingers through his slicked back hair. "Shay's an insomniac. He needs the bed that means he can get up and down a lot without waking me. He's always had the bottom bunk."

"And has he always had insomnia?"

"If that's what you want to call nightmares." He hesitates, before offering, "Why don't we have our own date now?"

"I'd like that."

I smooth my hand over the covers. They're messy and unmade. When I glance above my head, I can see that the top bunk is made with military precision.

I should have been able to tell which bed belonged to which twin.

The only thing out of place on the top bunk is a book, which is lying open: Angela Carter's *The Magic Toyshop*.

Eden's borrowed (stolen) it from my own book collection. I recommended it at our last book club for two.

Eden always quietly reads my recommendations, and that always makes something warm unfurl in my chest.

It's a rush, a unique type of intimacy, reading the same book as someone but also knowing that they're going to escape into a new world, simply on your word alone.

That's a type of trust.

Plus, we try to read side by side in bed together at night for half an hour. I never thought that I'd want that because my ex would have laughed in my face, if I'd suggested it. With Eden, however, it's my secret indulgence like eating ice cream from the tub or not wearing a bra on Sundays.

I cherish those quiet times in bed with Eden, before Shay bounces in to join us with D'Angelo prowling after him.

Before Eden, I didn't realize how powerful silence could be.

I nod at the book. "So, what do you think of it?"

Eden's gaze doesn't leave mine. "Beautiful. Dark. It shows how people can play each other like puppets. Sometimes, you can only start your new life by burning down your old one."

Perhaps, it wasn't the best book to recommend.

"I guess." I push a strand of hair behind my ear. "Did you do that? Burn down your old life?"

Something flickers behind Eden's eyes that I don't understand. "I thought about it. But I was the one who burned."

Uncomfortable, I'm hyper aware of the phoenix tattoo on his back.

I reach to cup Eden's cheek. "But you were reborn from the ash, right? You'll always be reborn."

He nods.

Then I notice that a sheet of folded yellow paper is sticking out of the book.

My face lights up. "You made notes!"

I reach for the book, grasping it by the corner.

"Don't," Eden says, alarmed.

The note flutters out and lands on my lap.

When Eden slaps his large hand onto the note, his hand covers my crotch.

I arch my eyebrow. "Hmm, that feels nice. I didn't know that talking about books was code for sex but I'm down with that."

Eden snatches his hand back, flushing. "Sorry."

I glance down at the note but I don't open it. If he doesn't want me to read it, then I won't embarrass him. Perhaps, it's a poem or the long promised chores rota for the household.

That would make D'Angelo happy.

Finally.

But then I see the underlined title that's scrawled on the top:

<u>Ten Reasons I Love Robyn</u>

My heart beats faster.

Joy soars through me.

He loves me…and for ten different reasons.

My face warms. "At a wild guess, this isn't a blog post.

That would kind of defeat the whole *secret relationship* thing we have going on."

When I glance up, my gaze meets Eden's unreadable one.

He moves even closer to me on the bed. He takes the paper from my hand, pushing himself up and placing it back in the book like it's a relic.

He stands with his back turned to me.

Shit.

"I can't say these things out loud," he finally says, still turned away. "But I can put them down on paper."

I clench my hands on my lap. "I didn't mean to see it like that."

"It's good. Now, I don't have to work out how to tell you. I could add them to our Guide. I've been trying to work out how I can become a part of your Guide. I want to fit in this relationship. I need to find my place."

"I'd love that. It'd be perfect. D'Angelo already has the smutty stickmen drawings sorted."

"And Shay has all the kinks that he wants to explore with D'Angelo and you written at the back with marks out of ten."

Wow, thorough.

I should have known that Shay would do something like that.

The muscles in Eden's strong shoulders bunch, and it looks like the phoenix on his back taking flight.

"This is new to me. These feelings." When Eden turns back to me, I'm floored by the depth of emotions in his beautiful eyes. "I didn't think that I'd care for anybody but

Shay. But you're different. I know pain, but you make me feel like I may learn to feel pleasure too. I want to try. I need to know that there's more to life than surviving suffering."

My throat is thick with tears.

I leap up from the bed and grasp his arm.

Careful of Eden's injured shoulder, I pull him around to face me. "I promise, we'll work this out together. There's so much pleasure in the world. I don't only mean the sexy kind. Hell, you already have a pet squirrel and a book club, as well as a family and a home here. I know that it's not the job that you hoped for, but tomorrow, we'll go to the rink when the guys are fitting in some practice over the weekend, and I can start introducing you to staff. That way, it won't be overwhelming, when the PA role begins on Monday. I think that you'll be surprised how much you'll shine."

Eden looks troubled. "I don't know anybody."

His social anxiety is going to make this tough for him.

I'm going to figure out a way to make this work. The fact that he's been brave enough to take this on and is holding himself back from complaining, makes me respect the hell out of him.

"I'll be with you," I reassure him. "If we do the introductions one to one, then it'll help. Normally, you can do correspondence however you like. I'm guessing that you'll prefer online. Most of the time, you can work from home. Already, you help me with research. You're organized and committed. You have a player's perspective on hockey."

Eden's eyes dance with amusement. "I'm hiring you as a cheerleader."

"It's okay, I come free with the job." I go on tiptoes to kiss him, deep and tender. I will him to believe me. "You're smart. You can beat your brother at chess and poker, and he's a genius. You're going to kick ass as a PA."

Eden's eyes darken. "I fucking adore you. There, I said it. I'd like to make this my big night too. I want you to be my first and also my last. *My only.*"

My breath hitches.

His only.

Eden doesn't speak much. So, when he does, you need to listen.

What he's just confessed is more powerful than a marriage proposal.

How can I turn it down?

Why would I want to?

My pulse is roaring in my ears. My eyes sting.

When Eden reaches to wrap his arm around me, I catch sight of the black roses with thorn tattoos that wind around it.

He won't only know surviving suffering.

It's time to show him pleasure.

"I want to be that for you so fucking much," I murmur.

Eden studies me for a long moment, before he nods.

"Undress," he commands.

He lets go of me and watches with hungry eyes, as I wriggle out of my cotton, green dress. Then he drops his hand to my hip, before kneeling and dragging my lace panties off for me.

Somehow with Eden the gesture is gentlemanly.

I step out of my panties.

He stares up at me for a long moment, tracing teasing circles on my hip. "May I?"

I nod.

He leans forward, pressing a reverential kiss onto my clit. I open my legs with a sigh, as he swipes his tongue down my pussy.

I clench my hands in his hair, struggling not to come just at the sensation of his tongue circling my clit.

Then I urge him to stand up because I want this to be about *his* pleasure too. He looks confused but lies on his back on the bunk bed.

He pushes the cover back, looking satisfied when he holds up a condom that was hidden underneath the messy bedding. "Shay always leaves them lying around."

"Fuck, this is your brother's bed."

"Revenge for all the times he fucked people in *my* bed at college."

I laugh, swooping to capture Eden's plush lips that have *almost* quirked into a smile.

"Revenge will definitely add some spice." I bend to drag Eden's joggers down, which catch on his large cock that's already at half-mast. *And is gorgeous.* "But I know where I want to start. Let's see if your piercings make you as sensitive as I hope they will."

Eden's breathing picks up. His pupils are dilated.

He likes the thought of that.

I straddle his hips, deliberately wriggling my bare ass

against his hard cock. I lean down and lick over his pierced nipple.

Instantly, it peaks.

His chest begins to rise and fall rapidly.

He doesn't need words.

He's beautifully responsive without them.

I alternate flicking and rubbing over each of his nipples, while leaning over and licking. I let my hair sweep across his skin.

Every time that I lick, Eden's breath hitches in an adorable way.

His pupils are blown wide.

I glance at him from underneath my lashes. "Okay?"

He nods.

Eden's nipples are just as sensitive as I'd hoped. I bet that I could get him to come merely by playing with them alone.

But not tonight.

I have a different use for his cock tonight.

When I tap the silver piercing on his right nipple, his dick twitches beneath me.

"Robyn..." Eden murmurs.

He tangles his hand in my hair, tugging me up to kiss me, passionately.

Our tongues twine.

Eden smells freshly of sweet vanilla.

I moan, as his hand tightens in my hair. Then I break away, and he loosens his hand in my hair, stroking down my neck.

I shiver. My skin tingles.

When I reach beneath me to run my fingers over Eden's cock, he groans.

He feels as hard as steel underneath the velvety softness. I'm fucking wet too.

Our gazes meet, and it's electric.

I'm glad that we waited, until we knew each other properly to do this because it means so fucking much to Eden. Shay isn't the same as his brother, nor is D'Angelo.

I've spent plenty of nights with different partners that didn't mean anything romantically to me because sex is fun, stress relief, or feels so fucking good.

Yet Eden has never had a girlfriend or a one-night stand.

When he passes the condom to me, it feels like a sacred ritual.

I bend to kiss him again as I sheath his cock.

"I love you," I whisper.

Eden's eyes widen.

Then he smiles.

He fucking smiles.

At the same moment, I rise up and slowly lower myself onto his dick.

I gasp. "Hell, you're big."

He takes a shuddering breath, tightening his hold on my hip.

"Fuck…" His eyes are wide with wonder.

He stares at me like I'm a goddess.

He feels incredible, stretching me. I bite my lip, tossing my hair over my shoulder and arching my back.

I rest my hands on Eden, pinning him down. I ride

him faster and faster, ignoring my tired muscles. He's still hurt. I'm going to do all the work.

He's dominant, but this is about me taking care of him.

I'll show him how much pleasure I can give him but also, how easy this can be. He doesn't need to *give* or work every time.

Eden spends his life caring for everyone else.

Sometimes, he can lie back and let someone else ride him to the best orgasm of his fucking life.

Eden reaches up to cup my breast. His eyelashes flutter closed. "I'm going to... This feels..."

Neither of us are going to last long.

I don't want us to.

My sweaty hair hangs over my face, as I lean forward now, desperate to kiss Eden again.

He eagerly accepts my kiss, looking overwhelmed by the sensations.

His eyes open and meet mine.

Ecstasy is winding through me as well, coiled tightly through me. I can control everything in this position: the speed, angle, and rhythm. I'm positioned on top in such a way that my clit is being rubbed on each downward thrust.

Sparks fly through me, making me shiver.

"You're beautiful," Eden murmurs like he can't hold in the words. He's panting. The pulse is fluttering wildly in his throat. "When I'm healed, I can't wait to bend you over this bed and make you come, over and over and over and..."

Then his back arches, and his hands clutch at the sheets.

He groans as he comes.

I balance with one hand on Eden's chest, and with the other, I touch my clit, rubbing circles to help tip myself over the edge.

"Fuck, fuck, fuck..." I scream.

I come, staring into Eden's eyes — seeing the spark of pleasure. And hoping that tomorrow, I can protect him from pain.

CHAPTER TWELVE

Rebel Arena, Freedom

Eden

MY ARM IS TOUCHING Robyn's.

We're in public.

After last night, I want to be holding her hand. But this...the brush of our arms, as we both lean against the boards of the rink and watch Shay and D'Angelo practice on the ice...is enough.

It's everything.

I feel relaxed and comfortable in our relationship for the first time.

I didn't realize how much I needed to feel that she wanted me in the same way that she does the other two men.

And she does.

Fuck, does she.

Last night, she made me feel...*something*.

A spark.

She's dressed in a woolen fuchsia dress, her warmest coat, gloves, and sturdy boots.

I'm so aware of her that the hairs are standing up on the back of my neck. My skin goosebumps.

I push my gloved hand into the pocket of my long, gray coat, which hangs over my leather trousers, in an attempt to stop myself from reaching for Robyn.

A thrill of excitement rushes through me, as I lean against the glass.

I scrunch my nose at the smell of the arena. It's the scent of my salvation: the bite of cold air mixed with sweat and rubber.

There's a pain deep inside this time though.

It's not my cracked ribs, or the deep throbbing of my temples that's been growing worse over the last few days. I can barely open my eyes against the bright light of the arena.

I can cope with the physical pain. I won't make the others worried with my shit. They have enough else to deal with, including that journalist who's threatening them and the start of the season.

They've never been under this level of pressure before.

It's Shay's chance to shine but also potentially, to explode into a supernova and be destroyed into a black hole.

See, sometimes I listen to my brother's geek talk.

SECRETLY PUCKING

The pain, however, is because I'm on the wrong side of the glass.

My real place on the ice with the Bay Rebels has been stolen from me.

I have no one to blame for it. The players who violently caused my concussion were assholes who deserved to get into trouble but they didn't know about my history of head injuries and concussions.

They couldn't know that they were ending my career.

I've had therapy, which I've struggle with, for years to untangle that nothing that happened to Shay and me as kids was our fault.

I can't be angry at my biological parents forever.

I don't even know their names.

Sometimes, life is just shit.

On the other hand, there's always something precious, worth caring for, and protecting, even in the midst of that shit.

For me, it's always been my twin.

Now, I have Robyn and D'Angelo too.

Yet seeing myself as a spectator who is separated by glass from the ice hurts like a bitch.

I grit my teeth.

This is strange.

Overwhelming.

Wrong, wrong, wrong.

It feels like ants are crawling beneath my skin.

"I've arranged a one-to-one later with the operations manager." Robyn glances down at the file in her arms, which I helped her to organize, before breakfast. "Half an hour, and we'll make our way there."

"Good."

I feel sick. My heart starts to pound.

I'm glad that my hand is in my pocket, so she can't see that it's shaking.

"It's in Dad's office, which you know," Robyn says, casually. I know that she arranged it like that to support me. "The meetings are all one-to-one. I've started with the nice guys first, so that we can build up to the…"

"Dicks?"

"I'd have gone with assholes, but yep, that's about it. It's a well-known management technique. Start with the soft nuts and move on to the tough ones to crack."

"Sounds painful."

"Sounds like something D'Angelo would check on one of his kink lists."

"In triplicate." I pull my hand out of my pocket to count off on my fingers. "Signed, double checked, and filed."

D'Angelo is the most thorough and organized man I know.

And *I* love filing.

My gaze darts back to the ice, when I hear Shay laugh.

What the fuck is he doing?

He shouldn't be goofing around. This is practice time. He knows the rules of the ice.

If I was out there with him, he wouldn't dare mess around.

I glare out at the rink.

D'Angelo leans against the far boards, watching Shay skate. There are deep shadows under his eyes. He looks exhausted.

He's encouraging Shay, calling out the mix of criticism with an edge of praise that makes him the best mentor.

When D'Angelo catches my eye, he touches his fingers to his head in a mocking salute.

I ignore him.

Shay isn't being the best mentee.

I scrunch my brow with concentration.

Shay sprints across the ice in a blur of sprayed ice. He's fast and he makes it look effortless like always.

Yet I grew up on the ice with him; I know that he's not pushing himself.

That's not fucking okay. I'd be kicking his ass, if I was out there.

He's distracted and showing off. I can't tell if it's for Robyn or D'Angelo.

I bet both.

I click my tongue.

"Shay," I yell. My eyes are as hard as steel. "Concentrate."

Shay's gaze snaps to mine. He looks sheepish, and his smile fades.

He nods, before his expression becomes determined. He begins to skate with a new physicality and vigor.

Better.

Robyn shuffles even closer to me. "Wow, tough coach."

I shrug. "The first game is on Tuesday. He needs to

give one hundred percent. He shouldn't slack off because he's flirting."

"He always looks mesmerizing on the ice to me. Who's he flirting with?"

Can't she tell?

I nod my chin at the two men who are now fully focused on their practice session. "They're both distracted."

"I mean," Robyn watches as Shay skates past us, "your brother still looks better than ninety-nine percent of the other players in the NHL. No need to bust his balls. I bet that he's still sore from last night. I'm impressed that he's out there skating at all. It shows dedication. Anyway, until you barked at him, he looked like he was still glowing with whatever D'Angelo did to him."

"He was glowing with thoughts about what he'll be doing with *you* tonight." I turn to give her a long look.

"What?" Robyn appears confused.

"It's Saturday. His turn to take you on a date."

It hits me then.

Robyn doesn't understand.

She doesn't know how excited Shay is about taking her on a date, enough to have woken me up at four a.m. because he couldn't sleep and even agreed to go to the gym with me to get out his energy.

She doesn't truly understand that he's never had a true relationship before.

That he's never felt loved in the same way that I haven't.

We've only had each other.

Shay's told her, but there's a difference between hearing and understanding, deep inside.

Robyn smiles. "I'm looking forward to it as well. Should I wear my leathers? Is he taking me on his motorcycle again?"

She sounds hopeful.

But then, Shay fucked her over it last time.

I shake my head. "I can't tell you anything else. He made me promise."

She pouts.

Cute.

"Just dress warm," I advise.

"Tease."

I wish that she knew the impact she had on my brother.

The way that Shay's face lights up when her name is mentioned, or how every morning he lip syncs to her, as she sings in the shower in the bathroom next to our bedroom, thinking up even more outrageous dances and trying to make me laugh.

How he wanders up to me, suggesting ways that we can all have fun together.

I've never seen him so happy.

I could spend my life with this new family of ours for that reason alone.

I bet that Shay only has one reason that he loves Robyn: *She's my sunshine, and I'm hers.*

Of course, I have ten.

Last night, I thought that I'd burst into flames with

embarrassment, when Robyn found my reasons on the piece of paper folded inside my book.

They were private.

Writing things down helps me to process them.

Feelings make more sense, when I see them in black and white.

D'Angelo realized that quickly. He allows a lot of our communication to be written or online.

I've slowly made a list, adding to it each day.

<u>Ten Reasons I Love Robyn</u>

1. She wants me as much as she wants my twin. I am not a shadow with her.
2. She makes me feel worthy.
3. She's kind.
4. She listed all the ways that I'm more talented than my twin. I think she even believes they're true.
5. She's beautiful.
6. She makes me feel seen.
7. She loves and respects books. And cats.
8. She's not abandoning me because I can't play hockey anymore.
9. She's smart and funny.
10. I can't imagine a future without her in it.

I CAREFULLY COPIED my reasons into Robyn's Guide under D'Angelo's stick drawings. I signed my name underneath because it felt like a legal document.

Can you make your love official?

Robyn taps her file. "Hey, do you want to get a couple of photos here at the rink? I'll add them to the Bay Rebels social media later. I'm building a different page for each of the players that fits their characters. They're already building a big fan following. Your relaxed photographs from the kitchen have gone practically viral. The fans love them. You're super talented."

See, she believes that I'm talented.

Warmth unfurls in my chest.

I pull my phone out of my coat pocket. I switch it to camera. When I point it at the rink, my shoulders relax.

For the first time, I don't feel like I'm separated from the ice.

The sensation of crawling ants subside.

Like this, I have a purpose. I'm in control.

I focus on Shay. His golden hair tumbles out of his helmet around his face. He looks intense and lost in his skating now.

He looks like he was born to do this.

I take the photograph.

Suddenly, strident voices disturb me, before I can take another photograph.

I frown, lowering the camera.

My breathing becomes ragged. My pulse spikes.

A crowd of men and women in designer power suits — who I don't know — are striding toward us past the cold metal benches that line the ice rink. They're looking at both the arena and D'Angelo and Shay like they own them.

I shove the phone back into my pocket and cross my arms.

"You said that the meetings were going to be held in coach's room." Betrayal and hurt flood me. I don't let them show on my face. "Individually."

"They are." Robyn sounds panicked. "These are the assholes...the tough nuts. I don't know why they're down here right now. The guy with the silver hair and beard like Santa if he was a thin, ruthless, billionaire is the senior board member, William Bronwyn."

"Who's the man next to him?"

My breathing is too quick. I struggle to get my anxiety under control.

It's like drowning.

"I don't know." Robyn stands in front of me, plastering on a fake smile. "But I don't like the sneer on his asshole face."

She takes a step forward, effectively blocking the crowd of board members and senior managers.

She's a brave woman.

I should add that to my list.

Reason eleven.

"Down here to enjoy the practice?" Robyn smiles. It's not the type of smile that she offers me. I can tell the difference. "As you can see, these two are so dedicated that they're fitting in an extra couple of hours. The captain mentors all the new players and—"

"Hardly *enjoying*," the man at Bronwyn's side sneers in a pompous tone. My jaw clenches at his rudeness for cutting off Robyn. "It's not dedicated to do your job. We're working on the weekend as well."

Robyn's smile dies. "I see that. Sorry, we haven't met."

"Silas Anderson." The man is in his forties, small and horse-faced. His ginger hair is neatly parted. "And you're the coach's daughter."

Robyn's eyes flash with anger. "I'm Robyn McKenna. You can call me Ms. McKenna. I'm not a kid and I don't let myself be defined by the men in my life. I'd appreciate it, if you didn't either."

The crowd of management and board members are murmuring now and staring at her, but she holds her nerve.

Finally, it's Anderson who backs down. "My mistake, *Ms*. McKenna."

"Bronwyn." The senior board member holds out his hand like it's a weapon, and Robyn shakes it. "When was it that we last met? That charity thing for something or other in Pittsburgh that your husband was championing I think."

Robyn's lips pinch. "*Ex*-husband."

Bronwyn's eyes twinkle with a dangerous intelligence that tells me he knows exactly what he said. "Ex, of course. Such a messy affair, all over the news. Shame that it's now involving our club. He's suspended, isn't he?"

"Not my business anymore. Only the Bay Rebels is."

"And you." Bronwyn turns to me with a sympathetic

smile that doesn't meet his eyes. "I know who you are, of course. How are you doing, son?"

I wince on the *son*.

I hate it when men call me that.

Hate it.

My heart hammers even harder in my chest.

"Fine, sir," I answer, stiffly.

It's hard to force my tongue to form words.

I can hear the whispers from the group.

...The kid who took the fall...the untalented twin...scandal...

I force my expression to blankness.

Bronwyn studies my sling that's been signed like a cast by the entire team. "Looks like you have a lot of friends. That's well signed. Look, I want to say that what happened to you was a terrible break. Hockey is a tough sport, son." His gaze flicks to the rink, and he watches Shay, admiringly. Shay is slowly skating laps. Both D'Angelo and Shay are looking over at the crowd of people who've surrounded Robyn and me with concern. "Not everybody can be as natural a star as your brother."

There's a cold ball of ice in my stomach.

I feel like I'm shaking apart.

Yet there are flaming words in my throat.

I'll be burned to death, if I don't say them.

But silence...no comment...

It's Robyn's rule.

Robyn is looking at me now. I think that she's saying my name.

"The Prince twin who hasn't been a disaster is going to be a big money spinner," Anderson is now explaining to the board members. "He's handsome, which appeals to the female demographic and is good for both sponsorship and merchandise. The way that he scores, however, is the key. If we keep playing and winning games like this, then there's a chance that the team can be saved on gate fees alone."

"But we can't afford any more...*noise*." Bronwyn looks away from Shay to gesture at me. "The focus of this season needs to be the games that are won and not scandals, messy personal lives, and broken heads."

That's it.

My eyes flare. I step forward.

I'm going to break Robyn's rule. I'm probably going to get us all in trouble.

Yet I have a voice off the ice now. I'm learning that.

And I'm going to use it.

I'm towering over all these men in suits.

For a moment, something like fear skitters in Bronwyn's eyes.

"I didn't fall." My voice is low and hard. "I was attacked illegally on the ice, while playing for *your* team. My career was ended. That's not *noise*. Players have real lives because we're not robots. *We're not slaves*. And I'm not your son."

CHAPTER THIRTEEN

Captain's Hall, Freedom

Shay

SOMETIMES I THINK Robyn can't become more beautiful.

Then I see her in the starlight and I know that she's never going to stop growing more beautiful in my eyes.

I rub my hands together against the cold of the night, shivering.

I'm only wearing a red sweater and black jeans. My leather jacket is wrapped around Robyn's shoulders, as I lie next to her on the blanket on the flat roof of Captain's Hall.

The tartan blanket is surrounded by purple cushions

that I've borrowed from the lounge. To my side, stands a small, blue cooler.

Our shoulders are touching, as we lie on our backs, looking up at the black velvet of the sky with its map of stars.

The night is clear. The crescent moon is bright.

I found this flat section of roof, when I was restless during training camp one night. I clambered through a skylight and explored this new world, feeling finally at peace.

Eden busted my balls for it the next morning.

It was something about how I could have *fallen...broken my neck...spanking.*

Blah, blah.

I wasn't paying attention. I was trying to work out how to find a safer route back onto the roof.

In the end, I asked D'Angelo, and like the brilliant friend that he is, he waved his hand like it was the easiest thing in the world and paid for a ladder to be installed.

Now, I'm sharing my nighttime refuge with Robyn for our date.

I want to share the stars with her.

They're how I escape.

I connect with the universe.

It's the feeling that there's something bigger out there. It helps me hold faith, even when people feel small and cruel.

I pillow my head on my hands, before turning to study Robyn.

My jacket looks better on her than it does on me. I love seeing her in leather.

She's fucking hot.

She's dressed in an emerald sweater that matches her eyes and woolen black skirt with sexy little leather belt that is full of possibilities.

Robyn's been buzzing ever since we came back from practice at lunchtime, glowing with pride about how Eden stood up for himself against bastard management.

Eden has been more silent than normal but it was like he'd grown six inches, and we always wished that we could do that.

I'm proud of my brother.

He's never spoken to strangers like that in his life. He usually lets me do the talking.

Having to practice without Eden, as if he was separated from me on the wrong side of the glass, was tough. But then, he called me on my bullshit. He always knows, when I'm slacking off.

Of course, he doesn't know what it's like to skate, when your arse is still aching from being fucked for the first time the night before and you're jittery with excitement over your plans for your date with your girlfriend.

It's no excuse.

When Eden yelled at me to *concentrate*, I realized that he's not separated from me, simply because he's not skating.

We're still in this together.

Then he spoke up to defend us against the board and senior management, and I saw a side to him that I haven't since he took my hand and saved me from the couple who hurt us.

Yet I always knew that it was inside him.

Now that he's no longer in my shadow, he has a chance to show it.

To shine in his own right.

This transition period will be hard, but hope bloomed through me that Eden is going to find his true voice for the first time in his life.

Robyn turns her head toward me. Our faces are so close that our noses are almost touching.

I'm comfortable and relaxed.

"Your brother was incredible today." Robyn's eyes are bright with pride. "His words just burst free from him. He was fucking amazing."

"You knew that we were trouble." I grin. "Rebels."

She kisses me, petal soft. "My rebels."

"Always, love."

Robyn's eyes become clouded with worry. "Of course, he also put himself — and me — on top of the board and senior management's shit list. They hate us now. It's tradition to act like they're gods, but really, they're the puppeteers."

Cold dread washes over me.

I reach for Robyn's hand, entangling our fingers. "The whole team is behind both of you. You know that, right?"

She squeezes my hand. "It was worth it. Eden's right. I also learned that what they care about most is winning. We're safe, as long as you continue to be…"

"A scoring machine?" I arch my brow.

No pressure then.

My chest is tight.

Hockey is my life. It's what I'm best at. But this is my first season.

What if I screw up?

Yet D'Angelo hasn't stopped being at my side either for hockey or as a boyfriend. I thought that his aftercare would have ended on the night of our date but I was wrong. He checked in throughout today to see how I was feeling, to chat about what we'd both enjoyed, and whether we'd change anything next time.

I've never fucked anyone who communicates so well.

Robyn chuckles. "I may steal *scoring machine* as you nickname on social media. It's good."

"I thought that my brand was the English hockey royal."

"Who's also a scoring machine." Robyn looks at me searchingly. "So, how did it go with D'Angelo last night?"

Joy surges through me at the memory of my date with D'Angelo, from the way that he watched a movie that scared him for my sake, trusted me enough to talk about his past, then bent me over the couch and showed me a way of fucking that I'd never experienced before and that made me see stars.

And my favorite part of the evening…?

The way that he wrapped me in a blanket, before we fell asleep together cuddled on the couch.

No man apart from my twin has made me feel so loved or wanted.

I push myself up onto my elbow. "It was bloody

incredible, love. Plus, Jude promised to give me my first proper piano lesson tomorrow. I never thought anybody would care enough about me to teach me music."

"Eden said that you'd sent him some interesting emojis about the date, a peach and an eggplant."

Of course he did.

I wink. "Jude knows how to use his eggplant, and I know how to use my peach."

Robyn laughs. "I can bear witness that both of those things are true. I'm one lucky woman to have both *your* peach and *his* eggplant."

I run my fingers down to play across my crotch. "My eggplant is feeling left out. You own it too."

Robyn wrinkles her nose. "Perhaps, we should stop talking about produce."

I reach for a cushion and adjust it under her head to make her more comfortable.

Eden gave me one word of advice for this date.

One word answers are sort of his thing.

Nests.

I have no bloody clue what it means but I'm doing my best with the blanket and the cushions from the lounge. Robyn settles back with a happy sigh. So, it appears to be working.

I never thought that I'd be taking dating advice from my brother.

Talking about that...

I sit up cross-legged next to Robyn. "So, it turns out that I wasn't the only one on a special date last night. Not only did you somehow escape singing at a karaoke evening, which I want to come to next time, but you then returned home and saw Dee. He introduced you to Puck."

Robyn's eyes twinkle. "I didn't know that he'd named his cock."

I chuckle. "Seriously, it was huge—"

"It was."

"Stop it, love." We're both laughing now. "I'm trying to be sincere and serious and that doesn't happen often. I meant that it was huge for him to get close to you like that. We both had our first times on the same night. See, twins truly are mystically connected. Want me to read his mind for you?"

"That's you being sincere and serious?"

"Impressive, right?" Playfully, I press my hand to Robyn's forehead, pretending to concentrate hard. "Shall I read your mind? Hmm, you're thinking...*that I can't read your mind because I'm full of bullshit but that I look hot in these pants*. Oh, interesting, you're also imagining what I look like *out* of these pants and then...naughty girl. But then, I'm a bad boy."

She narrows her eyes. "Almost."

To my surprise, she grabs my wrist and sits up. She drags me over her knee in a move that's smooth enough to tell me that she's done it before.

Or has imagined doing it.

My breathing picks up, and my dick hardens.

Fuck, I've hoped that she'd do this so many times.

I rub my clothed dick against her legs, letting her know how hard she's making me.

She gasps as she rests her hand on my ass. Then she teases me, rubbing in circles.

"This is what happens to bad boys." She hesitates, giving me time to back out.

Fat chance.

Instead, I push my arse up, encouragingly. "They get massaged…?"

She huffs in outrage.

I hide my smirk in my arms.

"Brat." When Robyn spanks me, it sounds loud in the silence of the night.

I can barely feel it through the denim of my jeans, but it still sends a satisfying warmth radiating through me.

How can I encourage her to lower my pants and spank me on bare skin?

I need her hand slapping, skin on skin: the connection.

Instead, she smacks me rapid fire, from one side to the other and down to my thighs.

I breathe out, letting the sensation wash over me.

Robyn pushes my sweater up and traces circles on my lower back.

I sigh, needing her touch.

But then, she stops.

"Except, you're really my good boy." She traces down the seam of my jeans, lower and lower to my balls. I whine at the intensity. "And you *can* read minds because I've been thinking all night about how hot you look in these pants."

My eyes widen, as she yanks up the back of my jeans,

tightening the material even further to the point of pain, pushing my thighs wider.

"Just lie there and let me show you how good you are," she murmurs.

She strokes and teases across my arse, which is sensitized now by her spanking, tickling and caressing me.

She plays her fingers down to my balls and sensitive thighs.

It's an exploration and a worshiping.

What is this?

I give pleasure to other people. I don't get adored.

I'm breathing too hard.

Yet I'm smiling and laughing, as she tickles my balls.

"Love," I gasp, squirming.

"Yes?" Robyn asks, trying for innocent.

"What are you doing?"

"Being sincere and serious."

I'm going to need to watch this one. She's brilliant.

When Robyn presses at my taint, and pleasure shoots forcefully through me, close to making me come in my pants, I decide that I've had enough punishment.

At least, if I don't want to spend the rest of this date with the front of my pants uncomfortably cold and sticky.

Laughing, I squirm off her knee onto the blanket.

"Hey, my prisoner is escaping," Robyn protests.

"Madam Kidnapper up to her old tricks, I see." I sit up, struggling to get my breathing under control. Robyn is eying how hard my cock is in my pants with satisfaction. She's earned her smug look. "But I always turn the tables."

I twist to her and push her gently back onto the blankets, pinning her wrists.

We're both looking up at the stars.

"Isn't it amazing up here?" I murmur.

She nods. "You truly love stargazing, huh?"

"Dee and I used to do this in college. Well, not the spanking and pinning down stuff." I flex my hands around her wrists, and she works to push even closer to me, until our legs are tangled and her gorgeous breasts are pushed against my chest. "We couldn't afford to go to the pub or many parties, and Dee hated doing that anyway. So, I found a way up onto the dorm roofs. It was forbidden, but as you know, I'm a bad boy. I'd take a beer and my headphones, and Dee would bring a book. Did you have a place that was like a refuge to you at college?"

"For a while, it was D'Angelo's dorm room. For him, it was mine."

I stare up at the stars.

Here in Freedom, the skies are much clearer than they are London. I can make out the constellations much better like finding old friends.

"Since I was a kid, I was obsessed with the stars, while Eden was obsessed with myths. We both had our different defenses and ways to escape. We'd sit there, and I'd point out the stars to him, each with their own ancient myths like... You see the string of stars up there that looks like a cooking pan?"

I move both of Robyn's wrists into one of my hands, so that I can point at the stars.

"Uh-huh." She watches where I'm tracing.

I glance at her sideways, in case I'm boring her. But she looks spellbound.

An unusual emotion floods me.

I puff out my chest, pointing more confidently at a second set of stars. "Then this smaller set like another pan…? The first one is called Ursa Major, which is Latin for She Bear. The second is Ursa Minor. The story goes that Zeus, the horny bastard, fell in love with a beautiful princess called Callisto. But Callisto was sworn to remain a virgin. Zeus seduced…read forced himself…on her anyway. When her pregnancy was discovered, her baby was taken to be trained into a hunter, while she was turned into a bear. His prey."

Robyn looks transfixed. "That's horrific."

"The Greeks didn't mess around." I study the mother and son, forever caught in the stars. "As a man, he didn't recognize his mum. She was a beast. He was going to kill her…"

Robyn gasps. She looks as wrapped up in the story as Eden always had been. I didn't know when we were young, whether it was the chance to hunt our parents, having been taken away and raised to be strong enough to battle them, that really interested Eden.

Eden is stronger than me, mentally.

He's also darker.

"Zeus realized what was about to happen and turned them both into constellations to save them," I reassure Robyn.

Robyn huffs. "Save them? He screwed up the princess' life in the first place. Why wasn't Zeus the one who was kicked in the balls? I'd have thrown his ass into the stars."

"I'd love to see that." My lips quirk. "There's a lot more to the stars than people think."

"I know that you're really a scientist." Robyn turns to look at me with an unsettling intensity. "Eden said that he wanted to be a vet, before you trained as hockey players. Do you ever wish that you were an astrophysicist?"

I give her an insulted look. "My degree didn't fall out of a cereal box, love."

"But you're not working as a scientist."

"I still could. Never say never, right?" I steal a taste of her delicious lips. "Now, I heard an interesting story about food play from Jude. And you kindly brought home vanilla ice cream for me on what Jude insisted…many times…were his highly expensive leather seats. Fuck, it's a beautiful car."

She blinks at me, confused.

This is the part of the evening that I've been looking forward to.

I can't wait to taste her sweet pussy.

I live for tonguing her.

I let go of her hands and sit up. I edge toward the cooler and drag it closer to me. Then I open the lid, as anticipation thrums through me.

I lift out the tub of vanilla ice cream.

Joy settled over me, warm and unexpected, when Robyn had remembered me, bringing this home.

I saved the ice cream though because I knew how I wanted to use it.

Well, some of it.

It's going to taste even more delicious eaten off my Robyn.

She's watching me with wide eyes. Her chest is rising and falling.

She looks perfect with her hands raised above her head. She hasn't moved them from where I put them.

I smile at that.

My jacket is spread around her.

"Don't move," I murmur.

I lean over her, pushing up her sweater. Gently, I pull her breasts out of her lacy bra

Her breath hitches.

I lean down and kiss her right tit in worship.

I slide my hand down her stomach, and she shivers. I swirl my thumb around her bellybutton, bunching her skirt at her waist.

"I'm going to pull your tiny panties down because I want to see your pretty pussy." I tease my fingers underneath her panties, snapping them.

Robyn's pupils become dilated. "Don't rip them. I'll run out of them at this rate."

I laugh. "D'Angelo's an animal."

I ease Robyn's panties down her hips and ease them off her ankles.

I wave them around to show her that they're not damaged, before deliberately shoving them into my jean's pocket.

"What…?" She splutters.

"Souvenir." I pat my pocket. "Something to smell, think of you, and wank into."

Robyn blushes. "Pantie thief."

I snap the lid off the ice cream and groan at the sweet scent. I lean down and lick over it.

It's delicious, but not as delicious as Robyn.

I run my thumb through it, before holding it up to her mouth. Eagerly, she sucks my thumb between her lips like it's my cock.

My breathing becomes ragged, as she twirls her tongue over my thumb. I push it in and out of her mouth, and she moans.

At the same time, I balance the tub on the blanket next to her stomach and trail the fingers of my other hand through the ice cream.

The cold makes me draw in a sharp breath. It reminds me of being on the ice.

I'm at home in the cold.

Robyn's skin is like fire, however, when I trail my fingers around her hot breast.

"Fuck." She lets go of my thumb in her shock.

I cup her cheek. "Color?"

I know that she loves temperature play but I still want to be sure that she's all right.

"Green." She watches me with glassy eyes.

When I glance down at her pussy, I can already see that she's glistening and wet.

I lick my lips.

"I'm going to kiss this ice cream off your sweet tits." I

bend my head, and slow and languorous, lick around her breasts.

Then I flick my tongue over her peaked nub.

She whines, arching off the blanket.

I lick her thoroughly to make sure that my tongue has cleaned and warmed her. Then I scoop up more ice cream and smear it down the curves of her stomach. When I reach her bellybutton, I hesitate.

She stiffens, before she shudders at the icy sensation.

"Cold," she hisses. "F-f-fucking c-c-cold."

I tease her, hovering my tongue over the trails of melting ice cream.

I look up at her through my long eyelashes. "My tongue is at your service. Do you want me to get to work and warm you with it?"

"Fuck, yeah."

I push myself up, just once, and kiss her on the corner of her mouth.

Her eyes crease, as she smiles.

Then I work myself down, dedicated to licking the melted ice cream down her stomach.

I lick, kiss, and suck.

Robyn shivers. "Shay, don't stop. Just like that, please…"

I work harder, sucking the ice cream from her bellybutton.

After the cold, I know that my mouth must feel doubly hot. She'll be shaking apart with the sensory overload.

But she's not quite where I want her yet.

Mischievously, I dip my index finger into the melting ice cream, before I slide even further down her.

I love her pussy.

I part the folds gently, kissing her clit almost in apology.

But I'm going to make it up to it.

Many times.

"Oh, shit," Robyn whispers, as if she knows what's going to happen.

Her thighs are shaking.

Then like she can't stop herself, she lowers her hands and buries them in my hair, tugging hard. She pushes my face against her pussy, and I take a deep breath.

Her smell is everything.

I've always adored being between a woman's thighs.

When Robyn finally yanks me back by my hair, sending delicious tingles through my scalp, I glance up at her.

"You're going to taste like my favorite flavor, love," I promise. My index finger drips the ice cream over her clit, and she moans. She's shivering from the cold on her most sensitive part, but it's making her fucking wet. "I can feast on you all night."

I suck her clit into my mouth, and it bloody does taste like the best thing in the world.

Vanilla, love, and Robyn.

My Robyn.

When her back bows, I hold her down.

"Fuck, Shay…" She clutches the blanket in her hands.

I don't stop sucking.

At last, Robyn comes, screaming so loudly into the silent night that D'Angelo and Eden must be able to hear inside the house.

I lick over her but I don't raise my head.

I don't touch my cock, which is so hard that it hurts. Because all my focus is on this woman's pleasure, who tastes like heaven.

I'm going to feast on her all night.

And I'm going to make her come…all…bloody…night.

CHAPTER FOURTEEN

Captain's Hall, Freedom

S hay

ENTHUSIASTICALLY, I lay my hand on the Steinway piano's keys, ready to try out my very first chord.

First *official* chord.

I've been sneaking into the lounge to pretend that I can play D'Angelo's grand piano like a virtuoso for days in preparation for my first lesson, despite the fact that touching it without his permission is forbidden.

But then, I've always been a rule breaker.

D'Angelo had better not think that us dating is going to change that.

I've been thrumming with excitement all day, waiting on this lesson.

Now, it's Sunday evening, and the moon shines through the windows over the crackling fire that's burning in the marble fireplace.

He's spent the last hour teaching me basic concepts like the layout of the piano, adjusting my posture, and showing me hand positioning.

I can't stop smiling.

I knew that I could trust D'Angelo to give me this. I didn't think that a partner would want to put in the effort of teaching me, when he's not getting any pleasure back.

Although, I'm giving D'Angelo a headache.

I'm only dressed in a scarlet t-shirt and black jeans. For him, D'Angelo is just as dressed down. He's stripped to suit pants and a blue shirt. It's open at the neck.

He's not even wearing a tie.

He's rolled back his sleeves to reveal his strong forearms that I bloody love but not more than I love his elegant fingers.

Fingers, which are tapping on his knee now like he wants to adjust *mine*, and I haven't even played the chord yet.

My smile fades.

Have I got it wrong?

My knee bounces.

"Sit still," D'Angelo barks.

"That has to be a record," Eden's voice rumbles from behind us on the couch. "Sixteen *sit stills* in a single hour."

"These music lessons are either going to lead to them killing each other," Robyn says, "or glorious, rough sex."

"Audience participation is not required," D'Angelo grits out.

"For the killing or the rough sex?"

I chuckle.

"For the music lessons," D'Angelo growls.

I glance over my shoulder at Robyn and wink. "They're being supportive."

Robyn is cuddled in Eden's arms, which appears to be her favorite place in the evenings. They're both sprawled on the crushed velvet couch with Robyn's head resting on Eden's shoulder like he's a plushie.

They look relaxed and like they belong together.

I'll never get bored of seeing them like that.

Robyn's red hair hangs in waves over her **MURDER PAWS** black cat t-shirt, which I know is one of Eden's favorites. She's been holding her phone in front of her and reading through messages so close to her face that it's as if she's reading them with her nose.

Eden's clutching a cup of tea, content to simply sit and watch everything that's going on like usual.

"Is that what we're calling it?" D'Angelo drawls. "I call it comfortably sipping on tea, while counting the number of times I tell your twin to *sit still*, *concentrate*, and *maintain posture*. And you, principessa, when not throwing out snarky comments, are in a three-way WhatsApp with your brother and Neve, plotting ways to take down Melanie."

Robyn opens and closes her mouth. "Mostly, but for

the sake of transparency, it also includes discussion of the best new sex toys."

"What respectable three-way wouldn't?" I smirk.

D'Angelo snatches me by the chin, and my stomach swoops.

He turns me back to face the piano, adjusting my position. "Sit still. Concentrate. Maintain posture."

"Is this okay?" I ask, looking down at my hands.

Unexpected nerves swirl in my stomach.

D'Angelo is strict and demanding just like he is on the ice but he's a brilliant teacher. I don't want to let him down.

Music has always been one of my escapes like the stars. I fucking love it. But that doesn't mean that I have the skill to play it, right?

As if he can read my thoughts, D'Angelo runs his thumb lightly across the back of my knuckles, steadying my hands.

The gentleness of his touch, however, is not in keeping with his words. "I said that I'd teach you and I will. Now, play the chord. I should have got a ruler to rap against your knuckles, but you'd only enjoy that too much."

"You know me too well, darlin'." The tension bleeds from me.

I push down on the keys, hard.

Discordant noise echoes through the lounge.

Triumphant, I look delighted. "I did it!"

Why is D'Angelo wincing?

"Almost." He carefully adjusts my hands. "Try again. The white key next to that one. There…"

I lick over my lips in concentration. "Got it."

"Softly this time," D'Angelo says, hurriedly. "Like you're making gentle love to the piano and not rutting it."

I choke on my tongue "When do you make gentle love?"

D'Angelo's gaze becomes dreamy, and I'm certain that he's thinking of Robyn. "You'd be surprised."

Will he ever look like that when he's thinking of me?

I nod, letting out my breath.

I loosen my shoulders like I would before taking a shot on goal. Then I force myself to depress the keys softly.

This time the sound that I've coaxed is pretty.

"Oh…" I beam. Pride surges through me. "You mean like that."

D'Angelo's smile is fond. "Near enough. You've done well today."

I cast him a disbelieving look. "I mean, sixteen *sit stills*…"

D'Angelo's lips twitch. "I was betting on at least fifty."

"How did you become so good, Jude?" Eden asks. "You could be a concert pianist."

D'Angelo flushes.

Praise doesn't do it for him in the same way that it does for me. I also recognize the signs, however, of someone who's spent a long time without approval from people who he respects.

"I couldn't." D'Angelo pushes his curls back from his face. "My sister, Maria, was the true prodigy in the family. We both learned from the same teacher, but she's the one who went on to become a musician."

My eyes widen. "That's bloody brilliant. Do you still…?"

"I don't want to talk about it now," D'Angelo says, abruptly. "This is your lesson."

My chest tightens.

I pull my hands back from the keys. "Thanks for this. It means the world to me. How about you give me a demonstration of how it's meant to be done?"

D'Angelo leans closer to the piano like he can't stop himself. He effortlessly dances his hands up and down in scales all the way from one end of the piano to the other.

I stuttered over a single scale earlier.

I roll my eyes. "Now you're just showing off."

D'Angelo flashes his canines at me, already buzzing with the joy of the music. He's like this every evening that he plays.

I expect him to begin to play Mozart or some such shit.

Instead, he bursts into "Dance Monkey."

Robyn laughs.

"Fuck, how fast are your fingers moving?" I watch him, spellbound.

D'Angelo's curls hang over his face. He's lost in the music.

How he's playing now? Emotional, intense, with rhythm?

This is making love to the piano.

He's playing without sheet music. I think that he's making it up on the spot.

Like this, he makes me breathless.

SECRETLY PUCKING

When Robyn starts to sing, I grin and join in as well.

I barely stop myself from jumping up and dancing. But I don't want to miss a moment of D'Angelo's performance.

I think he's wrong. No matter how good his sister was, D'Angelo's also a prodigy.

Being sent to that fucking brutal discipline school may have fucked up his music career in a way that I don't understand yet. But I love that he can still play and find happiness in expressing himself.

I love even more that he can share it with us.

I can see Eden out of the corner of my eye stand and stalk to join us at the piano, leaning on it.

Robyn is still singing, as she hangs around my neck and kisses my cheek.

I sing louder to encourage her, and now, she's singing just as loudly as I am.

When D'Angelo finishes, breathing hard, he looks dazed.

For a moment, he appears lost and confused.

He blinks, as he realizes that he's now surrounded by us all.

Eden and Robyn clap, and I whoop.

"That was incredible, professor." I slip my hand onto his thigh and squeeze.

D'Angelo's gaze refocuses and becomes wicked in a way that I've grown to love and fear. "Professor...? Although I believe that you can be taught to be my *good boy*, you have been rather a naughty student today."

I gape at him. "Harsh."

He nips my lower lip, deepening the kiss.

Then he whispers against my mouth "Feel like role playing?"

Oh, that makes sense.

I relax, as heat washes through me.

I've wanked to fantasies of this exact roleplay at least ten times.

I kiss D'Angelo, before turning to capture Robyn's lips. "Fuck, yeah. What about you, love?"

Robyn scrunches up her nose adorably. "I've always wanted to be a professor."

"Aren't you another student?"

"She's not the one who can't sit still, concentrate, or maintain his posture." Eden's expression is serious, but his eyes are dancing.

I give him a betrayed look. "Hey, what about the bro code? Circle of Twins?"

Eden crosses his arms. "I'm not your brother. I'm..."

"A dick?"

To my shock, D'Angelo sweeps to his feet and then snatches me by the arm. He drags me up by the elbow to my feet.

Then he spanks my arse.

I yelp.

Through the denim of my jeans, it doesn't hurt.

But my ego is bruised.

"Apologize for your rudeness," D'Angelo says, sternly.

"Why?" I narrow my eyes.

D'Angelo slides his hand up from my elbow to the

back of my neck and then shakes me in a way that makes me melt against his chest.

I feel so turned on that I can hardly fucking breathe.

"Because," he whispers into my ear; my skin tingles, "you're practically coming in your pants at even the thought of it. How hot are you finding this?"

"Bloody hot."

"Don't forget your safe words."

"I won't."

D'Angelo pulls back from me and slips seamlessly back into character again.

If every one of my lessons ends in this type of motivating group scene reward, then I'm going to be a virtuoso myself by the end of the season.

"I'm sorry, Professor Puck," I singsong.

D'Angelo spanks my arse again.

Robyn is trying hard to smother her laugh behind her palm.

"What?" I pretend innocence.

Eden arches his pierced brow, which for him, is like an entire sentence long answer.

And it means that I'm screwed.

"Isn't that your name?" I pretend to think about it. "Wait, is it Professor Catitude? Smallwood? Buttz? Or..."

"Before you use up all your wit, and my spanking hand, in one go," D'Angelo says, dryly, "you'll simply call us all *professor*."

He stops all my bratting fun.

"Yes, professor."

"I have an idea." Eden's eyes glint. Shit, I shouldn't have mocked the squirrel. "He needs to be taught a lesson."

"Traitor," I hiss.

Eden's stormy eyes only darken. "I gave him detention twice today. Don't go easy on him."

I definitely shouldn't have mocked cats either.

Eden picks up one end of the piano stool, and Robyn helps him to shuffle the other side into the middle of the lounge.

Anticipation buzzes under my skin. What are they planning?

D'Angelo's expression becomes dominant. "Excellent."

He steers me by a hand at the back of my neck toward the stool.

Robyn shoots me a smile, before kissing me. Then she drops to her knees, unbuttons my jeans and drags them to my ankles along with my boxers.

"Professor, this is so sudden," I gasp, playfully.

Robyn pulls my jeans and boxers entirely off with a waggle of her eyebrows, before leaning to lick a stripe up my cock that's already at half-mast.

I shiver, swallowing when she fondles my balls with one hand and suckles at the head of my dick.

"Take what's coming to you." D'Angelo reaches up to tug on my hair, and I whine. "You deserve this punishment. You earned it."

"I agree," I pant, as Robyn runs her tongue along the sensitive underside of my cock, which feels like bloody heaven. "I f-f-fucking did."

I can definitely get behind that.

Then D'Angelo pulls something out of his pants' pocket and tosses it to Robyn.

A condom.

That's D'Angelo, always prepared.

Robyn fumbles her catch with an awkward shrug. Then she opens the packet and rolls the condom onto my cock.

I watch her with blown wide pupils, as she pushes herself up from her knees. "Now you're dressed appropriately, Shay."

Eden stalks to stand behind Robyn. He wraps his arms around her waist, and they whisper to each other.

They're close and intimate. They have been since Friday night. They've barely been apart, except for Saturday night, when I was lucky enough to get her to myself.

Now, we're going to be together in a group. It feels so fucking right that my blood sings and my bones ache.

D'Angelo shoves me toward the stool. "Lie over it on your back. Spread your legs. Don't talk. Don't move. Your bratty mouth has said more than enough. You're going to do something useful with it by bringing me pleasure."

Except, doing that will bring *me* pleasure.

D'Angelo knows that.

He still waits, giving me time to safe word.

I don't.

Instead, I smile as I lie on the piano stool. Caught between the man and woman who I love is exactly where I want to be.

Robyn is kissing Eden. She slips her hand inside his joggers. She's moaning as she wanks him.

My cock is already hard and curving onto my stomach.

D'Angelo drags me so that my head hangs off one end of the piano stool.

He's still dressed — I'm the only one who's half undressed — but he undoes his trousers and pulls out his cock, which is already hard.

It also looks much larger from this angle.

I've never sucked a cock like this before.

The first time, Robyn was helping and guiding me.

My gaze becomes steely. I want to be able to do this.

The thought's making me as hard as knowing that Robyn is going to ride me at the same time.

D'Angelo leans down and grips my cheeks. He presses for me to open my mouth. Then he's pushing his cock in, slow, steady, but unrelenting.

I choke, but he doesn't let up.

Eden is panting. His breath is ragged like he's close to coming.

Somone's kissing above me.

I'm like an object, however, being fucked in my mouth, held by my hair. I can barely breathe, but the taste and feel of D'Angelo, while Robyn's small hands pluck at my nipples and caress my stomach, is enough to make my mind feel like it's filled with cotton wool.

Suddenly, a wet, tight heat sheathes my cock.

It's perfect.

Robyn begins to ride me, hard.

My cock is her toy.

"Fuck, fuck, fuck," Robyn gasps.

"Language, professor," Eden chides.

D'Angelo huffs a laugh. "Careful, or he'll be giving *you* detention, principessa."

How is D'Angelo not even out of breath? He's fucking my mouth in long, controlled thrusts.

My throat and cock are being used. It's overwhelming.

Spread your legs. Don't talk. Don't move.

As pleasure winds through me, and I can hear it winding through my brother, D'Angelo, and Robyn in the changes in their breathing, gasps, and moans, I feel calmer and more settled than I have since I came to America.

It doesn't matter whether I come.

What matters is that I'm caught here in the middle of a group of people who are taking pleasure from my body.

Who I love and who love me.

And that's the most beautiful music of all.

CHAPTER FIFTEEN

Captain's Hall, Freedom

*E*den

It's Monday morning, and I'm sitting at the desk in the study in Captain's hall. The desk is heavy, rich mahogany. I run my hand over its smooth surface. It looks like the fancy type of thing that a CEO would own.

Or D'Angelo.

It's his gift for me officially starting as his PA today.

None of my bosses at the cleaning firms bought me a gift.

D'Angelo is currently my number one boss, especially

as he also bought me my own computer, iPad, and phone, and is allowing me to order as much stationary as I like.

I'm planning on ordering moleskin notepads and a professional color-coded document organizer, which I dreamed about owning in college.

Of course, my favorite thing about this desk is that I asked for it to be pushed up against the window next to Robyn's desk.

Hers is pine and cluttered with papers, empty wine glasses, and at least six different phones, as well as a hands free set, which is looped over her ear. She's been excitedly talking into it for the last hour to different journalists.

Yet she appears to understand her own chaos.

I think.

She's good at her job.

The study's walls are painted deep green, and the floors are oak. A circular light that looks like a flower blossoms from the ceiling, and a matching light sprouts next to the desk.

A lime couch rests against the back wall, beneath photographs of the hockey team with D'Angelo at the center and Shay smiling next to him.

Underneath, are the staff, including Robyn, Cody, and me.

On the wall closest to the desks are ranks of filing cabinets, a black board that I've divided into D'Angelo's schedule for the next week, and a bulletin board.

Robyn's currently using the bulletin board for pinned to-do lists, cut out magazine and newspaper articles, as well as inspirational quotes.

D'Angelo looked like he was sucking a lemon, when he saw this morning's quote: *Sing like no one is listening. Love like you've never been hurt. Dance like nobody is watching.*

D'Angelo arched his brow. "Shay definitely does that."

"Hey," Shay laughingly protested.

"And I'll always be watching when you dance."

Robyn smirked. "Voyeur...or stalker."

Can you love like you've never been hurt?

Can any of my new family?

Yesterday, watching Shay's dream of learning the piano come true, D'Angelo's patience with him, then how he could be spanked and used but not hurt...I'm coming to believe that it's possible.

Touch doesn't have to mean pain.

I glance out of the window at the rolling lawns and trees, which lead to the haze of Captain Forest beyond.

I furrow my brow, as my temples throb. My eyes feel tired. I squint against the light.

Would Robyn mind if I closed the drapes?

I pick up my mug of Earl Grey, which has pride of place on my desk. I take a sip, sighing in satisfaction.

Hot and strong. Just as it should be.

I warm my hands around the mug because they're cold. They have been since I was injured.

I can't seem to keep my hands or feet warm at the moment. I also can't seem to shake this concussion that's making me feel like shit.

I don't let it show on my face.

I have work to do. I can handle it.

I run my finger over the red, golden, and black lines of

the phoenix with a dramatic tail and wings, which is printed onto the white mug.

It's my tattoo design.

It fucking drove the breath from me, when Robyn and Shay presented me with it this morning.

They'd had it printed as a good luck gift for my first morning.

Have I ever received so many presents that were just for me before?

I share a birthday with Shay. We always got presents together.

Yet this mug and the desk are only for me because I'm starting a new role.

It makes me even more determined to do my best.

I place down my tea and flick open the file in front of me, running my finger down the timings for the games this week.

The first one is on Tuesday against the Dallas Stars.

Since breakfast, I've been looking through D'Angelo's schedule, memorizing it and trying to figure out ways to make it more efficient for him.

He's going to be working hard this season.

It'll be tough to hold him together, but I will because his team needs him.

The Bay Rebels must win their opening games to keep the board and senior management on side.

Robyn ends her call, then she brushes her hand against mine. "Isn't it awesome that we can work together like this?"

"As long as you don't steal my stationary."

She laughs. "I make no promises. Plus, your brother has already been stealing your post-it notes. He plans to use them to torment D'Angelo. Has he always been a prankster?"

I shake my head. "Shay didn't have anyone in his life who gave him such fun reactions. He didn't have a best friend either."

Robyn taps her phone. "I'm not being too noisy, right? Can you still concentrate."

I nod. "I'm used to Shay."

I don't tell her how much my head is hurting. It's been getting worse all morning, a sharp migraine.

It's less than an hour before we'll break for lunch. I'm not ruining my first day, when the others went to such an effort to make it special for me.

They bought me my phoenix tattoo mug.

"I thought that you'd short-circuited D'Angelo this morning." Robyn hunts through her papers like she actually has a system. "You know the way that you stopped him at the door to pass him Gatorade, his rearranged daily schedule, and even healthy, made from scratch lunches for Shay and him. You're making life hard on yourself to be that good on your first day. You should have started out kind of incompetent and then you had somewhere to go. At this rate, you'll need to be running for President by the end of the year."

"I can't; I'm English," I deadpan.

"My mistake." Robyn traces a finger down my cheek, before turning my head and stealing a quick kiss. "I like this. I've spent too much time feeling alone. When I studied for my PhD, it felt so theoretical. It was hard to make friends, when Wilder didn't like me seeing people who weren't part of his social group, which meant *his* friends, the hockey team."

"I've always been alone apart from Shay. This feels like I'm in the college library, but instead of working by myself, I'm finally like the other people who I watched."

Robyn's brow furrows. She doesn't understand. How could she?

It's hard to explain. The words won't arrange themselves.

"The students. Everybody else. Others." I have one more go. "*Real people.*"

"You are real." Robyn clasps my hand. Maybe I am. When she touches me like this, I feel that I could be. "And I'm sitting with you now. I wish that I could have been your friend back then. I would have been."

She wouldn't.

I don't tell her that.

"Jude says that once I'm settled in, he'll tell me about the admin role in his charity as well," I say.

Robyn's expression brightens. "You'll be great at that. The kids there will love you. Anything that I can help you with, just ask. Hey, do you want to see your photos on the pages that I created?"

I sit forward to look at the computer screen that she turns to face me.

"This is Shay's page," she tells me, proudly. "Look, there's the photo that you took in the kitchen. It has the most views, and I'm not surprised. Not only does he look fucking gorgeous, but you've captured the *real* Shay and not the volatile hot tempered player who people see on the ice."

I study the page.

It's filled with information on Shay's English background, showing him as playful, relaxed, and fun.

There's an interactive quiz and a video of the arena.

"It's impressive." I mean it.

Robyn smiles, before clicking through onto another page. "It links to new merchandise."

I swallow, as pain twinges through my shoulder.

Robyn looks concerned. I wasn't able to hide the pain well enough.

"Is it your shoulder or your ribs?" She asks. "Can I get you more pain meds?"

She looks ready to leap out of her seat.

I shake my head, but that only makes the pain lance through my temples worse.

I'm dizzy.

"I'm fine." My vision is blurry. I struggle to focus through the involuntary tears at the screen. "D'Angelo's page looks different."

Robyn tears her concerned gaze away from me after a long moment. "It suits his commanding leader of the team feel versus Shay as a rising star. So, suits and cold but elegant stances with arctic blues and statistics. But I was planning on…"

I don't hear what she's planning.

Her words fade, blur, bleed into each other.

My ears are ringing.

The pain swells into agony.

I hunch my shoulders, gritting my teeth.

I can bear this.

Take it.

It's only pain.

Dee, dee, don't close your eyes. What if you don't wake up? What if you leave me alone with the monsters?

My eyes scrunch shut. I can't help it.

I'm sorry, Shay. I'm sorry...

My mind's muddled.

Where am I? What's happening?

Without meaning to, I tip forward against the wave of exhaustion. I grimace, as my arm in its sling is caught against the front of the desk.

I hear a panicked cry.

Am I alone with the monsters?

Then everything turns black.

CHAPTER SIXTEEN

Captain's Hall, Freedom

*E*den

"I DON'T NEED A DOCTOR." I clench my jaw.

I'm lying in D'Angelo's large antique, silver bed. Even though his drapes have been pulled closed to reduce the light in the room, I can barely open my eyes.

My head throbs.

I try to sit up.

Shit, I'm dizzy.

I collapse back onto the silk pillows.

I can't fully remember how I got up here.

I think that D'Angelo and Shay carried me between them.

I grit my teeth.

Why did Robyn have to call them back home on their first day of the season?

I could have had a quick rest on the desk. I'd have come round after a bit.

When you pass out, it's like that.

You come round with a dry mouth and migraine headache.

It's no big deal.

"Humor me," Michael says, dryly. He checks my pulse. His hand feels hot against my cold wrist. "You've made your feelings clear four times now. But still, here I am."

"Surprisingly, when you collapse over your desk, it worries the people who love you." Robyn's sitting with her back against the headboard.

She pushes a strand of hair gently behind my ear.

She looks concerned.

D'Angelo's expression is shuttered, however, as he leans against the wall beside the window, studying Michael closely as he works.

D'Angelo's dressed in his suit from this morning, but his shirt is buttoned wrong and his tie is askew like he got ready in a frantic rush when he received the call from Robyn.

"I don't need a doctor," I try again.

Shay shoots me a glare. He's pacing from one side of the bedroom to the other.

His red t-shirt is on back to front. He looks like he got changed in even more of a hurry at the rink than D'Angelo did.

I swallow.

I didn't want to worry them or ruin their first day.

I failed.

Michael gives me a stern look. "You're not actually refusing a doctor, are you? And I'll point out again that between us, who's more medically qualified to judge if you *need* a doctor? Cody would stop feeding me his delicious cream cakes, if I let anything happen to you. He likes you."

Robyn wrinkles up her nose. "Tell me that's not a euphemism."

"Yes and no."

When I lick over my dry lips, Shay rushes to the bedside table and snatches up a water bottle. He holds it to my mouth, and I take grateful sips.

"Better?" Shay places down the bottle.

Our gazes meet, and my heart feels like it's breaking, when I see his anxiety.

He knows what this is about.

But neither of us want to voice it.

Dee, dee, don't close your eyes. What if you don't wake up? What if you leave me alone with the monsters?

As kids, when Shay learned to speak, every time that I was hurt, ill, or starving and would pass out, Shay would desperately shake me and say that.

Except, we knew who the monsters were.

They were real.

Shay perches on the edge of the bed, meeting Robyn's gaze over my head.

I don't know what their glance means.

Are they thinking about me?

"I'd be fine in my own bed," I offer.

D'Angelo crosses his arms. "You're not lying in that cramped upper bunk bed with cracked ribs, injured shoulder, and severe concussion. You never should have been. You're all in my bed for the moment, where I can keep an eye on you and make sure that you don't do anything like faint."

Faint?

Fuck that.

"I'm not delicate," I say, low and rumbling.

D'Angelo snorts. "I know that."

"But you have been masking your pain," Robyn replies. "None of us knew that it was this serious."

I wince.

"You're staying in this bed." Shay tilts up his chin. "And you're letting yourself be cared for, Dee. Don't be bloody stubborn."

"Independent," I mutter.

"In actual fact," Michael takes a step back from me, tapping notes onto his phone, "suffering from severe post-concussion symptoms."

"What does that mean?" Shay's eyes widen.

"It means that I wish you would agree to come into hospital." Michael arches his brow.

I shake my head.

"Eden," D'Angelo straightens, "you're my employee now. There's no concern over cost. I had extensive medical insurance written into your contract and luckily, you're now covered. Even if you weren't, I'd pay for anything that you needed. We're family."

Despite the throbbing pain that radiates down from my head to my neck and shoulders, happiness glows through me.

For the first time, I relax in D'Angelo's bed.

Family.

"Thank you," I say, gruffly.

"Yeah, cheers, darlin.'" Shay bounces off the bed and launches himself across the room.

He grabs the sides of D'Angelo's face to hold him in place as he claims his lips, fast and hard.

D'Angelo splutters for a moment in shock, before dragging Shay deeper into the kiss. Then he drags him away by the hair.

They both share a small, intimate smile, before growing serious again.

Robyn slides her hand to rest on my arm, which is in the sling. "So, what happens now?"

"Now," Michael replies, "Eden can come into the hospital as an outpatient, so that I can run tests to evaluate brain, autonomic nervous system, vision, and vestibular function. I'll create a custom treatment plan. I'll talk to a neuropsychologist and neuroscientist. You'll need physical and cognitive therapy to repair the damaged pathways."

That's a lot.

Why can't I just shake it off like all the other times?

I'm going to be okay, right?

Robyn's eyes are gleaming with tears. "Shit, that sounds… I mean, he'll recover…?"

Michael won't meet her gaze.

Fuck.

Michael starts for the door. "I need to get back to the hospital and talk with my colleagues in the right department."

"Mike," D'Angelo says, sharply, "he *will* recover."

"We're all going to do our best to make that happen," Michael replies. "As your friend and not your doctor, however, I'd like to say two things. Don't rush the pace. And also, think about therapy. Because the reason that this is so serious is the large number of previous injuries that we discovered, when you were in hospital before, to your skull. The ones that were untreated from childhood. Whatever caused those, if you haven't dealt with it…it's going to fuck you up."

Michael is the only doctor who I don't mind being around. He says things like *fuck you up*.

I glance at Shay. He's white as a sheet.

I wish that I could wrap my arm around him. But then, D'Angelo does, and I find that I'm okay with that.

"Can Code work as his physical therapist? Paid, of course, and around his Bay Rebels duties," Robyn asks, quietly. She glances at me. "Would you like that? I thought that you'd prefer someone who you know. Rather than going to the hospital, Code could come and do the work with you here."

Robyn's always thoughtful and kind.

I nod.

Michael slips his phone into his pocket. "I'll ask at dinner tonight. He'll say yes because he's already sent me three texts asking how Eden is and whether he can come round here and see him. I'll put him off until tomorrow, so that you can get some rest. And I mean it, about the rest."

D'Angelo walks to the door, patting Michael on the shoulder. "I'll make sure of it. We'll be waiting on him hand and foot. I appreciate you coming out and doing this for us. It means a lot."

Michael's expression softens. "Robyn's family, and since she's chosen you all to be hers, then you are too. My husband and I look after our family and friends. I know my way out."

"Tell Code that I'll phone him later," Robyn whisper yells after Michael's retreating back.

Pain still lances through my head.

Robyn strokes down my cheek in apology. "We'd better keep our voices down."

"Okay, love," Shay mouths silently, before shrugging out of D'Angelo's hold.

He approaches the bed again, before burrowing under the covers and lying as close as he can to me.

I thought that he would, after Michael's comment about therapy.

Shay hated the therapy that our parents sent him to.

Just because he could talk about what happened, didn't mean that he wanted to.

Or could.

He lies with his head on the pillow next to me. Our golden hair mingles. He lifts my hand, staring at the way that his fingers entangle with mine.

D'Angelo watches us from the doorway. "So, how do you think your first day went as my PA? Just boring admin stuff like I promised, right?"

Shay tightens his hand around mine. "Don't make me laugh. I'm too angry."

My heart speeds up. My mouth feels even drier.

I made Shay angry...?

He's shaking.

This is the opposite of what I wanted. I wanted him to relax and enjoy his first day of practice, before the big game tomorrow. Shay is meant to be able to focus on his hockey, now that he doesn't have to support me on the ice.

Instead, he's here worrying and *angry* about me.

How have I screwed up?

"Not now," Robyn says, firmly. "Let him rest."

Shay turns his head on the pillow and reluctantly, I turn my head as well to meet his burning gaze.

Except, I can see now that he's using rage to hide his fear.

He usually does.

He's terrified.

"This is serious, Dee," Shay whispers.

"I know."

"Do you?" Shay's expression hardens. "Did you listen to what Mike said? Do you have any idea what it did to me to see you collapsed on the ice that day? To not know if you'd wake up? To see you in that hospital bed? Then to get called off the ice today and told by coach that you'd collapsed *again*. I thought that you were going to die…"

Shay chokes on tears.

I feel sick.

"Shay." I pull his hand close to my chest. "I'm right here."

He always needed this: to feel the rising and falling of my chest.

The steady *thud — thud — thud* of my heart.

It was the only way to know that I was alive, when my eyes were closed and I couldn't talk.

For years, I'd wake up from sleeping and find that he'd lain over my chest just to be certain that I was alive. He couldn't sleep otherwise.

D'Angelo's lips thin. "Mike's right about the therapy for both of you. Why in the hell didn't you say anything? You must have been feeling like shit for days."

Bewildered, I blink. "It's only pain. You were busy. Today was important for you."

"You're important," Robyn bursts out. "More important than hockey or fucking anything."

I stiffen in shock.

"We'll find a way to prove it to you." D'Angelo looks determined. Then his gaze sweeps across Shay as well. "To both of you. But for now, I have to say that as Shay's Dom, I need to know how this impacts you. I'm beginning to think that perhaps we all should stop holding onto secrets. I don't exclude myself from that. But this isn't about me right now. We have a right to our pasts. No one should feel pressured to share more than they're comfortable with. But I have a responsibility to Shay and to uphold that I have to know about things as serious as this. For your sake, Eden, if you can't share this with strangers, then consider that you should with friends. Will you trust us?"

My chest is tight. My eyes burn.

I can't speak.

I glance between D'Angelo and Robyn.

They're not looking at me like they're judging me.

Pitying me.

Thinking of abandoning me.

Is it compassion? Understanding? *Love?*

I turn back to Shay. He's ashen, and a tremor runs through his hands.

This isn't only my secret.

It's Shay's as well.

D'Angelo does have an extra duty toward Shay, however, and protecting my twin matters most in the world to me.

What if D'Angelo triggers him because he doesn't understand?

I've never spoken about this to anyone.

I've never let the words free.

Perhaps, if I do, then *I'll* be free.

Shay won't be alone with the monsters anymore.

I turn my head, lying straight on my back. I'm still as a statue.

I learned to do this.

It helped to stop myself being noticed. Shay was never able to learn the same trick, even though he tried really hard, as far back as I can remember, to copy me.

I can't look at anyone as I tell them.

I stare up at the ceiling instead. I study a thin crack between the thick plaster.

Has D'Angelo lain here and noticed it before?

"They locked us in this dark room with a mattress on the floor." My voice is steadier than I'm expecting it to be. I don't know where the words are coming from. I feel like I'm floating above my body. Maybe somebody else is speaking? I can hear Shay's ragged breathing and feel how tightly he's clinging to me. "I was happy, when they dragged me away from Shay and into the room next door. He was crying. I could hear him. But they weren't going to hurt him. He was safe and he wouldn't see…"

"Dee," Shay sounds broken hearted.

Like he did back then.

"They liked that I didn't speak. Perhaps, they thought that I'd never be able to tell. They thought that it was funny and made a game out of trying to make me say things. They said they'd stop if I did. But I wouldn't have, even if I could. Because their game kept them choosing me to play with and not Shay every night."

"But I wanted them to choose me." Shay's sobbing. The front of my t-shirt is wet. "I begged them to."

"I know." And fuck it, I do. "Therapy will do fuck all. Our parents and therapists thought that Shay was the unbroken one because he spoke. Because he smiled. But his words and smile are a shield. It was harder for him to listen to me being hurt through that wall, the slaps, thumps, and...all of it."

"I had to sit with you after," Shay whispers, "when they carried you in, bruised and not moving. When I saw you on the ice...or heard about you from coach today...it made it all rush back. I was terrified that you wouldn't wake up, just like I always was back then."

"You're both here with us now," Robyn says, although her voice is wavering like she's holding back tears. "I can't even begin to understand what you've been through. But I'll always be here to listen, and it's clear that this current concussion is traumatic for both of you."

"What's clear," D'Angelo growls, "is that I'm going to find the people who did this to you and destroy them. Until then, please believe that I'll keep both of you safe. I protect my family. You're not in this alone anymore."

Slowly, I feel less numb.

I blink, swallowing.

I don't think that I've ever spoken this much. At least, never to someone who isn't Shay.

Yet if they're family and want to understand both Shay and me, then I need to get these final words out.

I may never feel able to again.

"People think that you're broken if you don't speak." My throat burns. My skin itches, and I wish that I could trace across my rose tattoos. "But not being seen and heard is safer. Shay likes the spotlight. No one notices how damaged you are, when you're in it. He's always been desperate to please our adoptive parents, college teammates, and women…so that we wouldn't be sold, thrown away, or hurt again. Physical pain is nothing. Emotional pain is what breaks you."

CHAPTER SEVENTEEN

Rebel Arena, Freedom

Robyn

I WRING my hands together in my warm gloves, pacing the side of the rink. I try to ignore the roar of the crowd, chatter of the commentator, and the bite of cold air mixed with sweat and rubber.

I *really* try to ignore the bank of journalists and photographers from the press.

I've been deliberately not catching Melanie's eye for the last couple of hours.

This is the opening game of the season against the Dallas Stars, and every seat in the arena is filled.

The atmosphere is buzzing.

Have I ever been at a game with this level of both pressure and excitement?

It's electric.

No one expects the Bay Rebels to do anything but lose.

Yet the score's **4 — 4**.

They could truly win this.

It's the start to the season that the Bay Rebels, Dad, D'Angelo and Shay need.

It's the start that myths are made of.

The crowd are cheering every time that the Bay Rebels gain the puck.

They're going crazy, every time that the players make a shot on goal.

And by players, I mean D'Angelo and Shay.

They're on fucking fire.

They've scored twice each.

Five minutes left...

My heart is beating fast. I'm shaking with adrenaline.

I watch a Bay Rebels dark haired defenseman, Atlas, shut down an attack by the Dallas Stars, stopping them from scoring.

"Yes!" I yell.

It's so close. It's a tough game.

I pull my long, woolen coat around my emerald dress, glad for the scarf that Eden wound around my neck, before I left for the game.

It's one of Eden's gray scarves. I turn my head to take a deep, sniff of his sweet, vanilla scent.

It's comforting.

I hated leaving Eden behind, but despite his protests that he was *fine* (I'm not going to believe that again any time soon), the memory of him collapsed over the desk, while my heart almost burst through my chest in terror, made me firm my determination that he couldn't come out to the arena.

He'll be watching from his place on the couch in Captain's Hall.

"You're thinking about the twin again." Neve nudges me with her elbow.

I rub my arm. "Ow."

If there was a sport called elbow nudging, Neve would be an Olympic Champion.

Underneath her open military style floor-length coat, she's wearing what I'm coming to call her *game night* Emo t-shirt:

SPOILER ALERT: I DON'T CARE.

I bite my lip, as D'Angelo passes the puck to Shay.

They're totally in tune with each other.

They're like a fucking machine.

It doesn't matter who scores. They're doing this together.

They're doing this for Eden.

For me.

For the whole of Freedom.

Neve nudges me again.

"Double ow." I still don't look away from the rink.

"The virgin twin who you fucked, rather than the one who's everybody's fucktoy," Neve whispers.

"Neve," I hiss, hushing her.

I glance around myself, hoping that no one's overheard.

"I could be talking about the Addaman twins." She smirks.

"That's worse. The Addamans are in their nineties and assholes."

"Hey, don't be ageist or anti-asshole." Neve gives me a long look. "And don't avoid my question, Robyn Hood. I'm right, aren't I?"

I sigh. "Of course I'm worried about Eden. It was fucking terrifying to see him pass out and… It reminded me of Mom, you know?"

Neve's expression gentles. "Yeah."

My chest is tight. I focus on the blur of players who are battling it out on the rink.

Three minutes…

"He's so hard to read. I've never met anyone like him. He's stoic and acts like nothing's hurting him. But just sometimes, he'll tell you something and…"

I shudder, thinking about what Eden admitted, after Michael had checked him out medically.

I have the feeling that Eden told us mostly for his brother's sake, as if he wanted us to know that Shay was more broken than he pretended.

It's like he felt obligated to make sure that we knew enough to be careful of Shay without realizing that D'Angelo and I are going to be just as careful with him.

D'Angelo exchanged a troubled glance with me.

If D'Angelo was protective of the twins before, he's a hundred times more now.

I've never seen D'Angelo and Shay being as fierce and fearless together on the ice as they're being tonight. Perhaps, the trust that they've shown each other over the last few days has connected them in their play.

The crowd are going wild for them.

I glance to my right, watching Dad who's standing by the benches to get the best vantage point and view. He's dressed in a smart black suit with the team's official tie.

My eyes narrow, when I see Silas and Bronwyn flanking him like the hockey mafia.

Dad is animated as he watches the game, gruffly shouting and waving his arms.

Silas' lips are pinched. But Bronwyn is smiling.

My shoulders are tense, however, with nerves.

A draw isn't enough.

We need to win.

Two minutes...

"Eden's English." Neve shrugs. "Just give him some tea, talk about soccer, and make sure that your humor is dry, ironic, and sarcastic."

Actually, that'd work.

D'Angelo weaves around the rival players toward the goal.

My mouth dries, and my hand instinctively rises to touch the golden pendant of a jersey that lies around my neck. My guys gave it to me because our relationship is a secret but they still want me to have something of theirs to wear during games.

I smile as I trace over the pendant.

"Anyway, Code and Mike are over at Captain's Hall,

keeping Eden company and checking that he doesn't collapse again from all the excitement." Neve crosses her arms. "The most that will happen will be that he'll collapse from boredom. Mike will feed him hummus and drone on about old guy shit like classical music and the rising cost of insurance."

"The horror."

What would Neve think about D'Angelo's piano concerts for us in evenings? She'd probably categorize them under her *boring old guy shit*.

What would she say about D'Angelo's classic car?

I know that one.

I bite the inside of my cheek to stop myself from telling her because there's a ceasefire between my best friend and D'Angelo...but that's it.

"Huh, did you stick something into their asses to get them to skate that fast and score like this?" Neve studies the way that D'Angelo is barreling toward the goal with serious intent. Then her expression becomes dangerous. "Try ginger for the second game on Thursday."

I wince, and my asshole clenches in sympathy. "Thanks for the figging tip. I'm sure that D'Angelo will be even more grateful."

See, only a ceasefire.

I can't look away from D'Angelo. He looks unstoppable.

An ice god and his prince.

One minute...

Can D'Angelo do it?

"I'm actually going with positive reinforcement as a

motivator." I don't look away from the ice. Shay is on the other side of the goal to D'Angelo, backing him up. The atmosphere is charged. "They've both scored two goals so far. Whoever scores the most over these opening three games gets to choose to share with me one of their…"

I glance over my shoulder.

These phone calls and texts from Melanie have made me paranoid.

I snatch Neve's hand between mine and use our trick from high school, when we wanted to talk about how much of a dick a teacher was being in front of them or what guy had the tightest ass in the middle of English without anyone knowing.

Perhaps, I can understand now why the teachers separated us in most lessons.

I spell out the word on her palm: **KINKS**

Neve's eyes widen, before she turns to the glass and begins to holler, enthusiastically, "Come on, Shay. Get your ass into gear. Eyes on the prize!"

He glances over for a moment, before to my shock, starting to skate even faster.

D'Angelo passes Shay the puck.

My heart is my mouth. My pulse is racing.

Please…

Shay raises his stick, aiming at the goal.

If he scores, Bay Rebels have won.

He shoots…

And he scores.

"Yes!" I scream.

The crowd bursts into applause, as the siren sounds, ending the game.

Neve fist pumps. "Kinky for the win."

I let out a choked sound, struggling to stay standing.

They did it.

They've won the opening game of the season, and the world has seen that the Bay Rebels are no longer *losers.*

CHAPTER EIGHTEEN

Captain's Hall, Freedom

*R*obyn

I STARE AT THE BEAUTIFUL, tight globes of D'Angelo's naked ass.

I can't look away. I'm mesmerized.

"Gorgeous," I murmur.

I'm sure that I first fell in love with D'Angelo at college because of his breathtaking ass.

He turned up at the college Halloween party naked apart from a pair of horns on his head.

D'Angelo looked spectacular in that costume.

A horny devil.

My devil.

Or fallen angel.

I bite my lip, running my finger around the rim of my coffee mug, as I stare at D'Angelo's long, athletic legs, strong back, and the way that his ass is framed by the **I'LL FEED ALL YOU PUCKERS** blue hockey cooking apron.

The apron is the only thing that he's wearing.

Eden was insistent that D'Angelo borrow it to protect his…manly bits…while he cooked.

D'Angelo pushes the sizzling bacon around the frying pan.

I wrinkle up my nose at the delicious scent.

There's no better smell in the world.

Apart from — possibly — D'Angelo himself.

The scent of D'Angelo naked and cooking bacon should be bottled.

It's enough to distract me from how early it is.

We're determined to fit in some time together, before D'Angelo and Shay leave to practice at the arena, and I must focus on the intense press interest in the Bay Rebels after their spectacular win against the Dallas Stars.

Would it be a fair rule that all men should be unclothed in the house?

Shay would go for that in a heartbeat.

Sometimes, it's a struggle to get him to put on clothes after he's had a shower. He prefers to saunter around with or without a towel.

"You're drooling." Eden arches his pierced brow.

Eden's sprawled next to me on the bench at the oak table. He's wearing a gray t-shirt and joggers. His hair is slicked back, but a single golden strand falls over his eyes.

Morning light streams through the wide, bay window

behind the oak table. The table is already laid with pastries, fresh rolls, and toast.

I smile, relaxed and happy.

Yesterday was a good day. The win in the game was an important one.

I'm never going to forget the way that D'Angelo walked back into the house with his arm around Shay's shoulders, smiling with pride, or how Shay glowed like the sun.

Then Eden's joy, when his gaze met his brother's.

This success belongs to all of us.

And last night...hell, we celebrated.

Eden needed to watch, as Michael hasn't cleared him yet. He appeared to enjoy sitting on the chair by the bed, however, jerking himself off in long, twisting strokes to D'Angelo fucking me.

I smile, dreamily.

I'm sore in all the right ways...and places.

I instinctively wipe at my mouth. "I'm not."

I can only see the back of D'Angelo's head but I can still tell that he's smirking.

He shifts the weight on his legs. I'm certain it's so that the muscles in his ass flexes.

I swallow.

Now, I'm drooling.

"Perhaps, I didn't expect to come down to our celebratory breakfast and find the naked chef in my kitchen," I point out. "But I approve."

D'Angelo glances over his shoulder at me.

"I decided that we shouldn't wait for the reward until

three wins, after yesterday's stellar performance. I can be generous and I'm not one for delayed gratification," D'Angelo drawls. "At least, not for me. I rather enjoy other people's."

His gaze slides to Shay.

Shay will definitely be sore in certain places this morning.

Shay doesn't seem bothered. In fact, he seems so hyper with energy that he doesn't notice that D'Angelo's talking about him.

Shay's too busy — and has been for the last half an hour — excitedly recreating the game with his hockey stick in hand. He's wearing his black silk pajamas that D'Angelo bought him.

I wince.

This is going to end well...*not*.

"He was like a bloody god." Shay leaps onto the counter, swinging his stick for emphasis, barely missing the fruit bowl. Eden's cheek twitches. D'Angelo appears to have a sixth sense about Shay's disasters and destruction of his kitchen, which is admittedly a daily occurrence. He switches off the cooker and turns around, crossing his arms. "Our captain dominated on that ice. He has the puck. But there were only minutes to go. My heart was fucking hammering in my chest. I couldn't see anything but the goal. I *had* to score."

He throws himself off the counter, wielding the stick like a sword.

"Shay," Eden warns.

I'm caught up in Shay's excitement.

I'm back there.

Please let them score...

It's like Shay can't hear his brother. "*One minute.* All I'm thinking is one more goal. That's it. I can't let Robyn down. *I won't.* Then...like the bloody legend that he is... our captain here passes."

D'Angelo stays silent, but his cheeks tinge pink.

"And I'm thinking..." Shay darts forward, leaning on the table and slamming the stick perilously close to the vase of roses. I dive forward to steady it, before it can fall. Shit, that was close. "...I'm the fucking English Ice Prince. So, they all think that we're losers and misfits...? They want to fire the people who I care about? I'm going to show them." He bounces up and down on his toes. "So, I take the shot and I..."

Eden stands and rests his strong hand calmly on Shay's shoulder.

Shay steadies and stills without his twin needing to say a word.

Shay lowers the stick and relinquishes it, leaning it against the table. "Sorry, I don't mean to get hyper. I just do sometimes. You can tell me to shut up and sit down."

"I'd never do that." Eden's stormy gray eyes settle on me. "You shouldn't have offered him that second muffin."

I hold my hand out to Shay, tugging him out of his brother's hold, until he's perching on the bench next to me. "Shay scored the winning goal. He earned it."

Shay flushes. Then he slips his finger gently under my chin and kisses me, petal-soft.

Somehow, I feel that he needed to hear that.

I wish that Eden had allowed him to get to the end of his story, even if it'd resulted in ten broken vases.

D'Angelo must agree with me because he says, "And what happens when you take the shot?"

Shay shrugs.

D'Angelo looks determined. "You showed incredible potential out there. It took the other team by surprise. Of course, it'll be harder in future games because the teams will analyze our play and be more prepared. Now, what happened next."

Shay ducks his head, looking pleased. He needs this balance: his brother's stern steadiness, but also, the praise and encouragement from D'Angelo and me.

"I scored and won the game," he says, quietly.

I tap my chin. "Huh, wasn't there some sort of bet going on…?"

D'Angelo rolls his eyes. "Here I am, making all this effort,cooking breakfast in nothing but an apron, and you focus on my lost bet. I still have two more games to even the score, you know."

I chuckle. "It's a hard life…just not for me."

Definitely not right now with these three gorgeous men around me, a bacon roll about to be made for me, and a won hockey match yesterday.

Shay brightens. "I won this round of the kink contest too! Are there real kink contests? Because I'd like to enter. If not, we should hold one every game."

Eden narrows his eyes. "That's up to Robyn."

Shay's lips quirk. "Of course, our mascot."

"Hey," I protest, "that's Seal. I'm more like…"

"Our good luck charm," D'Angelo offers. "Players are allowed to be superstitious. We could insist that you wear the same panties from the winning game to each game from now on or that we tap your shins with our sticks for luck."

"So, me wearing smelly underwear and having bruised shins will help?"

D'Angelo smirks. "I don't make the rules."

All of a sudden, I hear a noise outside in the hallway and the bang of the front door.

I freeze. "Shit, did you hear that?"

D'Angelo's shoulders straighten and he nods.

Eden's gaze becomes steely, as he exchanges a sharp glance with D'Angelo. Then he gestures at Shay and me to remain seated.

What on earth does Eden think he's doing?

He's black and blue, with eyes that still look strained with a headache. He's booked in for hospital appointments all afternoon to make sure that he gets the right treatment over the next few months.

Now is not the time for him to act like an action hero.

"Dee," Shay whispers, urgently.

He must be thinking the same as me.

Eden shoots Shay a look, however, that's flashing with such fire that Shay draws back.

D'Angelo raises his finger to his lips to keep us quiet. Then Eden and him stealthily prowl toward the door.

D'Angelo brandishes his spatula in front of him like a sword.

What does he think he's going to do to an intruder with that? *Flip them like a pancake?*

My breaths are quick and shallow.

Who the hell is out there?

A burglar? Wilder, my stalker ex? *Melanie?*

Shay pushes himself up, standing protectively in front of me.

At the same time, I slip my phone out of the pocket of my green dress and hover my finger over the emergency number for the cops, which I have on speed dial.

I needed to for my own safety, when my ex started to stalk me, even if I never called them.

The scandal would destroy my family all over again.

Please, don't be Wilder...

I can hardly draw breath into my lungs.

I feel lightheaded.

"Hey, guys," Cody calls breezily as he struggles into the kitchen laden under a heavy, pastel blue physiotherapy bag that matches his boardshorts. He's wearing his **TORTURER** t-shirt that Michael only partly bought him tongue-in-cheek to wear as the Director of Physical Therapy for Bay Rebels. He's carrying a balance pad under one arm and a foam roller under the other. "A little help here."

My eyes widen.

Am I hallucinating?

I can't be the only one to see my brother strolling into my kitchen like he's been summoned by the smell of bacon, right?

D'Angelo is frozen with his spatula still upraised.

Shay bursts into action, however, rushing forward to grab the balance pad from Cody, before Cody...ironically...overbalances.

Cody locks eyes with D'Angelo, and they appear engaged in a battle of wills about who will crack first and mention the fact that D'Angelo is naked apart from the apron.

Shay turns and strides to rest the pad on the floor next to the table, winking at me.

I struggle not to laugh.

D'Angelo slowly lowers his arm and looks like he wants to adjust his non-existent cuff links.

He says stiffly, as if he's dressed in his smart suit, "Good morning. Would you like some breakfast? I've made bacon."

Now that's class.

You know that someone has been raised in an elite family, when they offer an uninvited guest to join the meal, even when their own ass is hanging out.

Cody's eyes are twinkling. "I can smell that. Hmm, yummy. But I'm good thanks. I had eggs with Mike and..." Cody's helpless gaze darts to mine. "Where do I get a naked butler?"

Shay splutters with laughter.

"You don't," I reply. "Mike's far too possessive. The poor naked butler would find himself kicked out on his ass."

"Yeah, but what an ass."

"Read the room," Eden blurts. "We didn't know who

you were. You could have been attacked as a home invader."

Cody looks surprised.

Shay perches on the side of the table, swinging his legs. "You're lucky that I didn't think to grab my stick and was relying on Jude's spatula to save us. It shows that you don't always react like you think you would in the moment."

I smile. "You were all perfect."

Cody wanders further into the room, dropping the heavy bag next to the table. He crouches down and places the foam roller onto the pile.

He stretches, easing his neck. "I didn't mean to cause panic, naked or otherwise. Dad gave me a key after the…accident."

Of course he did.

Eden marches to the wall next to the fridge where his aprons hang, selecting a red one with **BURNED TO PERFECTION** in black lettering. He slips it over D'Angelo's surprised head but backwards, so that it covers his ass.

Eden silently ties the laces for D'Angelo.

"Thanks." D'Angelo cocks his head, studying Eden.

Eden gives him a small nod.

"Seriously, why are you here?" I watch as my brother kneels on the floor, unrolling a foam mat and opening his bag. "You know that I'm always happy to see you, but we weren't expecting you."

Cody chuckles. "Read the room, right? I'm getting that impression. Didn't you get my text, Eden?"

Shay groans. "I knew that it'd be a text miscommunication."

Eden's expression is stony. "It just said *8.*"

"As in *eight in the morning*." Cody taps his watch. "I need to fit this in, before my work at the Bay Rebels and your appointments at the hospital. I added a thumbs up emoji."

I groan, tearing off a piece of toast to hurl at Cody's head, and he dodges it. "The dreaded thumbs up emoji strikes again. Would you prefer an email next time, Eden? You know, something with full sentences like we're grown-ass adults."

Cody looks like he wants to give me the finger but is holding back under the weight of D'Angelo's dominant glare.

Eden nods.

"Now that's sorted, you'd better get on with your job." D'Angelo points at Cody.

"He means," I lean forward, squeezing my brother's shoulder, "thanks for doing this."

"Of course, you're all family."

D'Angelo turns back to the counter and begins to butter the rolls, ready for the bacon.

Eden cautiously approaches the mat.

Cody pats it. "Come on, I won't bite. It's Mike who's into that."

"TMI," I mutter.

"I feel your pain." Shay tilts his head. "D'Angelo's the one who sinks his teeth into me, usually my arse."

"Keep talking," D'Angelo says without looking around, "and I really will be tempted to."

My heart clenches, as I watch Eden kneel next to Cody.

He's stiff and tense but trying to hide it.

He's squinting against the light. I can see the furrow between his brows, which I now know to look for as proof of his headache.

He's not moving quite right either, as if his muscles are too stiff.

It's painful to think that he didn't say anything because he thought it wasn't important.

Because he thought that he wasn't.

I'm going to make sure that he never thinks that again.

"Do you want to do this somewhere else or is this okay here?" Cody asks.

"What are we doing?" Eden's expression is unreadable.

"Today, we'll only be talking, and you can look at some of the equipment and get familiar with it."

Eden's shoulders relax. "Then here."

"Don't look like I'm here to…ehm, torture you." Cody looks down at his own t-shirt. "Honestly, I'm good at my job. But Mike can be a grumpy dick and even though he let me practice my physiotherapy on him, when I was training, he still nicknamed me *Torturer*."

"Now we're filled with confidence." Shay steals my coffee and takes a swig.

"Hey." I steal the mug back and take my own drink.

I have a feeling that I'll need it.

Eden looks pale.

"Seriously, physical therapy can be fun," Cody promises.

Eden quirks a disbelieving eyebrow.

"What do you feel about virtual reality? There's a game that's really good for your needs. You can play it with a pair of glowing sabers."

Shay's mouth drops open. "Do I get to play?"

Cody's expression is dangerous; many people forget this side to my brother because he's freckled and looks like a sun blushed college student who wishes that they were surfing. "Unfortunately, it's not for sarcastic brothers who don't have any *confidence* in me."

Eden's eyes dance. "I get to play with the sabers."

"Normally, I'm the twin who enjoys crossing swords in this relationship," Shay grumbles.

"There's a problem." D'Angelo edges the bacon onto the spatula. "How are you going to do any treatment, if Eden can't — or won't — tell you his pain thresholds?"

Eden flushes, tracing his finger over his rose tattoo.

I wish that I could hug him, but he wouldn't appreciate me doing that in front of Cody. Sitting with my brother, who he doesn't know well, is already a strain for him.

Cody knows about Eden's social anxiety and is giving him space. I can see how careful my brother is trying to be, at the same time as professionally assessing Eden without making it obvious.

Cody rolls a ball toward Eden, and it appears to break him out of his reverie. He rolls it back.

"I must be smart because I've thought of that too." Cody taps the ball. "You can use a rating system from one to ten. One is mild pain like stubbing your toe and ten is..." Cody screams, falling onto his back and thrashing around.

"Fuck me." Shay jumps as much as I do, toppling off the table to land on the bench.

"Got that out of your system?" D'Angelo drawls.

"Demonstrations are useful." Cody pulls himself up to sitting again. He has a point. What would extreme pain even look like to Eden who's more used to being in pain than any of us? "The important thing is that when you do any exercise, you mustn't go over level four, *ever*. I hear that you're a bit of a gym bunny, as well as being dedicated and hard working. Normally, that's great. But in this case, you need to slow down and listen to your body. No keeping going, until you hit your limit, which I'm guessing is level ten, screaming and thrashing around on the floor...or getting dizzy and collapsing because that's a ten too."

Eden looks frustrated. "Then if I can't go to the gym, what can I do?"

"To start with you can walk."

"You love hiking on the trails around here. I'll go with you," I offer.

I love the idea of spending more time with Eden in the woods.

This time, hopefully I won't land on my face in a muddy puddle.

I'm a disaster around nature, but it brings Eden to life to be outside in the sunlight with the birds and animals.

So, I'll risk it.

"I can't do more than that?" Eden demands.

"Hey," Shay warns, "it's only been two days, since…"

"I know." Eden looks away.

"I can guess why you'd like hiking in the forest." Cody rummages around in the bag. "I love the beach and bay around my cottage and couldn't live anywhere else too. When I surf, it's like I'm in a different world. It's just me and the waves. Is it the same for you in the forest?"

I hold my breath.

Cody already sees himself as Eden's friend. But Eden doesn't appear to understand that.

If anyone can help him to understand friendship, then it's my awesome brother.

"Sort of," Eden cautiously replies.

"There's this large outcrop of rocks to the side of the beach. The seals like to bask in the sun there. Last year, there was this one dark gray seal, which was bigger than the rest with this whiskery head. I looked out for him every time that I went surfing. I named him Daddy Whiskers. Mike said that he sounded like a porn star."

This surprises a deep laugh out of Eden.

Eden looks as shocked as I am.

I love hearing Eden laugh and only wish that it was possible to make him laugh more often.

"I have a squirrel called Puck," Eden confesses in turn.

I try to sit still and not spoil whatever spell has fallen between Eden and Cody that they're able to talk this comfortably.

D'Angelo appears to be doing the same because he's

stopped making the bacon rolls and is watching the exchange intently.

Shay's eyes are wide.

"What's this Puck like then?" Cody asks, and I love my brother even more for the easy smile that he gives.

Cody's laid back nature and conversation has distracted Eden enough that he hasn't even noticed that Cody has guided him to lie on his front over the roller to keep pressure off his injured shoulder, while he starts to massage his shoulders and neck.

He's magic.

"Red fur, feisty, and cute." Eden rests his cheek on his forearm. "Reminds me of Robyn."

I can't hold back the snort.

Cody's eyes sparkle, as he works on Eden's back with nimble fingers. "Sounds like my sis. And you can build to jogging soon."

"I'll do it with you." Shay perks up. "Hear that, Dee? You can go running with me."

"I'm also going to teach you some easy ways to self-massage the pain and stiffness out of your muscles," Cody continues. "Although I bet that you'll have some willing volunteers to help as well."

"Of course," I say.

"I can do it myself," Eden replies, suspiciously quickly.

My eyes narrow.

Doesn't he like my massages?

Okay, I suck at them.

But still…he could at least pretend, right?

"I volunteer!" Shay says, dramatically. "Massage is my specialist subject."

"And here I was hoping that it was hockey." D'Angelo turns back to finish the bacon roll.

At last, he carries it across the kitchen to me, and I make grabby hands for it.

"She's serious about her bacon sandwiches," Cody says. "We used to have contests about who could eat the most."

"I always won." I snatch up the roll off the plate.

"She also won, when it came to ice cream and pancakes."

I take a large bite.

My eyes almost roll back into my head; it's fucking good. "I think I just died."

Shay claps. "Total respect, love. I could watch you eat all day."

D'Angelo preens. "Only because I'm such a good cook."

I ready for my next delicious bite, when all of a sudden, my phone on the table vibrates with a message.

I frown. I bet that it's Dad.

I know better by now not to ignore his messages.

Yet when I click on my messages, it's from Dad but it's only a link to an article. Normally, I'd never click on a link but I recognize it.

It's the Peninsular Daily News.

Melanie's published her article on D'Angelo.

My heart speeds up, and anxiety spikes through me.

If Dad's sending this to me, then it has to be bad.

D'Angelo prowls to my shoulder. "I know that look. What's the bad news?"

I click on the link and then stare at the article for a stupidly long time or at least, stare at the photograph.

The article isn't what I was expecting. It's only the headline and a single photograph.

But what a picture.

I'm barely able to look away because of how impossibly beautiful D'Angelo looks in it…but also because of the man on his knees in front of him.

D'Angelo is dressed in the hottest possible ringmaster outfit, complete with top hat and whip coiled at his side.

The man kneeling obediently in front of him in nothing but glittery yellow shorts is wearing a golden lion's mask. It's a good choice of outfit for him because he has a shock of golden curls.

I can just make out a kitten tattoo with rope binding it around his upper arm.

"Melanie published the article. She's still a bully." My gaze flicks to Cody's face.

His eyes flash with rage.

Except, I'm the one who's shaking with it.

It's my job to protect D'Angelo from this type of press. I'm his shield.

But I didn't protect him.

Yet how could I? I don't even know what this picture means.

Why is this a secret?

Still, it smarts. I couldn't stop Melanie, when she hurt my brother and me. And I haven't stopped her from attacking D'Angelo.

My expression becomes determined. "I don't understand what she wants. Why's she so obsessed?"

"At the moment, she's trying to get our attention," D'Angelo replies. "By how you're shaking, it's worked. What's this deep, dark secret of mine then?"

He's playing it off as casual, but it's not convincing any of us.

"You're into lion taming," Shay answers, squinting at my phone. "How is being into roleplay a scoop? The public know that you're into stuff like this."

This photograph is obviously private.

D'Angelo has already taken enough shit about being openly bisexual, and stirring up the media at the start of the season about his sex life is petty and mean.

Still, why is this a *secret*?

Everybody already knows that D'Angelo is a wild playboy. There are photographs of him being spitroasted over tables in bars and dancing around poles already out in public.

I heard that there's also a sex tape somewhere.

I guess that I should track that down.

Purely for PR purposes, of course.

I hold up the phone for him to see. "When was this taken?"

I'm alarmed, when D'Angelo becomes ashen and doesn't immediately reply.

"Hey, you're okay." Shay dives off the table to wrap his arm around D'Angelo's shoulders. "You look incredible in that gear. Everyone will think so."

Cody exchanges a troubled glance with me.

Who's the other man in the photograph? Is that why D'Angelo's worried?

I'm going to kill Melanie.

"It was a fetish Christmas ball." D'Angelo taps his thigh, rhythmically in threes. He's increasingly anxious. "I don't know who took that photo because cameras were banned at the event. It was meant to be strictly discrete and private. It was just fun."

"We know." Eden stands, prowling to snatch a bottle of water from the counter. He unscrews its lid as he walks back to D'Angelo and passes it into his hands. "Drink."

D'Angelo obeys him, and it appears to steady him.

The twins stand either side of D'Angelo, flanking him. When he notices, it makes him straighten and the fire return to his eyes.

I shake my head. "I don't understand why she'd print this. I wouldn't be surprised if it didn't positively help your image."

"You don't understand," D'Angelo growls. "This is from a side to my life that I haven't fully shared with any of you yet because people trust me to keep them safe and their identities protected. People don't always understand our community and lifestyle. If Melanie truly has found a way to break into it and is prepared to reveal private individuals to get to me, then she's going to hurt my friends and wreck me. This so-called article is a threat."

"Fuck." Dread is heavy in my stomach. I hurl the phone onto the table, and it clatters away from me. "Why would she do something so toxic? Who's the lion?"

D'Angelo takes another swig of water. "I can't tell you.

It's the rule of parties like that, which you'll know if you're eventually invited. I have a duty to those who I dom."

I'm not jealous.

I love seeing how happy Shay makes D'Angelo. I don't even know how long ago he played with this other guy.

I know that it takes time to be trusted by communities and I've only just returned to Freedom. It makes me intrigued about being invited sometime though.

On the other hand, the thought that this connection could be what destroys the man who I love — all the men I love, as well as my own career — shoots fear through me.

"I get that," I reply. "And I respect the hell out of you for it. As PR Director, however, I can't protect all of us from this, unless I have the full facts. On top of that, this shit show is going to hit that guy too. It's not fair but it is what it is."

"It doesn't matter whether you're innocent and have never done anything yourself, you can still get caught in the crossfire." Cody's head is ducked.

I know that he's thinking about how he and I were haunted throughout our childhoods by Dad's scandal in the NHL.

The press didn't care that we were kids.

I press my lips together. "You need to reach out to him."

"I will." D'Angelo nods.

"Are you still in contact with him?" Shay tightens his arm around D'Angelo's neck.

To my surprise, I realize that it's *Shay* who's jealous.

Is his possessiveness because of insecurity?

Shay's fidgeting and not meeting D'Angelo's eye.

Is he still not able to believe that D'Angelo can love him?

Does he think that he's going to be abandoned…again? Thrown away like trash?

When D'Angelo looks at him, Shay plasters on a hurried smile, but I can see through its cracks, now that Eden has pointed them out.

I physically hurt inside, when I look at that smile.

D'Angelo's expression gentles. "Absolutely not. I haven't been in a romantic relationship…ever. I've been in love with Robyn since college. I've fucked a lot of people, but it's not the same thing, is it?"

Shay's lips quirk up, and he looks delighted. "Definitely not."

"I don't own the lion. I merely tamed him for a single night, as part of a performance for the ball. Neither of us were dating. He didn't have a dom, and I didn't a sub. That's all there was to it. I haven't played with him since."

"How do you know that Noah didn't sell the photo himself?" Cody demands. "I mean, he's a great guy, but people do out of character stuff, when they're pressured, scared, or desperate for money. Noah's from the tough side of town. It's pretty obvious that he's been struggling to—"

"How do you know that it's Noah?" D'Angelo shakes Shay's arm off his shoulder and stalks to Cody.

To my alarm, he drags Cody to his feet by the front of his t-shirt.

"Hey," I jump up, "let go of my brother and stop glaring at him with those murder eyes."

D'Angelo drags Cody closer until their noses are touching. "When your brother tells me how he knows—"

"Whoops," Cody smiles, sheepishly. "I'm glad that I don't have your job, Ryn. Sorry, I didn't mean to say his name."

"Who is he? And D'Angelo," I use my best authoritative voice, which I model on the one that Dad uses with his team, "let my brother go."

To my surprise, D'Angelo startles and drops Cody.

I'm going to use that voice more often. It's effective. Or at least, keep it as my secret weapon.

Cody smooths down the front of his t-shirt. "Sorry, Noah's name slipped out. I didn't mean to say it; I'd never have done that on purpose. I suck at this secrets business. But when you combine his hair and that tattoo…"

"Who is he?" Shay quirks his brow. "And when can I meet him?"

Cody glances at D'Angelo as if requesting permission.

D'Angelo sighs. "Why stop now?"

"He's the Bay Rebels nurse. You've already met him. He normally covers his tattoo, which I never understood. I saw it, however, during training camp, when he was showering. I liked the kitten."

Eden scowls. "The kitten shouldn't be bound in ropes."

"Noah *is* the kitten." D'Angelo pinches the bridge of his nose. "I'll never forgive myself, if the press' pursuit of me hurts him. His parents are traditional. They're distant, poor cousins of Anderson, the finance manager. Anderson is a prejudiced asshole and would fire Noah, if he became involved in a scandal. I know that his parents won't be accepting of him. If Melanie's threatening Noah as well, then we should…"

"Burn her alive." Eden's expression is unreadable.

D'Angelo blinks. "I was thinking more sue her, but your idea works too."

"We're going with suing, Dee." Shay shoots Eden a quelling look. "But why is this Melanie doing this? Why is she trying to ruin you?"

I'm shaking with anxiety.

What the hell is this all about?

I tried to find out through my sources, but no one is willing to talk about Melanie. On top of that, most of the magazines and news outlets are now looking positively on both D'Angelo and the Bay Rebels.

Is this a lone crusade?

Personal?

"When she rang me, when I was in Merchant's Inn, she demanded a full interview with D'Angelo," I say, thoughtfully. "It feels like blackmail to get you to agree."

"Then I'll do it." D'Angelo won't meet my eye.

He doesn't want to do it. He's agreeing for the sake of Noah.

A guy who subbed for him once.

He's going to do this interview because he's a good man and he doesn't want anyone to suffer on his behalf.

It's agonizing to have to shake my head because I can't let him do that.

This has gone too far.

"It's too risky." I reach for my phone, tapping back to my messages. What the hell am I going to reply to Dad? "Why's Melanie going to such lengths for this interview? Why now, at the start to the season? When senior management are on our backs? If she's prepared to cross this many lines already, then she must have a serious reason for wanting a live interview. She could spring anything on you. I wouldn't be able to prepare you for it. She could destroy your career and Bay Rebels alongside you."

"If she threatens to reveal Noah directly," D'Angelo meets my gaze, "then I don't care. He's only twenty-two. I'll do the interview to stop that happening. I'd do it to protect someone in both Bay Rebels and my community from losing their families and suffering…"

I know that he's thinking about what he went through at the hands of his own family.

Suddenly, my phone vibrates with a text.

Shit.

It's Melanie.

HELT (8:16): Live interview with BR captain 15:00 tomorrow before game. Otherwise, I'll publish secret number 2…

CHAPTER NINETEEN

Captain's Hall, Freedom

*S*hay

I'M CURLED AROUND ROBYN. We're lying on top of her violet quilt. She looks bloody gorgeous in a silk green suit. I play with her long hair, twisting it around my fingers.

Eden sits with his back against the wooden headboard on the other side of Robyn. He's alternating glancing between me with concern and at D'Angelo who's sprawled by himself in a heavy antique chair by the window.

I think D'Angelo's brooding.

It's like he has some bloody stupid idea in his head after yesterday that he doesn't want to taint us with whatever secret that journalist unleashes next.

Tough.

It doesn't matter what she says or what photograph she posts. We're going to stand by our captain.

Light streams into the bedroom through the floor length window, making D'Angelo's skin glow.

His black curls look even silkier than normal. I bite my lip, wishing that I could run my fingers through them like I am Robyn's hair.

Heat floods me, when I remember how he loves to yank me around by *my* hair.

He's a beast.

I smirk because that's just how I love my men, apparently.

D'Angelo — unsurprisingly — looks immaculate in his navy team suit and blazer with team tie.

I forgot my tie.

It's the one that we're meant to wear because it's covered with the official Bay Rebels logo.

I'm struggling to concentrate even more than usual. I'm on edge about the game tonight.

This season is huge for me.

Above me, the ceiling fan spins slowly.

I love Robyn's bedroom.

It's happy and welcoming like her.

The walls are painted a soft blue. Couches, a wardrobe, and a chest of drawers are surrounded by waves of books and abandoned chocolate wrappers.

I'm only wearing a white shirt, which hangs open, and black trousers.

There's an hour to go, until we need to leave for the rink.

I should be buzzing with excitement more than nerves. We all should.

Yet I can't even get myself to do up my shirt buttons because I'm waiting for what bombshell is going to drop next.

I hate that my first season is being poisoned like this.

Suddenly, my expression steels.

I'm not going to let someone do this to me. I've worked too bloody hard and been through too much to allow someone to play us like this.

I kiss Robyn's ear. "How much longer, love?"

She stiffens, glancing down at the phone clutched in her hand. "Three minutes."

I give an uneasy laugh. "It's like the countdown of doom."

"The sword of Damocles." Eden's heavy gaze lands on me. "Get dressed."

Half-heartedly, I reach down to do up the bottom button on my shirt.

"What if the time goes past when Melanie wanted the live interview, and she actually doesn't post anything else in revenge?" Robyn says, hopefully. "What if this has all been a bluff?"

D'Angelo snorts. "Wait, I know what this is called... optimism. Nope, wrong word, I meant naiveté."

"What did Noah say, when you called him last night?" I ask.

I feel cold inside, when I think about being quite literally unmasked like Noah could be. I haven't met the bloke, but he's a Bay Rebels staff member and that makes me feel doubly protective.

Plus, at least I'm sure that Mum and Dad would be fine with me being both bisexual and submissive. I only want to be able to tell them myself, when I next see them.

It's sick to have your sexuality, including if you identify as dominant or submissive, outed.

D'Angelo's fingers curl around the arms of his chair. "He cried. It was a hard conversation. At least, his parents don't know that it's him. *Yet.* Silas is a fucking piece of work and he'd make things hard for Noah's entire immediate family, including his younger brothers. I told Noah that he can call me anytime. If he's thrown out of his home because of this, I've offered that he can stay at my mansion. Do you mind?"

"Of course not," Robyn says, passionately. "Fuck, we'll do whatever we can. Cody says that Noah's a nice guy too."

"Yeah," I agree. I push myself up, vibrating with an energy that has nowhere to go. "Anything that he needs. You're allowed other friends too, darlin'. I'm sorry that I was a dick yesterday."

D'Angelo's lips quirk. "Maybe I found it hot that you're possessive."

I flush. "Maybe I just fancied being the kitten."

"Misuse of cats," Eden mutters.

Robyn pushes herself up to sit between Eden and me. She's staring at the phone, looking pale.

D'Angelo and I had practice at the rink, before we

came back for lunch. For the last couple of hours, however, Robyn's barely looked away from the screen.

D'Angelo checks his Rolex. "One minute."

"Fuck this," I burst out. "Why don't we just block the bitch? Or call the cops?"

"We can't," Robyn replies. "Hell, I want to. But blocking won't make a difference because Melanie will still publish anyway. And even if the cops are prepared to arrest a journalist, then the scandal that it'd stir up would be as bad as what she's doing to us now. She'd definitely reveal anything that she's uncovered on D'Angelo, along with Noah's name, if she knows it."

"We're being her puppets." Eden's stormy gaze meets mine, before it shifts to Robyn.

A look passes between them that I don't understand.

"Sometimes, you can only start your new life by burning down your old one," Robyn says like she's quoting someone.

I scrunch up my nose. "Is that Shakespeare or one of those boring dead guys?"

Eden reaches across the bed to poke me in the shoulder in outrage. "Take that back."

I should have known not to commit the Shakespeare sacrilege. "Boring dead guys like Dickens? Hardy? Tolkien?"

Why's Robyn giving me the death glare now?

See, these are the moments in polyamorous relationships that are never shown in television shows: when both your lover and brother are sitting looking at you with unimpressed expressions because you don't know a book quote.

I look at D'Angelo for help.

He only gives me a wicked smile. "One thing that you need to learn about Robyn is never insult a book. Since your brother treats them like his babies, you should know the same about him."

Oh, I get it.

I give a dazzling smile. "You know that I'm an ally. So, it was a bloody boring dead *woman*, right?"

Eden groans, covering his face.

D'Angelo shakes his head. "There's no saving your ass now."

Confused, I blink. "What?"

When Robyn's phone vibrates, she jumps. "Shit, a text from Melanie."

I stiffen, sucking in a breath.

D'Angelo leaps out of his seat and takes a stride toward the bed. He looks pale but determined like he's going to war.

What's the second secret about him going to be?

My heart aches for him.

It was like being punched in the gut to see the man who I respect and admire so fucking much having a side to him that's private and special splashed into the public eye.

Most of the comments online today have been about how hot he looked, although a lot were objectifying, and since they're from strangers and fans, crossed the line.

Debates about the size of his cock or *what holes* he likes to fuck or have fucked are wrong.

He's a real person. He doesn't deserve to be talked about like that.

I only know because Eden showed me quietly in the study at lunch. I hope that D'Angelo has kept off social media like Robyn insisted.

When Eden also showed me the trolls that he's been efficiently blocking, removing as many of the death threats and hate comments as he could, I understood why he's been worried.

Has D'Angelo been putting up with this on his own, before he employed Eden? Did he simply not tell any of us?

No wonder his reputation in the press as the cocky playboy pissed him off so much.

It damaged him in a lot of ways.

"Hang on." I hold up my hand, and D'Angelo hesitates. "What about if we look at this, but you don't? We're leaving for the big game in an hour. It'll shake you, which is what Melanie wants."

"What she wants," D'Angelo growls, "is to hurt me."

"Exactly," I press. "So, why are we letting her again?"

"I'm just going to…"

"Sit down," Eden orders.

D'Angelo sighs but sits on the end of the bed.

"We'll look." Robyn's chewing on her bottom lip. "And only tell you before the game, if you truly need to know. We'll crisis manage it like we did before. Then after the game, we'll work out a way to bring Melanie down."

I brighten. "Too right."

Robyn presses on the link in the text.

Eden leans over her shoulder.

At the same time, they both freeze.

"Fuck." Eden slams his hand onto his knee.

I startle both at his cussing and the way that he's banged his hand onto his leg.

"What the fuck is it?" I scoot even closer to Robyn, peering at the screen.

I tense, worried about what I'll see.

What's secret number two?

It's a photograph.

"Shay," Eden says, brokenly.

Robyn's gaze shoots to me in shock, before she tries to reach for me. I shy away from her touch, however, flinching.

I can't look away from the screen.

The blurred photograph is of a naked man who's curled in the fetal position on a bed. His hands are bound with ropes. It's dark, he's blindfolded, and his golden hair tumbles over his face, which is sweaty and wild in his distress.

He's weeping.

Tears streak down his cheeks underneath the blindfold.

For a long moment, I can't process what I'm seeing.

Then I'm thrown back to that night.

And everything comes crushing down on me so hard that I can't breathe.

It's me.

Blythe took photographs of me.

Eden's saying my name.

Shay, Shay, Shay...

D'Angelo's arms are around me. I'm being pulled against his hard chest.

I'm not responding.

I can't.

In this moment, I'm not here.

I'm panicking.

My hands are tied too tightly in ropes that are burning them, and I'm curling as tightly around myself as I can like I can comfort myself that way.

"Red," I mutter.

Immediately, D'Angelo releases me.

I scramble to the side of the bed and hurl.

I choke. My mouth is bitter with the acid taste of vomit.

I'm shaking.

Where am I?

I stare down at my hands. Why aren't they tied?

How am I free?

Did Blythe come back?

Am I still bad? Is that why she left me like that?

"S-s-sorry." I rub at the back of my mouth. I try again, weakly. "R-r-red."

"It's all right." A man's voice, achingly gentle. "I heard your safeword. You're being so good for me. You're okay. I've got you."

Good.

I'm good.

I let myself collapse back onto the bed. Someone's wrapping a soft blanket around me. Someone else is pressing water and then a chocolate to my mouth.

Slowly, as if I'm rising through thick treacle, I blink back to myself.

I feel exhausted like I've already played a full hockey game. My muscles ache.

I'm warm.

When I blink, looking around, I find that I'm surrounded by three faces.

"Shay," Robyn's voice wavers with tears, "are you back with us now?"

"I don't know what happened," I whisper. My throat feels sore. "Shit, I threw up on your carpet. I'll clean that."

"You won't," D'Angelo says, firmly. My head is cushioned on his lap, while Robyn and Eden sit on either side of me, holding my hands. D'Angelo's stroking my hair in a way that makes me bloody melt. "You had a flashback. Do we need to call coach and…?"

"No!" I yell, before adding more quietly, "I'm fine."

"You sound like me." Eden's expression is drawn and closed off.

I glance out of the corner of my eye at the phone that someone has collected and slid onto the bedside table like that can hide what we all know has been exposed to the world.

"You can't tell that it's you in the photo," Robyn points out. "Although, it's clearly another threat. Your submission is a beautiful thing. There's no shame in it. But what was going on in that picture…it's not what we have, right? It's…"

I think I may hurl again.

I'm numb.

I feel like I'm floating above my body and not in a good way. It's been years since I've felt like this.

I feel violated.

"He doesn't need to talk about this." D'Angelo's voice is tight with fury. "He was safewording in his flashback."

I swallow bile.

I never wanted to think about any of this again. But I know that I should have told D'Angelo and Robyn already.

Yet haven't I already needed to admit enough?

Do I also want them to know that I've had a Domme before, and she didn't want me for a real relationship?

That I was the one who was stupid enough to think that anyone could?

How can I not tell them now? *I've thrown up on Robyn's carpet.*

"Blythe was in her third year at university, when I'd just started my first year," I say, quietly. "She was wealthy and glamorous. You know what it's like when you're away from home for the first time. You go a bit wild for the first time. At least, I did. Blythe had the money to indulge me. I thought that we were dating. I was an idiot like that because I didn't know that she was a domme. I love confident, smart women. I just thought that she was like you, love."

I give Robyn a broken smile.

My gaze slides to Eden, who nods reassuringly and tightens his hold on my hand.

He knows how this story ends.

"I was fucking wrong." I lower my gaze. "I didn't have many girlfriends before college. Blythe made me feel special because she chose me. When it came to sex though, she was into all this stuff that I had no idea about. After a couple of weeks, she told me that she wanted to be my Domme. I didn't know anything about that. The things that she talked about mainly turned me on. But she didn't have a contract or do negotiations like we have. She did give me a safeword but she made me feel like I was weak and pathetic, if I ever used it."

"Then she was a fake Domme." D'Angelo's eyes blaze. "She was simply somebody lying and using that title to get away with being abusive and controlling."

"I wish I'd known that then." I struggle to draw in deep breaths, pushing down the panic. This is going to be bloody hard to say. "The night...when that photograph was taken...she was angry with me. I'd turned up for what I thought was a date. I'd bought her some fancy chocolates with money that should have paid for my meals that weekend. I may suck at it but I do try to be a good boyfriend and romantic."

"You're an awesome boyfriend." Robyn caresses down my cheek. Her eyes gleam with tears. "What's more romantic than stargazing?"

"Or cuddling, while watching horror movies?" D'Angelo valiantly tries.

I give a wet laugh. "Good try."

Eden's lips thin. "She didn't deserve anything."

"She didn't *want* anything." A tear slips down my cheek. D'Angelo wipes it away with his thumb. I struggle not to flinch. "She laughed when she saw the chocolates. She asked me what the hell I thought this was between us? Didn't I understand what I was to her? Hadn't she been clear enough, when she'd told me that she was my Domme? She threw my chocolates in the trash. Then she made me kneel and call myself a *stupid bitch* for thinking that dommes have romantic relationships with their subs. She made me call myself a *toy*. Then she punished me and she didn't stop, even when I…"

I can't say it.

I'm back there.

I can smell the cloying, jasmine scent of her pillow, as my face is pressed into it. The way that the rope burns my wrists. The coldness of her voice and the invasive feel of her hands, hitting, and hurting, and touching my smarting skin.

I don't want this.

I don't fucking want this.

Subs aren't loved…

Help…

Red, red, red…

"This fake Domme didn't stop when you called your safeword…?" Robyn guesses.

I shake my head. "She didn't give me any aftercare either. I didn't even know that it was called that at the time because she'd never given it to me. I felt like shit for days afterwards. I didn't know that I was in subdrop. Hockey practice was hell."

"I wish that you'd felt able to tell us this." D'Angelo runs his thumb down the back of my neck to the soft hair there, and I shiver. It's pleasurable and cuts through the fog in my mind, anchoring me fully in the present for the first time. "I understand why you didn't. We're only just getting to know each other. I'm older than you and have my own experiences on the scene. We'll need to discuss this because how can we safely play, if something I do triggers you? Is this why you think that if you screw up, we'll beat or abandon you? That you're not worthy of a proper relationship?"

I avoid his eye. "Can you blame me?"

"This isn't about blame. It's about understanding. Communication and trust. And just so you know, everything that abusive asshole told you is wrong. It doesn't matter if you're a dom, sub, or switch, you deserve love. Kink doesn't define you, and it's the genuine relationship underneath that's going to sustain you."

Now that I have this amazing relationship with Robyn and D'Angelo, which is nothing like the hollow feelings that I convinced myself I felt for Blythe simply because she was the first person to treat me decently, I know that he's right.

I fucking love them both, and they love me.

Sometimes, I stumble on the thought. But so far, they keep on proving it to me.

Like they are now.

"We're going to show you what it feels like to be properly cared for, loved, and protected in a way that only brings you pleasure and pain that takes you to a place of euphoria." D'Angelo grips me by the chin, forcing me to meet his piercing blue gaze. "How does that sound?"

My dick hardens, and a slow smile spreads across my face. "Bloody brilliant."

D'Angelo's hold on both my neck and chin tightens, and fuck, my dick is painfully hard now. "Can I show you what a *true* dom is like?"

"Who could say no to that?" I can't stop smiling now. I didn't think that I could feel happy like this, after feeling such distress after seeing one of the worst moments of my life splashed in the news. But my family are surrounding me, and I trust D'Angelo. It's a miracle, but I do. "Please."

Finally, he releases me.

Weirdly, I'm disappointed.

"You're always safe with us." Robyn leans down, and her hair sweeps across my cheeks, as she kisses me.

When she draws back, our gazes meet.

"I know, love."

Her brow furrows.

"In here you do." She presses her soft lips to my forehead. "But not in here yet."

She leans down, pushing my shirt aside to kiss over my heart.

I shiver. "It'll take a bit longer for my body to catch up, love. But it will. You make me feel strong for submitting, rather than weak. You *want* me and not only as some disposable hookup."

"I love you. And I want you for romance, washing

dishes, and a thousand shared moments, from the playful way that you wake me with kisses to the way that you keep D'Angelo on his toes by annoying him with too loud alternative rock music. Because that's what building a life together means."

Robyn kisses me again, long and deep.

When she draws back, she's glassy eyed, and I'm panting.

Yet Eden pours cold water over me with his next question. "Did you know that Blythe had taken those photos of you?"

Suddenly, I'm shivering for an entirely different reason.

I shake my head. "But then, she did a lot without my consent. I didn't always realize that at the time but I do now."

"How are we going to stop her?" Eden's voice is low.

Robyn shakes her head. "I don't know. But after this, it's the top priority. She headlined the photograph, saying that it's a hockey player. The press will be in a frenzy. You can't see much because it's a dark but…someone may still work it out."

Would D'Angelo mind if I threw up again in his lap? This is his game night suit. He'd probably be pissed, if he had to turn up under the cameras covered in vomit, right?

"Melanie must have paid big bucks for it." Robyn's eyes are cold. "You're a star now, and your ex partners must know that with how much you're in the news. There's a risk that all of your ex partners could get greedy and sell their stories."

Eden huffs. "At least being a loner has some positives. No kiss and tells."

While I was being wild, Eden was shutting himself up with a good book.

The only person to kiss him is Robyn.

Apart from Blythe, I had fun on most of my hookups. I adore sex. And I loved the freedom of life at university.

Normally, I wouldn't mind a naked photograph of myself turning up in a newspaper. I'm not ashamed of my body. I also don't care that I'm shown being tied up, as long as I consented to the bondage and to the photograph being shared.

But that night, when the photograph was taken (and I was both blindfolded and too distressed to even realize), I was being punished.

My safeword was ignored.

It's a night that I've fought hard to forget.

I don't want to see it and I definitely don't want anyone else to see me sobbing my fucking heart out because my trust was betrayed.

After my childhood, it's taken me years of therapy to offer my trust to anyone.

Did Blythe even know what she'd done?

Did she care?

I don't realize that I'm breathing too quickly again, until Eden's squeezing my hand.

"Breathe," Eden orders. "Slowly."

I take a couple of slow, steady breaths.

"Thanks." I shoot him a weak smile. "What happens if

someone does work out that this is me? I mean, with the Bay Rebels?"

"It'll affect sponsorship." Robyn looks thoughtful. "And the brand that we're building for you. Dad won't have a problem, especially if he knows the circumstances, but this is exactly the type of *noise* that the board and management warned us against. They want the focus to be on the drama on the ice and not our personal lives. This isn't our fault, but they won't see it that way."

"Do you want me to call coach and tell him that you have food poisoning? We have the vomit as proof." D'Angelo arches his brow. "You need to have your head in the game tonight. If you can't handle that..."

"I can. I will." I close my eyes.

My career has only just begun. I love playing for the Bay Rebels. The opening to the season has been brilliant.

Yet my own idiot self in the past could fuck it up.

"I said that *this isn't our fault*," Robyn repeats firmly. "I can see your expression, Shay. Both D'Angelo and you have been targeted. You did nothing wrong, then or now. Maybe this isn't about one person. It's about the whole team."

"We can work that angle tomorrow," Eden agrees. "Is Melanie threatening to reveal a third secret?"

Robyn nods.

"She won't get to." D'Angelo taps my cheek, and my eyes snap open. "I'm not allowing anyone else to be hurt like this — or risking your name coming out. So, I'm accepting Melanie's offer of the live interview. Whatever she intends to do to harm my career, me, or even the Bay

Rebels, I intend to face it head on. Rather that, than let her keep taking these shots at us."

"It's Thursday now." Robyn scrambles for her phone. "She wants to do the interview within the next week. It doesn't give us much time to come up with a plan."

"Then we better get thinking." My voice is steady again. My eyes flash. "This journalist has crossed the line so many times that she's erased it and no longer bloody knows where it is. Who knows what questions she'll ask? How she'll try and wreck Jude? All of us? If she thinks that she can manipulate us through fear, then she's wrong. Our drive to protect each other because of our love is much bloody stronger. I simply need to pull myself together and get through this game, before we find out who's really pulling the strings."

I know that I sound confident.

In control.

But inside, I'm still shaking.

Shattered.

I just hope that I can get through the second game of the season.

CHAPTER TWENTY

Rebel Arena, Freedom

*S*hay

MY BLOOD IS RUSHING in my ears. Adrenaline pumps through me. I'm high with excitement.

I don't see the crowds through the bright lights. I don't hear the commentator.

There's only the ice under my skates.

The goal in front of me.

And the puck.

I'm going to bloody score.

Win.

I'm not the man from that photograph anymore.

My hands tighten around my stick.

I'm not broken and bound.

I'm a star hockey player with an entire NHL team at my back. And I'm fucking *powerful* on my knees.

I skate faster, spurred on with a surge of excitement.

My heart is pumping. My pulse is roaring in my ears.

My lips are still tingling with the memory of the deep kiss that Robyn gave me before we left Captain's Hall for good luck.

"Now I'll be with you on your lips throughout the game," Robyn whispered, as her lips grazed mine on each word, "even if you can't openly blow me a kiss."

"Where's *my* kiss?" D'Angelo quirked his brow. "I'd never be cliched enough to blow you a kiss in the arena but I burn to shout your name every time that I score. So, how are you going to save us from that scandal and stop me from…?"

Robyn grabbed him by his tie and yanked him into a kiss that was as deep as mine had been.

Well, that was an effective way to shut up D'Angelo.

I'll remember that.

I lick over my tingling lips.

Robyn keeps on finding ways to worm even further into my heart. Now, she's branded onto my lips.

I scan the arena.

My chest is rapidly rising and falling. I take a moment to draw in a deep breath.

In this second game, the Chicago Blackhawks have been tough and ruthless.

The score is still **0 — 0**.

Despite everything that happened earlier with the photograph that ripped out my heart in a way that I'd allowed myself — or made myself — forget that I was capable of feeling, I'm in the zone now.

I've never felt this excited in my life.

D'Angelo looks like a bloody legend on the other side of the rink. He's passing the puck to the left wing, Grayson.

He's cool and in control. I've been rattled. But I can do this.

I can.

I need to.

Head in the game, Shay.

I can't help the way that my lips curl into a smile, as Eden's voice echoes in my mind. He may be watching from home but he can still bust my balls.

Hockey has always been my escape.

The moment that the puck dropped, I just played.

Ice instinct took over.

It was a relief.

Scoring my first goal on Tuesday was like a dream come true. I'm going to score tonight. I can feel it in my balls.

I put my head down and skate toward the goal.

I'm winning the bet. Anticipation tingles through me.

This next goal is mine.

I weave around the rival team's defensemen like they're not even there. They can't keep up with my speed. No one has ever been able to.

I skate faster and faster.

My shoulders lift.

I relax, feeling freer than I have in days.

I grin.

I'm open for a shot on goal.

I glance over my shoulder at D'Angelo.

He has the puck.

Our gazes meet.

He prepares to pass to me, and I ready myself.

All of a sudden, someone barrels into me, checking me hard.

"Fuck." All the air is knocked out of me.

My eyes widen, as I'm slammed toward the boards at high speed. In the split second that I have left, I struggle to tuck in my arms and chin to protect myself.

I can't hit my head.

I can't...

I twist to the side, grunting in pain, as my hip and shoulder take the worst of the impact.

Fuck, I'm going to be black and blue.

I grit my teeth.

I breathe heavily, struggling to control my rage.

I didn't even have the puck.

The defenseman was trying to spark my rage because of my reputation as a fighter. But I promised both D'Angelo and Robyn that I'd control my temper on the ice.

I can't spoil my image by being volatile.

I won't be a liability for the team.

Yet I'm rattled.

I should be used to this. Hockey is physical, and I like it this way.

Why does it feel different tonight?

Maybe because the pain that's radiating down my shoulder and across my hip is bringing back memories of Blythe.

I take a shuddering breathe.

I can't think of her.

Not during a game.

I struggle out of the heavy grip of the defenseman, who's still holding onto the back of my jersey, pressing me into the boards.

I swing around, trying to look cool, despite the volcanic rage bubbling inside.

Shit, it's Maddan.

He's a huge fucker with broad shoulders, mean eyes, and a prickly beard that looks like he's stuck a hedgehog to his chin.

He's known for playing dirty.

Was this attack planned? Is it part of the team's strategy?

I should have been paying more attention.

I struggle, managing to look past him.

D'Angelo is staring across at us, concerned. He's wheeling around to skate toward me, rather than the goal.

I can't allow that.

He has the puck now.

Maddan's trick won't stop the first goal of the game.

I subtly shake my head.

Immediately, D'Angelo understands what I mean. We've always had an incredible chemistry on the ice, even before I realized that I was in love with the man.

It makes us play in a way that I haven't with anyone else.

It's flawless.

When D'Angelo heads for the goal again, I let out a relieved breath.

Then Maddan towers over me, and I think that I've relaxed too soon. "I'm only trying to make you match your ugly brother. Let's get your arm in a sling." He shoves me back against the boards. I hide my flinch. "Didn't hit your head, right?"

He pats me on the shoulder that he's just bruised deliberately with too much force.

Bastard.

Trash talk doesn't normally get to me. But tonight, his chirps hit hard. Talking about Eden, whose career was ended by some dick just like Maddan, using his strength as a strategy to make me lose my temper, is too fresh and raw.

Especially when Eden is still suffering from those injuries.

No one talks about my twin like that.

I shove Maddan hard in the chest, and he lets go of my jersey.

I feel unmoored.

Fucking unhinged.

I don't know what my expression must look like, but Maddan raises his stick in front of himself defensively, skating backwards. "Prince…"

"Fuck you, Maddan," I growl. "Your Wikipedia entry only has two sentences: Will make a great coach one day.

The worst hockey players always do."

Maddan's small eyes darken with rage, before he skates directly at me. "Just like *your* coach, huh?"

I must have struck a nerve.

"Ever heard of the exception that proves the rule?"

"I'm going to fuck you up like your loser brother." Maddan swings for me. His fist connects with my jaw, and my head snaps into the boards. Stars explode, along with pain. "Then you're going to stay down, bitch."

Bitch...?

My mind's dazed.

Scrambled.

I can't think.

I blink, trying to focus.

He's shaking me by the jersey now.

My head throbs.

Where am I?

Stupid little bitch.

All of a sudden, I'm back there…

No, please, no.

I'm caught in a flashback.

I'm trapped in one of my worst memories because Melanie posted that photograph for everyone to see of me stripped and suffering.

"You're not my boyfriend." Blythe circles me on the bed. I can hear the click of her leather boots on the wooden floor. I can't see anything through the blindfold, which is soaked with my tears and uncomfortably scratchy. "Chocolates? Seriously? Stupid little bitch."

My breath hitches on a sob.

I bite my lip, tasting the blood where I bit through it earlier to keep in the cries, while she disciplined me.

What's the difference between discipline and being beaten?

I don't know. It felt the same.

It's close to Blythe's exams. I know that she's under pressure.

She said that she found hitting me *stress relief*.

If I can be strong and take this for her, then I will. I want to help her. I can at least get pleasure out of knowing that I'm pleasing her by serving her.

My ass hurts from the stripes of my own thick belt.

Blythe said that it'd be a good reminder if she used the belt from my jeans. I only own one belt, which she knows. So, I'll need to wear it.

I'll think of this beating every time that I wear my belt.

I'll remember the rules.

How can I forget them after…*this*?

I'm kneeling with my face pressed into the pillows. I hate the cloying, jasmine scent of her bedding. The way that the rope burns into my wrists, which are bound underneath me.

I don't want this.

I don't fucking want this.

Should I tell her? But wouldn't that disappoint her worse?

"What are you?" Blythe says, coldly.

I know what she wants.

She's trained me in this.

Still, I can barely get out the words. Why is this hard? But I feel heavy inside.

Wrong.

None of this is fun like it should be. Hadn't it started out that way with Blythe?

I'm not turned on by any of this. It's not hot. *It's hell.*

I am meant to feel like this? Why is Blythe even punishing me? Because I dared to think that she'd want to be my girlfriend?

"A stupid little bitch." My voice is flat and mechanical.

"That's right." Blythe slaps my arse, and I wince.

I'm sore enough already.

She runs her hand down my back possessively.

I shudder.

Then she trails the end of the leather belt along the backs of my thighs, where my skin is much more sensitive. The cold leather makes me flinch.

It hurts so bloody much to be hit there.

It's too much.

"Yellow," I say. "Please, yellow."

Blythe hesitates, before removing her hand and the belt with a sigh. "Pathetic. I expected better from you. You're being disrespectful by abusing your safeword like this. You can't only enjoy funishments and then not take real punishments when you've earned them. You're not meant to *like* this. Safe wording out is just bratting."

"I'm n-n-not…" I struggle to say.

That's not right…is it?

I can't think.

My heart is beating too fast. My breaths are labored.

My cheeks are streaked with tears, and I can't feel my hands.

"That's enough of a break." Blythe's hand is back on my arse, pinching cruelly. I whine. "You have such a cute arse. It's what I noticed first. All the girls on campus want to fuck you. You're such a fuck boy, aren't you?"

I shake my head, but she ignores me.

"You're not boyfriend material. But then, you need to learn this lesson. Men like you — subs — are toys to be played with for a couple of hours. You'll learn your place, right?"

I don't reply.

I can't.

Every word feels like another lash of the belt.

"Right?" She repeats with a deadly warning in her voice that I know not to ignore. "You know that I expect a verbal answer from you. Come on, this is part of your training."

"Yes, ma'am," I mumble.

She claims that she's *training me*.

She's breaking me.

My chest is tight.

I'm trapped in the black, which keeps me stuck in the spiraling thoughts in my head.

Everything is more intense like this.

I can't prepare myself for what she does next.

I'm shivering, hot and cold at the same time.

I told Eden all day excitedly about this *date*.

I *am* a *stupid little bitch*.

I dressed in my new crimson shirt, which I was forced to strip out of the moment that I stepped into her room.

That's one of her new rules.

I'm to be naked from the moment that I enter her dorm room to remind me of *my place*.

I bought Blythe chocolates, even though I can't afford them. Eden advised me not to, but I thought that he was worried about the expense.

He's never liked Blythe.

He has this furrow in his brow, whenever I mention her.

He'd hate her, if he truly knew what went on between us.

My brother and I have a code of check ins and codes for when I'm staying out all night.

Fuck, how long have I been tied up? How long has this punishment gone on?

Is she going to let me go home tonight?

I haven't sent Eden a text. He's expecting me back in dorms. He's going to freak out.

"Am I boring you?" Blythe snaps, sharp as a whip crack.

She's frighteningly close to my head now.

"N-n-no." I lick over my torn lip, which is bleeding again. "What time is it? My brother doesn't know that I'm... May I send him a text?"

"Are you kidding?" Blythe's voice becomes icy. "My friends all told me that I shouldn't associate with a poor scholarship student who doesn't even turn up to college balls, no matter how gorgeous he is...or how huge his cock. But I thought that you'd be trainable. Was I wrong to give you a chance? Are you such a bad sub that you can't even take a deserved punishment?"

Each word tears apart my soul.

Poor...huge cock...trainable...bad sub...deserved punishment.

I want to hurl.

I'm shaking.

Stop.

Stop.

Stop.

"N-n-no," I whisper.

The belt catches my calf, and I curl around myself in pain.

I thought that I could take this.

At the start, I liked Blythe.

She took me out to places, the movies, music gigs, and dinner. I believed that she cared about me as a man.

I hoped that I'd found someone who wanted to spend time with me like my brother did. For the first time, I'd be able to build a proper relationship.

Life's short, I know that. I refuse to live it in fear.

Only, isn't that how Blythe wants me to feel?

Frightened?

It's too much.

Panic screams through me.

"Red," I whisper.

The belt hits my hip.

Horrified, I wrench away.

She hasn't stopped.

Why hasn't she stopped?

My breaths are shallow. I'm frozen. I can't move.

Am I in shock?

"Red." I try again. "*Red, red, red.*"

I feel dazed. Light-headed.

I am saying it out loud, right?

Maybe she can't hear me?

Blythe whips me across my back, and a tear chases down my cheek.

She's meant to stop. *She promised.* She told me if I said *red*, then she'd stop.

She isn't.

My heart's breaking.

"Red, red, red," I scream it now.

But she doesn't stop.

She's heard me.

And I'm sobbing now. I can't stop.

Because the realization that Blythe's heard me, but my safeword means nothing to her, hurts me worse than anything that she's yet done to me.

She *wants* to hurt me.

This isn't about training.

Did Blythe ever intend to honor my safeword? Was it all a lie?

I panic for real.

Wild with fear, I struggle against the ropes. They're tied so tightly, however, that it only rubs against my wrists, flaying the skin.

I struggle and struggle and...

Now, rage surges through me.

All I can see is red.

White-hot rage burns through me. I can't stop it.

I'm cold.

Why am I cold?

My nose wrinkles up at the chemical scent of ice, mingling with sweat and rubber.

It slams into me then.

I'm in Rebel Arena on the rink in the middle of one of the biggest games of my life. A crowd of thousands are watching, along with millions at home.

Yet I'm still partly lost in the past. I can feel the sharp bite of my own belt against my skin and the even sharper pain of the betrayal, as Blythe ignores my safeword.

I'm confused.

And I'm devastated.

That mix transforms, as it has throughout my life, into anger.

I lash out against the person who's hurting me: Maddan.

Taken by surprise, he stumbles back, as I shove him in the chest.

I can hardly see him. I feel like I'm still blindfolded.

Yet I know that I'm hurling down my stick and ripping off my gloves. It's like someone else is doing it. Someone who's about to fuck up their entire career.

I can't stop myself.

I'm still struggling to escape those ropes and this is how I fight back.

Unexpectedly, someone is skating up to me and tugging me away from Maddan and the boards by the front of my jersey.

"Shay." D'Angelo sounds concerned. Then he turns to glare at Maddan. "Fuck off, asshole. Go cool down with a long, cold shower."

"He's crazy." Maddan glares at D'Angelo, before turning and skating back to his fellow players. "I'll fuck off and score."

I blink at D'Angelo, and finally, my vision clears.

D'Angelo's pulling me close like he's talking about strategy, but I can tell that he's shielding my face from the cameras.

Wasn't he about to score?

Why did he abandon his chance to win for me?

I can't help it. Blythe is still in my head. I can feel her.

"Make her stop," I whisper. "Red, red, *fucking red.*"

"She's not here anymore." D'Angelo slips his hand to the back of my neck. Unlike when Blythe would do that, however, I don't feel controlled. I feel loved. Because D'Angelo has always made me feel worthy of being loved. He speaks close enough to my ear that only I will hear, "You're safe. She can't touch you now. Robyn and I will always honor and respect your limits. I swear, you're not alone in this."

A sudden cheer goes up, and in horror, I peer past D'Angelo.

He's stiffened but is refusing to acknowledge the celebrations on the ice behind him.

The Chicago Blackhawks have scored.

Fucking *Maddan* has scored.

My heart sinks, when D'Angelo pulls away from me.

We're going to lose, and it'll be because of me.

CHAPTER TWENTY-ONE

Captain's Hall, Freedom

*R*obyn

"Arnica cream for your bruises." I wave the small tube at Shay. Then I raise my other hand. "And a cold bottle of beer."

I lean in the doorway to Captain Hall's bathroom.

The steam has misted the mirrored back wall. It's hot. Sweat drips down my neck into the collar of my cream shirt. I wish that I was wearing a skirt, instead of trousers.

Morning light streams into the room through the open window over the gleaming marble surfaces, blue walls, and free standing claw bath that's in the middle of the room.

I normally take showers in the spacious, walk-in shower in the corner of the room.

Where else am I meant to have fun singing?

Shay didn't come down for breakfast. He hasn't spoken to anyone since the Bay Rebels lost their game **0 — 1** to the Chicago Blackhawks

The game was a disaster.

It was agonizing to watch from the side of the rink.

It must have been even more painful for Eden to watch on the television.

I know that Shay blames himself.

Plus, Dad chewed him out for an hour. He kept him back by himself in his room after the game.

Shay was pale and shaky after that.

He went to his own bedroom to sleep as soon as we arrived back at Captain's Hall. It'd ached that he wanted to be alone.

I don't know what happened on the ice with that asshole defenseman but I'm sure that this has still got to do with Melanie's photograph.

He's rattled.

Wrecked.

"Cheers, love." Shay holds his hand out for the beer. I saunter closer and pass it to him, kneeling next to the bath on the cold floor. "If you'd only had a third hand and brought the new "Kaiser Chief" album, then that would officially make you the best girlfriend of all time."

I mock pout. "I'm not already? And three hands…think

what fun we could have with an extra hand. Sometimes, it feels like we need it in bed."

He laughs, but it's strained.

I study the dark bruise on his shoulder from where he was slammed into the boards last night, as well as the blossoming purple along his sharp jawline.

Before I can stop myself, I lean forward to kiss his sore jaw, and he draws in a breath.

I glance up, and our gazes meet.

"Does it hurt?" I whisper against his skin.

"Only when you kiss it." Shay's eyes flutter closed. "Don't stop kissing it."

I brush my lips as softly as I can across his jaw again like I can somehow erase the pain that he's in that way, but then, I draw back. "But how can you drink your beer, if I'm kissing you?"

"Priorities, huh?"

I smirk.

He takes a deep swig.

"So, I'm not doing as good a job as my brother does at hiding how much I need a drink then?" Shay takes another drink, studying me over the top of the bottle.

I shake my head. "D'Angelo is worried about you. He was all set to come in here with his typical overbearing brand of care that would probably involve *demanding* that you deal with whatever happened yesterday on the ice. Your brother has been anxiety baking since dawn. There's a whole basket of pastries downstairs waiting for you."

"I'm not hungry."

I fix him with a stern stare.

Shay's lips curl up at the sides. "I'll come down after I'm finished here and try to eat some of them. You can help me with the chocolate muffins. I just needed some time alone."

"Do you want me to go?"

"Not alone from you."

I smile, squirting some of the arnica cream onto my fingers, before dropping the tube to the floor. "Are you okay, if I rub this in now?"

He nods, and I lean over him.

I gently massage the cream first into his jaw and then his shoulder.

I know that players will get injuries every game. I've grown up around hockey players. I'm used to this.

Yet it's different this time because the fight looked deliberate.

My heart had been in my mouth watching it, especially after Shay was punched and his head was knocked into the boards as well.

He looked fucking out of it, and shit, I'd been shouting for Cody and the medics, even before Shay had his freak out on the ice.

What if Shay had the same problem with concussion as his twin?

Eden is surviving life after hockey, but would Shay?

I'd seen Noah for the first time in the arena then, recognizing his shock of blond hair. He'd been the first one of the staff to come running at my frantic calls for medics.

It was Dad who'd waved Cody and him back, assessing that Shay didn't need them.

I'd been shaking with anger and fear.

What if he was wrong?

I shoot Shay a careful look. "What happened out there?"

"Maddan." Shay pushes his wet hair out of his eyes. "The fucker was trying to get me to lose my temper. So, it's my own fault. I'm the one with the anger issues. They're simply using my reputation against me."

I frown. "*He* fought *you*. I'm proud that you didn't react."

"But I did." He looks away. "He triggered a fucking flashback. I mean, he wouldn't have, if I hadn't just seen that photograph or I'd had some time to process it. All those memories of Blythe...I'd pushed them down. Who could I even tell about them? Look at me. I'm this strong guy. Who would believe that this small woman was able to...?"

"Don't." My heart is beating fast, and my eyes burn with tears. "I believe you. We all do. It's not about gender. The moment that you said your safeword, she no longer had your consent." Emotions overwhelm me, and I deliberately turn my back to grab a sponge and give myself the opportunity to wipe away a tear. I came in here to cheer Shay up with beer and kisses. If he sees me crying — knowing Shay — he'll end up smiling and pretending that he's fine, simply to cheer me up. "What did Maddan do to trigger you?"

"More like what he said." Shay reaches up to grip my

chin and turns me back to face him. He brushes my cheek with his wet finger. "I'm not into most degradation play as you know from my contract, love. Jude has a way of mixing some in that I do like with praise and then that makes me melt. Well, that fucker on the ice called me a *bitch* like Blythe would, right after he'd told me that he was going to *fuck me up like my brother*."

"Now I wish that *you* had hit *him*."

Shay's eyes widen. "Shit, love, the official PR line really has changed."

"Don't tell D'Angelo. It can be our little secret."

Immediately, Shay's expression becomes troubled again. "I'm not that keen on secrets right now."

"Me neither."

He hesitates for a moment.

Then he adds, "My brother saved me, you know."

"What?"

"On that night, the one in the picture. He won't say anything because he never sees himself as the heroic sort but he is. He's always protected and looked out for me. He did that night as well. We had this code and lots of check ins, when either of us were out. Only, he never went out."

"I remember from the first night that we met. When you decided to come back to my room at the inn, you sent him a coded text."

"Smirking face emoji. Short and simple. Easy to send in any circumstance." Shay's gaze becomes hard. "And that's why Dee was suspicious, when I didn't send anything that night."

"You said that he didn't like Blythe. How didn't he realize that she was hurting you?"

I don't mean to ask, but Eden's observant.

Shay looks uncomfortable. "Because *I* didn't realize. People like her...abusers...are smart with how they reel you in. Eden tried to warn me about her, but I thought that he was jealous of the time that I was spending with her."

"Your brother would never be jealous, as long as you're happy."

"I know that now." Shay takes a long drink. "She left me alone tied up like that for hours, while she got ready to go out and meet her *real* friends. I think that she'd have left me there all night. So bloody dangerous. Eden knocked on the door, however, and I know how hard that must have been for him, when I wasn't answering my phone. She didn't care that she'd been caught, just laughed and said: *I'm going out, if you want him, take him.* And she let my own twin find me like that on the bed..."

"Shit," I breathe.

Shay pushes himself out of the bath for a moment, sloshing the water against the sides, and captures my lips in a kiss, which is hard and demanding.

He looks dangerous.

I forget sometimes that he and his brother are.

When he drops back into the bath, he looks more confident. "Eden became braver that night than he ever had but he never trusted anyone in college after that point. And I made sure that the world better watch out for the Prince Twins because I was never going to let myself be powerless again…"

I dip the sponge into the water and then lightly brush it over Shay's hard chest. "I know what it is to feel powerless, after being trapped in a marriage with a narcissist. This journalist is pulling at the threads of all our lives to try and unravel us. But we're not going to allow her to."

"We still lost the game, and it's my fault."

"No one thinks that."

"Coach does."

"Dad's a grumpy dick. The rest of the team doesn't. Even the press don't. You were punched in the fucking face. Most of the reports think that Maddan should have been sent to the sin bin."

"D'Angelo's disappointed in me."

"D'Angelo loves you. He knows the game well enough that sometimes other players can get in your head."

I caress the sponge in circles across Shay's chest again.

Shay relaxes back in the bath, bracing his arms on the sides and holding the bottle loosely. "Hmm, that's nice, love."

I run the sponge over his peaked nipples and deliberately ignore the way that his eyes become half-hooded.

Then I dip it lower over his abs.

A wet, naked Shay is a gorgeous Shay.

He stretches, caught between relaxed and turned on, which is exactly what I was going for.

Eden can cheer Shay up with muffins. I have other delicious methods.

I tease the sponge under the water and along Shay's thighs, skirting where I know he wants me to touch.

"Don't tease, love." Shay's hips hump out of the water.

His dick is already at half-mast and standing proud out of the water.

But I can do better than that.

"Hmm?" I say like I have no idea what he wants. I can be a mean woman. "With all your bruises, I'm trying to help you get clean. I'm being a good nurse. Now, lie back and let me take care of you."

I stroke the sponge down one of his muscled thighs and then back up the other. I circle in to his inner thigh, deliberately caressing across his balls like it's an accident.

He groans, dropping his head back. "Fuck, if nurses take care of their patients like this, then I'm going to be injured more often."

I tweak his nipple in retribution, and he yelps. "If you do that, then I'll only give you cold bed baths, and I don't think that you'll appreciate them as much."

"I'll like anything that means you have your little hands on my strong body, love."

Dangerous.

"What about if it's not my hands...?"

"What do you...?"

I smirk at Shay.

Then I lower my head and kiss the tip of his cock.

"Oh, fuck," Shay mutters.

I give his by now fully hard dick a single lick, before I drop the sponge and hold my hair out of the way. Then I lower my mouth over his shaft.

He hisses out a shocked breath.

I slide up and down Shay's cock, swirling my tongue along the head. My mouth is watering at the taste of his cock. It's silky and wet, so large that my jaw will ache later.

But I want more of it.

Much more.

I push down further, until my nose is just above the water.

"Fuck, Robyn..." Shay drops his beer, and I wince at the crack of the glass against marble.

I pull off his cock to shoot him an unimpressed look, as the beer puddles, staining my trousers.

He looks entirely unapologetic. "If you will look so sexy with your lips wrapped around my dick...and your mouth feels wet, warm, and perfect...you can't blame a guy for dropping his beer."

I laugh, playfully flicking water at his face.

"Hey, this is war." Shay sprays me with water back, giving a sunny smile. "And I have a weapon for you to polish."

"That was bad."

"It's your fault. You've turned my brain to mush. I need to cum." He wraps his hand around my hair and pulls me back toward his throbbing cock. "Tap three times on the side of the bath to safeword."

I come more than willingly, however, licking my lips.

I allow Shay to lower me back onto his dick, licking at the head and along the sensitive undershaft.

Then he fucks my face, slow and deep.

I take careful breaths out of my nose, as he increases the speed.

Shay's breathing is ragged, matching my own.

The water sloshes over the side of the bath.

I'm feeling lightheaded with the steam and the way that Shay's cock is knocking the back of my throat.

But I love this.

It's wild and spontaneous.

It feels like it's anchoring Shay back with me in the present.

"I'm going to — *love* — come soon," Shay groans.

I lift my hand to entangle with Shay's, where he's holding my hair. He's trying to loosen his hold and pull me off his cock. But I want to taste and swallow him.

He appears to understand by the way that I firmly hold his hand where it is.

Shay's hips stutter. Then he's coming.

"Robyn, f-f-fuck." Shay strokes over my hair.

When I remove my hand from Shay's, he finally pulls me gently off his oversensitive cock.

I haven't reached to touch myself.

My core is throbbing, but Shay brings me pleasure so many times that for once, this has been solely about him.

When I raise my eyes to meet Shay's, he's smiling widely. I find myself smiling back.

"I won the war," I declare.

"You did with your amazing mouth. I'm not even sad about it. I surrender, love. Long live the Queen."

"Well, well, look what happens in bathrooms, when I'm not here," D'Angelo drawls from the open doorway. I startle and swing round on my knees to look at him. "And I thought that it was only the singing of cringe inducing Justin Timberlake songs."

I raise my eyebrow, trying to look superior, before I realize that I still have sperm on my lip and hurriedly lick it off, flushing.

"Missed a bit," Shay mutters helpfully, leaning over to wipe at my lip.

I redden further. "Nope, also sexcapades. Come back at lunch for an orgy."

"I'll mark it in my diary," D'Angelo says, dryly. "Except, I won't. Because while you were up here having some clean but dirty fun, coach phoned and summoned us to his house for lunch. We all know that translates to us being fucked…and not in the sperm on the lips way."

CHAPTER TWENTY-TWO

Rebel House, Captain's Hall

*R*obyn

I SHIFT ON THE BENCH.

Have I ever been this uncomfortable before?

Probably, only that time the new, handsome headmaster in high school, who was trying to be friendly and *down with the kids*, called out to me, "Come into my office please, if you've got a sec."

I'd known that it was about Cody's fighting.

So, I plastered on a fake smile, replying loudly before I'd engaged my brain, "I have loads of secs."

We'd both frozen at the same time.

He'd blushed as deeply as me.

Plus, the rest of the corridor had erupted into giggles.

On the bright side, he was so flustered that he disappeared back into his office as fast as he could, and I escaped from needing to see him.

Cringe for the win!

Except, I don't think that there's an upside to this type of social embarrassment. It feels more like I can't breathe properly.

I'm fidgeting with my cutlery.

The sun is bright in the blue sky. I squint against the light, which glimmers over the lake like thousands of submerged stars.

Dad hasn't said anything about the real reason that he's invited us to lunch on the decking behind his boat house at the lake today.

He's like an ancient wolf biding his time to launch his attack on the new members to put them in their place…by serving barbecued chicken and drinking beer.

Dad's silver hair and beard are neat. He's dressed in black pants and a charcoal sweater with the sleeves pushed back. This is his laid back outfit, which he usually saves for the weekend.

Except, I can tell that he's on high alert.

Rebel House is Dad's boat house. It's the most iconic property in Freedom, but for me, it's my childhood home.

The old-fashioned house is huge, sprawling alongside the lake, as the jagged mountains loom behind it. In the distance, stands a private boat launch. A long pier disappears into the center of the water.

I'm sitting at a large, rough oak table that's set around the low, embers of the fire pit at the water's edge.

The table is laid with a feast of barbecued pork and chicken, along with beef shoulder. My mouth waters at the tangy smell of the barbecue sauces.

I wrinkle up my nose at the smoky scent, which wafts on the breeze. It stings my eyes.

D'Angelo insisted on dressing smartly in a navy suit with elegant arctic blue waistcoat. I'm calling it his *meeting the in-laws* outfit.

He truly does struggle with being around parents.

Shay, on the other hand, prefers to live dangerously.

Talk about a thrill seeker.

He's gone in the opposite direction and is wearing black leather trousers, a scarlet shirt, and his leather jacket.

He looks impossibly gorgeous.

Also, way too relaxed and happy.

He's sprawling back and drinking a beer like he's not the person who this meal is all about. It shows that he's new to Freedom and doesn't understand my dad.

Also, how optimistic he is.

In the taxi over to Rebel House, D'Angelo looked moments away from ordering the taxi to drive us to the airport instead.

"Why do meals at your dad's always feel like an execution?" D'Angelo pulled on his cuffs.

I snorted. "Probably because they are executions."

"And it's my head that's on the chopping block," Shay said, suspiciously brightly, "or my balls."

Surprised, I glanced at him, as he hummed and carded his fingers through his tumble of hair. "Don't you care about your head or balls? Because I'm kind of fond of them."

Shay shot me a smile. "Of course I do, love. But it's outside my control. I've had time to think. I did struggle on the ice but I shouldn't have my balls busted for mental health difficulties. What happened to me would fuck anybody up. Plus, having it put out there for everybody to see, when I didn't even know that Blythe had taken photographs, just before I had to play…I'm not going to blame myself for how I reacted. Coach yelled at me already for that. That's fair. If he wants to go at me harder today, then I'm ready."

"It's not right." My jaw clenched. "You weren't the only player out there on the ice. The team isn't made up of a single player. You can't be expected to win every single game. You were targeted by that defenseman."

"I'm proud that you didn't hit him back." D'Angelo caressed Shay's cheek. "Even if I wish that you did."

Shay laughed, lighter than I expected. "Me too, darlin'. So, let's simply enjoy some barbecue. It's beautiful weather."

I laughed. "You English and your obsession with talking about the weather."

Yet Shay does appear to be happy in the sunshine, sucking the barbecue sauce off his fingers in a way that goes straight to my pussy, and savoring his chilled beer.

He's carefully not looking at Dad, who's sitting at the head of the table.

The only positive to Eden no longer being a player is that he doesn't have to dance to Dad's tune and come to lunch today.

D'Angelo took great delight in saying that as *his* employee now, Eden was busy with work.

Of course, Eden still wanted to come to support his twin. Until, I played the *you don't want to faint face first into the fire pit* card.

Did I get Cody on the phone to back me up?

Maybe.

Did I also get Michael, his doctor on the phone…?

One hundred percent and no regrets.

Well, *some* regrets, but they mostly concern perming my hair in high school, wearing white jeans on the first day of my period (at least twice a year), and marrying Wilder.

D'Angelo and Shay are sitting either side of me with their hands resting on each of my knees. Their touch helps me to feel grounded and reminds me that I'm loved.

It helps because being back in my childhood home is tough, especially knowing that we're in trouble.

Dad is like a thundercloud. He holds his rage over your head, until he comes crashing down.

Cody and I could wait weeks, never knowing when he'd come storming down on us.

Except, he rarely rained on me.

He shone like the sun on me with his approval and pride. It was Cody who was seen as the screw-up who could never do anything right.

Yet my brother is talented and good.

He should always have been treated with love and respect. I know how much it hurt him that he wasn't.

My eyes burn with tears, as the pressure of waiting for Dad's calmness to crack and his real reason for inviting us today shudders through me.

Shay casts me a concerned glance, tightening his hand around my knee.

D'Angelo is already bone-white. He has his own triggers when it comes to parents but he's still supporting Shay and me.

He looks like he may hurl into his plate of buttered potatoes and salad, but he's managing to make polite conversation about classical music with Michael, who's sitting across the table with his arm slung possessively around Cody's shoulder.

I'm glad that Neve's not here to take the piss out of them.

They're getting seriously passionate about who's the better musician between Mozart and Beethoven.

"Beethoven was a genius who broke rules and created an entirely new musical era," Michael insists.

"But Mozart was a prodigy." To my surprise, D'Angelo's gaze slides across Shay and then me. "A foul mouthed brat but one who was so innovative that he was simply ahead of his time. His songs will be immortal. He's a legend."

Shay perks up. "Oh, like Jimi Hendrix."

D'Angelo huffs, but Michael nods.

Michael leans across the table and clinks his beer with Shay's. "Our rock fan wins the argument."

D'Angelo rolls his eyes.

Dad's simply watching them all in a way that's making dread curdle in my stomach.

It's like he's deciding whose throat to savage first.

When Michael notices, he casually leans over to add an extra spoonful of potatoes onto his plate. "Are you going boating this weekend, Austin?"

For the first time, Dad stops glowering. "On Sunday, if the weather holds up. I'll go out at dawn. It's good to be reminded that nature is much bigger than we are."

I let out a breath of relief.

Boating is the one topic that relaxes Dad.

It hurts Cody and me because boating is how Dad escaped from spending time with us after Mom's death. I still don't think that he understands how much he neglected us.

I raised Cody more than he did.

On the other hand, as an adult, I understand. In the calmness of nature, he found a way to grieve and heal.

Dad truly loved Mom. When she died, he didn't know how to cope and deal with suddenly becoming a single parent.

Yet Michael is wisely using the topic now to distract Dad. Never mind that Michael spent his morning saving lives. This here is some heroic shit.

Cody looks unsettled.

He slips out from under Michael's arm, before leaping up and diving around the table. He wraps his arms around my shoulders and hugs me.

I twist to hug him back. His hair brushes against my cheeks.

"Hey, Ryn," Cody whispers.

"Thanks for coming here today," I whisper back. This is familiar. Suddenly, I feel younger. I could be a teenager, hugging my kid brother as he sobbed in my arms for so many fucking reasons. "I know that it was short notice."

Dad didn't invite Michael and Cody.

I did.

I knew that Dad may control himself better with all of us here, and also, Dad needs to sort out his relationship with my brother.

Dad still hasn't properly apologized for treating Cody like the family fuck up for so many years. He has a lot of work to do to make up for the toxic way that he still talks about him.

"We always have each other's back when it comes to…" Cody pulls back from the hug to look significantly at Dad who's talking with Michael about the boat that he's recently bought.

"Yeah, we do."

I protect my brother, and he protects me.

I wish that didn't need to include from my Dad.

Most of the time, especially after Mom's death, Dad simply forgot us. But then, there'd be the times that Cody would be summoned to Dad's study, and the same fear that's now turning my bowels to water would make me hold his hand and insist that I'd go with him.

"Be a man," Dad would bark at Cody, despite the fact that

he was only a kid and barely came up to his chest. "You don't need to hang onto your sister all the time. No wonder you never get picked for any of the sports teams. Get inside."

Then Cody would be yanked out of my hold and dragged into the study by his ear.

The slamming of the study door always sounded like a punch.

I can still hear it.

Instinctively, I grab for Cody's hand.

Surprised, Cody's gaze shoots to mine.

No one can stop me holding his hand now that we're adults. It doesn't make him less of a man. It didn't then and it doesn't now.

Cody squeezes my hand back.

"It must be beautiful on the lake that early, coach." Shay takes a happy bite of his large sandwich. "I'd love to go out with you one time. I've never been anywhere like this. Guildford's so different."

"What in the hell makes you think that I'd take *you*?" Dad's voice is ice cold.

Shit, he's finally making his move.

He's savaging Shay.

Why did he need to reject Shay like that?

It's the same as he refused to take Cody boating, leaving him doing punishment chores, while taking me on the lake.

Shay chokes, and Cody leans to bang him on his back.

D'Angelo's gaze becomes flinty. "Don't worry, Shay. If you like the idea of boating, then I'll buy you a yacht."

My lips twitch, and Michael attempts to hide his own smile behind his beer.

Shay coughs again. "A bloody yacht?"

"Two then," D'Angelo says, casually.

Cody whistles. "And one for my sis."

D'Angelo arches his brow. "Done."

When Dad slams his hand down on the table, I jump.

Everyone falls silent.

The tension is palpable. The air is suffocating. The thunderstorm has finally broken.

"Buy yourself ten yachts, a Ferrari, and a mansion in the fucking Hamptons, I don't give a fuck," Dad barks. "Enough of this bullshit. Shay, what the hell happened in the game?"

So, Dad's decided on the direct route.

Shay looks like a deer caught in the headlights.

"Dad," Cody tries, "his brother has only just—"

"I'm not talking about his brother right now. Sit down, Cody. Stop hanging onto your sister's hand like... Sit your ass down."

Hurt flashes across Cody's face.

I squeeze Cody's hand. "You don't have to."

"It's okay." He leans down to hug me. "I'll be just across the table."

"Code didn't deserve that," I insist.

Cody's shoulders slump, but Michael welcomes him back next to him, slipping his arm protectively around his shoulders.

"I would appreciate you not talking to my husband in

that manner," Michael says low and steady. "You do not get to order him around."

"He's still my son," Dad replies. "And this is my house."

"Having him as your son is a privilege." Michael's expression is stern. His eyes blaze. "One that you may lose. We can leave very easily."

Cody sits straighter.

I love that he has Michael as his husband.

Dad waves his hand, dismissively. "This isn't about Cody's screw up this time. It's about Shay's."

Cody and I wince at the same time.

Michael tightens his arm around Cody.

"I'm sorry that I fucked up." Shay ducks his head. "But please don't bring anyone else into it, coach. Why are we talking about this in front of everyone? Wasn't being humiliated in front of millions of people yesterday enough punishment?"

"This is your captain, mentor, and PR Director. They need to be here," Dad points out. "I wouldn't need to have called his crisis meeting, if you'd been honest with me after the game. But instead, you wouldn't say a damn thing. Have you had time to think? I've had enough of this. We need to get your head on straight before the next game. You're our star player. We'll never make the play-offs, if you don't score for us."

"So, no pressure at all." I wring my hands in my lap.

"He should have pressure," Dad replies. "Hockey thrives on competition and high stakes. You need to be tough. If you can't handle that, then you can't handle the NHL."

Shay pales. "I can, coach."

"It didn't look like it yesterday."

"Back off," D'Angelo growls. "You've already roasted his goddamn balls once. What more do you want?"

"The truth."

I should have known that Dad would know that there was more going on. He was a player himself, before he became a coach. Just like me, he's been around this world too long to miss when something's happening in his team.

D'Angelo's lips thin. "It's private."

Dad launches himself out of his seat, leaning on the table. "Bullshit. Nothing's private on the ice. Don't you understand? This is all of your fucking careers on the line. If Bay Rebels doesn't perform this season — if it isn't seen to perform — then the board will fire me and every member of my staff. I have a responsibility to them and their families. Cody, Robyn, and Eden will lose their jobs too. Do you want that, Shay?"

Shay shakes his head, panicked. "I didn't do it on purpose. And I was going to talk to you tonight. I'd already made up my mind. I simply wasn't sure how. I don't think this is the right way but...someone deliberately mind fucked me before the game."

Dad's expression gentles with worry. "Have you told the security team?"

"It happened only an hour before we had to leave for the rink. We haven't decided how to handle it..."

"Then I'm telling you now," Dad says, firmly. "Tell security. No one messes with my team. Your safety is the most important thing to me. Robyn, are you in danger as well?"

"I don't know." I have to be honest.

Dad is looking even more concerned, as are Cody and Michael.

"That's it." Dad crosses his arms. "I want all the details — now."

"This person is targeting the private lives of Bay Rebels players," I explain. "Setting up smear campaigns."

"Melanie," Cody gasps.

Shay takes a deep breath, and I'm blown away by how fucking brave he is. "There was a photograph. It brought back a seriously bad memory for me."

Dad's eyes lighten with understanding. "Are you talking about that photo of Jude dressed up with the whip? What's the problem? I've had the misfortune of seeing at least a dozen pictures of him in the press over the years, which were lewder than that."

D'Angelo smirks. "Guilty."

"The other photograph," Michael says, softly. His gaze is troubled but understanding, as he studies Shay. "The one with…?"

Dad's eyes widen. "The blindfolded man is you?"

"Dad, he doesn't want to talk about it," I say more sharply than I think I've ever spoken to Dad before. He doesn't react, looking more sad than angry. But then, he knows what it is to be exposed in the press. The difference is that in his case, it was for doing something wrong on the rink. "This is strictly confidential. The person who took those photos didn't have Shay's permission."

Cody sucks in a shocked breath.

Slowly, Dad sits down. "I'm sorry. I don't know what to say."

"I don't know if it's illegal, but it should be." D'Angelo's expression is tight. "It's revenge porn. But worse, the journalist is using it as a threat or warning."

"It put me off my game." Shay tilts up his chin. "It won't happen again, coach. I hated most of my therapy in the past. But in this case, I think that I should try it. I don't know how to get past this. I never dealt with what happened to me at the time. If I don't now, then it could continue to affect me."

Dad nods. "I'll arrange it."

"Thanks, coach."

"Melanie Helt's always been a bully." Cody's eyes burn with a fierce protectiveness as he glances between Shay and me. "She knew that she could get a rise out of me, whenever she bullied Ryn at high school. Don't underestimate how dangerous she is. Even back then, she'd pick a victim, then sway most of class to target them, while not getting her own hands dirty. She could destroy someone innocent without even—"

"Innocent?" Dad crosses his arms. "Come on, this woman only threw childish insults at your sister. Don't you think that when I went storming down to the school in your defense I checked? What I found was that you were no innocent, Cody. I've never been so embarrassed, as when I demanded to know who'd been bullying my boy, until he limped home with black eyes each day, only to have your teacher tell me that *you* were the troublemaker who started fights. You were lucky not to be expelled. At least take ownership of your mistakes."

Shit.

This is exactly what Melanie manipulated everyone to think. It was the turning point in Cody's life that wrecked his relationship with Dad and led to years of being treated like he wasn't good enough.

And it was a lie.

Cody's lip trembles. "I do own it. But I was protecting my sister."

I reach across the table, and Cody desperately takes my hand.

Dad can't quite keep the look of contempt out of his eyes as he notices the gesture.

Cody stiffens.

"He was standing up for me," I insist.

"I thought that I was protecting your mom on the ice, when I got into the fight with the player that ended his career and could have killed him…and so, ended mine too," Dad growls. "It's not an excuse. You lost your temper because of some teasing, threw punches, then came home to cry about it like a—"

"Don't." My voice is cold. "Just fucking don't."

Dad looks startled. "I didn't mean… This is in the past, right? The point is that this woman is only doing the same thing now. Cody knows that what happened at school is forgiven. We've moved on from it."

"Have you?" Michael's voice is dangerously hard. He turns to Cody, gently lifting his chin. "Do you want to go home?"

Cody's breathing too fast; he looks dazed. "I don't want to leave Ryn."

"You do what's best for you," I say.

"Fucking run," D'Angelo mutters under his breath.

Cody shakes his head.

Then he looks up to meet Dad's eye; his gaze is fierce. "I need you to listen to me, Dad. I can't keep coming to see you here, if I don't feel safe. And the way that you speak to and about me, makes me feel really unsafe."

Dad looks even more startled. "What do you mean? I talk the same way to everybody. You should see the way that I kick Jude's ass. Plus, I've been breaking this newbie's balls…"

He points at Shay.

I wince.

I'm holding my breath, glancing between Dad and Cody.

Cody's needed to say this to Dad for years. But will Dad truly listen? Will he understand?

"It's not the same." Cody pulls his hand back from mine and clenches it. "*I'm your son.* The things that you say to me are toxic. They make me feel like shit. I know that I'm not as good or as smart as Ryn is. But I've still become a physical therapist. I may not be a jock like you hoped I would be. But I'm an awesome surfer. You've never come to see me in any of the competitions but…I'm good. I simply want you to spend some time with me, where you're not reminding me of the past. Try to understand that I'm not the same as you but that doesn't mean I'm worthless."

Dad takes a deep, shuddering breath. "I never thought that you were worthless, Cody. Hell, I'm sorry if I made you feel that way. I didn't want to see you fuck up your life like I did. I was worried, when you seemed so angry all the time, that you would. But I'm going to try. How's that, son?"

Cody looks like he's trying hard not to cry. "Good. I hope."

Dad's looking deeply uncomfortable. He doesn't do emotions.

Instead, he grabs his beer and takes a drink like he's looking for inspiration in the bottle.

"Do you want to go boating with me next weekend?" He mutters.

Cody and I freeze at the same time.

Dad's never asked him before.

"Michael as well?" Cody asks, carefully.

I don't blame him for not wanting to go alone.

Dad hesitates, before nodding. "Sure."

"Okay."

"And while we're boating," Michael's eyes gleam, as he pulls Cody against his chest, "you'll treat my husband with respect. He's an amazing man. If he decides that you deserve a place in his life, then you'll discover that. And it *will* be a privilege."

Dad stares at Michael for a long moment.

Inside, I'm cheering.

Michael has just out Alphaed the Alpha.

"This doesn't solve the problem with the journalist." Dad's gaze swings to Shay. "She did more than throw insults around this time. Plus, it impacted how you played. I can't have you distracted on the ice like that. I may have you sit out the next game."

My heart sinks.

Shay's leg nudges against mine, and I wrap my arm around his waist.

He's gone unnaturally still.

"There is no way," D'Angelo's words are icy, "that I am playing tomorrow without Shay."

"Remind me again who the coach is?" Dad sits down, glowering at D'Angelo. "You're like my son-in-law at this table, but on the ice, I'm the god in charge."

Unfortunately, it's true. Within the Bay Rebels, Dad holds the power.

"If Shay's name ever gets out attached to that photo," I say, "then it'll look like you're victim blaming. Not playing him in light of it will ruin both Shay and the Bay Rebels. It'll look like you're shaming him for being a sub. Whereas, if he's still playing, it'll look like Bay Rebels doesn't give a fuck about a player's personal life and is backing him, especially if we need to go after Melanie in the courts, as well as the woman who…"

"Abused me," Shay's voice is tight.

To my relief, Dad nods. "Do you want me to contact the cops? Make it official? We have a good lawyer too. We can make sure that everyone involved is prosecuted. I don't like to be on the defensive. We should go on the offensive, going after the journalist who's attacking the talented stars of this town's beloved team. You're right. I don't give a damn about your personal lives. She's the one breaking the law."

Fuck, I wish that we could do that.

Yet the scandal that it'd cause would put all of us under the spotlight. If we thought that press intrusion was bad now, it'd be nothing compared to what it'd be after a scandal like that.

We're just about managing to keep our relationship secret now. We couldn't then.

I doubt that Shay wants to have his past picked apart by vultures in such a public way after everything that he's been through — or his twin.

Is it fair that simply because you're a sports star or celebrity, when you're assaulted, you need to weigh up reporting it against the knowledge that everybody will learn every detail and you'll likely be torn apart in court?

"Anderson and Bronwyn already warned me, as PR Director, against allowing anything from the player's private lives destabilizing this season," I reply. "But it's still Shay's choice."

Shay looks down, and his golden hair falls over his eyes. "I can't do it, love. I'm not ready for everybody to be talking about me like that and to have to relive it over and over…it'd wreck me."

"How about we turn the tables?" A sudden thought shoots through me. "Why don't *we* investigate *her*? I've been drawing mainly blanks in the journalistic and PR worlds but that could be because people are scared of Melanie. No one dares talk. But we could hire someone professional to look into her."

"Is that ethical?" Dad asks.

"Is she?" D'Angelo drawls.

I turn to Shay, loving the flicker of hope that lights his gray eyes for the first time since that photograph of him was published. "We'll hire a team and get them working on this. We'll find out why she's targeting the Bay Rebels. How she's doing it. We're going to fight back. Then we'll be the ones with the secrets."

CHAPTER TWENTY-THREE

Captain's Hall, Freedom

D'Angelo

I sit with my back against the headboard of the bed in the center of my room with my legs casually crossed at the ankle. I'm wearing one of my favorite sky-blue Armani suits.

It's a fucking beautiful suit.

I sip at my caffe corretto, which is an espresso shot with a drop…or more than a drop…of brandy.

Delicious.

I lick over my lips, savoring the taste.

The early morning sunlight is barely struggling to

push through the drapes. It's never too early for this coffee kick, however, even if Eden would give me a disapproving look that I'm not drinking tea, and Shay would be babbling about some healthy smoothie shit that looks like toxic waste.

Only my principessa understands my love for coffee.

At college, we once debated starting a coffee appreciation society, which would mainly be an excuse to sit around tasting world coffees and deciding what cookies go best with them.

I take another drink, feeling far too relaxed considering the stress of the car crash of a meal at coach's house yesterday and the importance of the game later today.

Waking up this morning, however, I'm filled with a new determination.

I've survived my brother, parents, teachers at the discipline school, and bullies at college, all wanting to destroy me because of who I am.

Not what I've done...*who* I am.

I've never allowed them to.

I've survived. I've fought. And I'm still fucking standing.

So, no one is going to ruin me now for the same reason, let alone ruin men as sweet as Noah or Shay.

This new family that I've been building for myself can't be shaken by a journalist and the demons from our pasts.

My OCD has been pushing at me this week. My intrusive thoughts have been spiraling. Yet I can hold on because now, I'm no longer alone.

I'm the fucking luckiest man alive.

It's Melanie who's going down for hurting the people I love.

I take a last drink, before setting down my empty coffee cup on the bedside table.

This is how all mornings should start, especially since I have gorgeous men and women sleeping under the glimmering covers with me.

Of course, they're naked.

The early bird gets to put their pants on.

I smirk, holding the Guide loosely in my free hand.

"Let's see what fantasies my little ray of sunshine has added like this is a letter to a kinky Santa," I mutter, turning the page with a relaxed flick of my wrist. Then I lift my eyebrow. "Ten Reasons I Love Robyn."

I glance at Robyn.

She's lying in the middle of the bed, between Eden and Shay.

Shay's arms and legs are entangled with hers, whereas Eden is on the edge of the bed, tangled in the blankets instead.

I can't help the smile, when I see how Shay and Robyn's faces are so close that their long eyelashes are brushing. Her red hair is mingling with his golden locks. His hand with chipped black nails rests on her cute ass.

Shay's ice-white skin looks ethereal in the pale light, and fuck, I'm never growing tired of his tightly muscled body and broad shoulders. The way that Robyn's soft curves compliment his hardness is like poetry.

I love watching her sleep.

I refuse to accept that sounds stalkerish.

My lips thin, however, when I force my gaze away from my sleeping brats and start reading these *ten reasons* and realize that they're not Shay's romantic ramblings but rather, Eden's earnest pleas from the soul.

They're heartbreaking.

My brow furrows.

Eden loves Robyn because she doesn't see him as a *shadow...?* She makes him feel *worthy?* She listed the ways that he was more talented than Shay...and he *thinks* that she believes them? She's not *abandoning* him?

God, how could I have been so blind?

Eden spoke about how broken his brother was but he's spent so long protecting his brother that he can't see that he has the same issues.

It's not only physical pain that he hides.

My expression steels.

Eden is like a brother to me. I'm going to help him and that means making sure he knows that he has as firm a place in this relationship as the rest of us.

I can't help the slight laugh, when I see how Eden has signed his section of the Guide like it's a marriage document. He's as anal as I am.

No wonder he's such a good fit as a PA for me.

I honestly thought that we'd at least have had one argument over the best way to schedule appointments or line up notices on the bulletin board. Yet Eden is more organized than any professional I've worked with, despite his headaches and post-concussion symptoms.

To be fair, I feel like one of those politicians who have

their entire lives down to the diamond earrings that are bought for their wives' anniversaries, run by their far more competent secretaries.

I even found that Eden had marked Robyn's birthday in my diary with a gift symbol next to it.

I'm keeping him as my PA no matter if he genuinely demands a million dollars for his pay.

"Signed by Eden..." I shake my head with a quiet laugh as I snap shut the book and slip it onto the bedside table along with my empty coffee cup.

I hear Eden stir on the bed like some kind of baddass fae prince in a fairy tale who's woken up by his name being voiced, only one who's black and blue with his arm in a sling.

"Good morning." I study him.

Eden yawns, running his hand through his hair that's fallen over his face and instinctively slicking it back. "Morning, Jude."

He glances at Robyn, scanning over his brother and her like he's assessing what they need.

I know what they all need.

This is going to be an intense day.

A difficult one.

I'm going to make sure that we feel as connected as we can, before anyone tries to tear us apart.

I tilt my head in thought, before I lean to the bottom drawer in my bedside table. I pull it open and select a bottle of water based lube. Then I rummage around through my selection of sex toys, before I find what I'm looking for.

My eyes glitter wickedly, as I pull out the finger vibe. It's finger shaped, silicone, and purple.

I've noticed that's Robyn's favorite color in sex toy.

See, you should always want a man who's observant and thoughtful about those kinds of things.

Again, not stalkerish.

Eden sleepily sits up, and the sheet pools at his waist. "What's that? It looks like a witch's finger."

I hush him.

"It's not a witch's finger, but it is magic," I whisper. "Want to wake up our girlfriend in the best way?"

Or one of them…I have many creative, fun ways.

Eden nods, cautiously.

I look at Shay and Robyn who are still sleeping innocently.

Not for much longer.

I feel a little guilty, since Shay's insomnia was terrible last night. He was wandering the house until 3 a.m., before Eden and I cornered him in the kitchen, and I carried him over my shoulder up to my room. Then I put him in the middle of all of us, and he finally managed to fall asleep.

I know that Shay's freaked out by the memories that were stirred up by that photograph, as well as his anxiety about scoring in the game today.

Coach put the fear of god (or the devil), into him.

I could have kicked coach's ass for laying more pressure onto Shay's shoulders, even as simply a teammate and my mentee, let alone the man who I'm fucking obsessed with.

Shay's already beating himself up. He didn't need to be made an example of.

He was abused by that woman, and I don't think he realizes how badly. Perhaps, by being in this relationship with Robyn and me, he'll start to.

Of course, once it really sinks in what was done to him, it'll hurt worse, before he gets through to the other side, because he'll understand just how badly he was treated by so many people in his life who he should have been able to trust.

Instead, they spat on that trust and his love.

They betrayed him in the worst possible way.

People who pretend that they're doms, while using the title as an excuse to hurt people without their consent are the worst fucking assholes.

If someone has a red flag, it's not sexy. Red means stop in a scene for a reason.

I beckon to Eden with the finger vibe, which is strangely satisfying.

He rolls his eyes.

"It's a vibe," I explain.

Then I beckon to him with the violet finger again.

Eden's eyes darken with interest. He slides off the bed, wrapping the sheet around his middle without any care for the fact that he's exposing Shay and Robyn.

I share a long look with Eden, as he stalks around the bed to join me.

I enjoy having another dominant man in this relationship. Eden understands me with simply a look.

He quirks his pierced brow. "Are we tormenting them?"

"Tormenting with pleasure," I agree.

See, he simply gets it.

Although, he doesn't fully understand himself yet. This is new to him. But his dominance is an innate part of his personality.

I rarely get to play with another dom in bed.

It's always exhilarating.

I've always been good at being a leader. I loved mentoring Eden on the ice. I'm going to love mentoring him in bed even more.

Eden reaches forward, running his finger along the vibe. I let him explore the feel of it.

"It has different settings," I explain, showing him the button on the side. "They increase the vibrations. It adds an intense sensation to your touch. It means that since you're still injured, you'll be able to sit next to Robyn and barely move to get her panting. It's good because it's not bulky, so you can hit the sensitive spots and then let the toy do its…"

"Magic." Eden's eyes dance.

I grin, mischievously. "You always were a quick learner."

I reach for the lube and pump some onto my palm. Then I spread it over the finger vibe.

"Time for our girlfriend's special wakeup call." I gesture to Eden like I'm offering him the first dance at a ball.

He inclines his head, walking back around the bed, before stretching out next to our sleeping girlfriend.

I crawl onto the bed, hovering over Robyn and Shay.

I nod at Eden, and he takes up his place beside Robyn.

Lightly, I caress down first Shay's cheek and then Robyn's.

Her eyelashes flutter, then her nose scrunches up in the adorable way of hers. "Jude…"

Something inside me snaps at my first name *Jude* on her lips.

I growl, dipping to kiss her plush lips.

She opens them, making a small, surprised sound.

I deepen the kiss, and her pretty emerald eyes focus on me. She looks muzzy and still rising from sleep.

I kiss her awake.

Instantly, I hear buzzing behind me.

I glance around, as Eden rests the vibe on Robyn's nipple and begins to tease it. He's watching her face, avidly.

"Fuck." She jumps, but I press her back against the bed.

Her breathing hitches. She keeps her gaze fixed on me like I'm her savior.

She doesn't know that I'm the villain who set this up.

My lips twitch. "Something wrong, principessa? We're just waking up our Sleeping Beauty."

"You already kissed me," she gasps.

Robyn's struggling to talk already, as Eden swipes the vibe across her nipple, while using his other fingers to play with her breasts. The combined and unexpected sensations shocking her out of sleep are already driving her wild.

"Thanks for reminding me," I reply. "You need to be kissed somewhere else to truly awaken you."

I turn to Shay, who's lying very still like I won't notice that he's woken up and is watching the ravishment of his girlfriend with delight, if he doesn't talk.

I snatch his golden hair in my fist.

"Morning to you too, brute," Shay whines.

I lean closer to him, and his breathing speeds up. "Don't be rude. Kiss our girlfriend good morning."

For a moment, he looks puzzled.

He attempts to lean forward and purse his lips to capture Robyn's lips.

I'm mean enough to almost let him manage it.

They look adorable trying to have their Romeo and Juliet moment.

I don't think so...

I wrench Shay away by his hair.

"Hey," Shay protests like I've stolen his treat from him.

"Setting two." Eden doesn't give any more warning, before he turns up the vibe and distracts Robyn from protesting as well.

Robyn squeaks.

This is what I love about having a pincer attack of dominants in bed.

I smirk as I drag Shay down the bed. "I've already kissed those lips. Your breakfast is down here. You better show me how grateful you are for this feast."

I push Robyn's thighs apart, before directing Shay between them.

Eden trails the vibe down Robyn's stomach, circling her belly button. "Five."

She's crumpling the sheets between her hands. "I f-fucking l-l-love five."

She's going to love ten even more…actually, it's going to be more love/hate, but then, that's more or less how she's felt about me for a long time.

Shay's stroking up and down Robyn's hips as he settles himself between her legs.

I glance down his body.

His cock is already hard between his thighs.

"Taste her." I push Shay's face against her pussy, tightening my hand in his hair. "I want you to still have our girlfriend's taste in your mouth, when you win the hockey game this evening."

Shay groans, liking that thought as much as I do.

I know that we're both going to imagine his tongue in Robyn's pussy, every time that we pass the puck to each other during the game.

And I'm going to imagine fucking her myself when I score.

Shay licks down her pussy, then flattens his tongue and works harder, thrusting in and out of her like a miniature cock.

Robyn's humping her hips up and down now against his face like she can't stop herself.

I'll have to let Shay up to breathe soon.

But not yet.

He can hold on a little longer.

I lean forward and slide my own finger along her wet folds, pressing into her pussy.

"What...?" Robyn gasps. "Again."

"Good girl." I thrust my finger in alongside Shay's tongue like it's two cocks double penetrating her.

It's intimate and fucking hot.

I stroke Shay's tongue at the same time as Robyn's insides.

Shay whimpers.

Robyn's looking feverish; she's making these delicious moans that go straight to my balls.

"Ten." Eden rests the finger vibe over Robyn's clit.

Eden's gaze catches mine, and I nod.

Then he kicks it up to the top setting and the buzzing vibrations pulsate through it straight to her clit.

At the same time, Shay and I renew our efforts fucking into her pussy with our fingers and tongue.

Robyn hisses, arching her back.

Her breathing is labored and heavy.

I hold her leg down to stop her kicking and thrashing, but she's twisting her head side to side.

Then I can feel by the way that her pussy tightens around my finger, a moment before she comes with a scream.

Eden is relentlessly like I knew he'd be, holding the vibe at full power to her clit all the way through her orgasm.

"Eat up." I shove Shay even more insistently against her pussy.

I remove my finger and wink at Eden.

He presses harder with the vibe.

Robyn's clit must be oversensitive now.

"I'm awake." Robyn yells. "I'm f-f-fucking awake."

I laugh.

Eden switches off the vibe.

Robyn relaxes.

Eden lies down next to her, and she turns to kiss him. "That was incredible. But you appear to have grown a monster finger overnight."

"You like monster romance," Eden says, deadpan. "Aren't you happy?"

Finally, I drag Shay away from Robyn's pussy, allowing him to drag in a desperate gulp of air. He still gets in one final lick along her pussy like he's already missing it.

He won't forget the taste of her like I wanted.

He looks dazed but is smiling.

I loosen my hold on his hair, stroking over it, instead. "Good boy."

His smile widens.

I help him to sit up, massaging his jaw. I wipe my fingers over his lips and cheeks that are smeared and wet, helping to tidy him up.

"Okay?" I ask.

"Bloody perfect, darlin.' I'll happily wake up to using my mouth on Robyn or you every morning."

My eyes darken.

Now my cock is uncomfortably hard in my suit trousers. "If you keep making promises like that, then…"

"Yes…?" Shay teases, ghosting his hand over my crotch.

"I'll be immensely happy." I snatch his wrist and hold it more firmly against my crotch to show him how hard my cock is at the idea.

He sucks in his breath. "I can feel that, darlin.'"

But then, his thick cock is equally as hard between his thighs.

I quirk my brow. "Why don't we make ourselves mutually…happy?"

"Only if I get to watch." Robyn snuggles against Eden's chest, who's playing with her hair.

She looks sated and blissed out. She's watching us with a little smile.

Shay and I exchange a look that I know means we're going to put on a performance for Robyn, which is going to make her come a second time.

Shay brushes his hand through my curls with a sudden shyness like he thinks I'm a god and he hardly dares touch me.

My chest is tight.

I stay still, allowing him to lead.

His eyes are wide, as he brushes his fingers through my hair, reverentially. Then he scans my face in awe, before he kneels up and rests his hands on either side of my face. He draws me into a kiss, which is tender but possessive.

I slide my hand up his back, and he shivers.

Robyn is watching us kiss, and she's going to watch us…

All of a sudden, a loud obnoxious vibrating sound startles me out of my happy pleasure filled haze.

I frown, reluctantly drawing back from the kiss.

Shay follows me with his lips.

"Shit, sorry." Robyn scrambles to the far bedside table, snatching up her iPhone. "It's a text. Probably Dad; you know what he's like."

Sadly, I do.

"Tell him to go away. I have a cock to suck," Shay pouts.

"Don't tell him that," I say, quickly. "At least, leave out the cock sucking part."

Shay chuckles.

You can never be certain what Robyn will say. She has a talent for embarrassing herself.

And sometimes, me.

When Robyn gasps, I pull away from Shay altogether, however, and look over at her. "What's wrong?"

"It's from Melanie." Robyn's pale. "Another cryptic message. She says that she has more secrets and she'll publish them if—"

"I already agreed to do an interview with her," I burst out. "What more does she want?"

I couldn't allow everyone to be threatened and hurt.

As soon as that photograph of Shay was shared, I knew that I'd do whatever was needed to keep him or anyone else from being harmed again.

What if Melanie shared something from Robyn's past next?

The people in this bed right now are what matter to me.

"She wants you to do the interview live tonight before

the game," Robyn replies. "We can't allow this to happen. The press scrutiny will be huge at that time, and she's not giving us time to prepare for it. If she drops any surprises, then you'll be fucked up just before the big game."

I clench my jaw. "I guess that's what she wants."

Shay grabs my hand. "You shouldn't do this. She doesn't have the right to attack you on air and wreck your reputation."

I snort. "Don't worry, I've spent years doing a good enough job of wrecking my own reputation." He needs to understand. I can see by the way that Robyn is giving me an assessing look that she does. But then, she was brought into the Bay Rebels by her Dad to clear up my PR mess. Plus, she's known me since college. I tip up Shay's chin, stroking his jawline with my thumb. "You look at me like I hang the moon. But you shouldn't idolize me. I've made so many fucking mistakes. I've been beaten and disowned. I've spent years partying, drinking, and throwing away chances when…"

I look away.

Shit, this is hard.

"You look after us," Eden says, simply. "We'll look after you."

"That simple, huh?" I try to laugh and hide the tears in my eyes.

"That simple," Robyn says, firmly.

Shay tightens his hand around mine. "I don't only think that you hang the moon but the fucking stars too. That's saying a lot coming from an astrophysicist."

I chuckle, before letting out a surprised breath as Shay pulls me into a crushing hug.

"Why is she trying to hurt us?" Eden asks. "Why now?"

"Good questions." I pull out of Shay's hug, patting him on the shoulder. "Perhaps, she wants this interview because she's trying to get to all of us."

Robyn's eyes widen, and she shrinks against Eden's chest. "You think that she knows about us…?"

"Maybe." I fidget with my cuff links, three times.

If I don't, then the sick feeling spreads through me that something bad is going to happen. It's the same OCD feeling that I've been struggling with for the last decade.

The men are going to come, break in tonight, then…

I battle to recognize that it's an intrusive thought. It's not real. It won't happen.

I'm safe.

"I *am* doing this interview," I continue. "But that doesn't mean I'm going in there like the lamb to her wolf. I've got the team working to find out about her. Her behavior is shady and beyond normal journalistic parameters."

Robyn's brow furrows. "They won't have time to find anything out, however, if she wants the interview to be today."

Time to confess.

I plaster on a cocky grin, smoothing down my sleeve. "Then it's rather lucky that I took it on myself to get my friend who's a PI to look into her already."

"Legend," Shay breathes.

Robyn crosses her arms. "Since when?"

Here goes...

"Since the moment that she acted obsessed about me, before the season even started," I reply. "I rang him first thing this morning to gain as much information as I could. Finally, he came through for me. It took longer than expected because he kept getting blocked by someone powerful at every turn."

"The same as me." Robyn points at me. "Your morally gray ass is forgiven, if you managed to find something out that can save our asses."

"The PI, Garcia, told me that Melanie was kicked out of her first job on a city paper for lying and making up facts in her pieces, along with phone hacking. In her next jobs, she broke press regulations. She's known for it, as well as destroying celebrities' careers with smear campaigns based on rumors, while revealing secrets that she shouldn't be able to know." I give a slow, dangerous grin. "But I know more than that. I know some secrets of my own about *her*."

CHAPTER TWENTY-FOUR

Rebel Arena, Freedom

D'Angelo

I STALK down the low ceilinged tunnel in Rebel Arena that leads to Bay Rebels' TV studios where interviews take place both pre and post-game.

The narrow tunnel is in shadow. It's quiet and deserted, and I can only hear the pulse of my own heartbeat and the fast click of Robyn's heels as she struggles to keep up with me.

I'm dressed in my pre-game immaculate navy suit with team tie. I run my hands along my curls to smooth them into place.

I catch sight of my Rolex.

Ten minutes until my live interview with Melanie.

I bare my teeth. It's not in a smile.

Secrets will be revealed tonight — not mine.

Excitement buzzes through me. I'm fucking hyped, for the game, this interview…for taking back the control.

I'm done being the prey.

Tonight, I'm the hunter.

I glance over my shoulder at Robyn.

She's wearing an outfit that makes me smile because it's my favorite. She chose it for our first date. It makes her shine with confidence every time that she wears it.

It's an off the shoulder floor length emerald dress with a slit up the thigh that entrances me.

Fuck, it's hard not to simply grab her by the arm, throw her against the wall, and fuck her senseless, whenever she's wearing that dress.

I wrench my gaze away from her with difficulty.

I have permission from her to break the no comment and silence rule.

Brave.

She's letting me off the leash.

I can be the devil that I am, while masquerading under the cameras as an angel.

If Melanie thinks that she can be the puppet master here, then she truly doesn't know me.

What can I say?

I'm an asshole.

And tonight even my PR Director has given me permission to unleash my inner asshole because I'm fighting for the people I love, my new found family, and the future of the Bay Rebels.

Up ahead, I can see the bright lights of the studio around the curve of the tunnel.

Abruptly, I stop and turn to Robyn.

She looks surprised, as I stop her and push her against the wall.

She glances nervously up and down the tunnel to check that we're alone. She's shaking with anxiety. I know that she's facing a bitch who bullied her as a kid.

My expression tightens.

I understand about facing my demons.

I slide my hand to her throat to focus her attention on me. "No, look at me. Only me. We're alone. Right now, don't worry about anything else but my voice. Do you trust me?"

I can feel the way that she swallows underneath my hand. "Yes."

"Yes what?"

Robyn's pupils dilate. "Yes, Sir."

My cock hardens.

Fuck, I need this right now.

Robyn knows that. She always gives all of us what we need.

I flex and then tighten my hand around her throat. She doesn't look away from my eyes, as I'd ordered her not to.

I lean closer, brushing my lips across hers but not kissing her. "I love you, Robyn. I've known that you were the only woman who I could love since college. No one has made me feel so understood or like I could be myself around them. We could laugh at comedies together, watch your Disney movies, or chat about shit until 2 a.m. in the morning. When I wasn't with you, I was thinking of you. Hockey is my world, but you're my universe. This second chance with you is like being reborn. I'm not going to let anything or anyone threaten it." I reach up and touch the pendant that's hanging at her neck. "You carry me around your neck, principessa. But I always carry you in my heart."

I lean in and kiss her.

The fire between us ignites.

I push my thigh between hers, and her dress rides up. My dick presses against her hip.

She groans.

I draw back, licking across Robyn's sweet tasting lips.

When we win — in all ways — I'm going to fucking wreck Robyn tonight.

Her eyes widen like she knows what my wicked grin means…and she's excited.

Reluctantly, however, I release her throat, stroking over the skin. Instead, I drop my hand to her collarbone.

She shivers, as I caress her with my thumb.

"Garcia's been investigating Melanie and also Peninsula Daily News. He not only found good information on Melanie," I rest my forehead against Robyn's, enjoying this quiet moment, not knowing whether it's going to last, "he also asked some good questions like why she's so obsessed with me. He looked through Melanie's editorial articles. In the last three years, over a quarter have been negative smear pieces on me. He compared that to other sports sections that maybe hold a handful of pieces on me. She's single-handedly been behind pushing the agenda that I'm a cocky playboy loser."

Robyn frowns. "So, why…?"

"That's the question. As a local woman, why's she not supporting the team?"

"She's not a fan, huh?"

Okay, confession time…again.

The tips of my ears redden. "After she printed the first photograph with Noah at a play party where there shouldn't have been cameras, followed by the second picture from someone pretending to be a domme, I wondered if Melanie was in the BDSM scene. I didn't think that it was possible, since I didn't know her, as the community is small here. But what if she found a way to be invited into the parties in her typical lack of morals way, so that she could blackmail people, build up gossip, secrets, and connections…"

Robyn gasps. "That's disgusting."

"She's predatory. I wouldn't be surprised. At first, since Garcia thought that she was targeting me, I wondered…"

"If you'd played with her at a party." Robyn's eyes become steely. "Did you?"

"No fucking way. Plus, I think that she's only targeting me — or Shay — to impress someone else." I take a deep breath. I've waited to tell Robyn this because it's big. She knows the larger plan, but the reason behind it could break her heart. She's had that happen too many times already. "Garcia found years of evidence. I have a file that I can show you. It proves that they've been buying her expensive gifts, treating her to hotel rooms, meals out, and fucking her. Garcia was able to photograph them going into a hotel together. I bet that we can find a paper trail that he's been paying her too. In turn, she's been smearing Bay Rebels and me, while writing positive articles about him."

Robyn is still looking at me, confused. "Who are we talking about?"

I hate that I'm going to have to say his name.

I cup Robyn's cheek, and her gaze flies to mine.

"Talon," I admit.

"No," she whispers. Then she cries louder, losing her control, *"No..."*

Robyn struggles to escape my grip, frantic. Tears stream down her cheeks, and she sobs.

"I'm sorry, principessa."

"Wilder was cheating on me with *her*." She thrashes side to side. "How could he? He knew the same stories about Melanie that I've told you. He knew what she did to me at school."

I clench my jaw.

I don't know how yet...but I'm going to destroy Wilder.

"Talon's a narcissist," I reply. "He doesn't have the empathy to care about that and he clearly doesn't give a fuck about Melanie either. From what Garcia says, Melanie seems to be genuinely in love with Talon. Women seem to fall under the spell of a star hockey player, when they single them out and make them feel *special*. He abuses that position of power. She's being manipulated by him because she believes his love bombing. She thinks that she's in control but actually, she's *his* puppet. He only wants her for what she can print and the damage that she can do to his enemies."

Robyn looks devastated. "They've been hurting Shay and you to hurt *me*."

That's why I didn't want to tell her because I knew that she'd blame herself.

Yet I won't keep secrets from her.

At least, not more than I need to.

After these three games, I'm going to start letting her more into other sides of my world.

I asked her if she trusted me. Well, I need to trust her now.

Robyn tries to wrench herself away from me, but I don't let her. Instead, I clutch her to my hard chest, stroking her hair.

"Your ex is my rival," I reassure her, holding onto her as tightly as I've always wanted to. I'm never letting her go. "He's been finding ways to hurt me, ever since they beat the shit out of me with wooden coat hangers and called it *hazing*. This isn't your fault. The asshole is suspended; he can't get to us now himself. I guess that he thought he could manipulate one of the women who's dumb enough to think that they're special to him into continuing his stalking. Except, this time he's wrong. Our family is too strong to be torn apart by this. We're going to fight back. We're the rebels and not the losers, remember?"

Finally, to my relief, she turns her face up and gives me a watery smile. "Rebels forever."

I wipe the tears off her cheek. "Lucky for me that I'm dating a PR expert. You're in charge off the ice. Advise me."

Like me, she needs the control back.

I love that Robyn is a capable, independent woman.

I won't allow her ex and Melanie to steal that from her.

Robyn struggles to get her breathing under control. I scrunch up my nose, feeling antsy as she wrinkles my shirt by clutching her fingers tightly in the front of it.

It's not like I'm about to be interviewed in front of millions.

"How about you let go of my shirt?" I arch my brow. "Unless you have a portable iron."

She lets out a small laugh. "Sorry, can't have you looking anything but perfect."

She lets go, smoothing down my shirt, before pressing an apologetic kiss to my chest.

Then she pulls back, carefully checking her own cheeks for tears. "Do I look like I've been crying?"

"No."

Yes.

"Here." I carefully reach out and wipe away the smudged mascara underneath her eyes.

She gives another brave smile. "As your PR Director, here's what I think. Playing dead in this crisis hasn't worked. You need to stay calm and shape the narrative by putting your side of the story. The best PR doesn't sit around and wait for the news; it actively creates it. Melanie thinks that she's making the news with her ambush tonight. I'm certain that Wilder and her believe this will be a scoop about our polyamorous relationship. But when you go in there, you turn it on its head. You make *her* the news. You're the captain of the Bay Rebels, representing them before their third game. You're loved by the fans, and she's going to try and tear you down in their own arena. She'll end up looking like the devil, while you'll be the angel protecting the beloved team."

"My brothers," I reply, simply.

Robyn nods. "Melanie's fighting for a fake love, but we're fighting for family."

I grip Robyn's hand and turn to face the light at the end of the tunnel.

Determined, I prowl with her side by side down the tunnel toward the TV studio. "Then it's time that I face this battle, and I'm going to fucking win."

CHAPTER TWENTY-FIVE

Rebel Arena, Freedom

D'Angelo

I sit behind the arctic table that's shaped like a puck in the Bay Rebels soundproofed TV studio, which is emblazoned with the team's logo. I'm surrounded by electrical cables and cameras.

I blink against the lights that are directed into my eyes.

No one else has arrived yet.

Nerves swirl in my stomach. I tap on my knee rhythmically in threes to calm myself.

This is it.

I've never fought back against my public image,

despite how offensive I've found it, in front of millions like this before.

The press have ripped me apart for being a *playboy* or because of my bisexuality for six years.

Past PR Directors have advised me to keep silent and concentrate on my performance on the ice.

I've had to allow myself to be savaged.

For the first time, I get to bite back.

My nerves settle into excitement. I rest my hands on top of the cold table.

Robyn catches my eye and gives me the thumbs up.

I smirk, nodding.

Robyn's standing like my white knight in the opening of the tunnel behind the lights and cameras.

I don't need her to be in front of the cameras.

I'm her champion on the field of battle but I can still feel her lips tingling on my lips in the same way that Shay will be tasting her as he fights on the ice for her.

It's all about our Robyn.

She's the woman behind the throne, and we all know that she's the one with the power.

I glance over my shoulder at the glass wall behind me. During interviews, it gives a backdrop of the rink. I can just see the two teams starting their warmups.

The interview will be shown on screens above the arena. The crowd will see everything.

I twist back in my seat to face the room.

I've been in this room many times for post-match interviews as the captain. I hate them and I normally suck at them.

I drove past PR Directors to resign.

What did they say about me in those interviews? I came across as a *cocky, grumpy asshole…?*

Fair.

It could be because I *am* a cocky, grumpy asshole.

I don't like people asking me dumb questions, especially after the high of a game. I don't trust easily, and people can twist your words.

They use them to hurt you.

This week, however, Robyn's spent her evenings giving me short bursts of intense media training that's improved my interview skills.

I hope.

I take a deep breath, straightening my shoulders.

All of a sudden, there's a commotion in the tunnel behind Robyn.

Robyn and I stiffen at the same time, before I made a conscious effort to relax again.

"I told you to do it. When I say that I want something done, then it's fucking done, understood?" A harsh and entitled voice says. *Melanie.* Who the hell is she talking to like that? "Find out by the end of today or you're done in this business. You wanted to work with me, didn't you? Do you want me to share those screenshots? People aren't going to listen to your side of the story. So, be a good girl and fucking do your job. Okay, hun?"

I narrow my eyes.

No wonder people are scared of Melanie in the industry.

Melanie is no different to Wilder. She reels people in

with promises and love bombing, then turns on them, if they don't do what she wants.

People like her make me sick. Sadly, far too many bullies like her get away with it.

Not today.

Melanie strides into the studio, snapping shut her phone.

She's dressed in a pink power suit that somehow pulls off looking punky with its asymmetrical design. Her hair is streaked with silver. She's wearing a pair of large, distinctive looking diamond earrings in the shape of ice hockey skates.

A small group of men in black jeans and t-shirts trail behind her, looking miserable and uncomfortable.

They're keeping their distance from her and making sure to avoid her eye.

Several take up their places as camera operators or behind the lights.

"Don't fuck up the angles this time," Melanie snaps, and the camera operator closest to her frowns. "Stop making me look like I have a double chin. I know that you're doing it on purpose."

I snort in amusement, and Melanie shoots me a death glare. My amusement dies, however, when she targets the camera operator again.

She pokes him in the side. "This will be your last gig, if I don't like how I look. Are you fucking listening to me?"

He nods, keeping his focus on the camera.

A young, meek looking man with brunette hair and freckles who must only just be out of college is standing at her side. His shoulders are hunched, and he's nervously clutching a pile of files to his chest.

I bet that he's her PA.

Poor bastard.

Instantly, I think of Eden.

"Did you manage to set up that meeting after the interview?" She barks without bothering to look around at the man.

"I... I mean...yes, that is..." The PA stutters, fumbling with his files. He swallows and tries again. "He needed to make it half an hour later than you wanted but..."

Melanie takes a menacing step toward her PA, and he shrinks back. "You useless little idiot. I don't care what *he* wants. I employ you to make what *I* want happen. So, you'll get his ass back on the phone rearrange it. Understood, hun?"

The man wets his lips. "Mel, I don't think that he..."

To my shock, Melanie hurls her phone at the PA.

It hits him in the chest, and everyone jumps.

The man yelps, dropping his files. They scatter across the studio's floor along with the phone.

Robyn's eyes widen, and she moves toward Melanie as if to block her from attacking the man again.

The camera operators exchange disgusted glances.

"Don't call me Mel." Her voice is cool. "I'm not your friend. I'm your boss. Now, pick those up."

I stand up, clenching my fists.

I'd never treat Eden like this. I'd never treat any of my employees with disrespect.

When you have power over someone, it's easy to abuse it to make yourself feel big by demeaning them.

If you choose to do that, however, then it actually shows how small you are.

How many people treat others like this and don't think twice about it, simply because they're in a higher position, have more authority, or wealth?

How many treat people like tools or ruthlessly as stepping stones to their own success?

It's the opposite of what I practice.

While her PA scrambles on his knees to retrieve her phone and files, Melanie scans around the room like a shark. She smirks when she sees me and waves for me to sit down.

I adjust my tie, taking my time, before I do.

I hope that Melanie's going to ignore Robyn.

She doesn't.

"Raven, right? Nice to talk properly face to face. Wow, it barely seems any time since we were having such fun in high school. Have you lost weight, hun? Good for you."

I clench my jaw.

I can't wait to take this woman down. She thinks that she's using us...but we're using her.

I'm not nervous anymore. *I'm going to fucking love this.*

"It's Robyn," Robyn grits out. Melanie fucking knows that. "But you can call me Ms. McKenna."

"Don't be like that," Melanie says, sweetly. "This interview is going to be the best one this season. I expect it to go viral. I'm helping the Bay Rebels. You're the newest team in the NHL. You need the exposure. Romance and sex appeal can make a team explode globally. Don't you watch what's trending? You need to know how to package your gorgeous team. Haven't you seen the montages of their tight asses on BookTok? Atlas has his own fangirls, which doesn't surprise me. You're PR Director but you clearly don't know how to brand the team."

"So, what…? You're trying to help?"

"Of course. Just between us girls and off the record, let's be honest. You were only given the post as PR Director because of your Dad. You should have jumped at the chance to do this interview with me but look at what you made me do to get it. Your brother and you always were…slow."

Robyn reddens with rage, and for a moment, I think that she's going to blow our plan and simply tear Melanie apart right now.

Melanie fucking deserves it.

Instead Robyn shows badass self-control by giving a self-deprecating laugh. "We were different people in high school, right?"

Melanie looks surprised. "Right. I mean, nobody would have guessed that you'd have ended up married and then divorced to somebody like Wilder."

Robyn cocks her head, before reaching to touch Melanie's diamond earring. Melanie jerks back and the earring sways.

"This is nice," Robyn says. "It looks expensive. Did someone buy it for you?"

Melanie gives a nasty smile. "Someone who loves me."

"Hmm." Robyn turns away, strolling to stand against

the back wall. "It's unusual jewelery. Strange, but Wilder gifted me a pair just like that for our final anniversary before... I never wore them, and of course, I left them behind, when I divorced him. I didn't want any of his insincere presents."

Melanie pales.

Then she looks like she may hurl.

Robyn gives her a piercing look, before crossing her arms.

Melanie reaches up to touch the diamond ice skate like it's Wilder, before she can stop herself.

Then she scowls. "What's with those sissy pictures that you keep posting with the players messing around baking cookies, riding motorcycles, and smiling to camera like they're *normal* men? You have gods, but in the hands of a mortal like you—"

"We're happy to be in her hands," I interject, allowing my rage to cool to ice. "The fans enjoy seeing who we really are."

Melanie chuckles. *"Who you really are?* We both know that's not true." She strolls to the table. "Two minutes to go. Are you ready?"

I sit down. "How can I be, when you gave me no prep materials? Won't tell me what any of the questions will be? And blackmailed me into this interview?"

I don't keep my voice down.

Everyone in the room is now watching us.

Melanie glares at me. "I didn't... I mean, let's keep this civil."

How deluded is she? *Civil?*

"Of course," I reply, smoothly. "It's what you're known for. I was simply wondering something before we start."

She slips into the seat next to mine, patting her hair. "Shoot."

I lean closer, lowering my voice this time. "How many rules were you prepared to break to get this live interview? How many laws? And do you truly believe that Talon loves you, simply because he gives you the rejected earrings of his ex-wife and fucks you in hotels the same as at least thirteen other women of right now...and counting?"

Melanie gapes at me, before paling even further. Then pink creeps up her neck.

Wrong-footed, for the first time she doesn't know how to answer.

People like her always underestimate their prey.

I won't be Wilder's prey again.

"Wilder loves me," Melanie finally whispers back.

The fact that defending their love is her priority tells me all I need to know. She's going to be heartbroken, but I can't find it in me to feel any sympathy.

She's manipulated and bullied too many people. She's risked pulling Noah's life down around his ears and wrecking Shay.

She's hurt Robyn, and I will never forgive that.

My eyes darken. "How about *I* tell *you* a secret? Talon only loves himself."

Melanie hisses in a sharp breath, pulling away from me.

"Ten seconds," the camera operator calls out.

I compose myself.

My expression is a mask, but inside, I'm flying. I'm as exhilarated as when the siren is about to signal the puck drop.

Melanie, as I'd planned, however, looks frazzled.

She touches her earrings, before forcing her hand away. Her gaze settles on Robyn. She looks like she wishes that she could be anywhere but here.

Melanie's mouth twists, before she reaches up and wrenches the earrings out, dropping them onto her lap.

Melanie's PA is watching her with a confused expression.

She's falling apart in front of everyone's eyes. Any moment now, I'll have her falling apart in front of the world.

The camera operator raises his hand in silent countdown...

Five...

Four...

"He loves me," Melanie mutters.

I don't know if she's talking to me or to herself.

Who's she trying to convince most?

Three...

I catch Robyn's eye.

Robyn's expression is kind and warm. It fills me with strength and reminds me why all those years ago, I risked getting my ass kicked to bring her orange roses at college from the frat house.

I'd risk my life for Robyn. Sometimes, that scares me.

Mainly, I know that it's because she'd risk her life for me.

Two...

The blank eye of the camera stares at me.

I steel myself.

One...

"Good evening, Melanie from the Peninsula Daily News," Melanie says with a false cheeriness and wide smile. She's a good actress. "I'm here before the third match of the season between Bay Rebels and the Arizona Coyotes with the Bay Rebels captain, Jude D'Angelo."

"Hello." I give a fake smile of my own.

"Now, this is an exclusive live interview because you've agreed to talk about some things that are normally off the table, isn't that right?"

Oh, she's good.

"Well, Melanie," I take a steadying breath, "there are some things that have needed to be said for some time. I'm going to step up and be the person who takes the risk and does that tonight."

Melanie's eyes light with a horrible excitement. "Listen to that, folks. How exciting. I can't wait to hear what the man who has been labeled by some as the *puck boy captain* has to say."

"*By you.*" My expression is grim. "You called me that."

Her smile falters. "You can't deny that you have quite the reputation as the playboy. After all, we've only just published a photograph of you looking…well, some commentators have condemned the depravity. In my opinion, you look gorgeous and as capable of taming…"

She winks at the camera, "your lovers, as you do the teams on the ice. Do you have any comment on that?"

"My private life should never have been published in that way." My voice is frosty.

"At least tell us the name of the pretty lion boy. I'm sure there are many men out there who wish that they could be your boyfriend. Are you officially taken then?" Her eyes sparkle.

"I ask that you respect my privacy and the privacy of anyone who is pictured with me. Neither of us gave permission for that photograph to be printed, and it was taken illegally at a private event. Speculation is wildly inappropriate. I'm a sportsman. Aren't I here to talk about hockey? I'd prefer to keep this to talk about the upcoming game."

She smirks. "I'm sure that you would."

I keep my expression shuttered. But I'm goading her.

What she doesn't realize is that she's looking bad — I'm not.

Robyn taught me this. If I don't rise to Melanie's taunts, then she looks like the one who's taking things too far. Then the public will see through her.

Fuck, I hope that they do.

"Okay," Melanie says, brightly, as if she's regained the upper hand, "let's start with hockey then. Your team has had some limited success, but it must be hard to be captain of a team that's been called the *losers* since its creation."

"Again, by *you*." I cock my head. "Why don't you support your local team? Our fans here in Freedom are awesome. They support us with their whole hearts. We as a team love them back."

I look at the camera as I say this.

I'm not winning over Melanie in this. I'm talking to hockey fans everywhere.

Melanie squirms. "Do you prefer the term *misfits* instead? But isn't *loser* fair? How many times has Bay Rebels made the playoffs?"

I bite the inside of my cheek.

Melanie is smart and unfortunately, she's been obsessed with the Bay Rebels and me long enough to know my weak spots.

When I hesitate, she jumps on it.

"Don't worry," she attempts to sound pleasant, but I can hear the bite beneath it, "I'll jog your memory. It's zero."

I lean over the table. "I'll take ownership. You're right. We're a new team without the deep pockets and high levels of sponsorship that some of the other teams in the NHL enjoy. It's going to take time for us to get there. On the other hand, we have an exceptional team this year, and I have a good feeling that we're going to make it."

"Why is it so *exceptional*? Who's the stand out player who makes the difference?"

Anger surges through me, and my shoulders stiffen.

She's after Shay again.

I knew that she'd go there, but it's still hard to not react.

She's watching my face avidly.

I smile, glancing at the camera again. "The whole team

is on fire. I'm proud — I'm sure that all the fans are — of every player."

She can't hide the way that her brow furrows. "But it's Shay Prince, the twin whose brother had such an unfortunate fall on the ice that ended his career—"

"It wasn't a *fall*," I bark, before I can stop myself. She has a way of creating fake news and false narratives that makes me sick. "He was targeted and attacked from behind on the ice. Injuries like those shouldn't be a danger of playing hockey."

Melanie makes a mock sad face. "Tragic, when he's so young and just starting out...just like his brother. It must be hard on Shay, when he's Bay Rebels' top scorer. Is that why Shay had a breakdown in the middle of the last game?"

My gaze flies to Robyn's anxious one and then quickly away.

"That's an inappropriate question," I reply, carefully. "He needed support for a brief moment on the ice, which I gave him as his captain. There's nothing else to say. Move on."

The crew are shifting uncomfortably and glancing between themselves.

"But does this indicate that he has mental health problems?" Melanie presses.

My gaze becomes icy. "That's no one's business. You're crossing a line."

My words aren't to her. They're to the millions of people who are watching this.

I hope that they listen and understand.

"Was he distressed by anything that happened before the game?" Melanie presses. *She's really going to go here?* "Does he often rely on you for support? You mentor him, don't you? In fact, both the twins. Who else are you *close to*...?"

When her gaze shoots to Robyn, I get the tingling in my balls that tells me she's about to get Wilder's revenge on Robyn live on air by revealing our relationship.

Even though her diamond earrings are now lying in her lap, she's still under Wilder's spell enough to take this risk for him.

She's already made herself look like a bully for him. But she's going to take it further.

It's time that I step up to act like the angel who swoops in with my flaming sword and cuts down the devil.

No matter what comes from this, we can't sit back and let her continue to wreck everybody.

Shay and Noah have agreed that even if she reveals who they are in the photographs, then I have permission to take on Melanie tonight. Otherwise, for the rest of our careers in Bay Rebels (for Noah, it means the rest of his life), she'll be able to hold this over them.

This is the only way to take away her power.

A secret can no longer control you, if you don't fear it being revealed.

Wilder can't have given Melanie anything concrete to prove my relationship with Robyn, Shay, and Eden because otherwise she'd have used it by now. Plus, he knows that I'll ruin him with the evidence I hold on him about his hazing, if he does.

Melanie thinks that she can scare us with her hints and rumors. But we're going to ruin her credibility. Then she'll no longer be believed. She can claim that she knows who's in the photographs. That we're in kinky relationships with the Easter Bunny or Taylor Swift.

It won't matter.

Some people may believe her but enough won't.

"You know, there was another photograph..." Melanie arches her brow. "Do you have any comment on that?"

Is that a threat? A warning?

"If you're referring to the disturbing photograph that you published of a young man in distress," I reply, stonily, "then my comment is that you yet again appear to have crossed journalistic lines. They don't appear aware that the photograph is being taken. I would be interested to know if you had permission to publish it, and whether there was public interest to do so."

Out of the corner of my eye, I notice the PA shifting.

I bet that he knows more about this.

Melanie is looking at me in shock. She glances awkwardly at the camera, chuckling.

"Let's get this back on track, shall we?" She nervously adjusts her hair. "So, how are you feeling about the upcoming season?"

Satisfaction floods me.

Time to turn the fucking tables.

I sprawl in my seat, loosening my tie. "Oh, now you want to talk about hockey? But remember, we were going to talk about something special. I thought that we were getting there with your illegally obtained and published photographs. No? Well, how about the fact that you use them to shame and blackmail celebrities into doing interviews with you or even into giving you information on other people?"

Melanie looks wildly at the camera operators, gesturing for them to cut the interview.

They're grinning, however, and shake their heads.

They keep rolling.

The crew are looking at Melanie with contempt. Robyn's lips are curled into a smile, as she watches.

I stretch my arms behind my head. "It's rather like how you forced *me* into this interview and in order to protect my team, I agreed. I knew that you would character assassinate me, as indeed you have. I couldn't let you hurt my teammates, however, who are like brothers to me. I love Bay Rebels, Freedom, and the fans. But you Melanie, are poison. You hate, troll, and gain your money and fame by tearing down people with more talent than you'll ever have."

"Shut the fuck up." Melanie stands up, slamming down her hand on the table.

Her diamond earrings tumble to the floor.

"Hello," I say, calmly. "It's nice to meet the real Mel at last."

"Don't call me Mel."

Her PA snorts, before walking forward, casting a nervous glance at the camera. Surprised, I shoot him a questioning glance.

He passes me Melanie's phone. "It's all on there. The evidence. She does exactly what you say...to a lot of people. I'm sorry. I should have spoken up before, but she…"

"It's all right," I say, quietly, "you're saying something now and that takes courage."

"What the hell are you doing?" Melanie snarls.

Robyn walks to stand at the young PA's side, gently squeezing his arm. "The right thing."

The cameras are still rolling.

What are the players below thinking? How are the crowds reacting?

I can't look behind myself to see.

"I already have evidence that you phone hack and use shady methods to delve into people's pasts in order to ruin their futures." My eyes flash. "You're everything that's wrong with the press. As we speak, seven people have come forward wanting to press charges against you with my backing. I have the funds, as you're aware, to support them." I look hard into the camera. "What's the bet that after this interview, more people will come forward?"

The camera operator, who Melanie threatened to have fired, chuckles.

Melanie looks frantic, before she pushes her way out from around the desk.

Robyn gestures to the camera operator, and he moves to track Melanie with the camera.

Melanie was totally wrong about Robyn; Robyn is an incredible PR Director. She knows that this clip will make every news channel. It will likely flood social media. What she needs most is a reaction, and Melanie is giving her one now.

I adjust my cuffs. "I did say that there were some things that have needed to be said for some time."

When Melanie tries to escape down the tunnel, Robyn firmly stands in her way with the PA bravely at her side.

"I don't fucking think so." Robyn looks like a goddess, as she puts her hands on her hips. "You've made a career out of hating on people and wrecking their lives and legacies. There are so many keyboard warriors, male and female, who do the same like sheep. Well, this is your karmic retribution."

I grin. Now *that's* Quentin Tarantino worthy.

Shit, Robyn looks hot, standing there with that fierce expression and her red hair tumbling around her shoulders.

I hope that she doesn't ruin her big moment by falling over her own feet.

"Get out of my way, fat fox," Melanie snarls.

"Okay." Robyn gives a small smile, standing to the side.

The PA moves next to her, and Melanie elbows him, as she pushes through only to run straight into the arms of our security team.

"Let me go." Melanie struggles, as they hold onto her arms.

"I don't think so," I say, casually. "You've threatened and assaulted different members of staff on this premise. You're being detained, until the cops can arrive. It's our duty to keep everybody safe."

The camera operators, crew, and PA burst into applause.

Melanie's expression twists with outrage and shock. "Then I'll tell everyone—"

"I wouldn't say anything," Robyn says quickly, "before talking to your lawyer."

I glance at the cameras and then over my shoulder down at the arena.

The players have stopped their warmups and are staring up at the glass wall of our studio.

1 — 0 to Bay Rebels vs Melanie and Wilder.

Now, it will be Melanie's turn to have *the right to remain silent.*

Anything that she says, whether to throw out more rumors about our relationship or naming the other men in the photographs will only make her look guiltier, since she's being accused by a range of people.

She'll be as good as confessing.

Ironically, she'll have to keep our secrets.

Yet the footage will go out to every channel, her reputation will be destroyed, and I'll look like the Bay Rebels' angel.

Now, I just need to win the game.

CHAPTER TWENTY-SIX

Rebel Arena, Freedom

*E*den

I WATCH the rink with a piercing gaze.

I'm intensely aware of Robyn who's standing at my shoulder and hopping up and down, swiping her arm through the air like she's the one with a stick in her hand.

Or a sword, wand, or knowing her, an equally frightening monster dildo.

I don't think that she's aware she's doing it in her enthusiasm for the game.

I side-eye her.

Her hair bounces on each hop.

She looks too cute for me to tell her. Plus, I don't want her to stop.

"Pass, pass, pass!" Robyn chants under her breath.

I love the way that the golden jersey pendant at her neck glints in the light. I'm desperate to reach out and caress my fingers over it and then the sensitive skin underneath it.

She'd breathe out, shivering.

Then I'd turn her to face me and kiss her because ever since she was my first kiss in the forest, I've discovered that her sweet lips are addictive.

Is kissing a hobby?

Shay and D'Angelo do it enough for it to seem like an Olympic sport.

Perhaps, Robyn and I can practice *our* kissing every morning before we wake up and go to sleep after that magical half an hour, when we lie side by side in bed together by ourselves reading…

I can't think about that now.

I fucking love this woman.

I force myself to steel my expression.

Does Robyn understand what she does to me?

What she means to Shay and me?

This feels like a date, even if only our arms are brushing, as she jumps about in excitement like she's the one scoring imaginary goals.

She casts me happy glances.

It makes a ball of happiness glow in my own chest.

We're totally connected in a way that I didn't know

two people could be, unless they were twins like Shay and me.

Shay promised that this was possible. Finally, I believe him.

I straighten my shoulders, biting my tongue as my ribs protest.

I missed one game but I'm not missing any more.

I'm a brother, lover, and PA.

I'm on this team.

I'll fucking be beside the ice every game.

I no longer need to wear a suit to game nights, but this morning, I discovered a dozen designer suits laid out on my bed.

D'Angelo leaned in the doorway. "Consider them a signing on bonus. Any PA who represents my brand at events must look presentable. Anyway, you've exceeded all my expectations in the role. You're exceptional. You deserve them. Plus, although I'd never admit that anyone wears a suit better than me, you do look better in them than those tatty joggers."

I ran my hand along the soft sleeve of the closest suit. "Thank you. They're perfect."

D'Angelo tried to hide how pleased that made him with a disinterested expression. "There's a couple of coats hanging in the closet as well. I've also added a clothing allowance to your contract, so that you can choose your own stuff each month."

I stared after D'Angelo, wide-eyed, as he swept out of the room.

Best. Boss. Ever.

Perhaps, I should buy D'Angelo a mug with that on it…*or an apron.*

I find that I like the feel of wearing a suit.

Shay hates them.

"It's like wearing a mask," Shay whispered to me, as we lay on our bunk beds. "It took me such a bloody long time to work out who I was, and I'm still figuring it out. You know what it's like, Dee. We had to be whatever everyone else wanted, in order to survive. So, wearing whatever the fuck I like — leather jacket, ripped t-shirts, nail varnish — expressing myself, it helps me to know that I don't have to become someone else's doll. I can be myself."

Yet suits help me to feel the same just like my ink does.

When I slipped on my first smart suit, which D'Angelo gave me to wear to coach's house, it felt like my true self was finally shining through.

Does D'Angelo understand that?

I think that he does.

For the first time in my life, I *wasn't* wearing a mask.

I shove my hand in the pocket of the gray suit with a light silver waistcoat that I chose for tonight. The long woolen coat that I'm wearing over it, which D'Angelo chose, exactly matches my eyes.

I try to hide my wince from the brightness of the lights.

My head is throbbing.

I promised Robyn that it wasn't, so she'd agree that I could come here with her tonight.

But I couldn't miss this.

I'm not going to collapse again. I'm only at a three on the scale.

I'm nowhere near the *Cody dramatic overacting ten* on the scale.

My lips twitch at the memory of Cody's demonstration.

He's good at his job though because his exercises are helping. I don't mind him calling me. I'd even like to visit him and see the seals.

Is that what having a friend means?

I don't look away from the rink even for a moment.

It's the third match of the season between Bay Rebels and the Arizona Coyotes, and the atmosphere in the arena is electric.

It's so much louder standing here close to the glass than being forced to sit between Cody and Michael on the couch and watch on television.

On Thursday night, watching the game while Michael ate hummus and chatted about his broken boiler, I'd debated collapsing again.

It'd been a close call.

The noise of the game through the television is quieter. The screen mutes it. It slows the pace.

Rink side, the players look a thousand times faster, as if they're flying on a cloud of ice.

I rest my hand against the glass for a moment, before pulling it back; I can feel it trembling.

Or am I trembling?

It's so fucking hard, standing here in the middle of all

this noise. There's too many people and too much emotion that I don't really understand.

Yet I'm swept up in the excitement too.

I've never wanted Shay to win a game more. This is his moment to shine. Once, I thought that he'd be able to do that only if I stop holding him back. Now, however, I feel that it means he's been able to because I'm still at his side; I'm simply not wearing skates.

Shay and I can be independent without losing each other.

"Come on," I mutter under my breath, "focus."

Shay's already scored twice, but this isn't only about winning anymore. This is about Shay hitting that fucking puck into the back of the net again and again and a-fuck-ing-gain, until the Melanies of this world can stop talking about his *mental health problems*, as if there's a stigma attached to that when there shouldn't be, and focus instead on the awesome ice hockey player that he is.

The type of player who could be the best in the NHL... if he's given the chance.

I take my hand out of my pocket to surreptitiously rub over my temples.

"Headache?" Robyn finally stops recreating the action on the ice with her hands and glances at me.

Obviously, I wasn't sneaky enough.

"I'm fine."

"Your head really isn't hurting, right? Tell me if you need to sit down on the benches or take a break somewhere quieter. It's wild in here tonight. We should have brought you something to cover your ears. You could have stuffed them with cotton wool or something."

"I'm not sure that would have fitted with me looking presentable."

Robyn chuckles. "The Bay Rebels have scored three goals, and the Arizona Coyotes have yet to score. Before today, nobody thought that our team had a chance. I mean, nobody thought that they'd even get near the puck. You could have turned up naked, and the fans would have cheered."

I arch my brow.

Insulting.

She flushes. "That didn't come out right. If you'd turned up naked with your tight ass on display, then they'd have cheered and probably, coach and the financial manager would have been delighted that we'd earned the most in Bay Rebels' history."

"But not me, when I was arrested like Melanie was."

She smirks. "We all need to make sacrifices."

D'Angelo — my captain, boss, *hero* — has the puck in the offensive zone again and is moving it around. Shay is more keyed into D'Angelo's instincts and plays than ever before and is closing in on the goal, putting pressure on the defensemen. He's positioning himself to be ready for D'Angelo's pass and get in a quality shot.

Their chemistry together is clear on the ice, but most people will think it's as teammates.

I haven't seen either of them playing so fiercely before.

But then, it must be because of the interview.

The crowd cheers.

The fans are hyped up, wild with excitement and aggressive support for the team after the scandalous interview with Melanie that'd been screened over the arena.

I'd been stiff with a mix of anxiety and anticipation, watching the interview play out and not being able to do anything about it.

Shay, forced to do his warm ups under the spotlights, had been worse.

When Melanie mentioned Shay, however, the rest of the players on *both* teams skated to surround him in a supportive circle, partly to screen him from the cameras but also to show their solidarity.

My heart swelled.

Melanie thought that she was tearing Shay and me down with those comments.

It shocked me to look around the arena, however, and realize that she actually made us a home here.

We're from England but now, we're accepted in America.

Freedom has adopted us.

"They've done it, you know." Robyn lifts her gaze to mine. "*We've* done it. When I saw the way that D'Angelo handled himself in that interview — his strength and leadership — I knew that not only had we won the game against Melanie and Wilder, but D'Angelo would swagger down here and lead his team to victory on the ice as well."

"He does swagger."

"Yep." Robyn's eyes crinkle. She turns to me. She looks

like she's struggling not to reach for my hand. "That suit looks good on you. Perhaps, *you* should swagger more."

"I'll give it a go."

"You do that."

When the crowd erupts and the goal horn sounds, my gaze snaps back to the rink.

"Shay scored again!" Robyn cheers.

I clap.

Then I glance at coach, who's standing by the benches and watching the game like a hawk. I let out a breath of relief, when he punches the air in celebration.

Robyn's dad is a tough man. I don't want Robyn to know how much he triggers me.

D'Angelo finds it harder to deal with coach than I do because he's constantly trying to also win his approval.

Shay is caught somewhere between puppy like hero worship because coach was once a star player, but at the same time, it causes Shay pain whenever he disappoints coach.

I know that I've already disappointed him.

I could never have been the player that coach wanted.

Yet Robyn loves her dad. He's her family.

Plus, coach is giving a chance to people like Shay who other teams in the NHL team wouldn't have signed.

I don't need the man to like me. But I do need him to leave us alone.

He has too much power over our lives.

I glower, noticing Bronwyn and the ginger haired Anderson sitting on the benches beneath coach. They look caught up in the excitement of the game, although

Bronwyn appears more pleased that we're winning. On the other hand, Anderson's expression is sour.

Robyn follows my gaze.

Then she pulls a face. "Those assholes will need to back off for a little while at least now. They'll hate that Melanie's interview created *noise*, but at the same time, she'll look like the obsessed stalker who created it. D'Angelo is the guardian angel of both Shay and the Bay Rebels. They're only minutes from winning this game, then for the start of this season, we're untouchable."

"And we can breathe again."

Robyn leans up, as close to me as she dares in public, as play starts up again on the ice.

I grit my teeth not to react, as her breasts rub against me.

"We can take a breath, recover, have fun together." Robyn's lips are against my ear, as she whispers, "And love."

Is it the feel of her pressed against the front of me, which has made my cock harden?

Yet it's word *love*, which makes my cock twitch.

She pulls back from me with a happy hum like she knows the effect that she's had on me.

I blush, glancing down.

Why did D'Angelo choose suits with such tight trousers? But then, all his suits are tight.

Shay told me with a smirk that it's because D'Angelo likes to show off his ass, since his ego is as big as his dick.

I hurriedly push my hand into my coat pocket and wrench it shut to cover my front.

Robyn's biting her lip like she's trying to stop herself from laughing.

At least there's no one else close enough to see...

"Hey," a quiet voice says behind me.

Startled, I twirl around. I back up a step.

My heart speeds up. I tighten my coat around myself even more.

A short but athletic man with tanned skin and rich, amber eyes is standing with his hands nervously clutched in front of him. He looks maybe a year older than me and is dressed in the medical staff uniform with Bay Rebels logo.

Robyn glances at him. "Is there a problem? We didn't call for assistance. Unless you're not still feeling okay, Eden?"

"I'm fine." I study the man.

He looks more awkward than I feel.

I don't recognize him.

But then, all of a sudden, I do.

It's his *hair*, which I recognize, a wild tumble of golden curls.

He's the lion who'd been kneeling obediently in the photograph in front of D'Angelo in nothing but glittery yellow shorts, while wearing a golden lion's mask. He had an awesome tattoo, even if kittens should never be bound.

He *is* the kitten.

"This was a mistake," the man mutters, turning on his heel.

"Noah," I force myself to say.

Noah turns back. His smile is tight. He looks sick with nerves.

Noah's gaze darts between Robyn and me like we're going to attack him at any moment. His fear makes my own settle.

"I've been watching you most of the evening, trying to work up the courage to come and speak to you." He runs his hand though his curls, making them even messier. "I thought that with us all working, it'd be good cover, you know?"

Robyn's eyes widen. "Oh, I see. I didn't know that you knew that we knew that—"

"Before you become even more lost in that sentence," Noah's lips twitch, "let me explain. Jude told me about what's been going on. He wanted me to have equal say in it. He told me that different players were being targeted and that you were the one being sent texts, Ms. McKenna."

"Call me Robyn," she says.

Noah smiles, shyly. "Thank you. I'm not ashamed in any way about…" He glances around us, and even though no one is close to us, his lips still thin. "…who I am. It's only toxic gendered roles that make people think men can only be one way. But my family won't feel the same. Especially, some of my wealthy, extended family like Silas who have a lot of power in Bay Rebels and within this town. You know that."

Robyn clenches her jaw. "Yeah, I do."

"Why are you talking to us now?" I ask.

Is Noah frightened of us? Does he think that we're going to reveal his secret? Ruin his life?

Noah hugs his arms around himself. "I trust Jude. I'd never play with someone who I didn't. He's been a nightmare for the hockey team for years. Silas has ranted about it a lot. But within the community, Jude's respected. He looks out for people who are new on the...well, you know. He makes sure that no one's taking advantage and that everyone can come to him for advice or support." I frown. Why hasn't D'Angelo told us this? "He never pushes people's limits or does anything without negotiation and contracts..."

"Let me guess, in triplicate." Then Robyn adds to cover herself, "You should see how anal he is about the paperwork with poor Eden here."

Noah shoots me a sympathetic look. "You must be a true saint to be his PA."

"I'm lucky." I tilt up my chin.

Noah arches his golden eyebrow. "It looks like you both are. I'm glad. Look, I'm risking coming to talk to you because I needed to say this. Fuck, it's taken a lot to get myself to. He told me that he trusts you. He doesn't trust many people in his life outside... Well, that's none of my business. The point is that if he says you won't tell anyone about this, then I'm going to take his word for that. He's a good man."

I'm really starting to believe that now.

Still, I blink.

Noah's putting his entire life in D'Angelo's hands.

Because of his faith in him.

Robyn's staring at Noah with the same amazement as I feel.

"I didn't think that you'd dated him," Robyn blurts.

Noah chokes on a laugh. "*Dated...?* Shit, I'd be so lucky. Everybody wants to date Jude. I mean, pretty much the whole of Freedom. But he never dates anyone. As his PR Director, you should probably know this. If you're lucky, then you get a couple of nights, but it's normally..." His pupils dilate, and his tongue darts out to wet his lips. "... like the photograph, one incredible night, which he makes mind-blowing. You know that it won't be more, going into it. He never leaves anyone unsatisfied or unhappy."

Robyn's own pupils have become dilated like she's lost in her own memories of times with D'Angelo.

"Are you still in danger because of the photograph?" My guts churn with unease.

Noah's gaze immediately slides back to Anderson. "I don't know."

"We'll protect you," the words are out before I realize that I mean them.

Normally, I can't talk to strangers like this.

Somehow, the joint danger that we've shared makes it easier. Also, there's an edge of shameless sunniness to Noah that reminds me of Shay.

Except, he's shyer. Also, more anxious.

I hate that it's because he's still living with his monsters, while I managed to get Shay away from ours.

I'm not trapped in the dark with them, and Shay's not still banging desperately on the door to get to me.

I turn a hard glare on Anderson.

Noah appears shocked. "You don't know me."

"It's like you said," I reply. "Obviously, you trust and respect Jude. So do I. If you're important to him, then you're important to me."

"D'Angelo said that he'd offered for you to move into his mansion." Robyn's gaze is flicking between Noah and me. "Perhaps, you should think about taking him up on that as a lodger. It would give you a chance to work out a way to gain some independence from your dad. Perhaps, he'd object to it, if D'Angelo was living there. But the building's empty right now."

"It's hard to feel safe, when it's your own family hurting you," I say.

Noah pales. "They d-d-don't…I n-n-never said…"

"It's not wrong to ask for help," I continue, firmly.

Robyn taught me that.

She's giving me a soft smile.

It fills up the numb, hollowness inside me.

I said the right thing.

I did, right?

I seem to have because Noah nods.

"I'll think about it." He pushes his hair out of his eyes. "Thank you."

All of a sudden, the excitement in the audience ratchets up again.

I turn back to the rink. "Come on, Shay."

Shay's heading for the goal again with laser focus.

He's fucking soaring...

He's scored four goals already.

Let him score again and again and...

A defenseman is just behind him.

My heart is beating fast.

Shay weaves around the final defenseman. Then he raises his stick, aiming at the goal.

"You can do it," I whisper. "You can fucking do it."

Shay shoots…*and he scores.*

The audience ignites into applause, whooping, and celebrations.

I don't look away from the rink, however, where the team are raising their sticks in celebration with D'Angelo leading them.

Shay isn't with them, however, he's skating toward *me*.

I move toward the glass, pulling my hand out of my pocket to rest it against the glass.

Shay slams into the glass, making it vibrate.

He's grinning so widely that his mouth must hurt.

He rests his hand against the glass on the other side. His gaze doesn't look away from mine.

"That one was for you, bro." His gaze still doesn't look away from mine.

The cameras are on us now: twins with our hands touching on each side of the glass.

I know what he's doing. He's making sure that I'm seen tonight.

I'm not his shadow.

He's honoring my sacrifice.

All night, he's been playing with such fierceness because he's been scoring for all of us.

It's never been just about him.

My heart soars.

We've won. We're together. And Shay and I have finally found our new family and home.

A place that we both fit.

When Shay's gaze slides to Robyn, he pulls his hand away from the glass and touches it to his neck.

Robyn flushes, reaching up to touch the pendant.

Shay winks. "I won the bet tonight."

CHAPTER TWENTY-SEVEN

Captain's Hall, Freedom

*R*obyn

How LONG IS Shay going to take to prepare the scene for his choice of kink? He does deserve this reward for winning the bet.

Yet I've been on edge for hours.

What will he choose?

Shay's checklist is a sea of *tried* with only a handful of soft limits (and three hard limits). When Shay filled it out, D'Angelo looked concerned at that.

I'd expected negotiations to be boring. Apart from

D'Angelo's paperwork obsession, I've been finding it hot as hell.

D'Angelo set us one task: *Describe your fantasies.*

Eden's gaze met D'Angelo's at that, startled. But then, he nodded.

I can't wait to find out what Eden wrote.

Right now, D'Angelo is keeping those responses to himself. He folded them up and stapled them into the Guide, before stamping them with a single word:

CONFIDENTIAL

When I demanded to know why, he smirked.

"You're even more desperate to know what they are now, right?" D'Angelo tapped the Guide. "To explore them? Act them out together?"

That man's the devil…and I love it.

Yet tonight, it's Shay's turn to share his favorite kink with the rest of us, picking one that doesn't break any of our limits.

I'm certain that it's going to be fun.

I love knowing my lovers' desires, needs, and what makes them tick.

They work hard at bringing me pleasure. It empowers me to find ways to bring them pleasure back.

Tonight is one of celebration, and I'm going to make sure that Shay gets his reward.

I turn underneath the spray of the shower, letting the gushing water hit my face. The steam smells of the rose scented shower gel. The water pounds against my bare skin like a refreshing waterfall.

I love this spacious, walk-in shower. It's my one indulgence each day.

My muscles ease. I roll my shoulders, sighing.

The room is dark. It's lit only by the pale moonlight that streams across the bathroom's gleaming surfaces and free standing claw bath.

The steam has misted the mirrored back wall.

I'm still hyped from the Bay Rebels' victory. It's been a couple of hours since we came back from the arena. Seeing Shay score goal after goal was as fucking thrilling as watching D'Angelo finally take down the woman who bullied me.

Doing it with Eden at my shoulder made it perfect.

These men don't try to control, tame, or change me.

They support me.

I can see a genuine future with them, which is terrifying but also, fucking exciting.

I'm singing Justin Timberlake's "SexyBack" enthusiastically. My voice echoes against the walls.

I should be opening games with this song, right?

I giggle, singing even louder, lost in my own fantasy.

Hell, D'Angelo's face would be priceless: cold and horrified.

I sing louder to spite the imaginary D'Angelo.

"I'm honored to witness such a special performance, especially since I've only seen Shay's version," D'Angelo drawls

I spin in shock, wiping the water out of my eyes.

I snap my mouth shut.

Fuck, have I sung D'Angelo into existence? A ridiculously handsome…naked…D'Angelo who's casually walking into the shower to join me?

My cheeks redden.

"What are you doing?" I demand.

"Joining you in the shower." D'Angelo presses his hard body against mine underneath the spray. "Wondering if you need somebody to wash your back."

I narrow my eyes. "If you do that, we both know that within moments, it'll lead to less getting clean and more getting dirty."

"I'm not seeing the problem, principessa."

"You're meant to be waiting downstairs for whatever the twins are planning."

"Am I?" He tweaks one of my nipples like that'll distract me from his utterly unbelievable innocent act.

Yet the way that the water runs down the strong planes of his body, between his powerful pecs and abs to the V that leads to his cock, which is already at half-mast, stops me from actually pushing him out of the shower.

Who could push a wet D'Angelo away?

He's irresistible enough when he's dry.

I tuck one of his wet curls behind his ear. "They're setting things up in the kitchen. They'll be pissed that we're starting without them. Actually, they'll probably be turned on and find it hot. Still, they told you to—"

"I don't take orders." D'Angelo's lips are suddenly on mine, hard and demanding.

I gasp into the kiss, before I melt into it. He pushes me back against the hard wall of the shower.

The water pounds down onto both of us, as he winds my hair through his hand and holds me tight into the kiss.

But I don't want to escape.

This is perfect.

Finally, he draws back. I'm panting.

Our gazes meet.

"I've already *waited* for nine years, pining and hiding my love for us to get to this point. We still have to keep our relationship secret." D'Angelo slips his hand close to my scalp and then tugs. My eyelashes flutter at the delicious sensation. "You're the only woman who I've loved. The only one who I'll ever want to be with. I go to sleep with thoughts of you running through my mind, and when I wake up, you're the first person who my brain conjures. You've bewitched me, principessa. So, I can share you with these other men because they fit both our needs. But you'll still always be mine."

My breath catches.

Fuck.

"And you're mine, Jude," I say, fervently.

Now, it's his turn for his breath to catch. His long lashed eyes are wide with awe.

His cock fully hardens against my thigh.

It's evidence of how much he loves hearing his first name on my lips.

One day, I'll test if he can come by that alone.

I shiver at the thought.

But for now...

I kiss him, deep and slow.

He tugs on my hair again, and I slide my hand down

his back. His skin is slippery against mine. It feels amazing to press my wet body against his.

We're both breathing hard, as I finally pull back.

"How much time do we have?" I whisper.

He strokes his thumb down my chin. "As much as you want, principessa."

Shit, how does he do that? Always make it about what *I* need?

I smile, pressing another quick kiss to his seductive mouth.

Right now he looks more like Lucifer tempting me to fall with him, and I would in a heartbeat.

Yet it scares me.

The rest of the season is going to be tough because of both the interview and the success in two of the games, along with the intense press interest that it's created in the Bay Rebels.

I don't think that my men have any idea how much of a nightmare it could be.

In the eyes of the world, D'Angelo is now the team's angel.

If they perceive that he breaks that, then Lucifer's fall to hell will burn his wings.

I never want to see that happen to my glorious man. D'Angelo has already survived too much.

"How about...?" D'Angelo's eyes gleam. "We save time by you washing my hair?"

He drops to his knees in front of me, and my breath stutters.

How can D'Angelo look more dominantly in control kneeling in front of me than when he was standing?

He looks up at me through his lashes, as water catches on them like glittering tears.

I turn down the spray.

"What's wrong?" D'Angelo rests his strong hands on my thighs. "Don't you want to serve me? I may be a hockey captain but inside Captain's Hall, I'm a man. A man who fucking needs you more than my next breath. I'll drown for you." Then he licks up my thigh, and I jump. "And I'll wash you."

"Oh," I breathe. "Fuck, yeah."

"Widen your legs." He squeezes my thigh. "I want to be thorough. I am a perfectionist."

I widen my stance, as I reach for the rose scented shampoo that's hanging to the side in the basket.

D'Angelo rakes his nails lightly down my hips. I'm struggling to stand still under the onslaught of sensations, hurriedly opening the shampoo and squeezing a large dollop onto the top of D'Angelo's head.

D'Angelo huffs. "Romantic. Don't get it into my eyes."

I bite my lip to stop myself chuckling. "Sorry, I promise to be careful. I haven't had experience washing the hair of a man on his knees before."

"You should get used to it with Shay. I already washed his hair like this in the shower today. He'd melt if you did it."

I reach to rub the shampoo through D'Angelo's curls. I should offer to do this every day. His curls feel like silk.

"Huh, shower sex twice in one day. Are you going for a record?" I smile.

"There's not time to make that record today, but we could try next weekend. Of course, Shay used his pretty mouth to wash me like I am you. Every time that we stand next to each other in the showers in Rebel Arena's locker room, I wish that I could push him to his knees and make him take me in his mouth like he does at home…in front of the whole team. He's getting better at taking my cock. I'm going to train him, until he can deep-throat me without choking, although I enjoy it when he does. His eyes look even more beautiful with tears glistening in them."

My heart speeds up, and my core throbs at *that* image.

"Fuck," I hiss.

I'm desperate to reach between my own thighs and touch myself.

To distract myself, I massage the shampoo into D'Angelo's hair, and he pushes into my touch.

I don't know that he realizes he's doing it.

I love that I'm having this impact on D'Angelo.

Noah said that *everybody wanted* D'Angelo.

They all want to play with him.

Date him.

Have him for more than one night.

Yet he's the man who's waited nine years for *me*.

He loves me.

And now, he's on his knees, while I'm washing his gorgeous hair and he's tonguing across my pussy like it's his reward for winning the hockey game.

Jude fucking D'Angelo is between my thighs, where he always should have been, and I could burst from joy.

Also, from pleasure.

I tighten my hands in his hair to control the waves of pleasure that are making my knees buckle.

D'Angelo chuckles against my pussy, and the vibrations feel amazing.

I don't know if I want to wash his hair faster or slower because he's matching my speed with his tongue.

When he scratches down my thighs, I whimper.

Then he flicks his tongue against my clit, and I dig my fingers into his scalp. He sucks on my clit, and I pull on his hair.

He moans, and the vibrations rush pleasure through me.

I close my eyes, throwing back my head.

I force myself to continue massaging his hair, as he spreads my folds with his thumbs and licks down my pussy.

I gasp, flexing my hips as much as I can to encourage him.

I'm almost there.

It's electric, buzzing through me.

"Fuck, that's..." I grind against D'Angelo, and he grabs the back of my thighs to pull me even harder against the aggressive licks of his mouth. "...keep doing that."

How is he breathing?

It's like all he needs to live is me.

"I'm going to..." I'm lost in the sensation of his tongue

between my thighs, his hands holding me steady, and the water raining down on us.

"Jude…" I scream, as finally, I come in wave after wave of ecstasy.

D'Angelo continues to lap at my pussy through it. Then he stands up fluidly, pinning me against the wall.

His eyes are dark. "I love you, principessa."

When he kisses me, I can taste myself on his lips.

"I love you too," I whisper, between kisses.

I'm sated, shaking with aftershocks.

That was fucking incredible.

D'Angelo's expression is devilish, as rivulets of shampoo wash from his hair. "But you did get shampoo in my eye. So, I think that we'll just have to keep on practicing this, until Shay calls for us."

"W-w-what?" My eyes widen.

D'Angelo drops to his knees again, before looking up at me with a wicked glint in his eyes.

He kisses my inner thigh, and I shiver. "I've changed my mind. Why don't we go for that world record?"

CHAPTER TWENTY-EIGHT

Captain's Hall, Freedom

Robyn

"I STILL THINK that we could have made the world record for orgasms in one hour." D'Angelo sounds grumpy, even as he looks impossibly gorgeous with water trails running down from his wet curls and onto his strong shoulders.

Despite sounding like a disgruntled cat after a bath, however, he must be feeling as mellow as I do because he's actually carrying me nestled in his arms bridal style, rather than flung over his shoulder.

His bare feet pad on the wooden floors of the corridor. We're both naked.

Perhaps, I'm getting too comfortable with the Shay method of walking around without even a towel.

Shay's rubbing off on me.

Of course, I'm hoping that he'll be doing some of that in a couple of minutes.

But there didn't seem much point in getting dressed to only strip off again, as soon as we find out what the twins have planned.

Although, if it turns out that Shay wants to share a clothing fetish (and I've wondered about him and leather), then I guess that we *will* be getting dressed.

I hope that he's into corsets.

I'd love to dress Shay in one because it'd be beyond hot to see him restricted in a pretty red lace corset with ribbons, struggling to breathe, while D'Angelo fucks him, and I ride his face.

When my face flushes, D'Angelo gives me a speculative look.

Sometimes I think that he truly can read minds.

Or maybe, only people's kinky thoughts.

Hell, can you imagine if that was a superpower?

Captain Brainkink.

I grin, resting against D'Angelo's hard chest, as he carries me toward the kitchen. "What is the world record anyway? You were incredible. Four times in one shower... Fuck, look at my skin. I'm half prune now."

"You look more like a mermaid. Let's continue the romance and say that's why I'm carrying you. You don't have legs."

I scrunch up my nose. "Is that romantic?"

"More than imagining that I was going down on a wrinkly prune. Sadly, you'd have become a complete one, if we'd actually rivaled the world record, which is sixteen orgasms…"

I perk up. "That's a lot, but with the three of you guys taking turns, we could manage it. Five each and I'll be kind and let you rest, while I do the work on the final one. What do you think?"

Sixteen orgasms in one shower is life goals.

When I glance up at D'Angelo, his expression is devilish; my mouth dries. "Let me finish, principessa. It's sixteen for men, and *one hundred and thirty four* for women. That's not in a shower but in a single hour, which is close enough. You know that I'm ambitious, however, so we can—"

"Hell, no," I say, startled. "Some fantasies should stay as fantasies. And that's one of them."

D'Angelo chuckles.

When he pushes open the kitchen door, my eyes widen, and D'Angelo hisses in his breath.

Because this is definitely *not* a fantasy that should remain one.

Sweet smells waft through the kitchen of fresh bread and pastries. The kitchen is flooded by silver moonlight through the wide, bay window behind the oak table.

The lights are on low.

To my surprise, the table is laid with delicious breakfast foods: muffins, rolls, bagels, and platters of fruit and berries.

Eden must have been baking, even though it's night,

and I know that he's exhausted after the tension of this long day.

My heart melts.

The *fantasy*, however, which should definitely not stay as a fantasy is the two men who are standing next to the table at attention.

What's the only thing that's better than a golden haired naked man with sharp cheekbones, winter gray eyes, and eyes flecked with gold?

His twin standing naked next to him.

"I've decided," I breathe, "that I *love* dating hockey players."

D'Angelo tightens his hold on me. "Ditto."

His heated gaze is fixed on Shay.

The only thing that the twins are wearing is an arctic blue bow tie.

Shay gives us a sunny smile, and suddenly, it doesn't feel like night at all. "Two naked butlers at your service."

Eden's expression is stony.

It makes my lips curl up.

Instantly, I know that this is his brother's idea, but he's going along with it because he knows that it'll please both Shay and me.

Inside, I have a feeling that he's baffled by most of Shay's ideas, and would have suggested curling up with a book and cup of tea.

Eden's body is a map of bruises in purples, greens, and yellows. His arm is still in a sling, and he's squinting in a way that I've come to recognize means that he has a low level headache.

But he wants to give me this.

He needs to be part of tonight's celebration. He needs to have that choice.

I trust now that he has Cody's scoring system that he'll tell us, if things become too much for him. He can't unlearn a lifetime of hiding or disregarding his pain. But I can show him that he's important and fully part of my life.

"What's all this then?" D'Angelo drawls, carrying me over to the bench.

He lowers me onto the seat.

"Midnight breakfast. Don't tell me that you haven't heard of it? It's sort of like a midnight feast but a British tradition," Shay replies.

I don't believe him.

By the way that D'Angelo snorts, neither does he.

"It's an eccentric English thing," Eden deadpans. "Like cheese rolling."

I scrunch up my nose. "What?"

"You roll cheese down a steep hill, then tumble down after it trying to catch it."

"You made that up."

"Did I?" Eden's eyes dance.

D'Angelo leans back against the table. "We didn't win the three games, cucciolo. Naked breakfast was meant to be a reward for that."

Shay's shoulders slump. "Sorry, shouldn't I have done this? I just thought that it was my fault that we lost the second game. It didn't seem fair that Robyn didn't get to enjoy…this…because of my…"

"Hey," I leap up and rush to Shay, grabbing his hand

between mine and leading him to the table. "It's not your fault that you struggled in that second game. Plus, you scored the highest amount of goals. You won the bet. So, tonight is your choice. If this is part of it, then I'm seriously grateful. Lucky me, two buff naked butlers and a delicious feast."

Shay exchanges a glance with Eden.

"Well, my main thing that I'd hoped we'd do is for later. First..." Shay sits down on the bench and pulls me onto his lap. My eyelashes flutter at the sensation of my bare skin against his and his cock that's already hardening beneath me.

He picks up a strawberry, before dipping it in honey and holding it to my lips.

I moan, as I take a bite of its sweetness.

I suck at Shay's fingers, seeking the sweetness of the honey.

He nibbles and licks down my neck. His hair is soft against my sensitive skin.

His hard dick pokes against my ass.

Eden strolls to the table, picking up a fancy porcelain black cat teapot.

It looks vintage.

"Ma'am," Eden says, politely, hovering with the teapot over a matching cat teacup, which is laid in front of my place.

A strainer rests over the cup.

So, Eden's taken the time to make traditional looseleaf tea. I never have the patience for that. I barely have time most mornings to allow a bag to dip its toes in boiling water, before I'm chugging it down. Whether milk has a chance to join in the fun, depends on whether I've remembered to buy any.

At least, that was before I began to be spoiled by Eden's breakfasts.

I nod. "Now I really feel like I'm being served by a perfect English butler. You're like a naked Jeeves."

As Eden leans over to pour the tea into my cup, I can't look away from his long cock and the perfect V that leads to it because it's close to my face.

I become wet.

I'm not sure this would be a scene in a *Jeeves & Wooster* book. You know, the one where the butler turns up to breakfast naked and then his boss gives him a blow job, while he pours his tea.

Perhaps, I should reread the books, in case I missed it.

Maybe it's in the one that's titled *Joy in the Morning*? Or maybe *Thank You, Jeeves*? *Very Good, Jeeves*?

Mating Season?

I really do need to reread those books.

Of course, it could be in the fan fiction.

"Thanks." I watch, as Eden pours the tea like a professional.

He places down the tea pot, before removing the strainer with the caught tealeaves. "Milk?"

"A dash."

He picks up a small jug and adds the milk for me.

Eden never looks away from my face. How can he make serving tea so erotic?

My skin prickles.

I know that it matters to Eden what I think of this tea.

I make a show of picking up my cup and taking a long drink.

Except, I don't need to act.

My eyes widen, and I moan. The gentle but citrus smell and taste is delicious.

"Fuck, that's good." I take another drink. "What is it?"

Eden gives a pleased look. "A mix that I created based on what they'd have drunk in Jane Austen's books in Georgian England. They went to teahouses in Bath to meet up in their versions of dates. I thought that it'd be romantic."

A warm feeling spreads through me. "It is. This is very special."

"My brother always makes a bloody good cup of tea," Shay says, happily.

I take a deep breath of the tea's fruity aromas. "I'm adding it to your list of talents." Eden looks even more pleased. "I know that you said you wouldn't be D'Angelo's butler, but look at that, a position has just opened up to be mine. Would you consider…?"

"I'll take it," Eden replies.

Eden replied so fast, when normally he takes a while to weigh his words, that I have an inkling that this role-play is one of the fantasies on the list that D'Angelo stamped **CONFIDENTIAL** in the Guide.

Eden places down the teapot, before striding around the table to sit on the opposite side. "Did you get Shay's text? I got the idea from my brother that the point of our…" He gestures at his bow tie. "…was that only we were naked. The clothed and unclothed. Now we look like three naked butlers and a maid."

"I'm no one's butler." D'Angelo tears off a piece of muffin and munches on it. "And our mobiles aren't waterproof. I was too busy making Robyn come...four times... to look at texts."

"Four times?" Shay humps against me in a distracting way. "I'll simply have to work hard to make her come again."

"Fuck..." I turn to lick across the seam of his lips, before kissing him.

When I open my eyes, Shay's are glassy.

He smiles, tracing circles on my thigh.

He nuzzles against my neck, and I sigh in delight at the sensation.

D'Angelo watches us together, dropping to run his hand along his cock in feather-light strokes. He's already getting hard again.

"What was the text?" How does D'Angelo manage to sound so coolly unaffected?

Eden cocks his head. "I don't know what it meant. Shay only wrote four letters: GNRN."

Shay's chuckle sends delicious vibrations against my skin, where he's still nuzzling my neck.

At last, he raises his head.

"Get naked right now," he purrs seductively in explanation.

Eden looks taken aback, before his gaze shoots to D'Angelo. "Did you want to poke the bear?"

"Maybe," Shay says, mischievously.

He so does.

When I glance at D'Angelo's dangerous expression, I realize that he already has.

D' Angelo stands up and towers over us. "Giving me orders...? That's your first mistake, cucciolo."

"Only my first...? Awesome, I'm doing better than I thought I was."

I can't hold back the giggle.

Whoops, now D'Angelo's dark look is directed at me as well. "And that's *your* first mistake, principessa."

"Hey, she can't be in trouble for finding me funny." Shay slips me off his lap onto the bench, passing me a strawberry as if in consolation.

He slides across the bench and stands to kiss D'Angelo in apology, even though we all know that he's only playing at us being in trouble.

I think.

I dip the strawberry into the runny honey, before shoving the whole thing into my mouth

Eden stares at me. "Now you do look like Puck, my squirrel. Your cheeks are puffed up. Cute."

I blush and struggle to swallow.

"Thanks," I squeak.

D'Angelo slips his hand onto the hollow of Shay's back, and Shay rests his head on D'Angelo's shoulder.

"Do you like my bow tie?" Shay presses a small kiss to D'Angelo's collarbone. "I thought that we had to be loyal to Bay Rebels."

"Very smart." D'Angelo winks at Eden. "Presentable."

"You're getting media savvy," I reply. "On brand even as naked butlers."

"We learned from the best, love." Shay leans into D'Angelo's touch, as he pets his hair.

Standing together like this, it's obvious how much taller D'Angelo is.

When Eden fidgets, which is unusual for him, my gaze shoots to him.

Then he pushes something toward me, which has been laid out behind the pots of jam and spreads.

Confused, I reach for the book, then my eyes widen with understanding.

It's a thin, pretty book that looks like a hockey strategy book in arctic blue and white with lines, arrows, and arcs on the front.

There's also a crude puck and hockey stick.

It's my Guide.

I don't speak because I've become better at judging Eden's silences.

Sometimes, he takes some time to work out how he wants to phrase something or maybe, to put the words together.

What he wants to say appears to be important to him. I give him the time that he needs.

"I added something to my ten reasons." Eden looks down.

Concerned, I flip open the Guide to the page with the <u>Ten Reasons I Love Robyn.</u>

My favorite purple glitter pen rests in the middle of the book.

I scan down the reasons. "Nine, she's smart and funny. Ten, I can't imagine a future without her in it…"

Then I notice that Eden's added a number eleven with my glitter pen:

11. With her, I have a voice.

My eyes burn with tears. "I love you. I have more than eleven reasons why. I don't even know how many. I couldn't write them down. But you know what…?"

I snatch up the pen, before turning over onto a fresh page.

Then I write on the top of the page:

A GUIDE TO LOVING HOCKEY PLAYERS

"This should be the guide not only to dating but loving hockey players." I glance around at the three men in this room who have come to mean so much to me. "Simply because you're no longer playing hockey doesn't mean that it's no longer in your blood or your voice, Eden. Once a player, always a player." I reach across the table to entwine his fingers with mine. "My player."

Shay raises his head from D'Angelo's shoulder. "I added stuff too. Do mine now, love."

Why do I think that Shay's may not be as romantic as Eden's is?

"It's at the back of the book," Eden helpfully points out.

Wait, isn't that where Shay has his list of kinks that he wants to try out, including marks out of ten?

I flip to the back of the book.

Yep, there's the list with a complex scoring system that looks like the football scores.

"I circled my choice for tonight." Shay is vibrating with

excitement, and it's only D'Angelo's arms that are now looped around his waist that appear to be stopping him from bouncing on the spot.

What is it going to be?

I can't wait to find out.

CHAPTER TWENTY-NINE

Captain's Hall, Freedom

Robyn

I STUDY the Guide and grin, when I see that Shay's circled, underlined, and starred in his enthusiasm his choice of kink to share with me tonight: orgasm control and edging.

"Controlling your orgasms or mine?" I check.

"Mine." The tips of Shay's ears redden.

I settle more comfortably on the bench. The sweet smells of fresh bread and pastries cocoon me in the low lit kitchen.

Eden's sitting opposite me as still as a gorgeous gargoyle.

D'Angelo's eyes light up. "Dangerous choice, when you've been such a brat. I'm looking forward to this, cucciolo. Your cock is mine tonight."

"Ours," I correct.

Shay shivers.

He likes that.

"First," D'Angelo says, "it's important that I understand what you love about this. How does it make you feel? Why does it bring you pleasure?"

Shay looks confused. "No one's asked me that before."

D'Angelo's expression clouds.

He reaches to hold Shay firmly by the back of the neck. "They should have done. And I am. I want this to be a chance to prove that we're not the same as Blythe or anyone else in your life who has used you without respecting your limits and boundaries, abusing your trust. Can you be my good boy and communicate with me like I need?"

Shay's pupils dilate at the *good boy*. "Anything for you, darlin'."

His gaze darts to me like he wants to be certain that I'm truly listening to this as well.

And I am.

We need this.

We're not trapped in the dark of our pasts.

Even if people try to drag us back into the shadows, we can escape into the light of our present. We have each other and we'll always support each other.

Only, sometimes physical touch and closeness work more than words to show that.

Shay needs touch and sensation, as much as his brother struggles with it.

The difference is that Shay won the bet and is in control of everything that's happening tonight. He's sharing something precious with us.

He has the power here; he's not the powerless one, bound and sobbing.

If he sobs, then it'll be with pleasure.

"I want to understand," I say, quietly. "Because I'm going to run my fingers and tongue all over your body, until you're begging to come, and I want to know what that's going to do to you."

"Fuck." Shay's hips buck at my words alone, and I give a smug smile. "Do you want me to come already by your voice alone, love?"

Yes...

D'Angelo tightens his hold on Shay's neck to the point of pain, but that only makes him buck his hips again. "Coming is a privilege. One that I'll take away if you don't behave."

Shay's eyes become even glassier, as his chest heaves. "Yes, Sir."

D'Angelo and I exchange a glance.

Shay truly does love this.

"Speak to me," D'Angelo says, more gently. "And all of you, remember your safe words."

Shay licks his plush lips. "I love that my pleasure is in someone else's hands; that I've given up that much control to someone who I trust. Being teased and then denied, over and over…it's intense. Then when I finally come, it's like this tidal wave hits. But the best thing is having someone *say* that I can come and knowing that I can't, unless I have their permission."

I stare at him.

I get it now, and hell, the way that he explains it, I want to try that sometime too. I've played around with it in small ways but never to the degree that he's describing.

It sounds incredible.

"Who do you want to have the power? To give you the permission?" D'Angelo asks.

Shay's gaze becomes unexpectedly shy but darts between D'Angelo and me. "I'm both your pets. Robyn and you are my world — my everything. My cock's at your mercy. You're my gods."

My breath hitches.

D'Angelo's shoulders straighten like Shay's belief in him has given him strength.

I stand up, desperate suddenly to be closer to all my men.

I'm going to ruin Shay in the best way.

It's intoxicating to be handed power like this but know that it's going to bring your lover pleasure.

Shay's gaze darkens with desire, as I prowl toward him. "Fuck, love, you look like a deadly tiger prowling toward its prey…"

I flick my damp, red hair over my shoulder. "I'm actually a squirrel. Be afraid."

Eden's lips twitch like I've almost got him to smile,

which is as precious to me as anything that's happened tonight.

It always is.

Shay waves excitedly at his brother. "Come on, you know where the ropes are."

"Ropes...? You want to be tied and teased?" I reach Shay, and D'Angelo shoves him roughly into my arms.

Shay nearly overbalances but catches himself by looping his arms around my neck. "Hey, love."

His lips brush mine.

I can feel our combined, fast heartbeats and the warmth of our bare skin, as we're pressed together.

Out of the corner of my eye, I watch Eden stand to the far end of the long table, which is suspiciously empty of food and plates.

Huh, I should have noticed that. Clearly I won't be getting my sexy detective badge yet.

Eden ducks down and lifts a length of scarlet, silk rope that must be tied to the table leg.

Instantly, I can imagine what it will look like bound around Shay's ice white wrists. Heat rushes through me.

This is definitely a treat for me...as well as D'Angelo who looks like he's ready to devour us.

"Prepared, huh?" I quirk my brow.

"Like a Boy Scout." Holding the rope like that, Eden couldn't look less like a Scout. "There are ropes tied to the table legs on the other side for his legs."

"At least if I'm in bondage, you won't have to punish me for moving around, fidgeting, or breaking shit," Shay says with a grin. "I did have time to set this up, since you had the longest shower with Mr. Started the Night Without Us…"

I knew that would bite D'Angelo in the ass.

"Careful," D'Angelo growls. "I hold your orgasm in my hands."

Shay scrunches up his nose. "That sounds messy."

I tug Shay toward the table, and D'Angelo stalks after us.

I trace my hand over Shay's wrist as I drag him. I imagine the way that the silk will caress his skin, while it holds him in place.

I can't wait.

"Don't I get something soft to lie on?" Shay complains. "Dee, weren't you going to put a tablecloth down?"

Eden is stony-faced. "I'm not spoiling a tablecloth. Lie down."

Shay opens his mouth, shocked that his brother isn't backing him up, before he tugs out of my hold and lies on his back dramatically on the table.

He looks like a sacrifice with his hands above his head.

"Hell, you're edible," I murmur.

He's more of a feast than the food that's laid out next to him.

When Shay's gaze meets mine, his expression softens.

He lays his head down. "Come eat then."

D'Angelo strides past me. "If you insist."

He swaggers around the table, taking the rope from Eden.

I watch mesmerized at the way that D'Angelo pulls Shay's wrists together, massaging over them for a moment like he can't resist, before looping the rope around them. Then he weaves a pattern around them that's beautiful.

The ropework is like art.

Eden is studying D'Angelo intently as he works.

He's as fascinated as I am.

Does D'Angelo know more complex ropework than this? I'd love him to do such beautiful, loving bondage on me sometime.

D'Angelo glances up at me and catches my flushed cheeks. His expression becomes thoughtful like he's trying to work out whether it's because I'm turned on by seeing Shay having his hands tied, or whether it's because I'm wishing that it was *me* being bound, stretched out, and powerless, in Shay's position.

Actually, it's *both*.

"Fetch scissors from the kitchen," D'Angelo directs Eden, "and put them in reach, in case we need to cut him out quickly."

Eden nods and moves around the table toward the cabinets.

D'Angelo finishes his work, slipping his finger underneath the silk to check that it's not too tight and won't bruise. Then he ducks his head and his curls fall forward, as he kisses Shay quickly.

"Okay, cucciolo?" He says far more gently than I normally hear him speak to Shay.

It's intimate on a whole new level.

It's not sexual or even romantic.

It's caring.

"Better than I've been in a long time," Shay replies.

Why do I think he's not only talking about how he's feeling right now?

"Good." D'Angelo rests his strong hand over Shay's hand. "And soon, Robyn and I will make you feel even better than that. Of course, before then, I'm going to fucking wreck you."

"Looking forward to it, darlin'." Shay arches up, as if begging for D'Angelo or me to pay attention to his dick that's already hard against his stomach.

"Lie flat," D'Angelo commands, sternly.

Then he edges around the table.

"What now?" I ask.

D'Angelo cups my cheek; his thumb traces my lips. "Now we show our pet that we control his pleasure. Also, that he can trust us to keep him safe, even when he's at his most helpless."

"I could watch you tie up people all day. It's breathtaking. Can I help?"

D'Angelo shoots me a cocky grin. "Come on."

He ducks down. Then he snatches Shay's ankle, as if Shay's no more than a doll, and yanks it closer to the table leg.

Shay lets out a grunt that transforms into a moan, when he feels the silk rope looping around his ankle and binding it in place with intricate knots.

D'Angelo weaves the knots as elegantly as he plays the piano.

"Pass me the rope from the far side," he instructs.

I grab the rope that's bound to the table leg on the opposite side.

"Spread your legs as far as they will go." D'Angelo taps Shay's inner thigh.

Shay wiggles his hips on the edge of the cold table, spreading his legs. This must be a stress position to be bound on his back on the table but pulled taut like this.

I'm impressed that he's able to hold it.

He looks like a bound god.

Yet he thinks that I'm *his* goddess.

Shay's wrists are bound together with his palms held together, as if in prayer. Yet D'Angelo pulls his legs wide apart, until his thigh muscles quiver.

Good for access.

"Wider." D'Angelo taps Shay's thigh harder, and Shay obeys with difficulty.

At last, D'Angelo ties Shay's final ankle in place, checking that the rope isn't too tight.

Eden places the scissors down on the table with a thump.

Shay's panting now.

His muscles look impossibly strained. He's laid taut across the table.

D'Angelo stands, smoothing his hand along Shay's trembling thigh. "Will you be able to maintain this position?"

Shay's already sweating. "It's difficult, but I'm green. Also, I'm grateful for the hockey warmups that have made me this flexible."

"So am I." I smirk, leaning over to trace my finger down his crack, delighting at his shocked intake of breath.

I let out a surprised breath myself, when D'Angelo twirls me and kisses me deeply.

His dick is hard against me.

I realize that this is the first time that we've been like this together — naked at the same time.

Normally, D'Angelo is dressed in a suit or pajamas.

He tries to keep one layer or barrier between us, which allows him to hide how affected he is.

This time, however, we're equally stripped and vulnerable.

None of us can hide and we don't want to.

"Time to tease our pet." D'Angelo pulls me between Shay's spread legs.

Before I can reach to touch Shay again, however, Eden's arm loops around my waist from behind and splays across my hip.

"And time for me to tease *you*." Eden kisses down my neck.

D'Angelo arches his brow. "Color?"

"Green," I moan, as Eden strokes down toward my clit but stops short just above, tapping teasingly.

This is what I needed, Eden's touch as well.

My gaze is hazy, as D'Angelo leans over Shay to tweak at his nipples, thumbing over them, until they're rosy and peaked.

Shay attempts to twist away, his breathing labored, but he's tied so tightly that he can't escape from D'Angelo's tormenting touch.

Then D'Angelo kisses down Shay's neck at the same time that Eden kisses mine.

My legs feel weak. I balance with one hand against the table, while I wrap the other around Shay's cock.

Shay whines. "Bloody hell…"

There's enough pre-cum already that I don't worry about lube. I twist around the sensitive head of Shay's cock, before I start pumping him firmly.

He's trying to buck his hips, as his legs jerk against his bonds, but he can't move.

D'Angelo growls, biting Shay's neck in retaliation. "Lie still. Take it."

Shay stills, but his breaths are labored.

His eyes flutter closed.

Eden kisses my neck in earnest, sweeping my hair to the side. I can feel his hard dick nudging at my ass.

"He's not begging yet," Eden urges. "Work harder."

Shay's eyes snap opened, outraged. "Bastard."

D'Angelo's eyes flash. "Someone clearly wants to be punished."

Shay looks panicked. "Sorry, sorry, I meant…*traitor*."

I chuckle and I'm certain that I hear Eden hiding his own laugh against my neck.

D'Angelo's look is dangerous, however, as he stalks to his feet next to me. As punishment, while I continue to stroke Shay's cock, D'Angelo fondles his balls. The dual assault makes Shay flush with pleasure.

It's the type of punishment that Shay deserves every day.

His nipples are dusky rose where D'Angelo has pinched them.

Tied down like this beneath me, I can see Shay's nuances of expressions.

In the throes of denied ecstasy, he's devastatingly handsome.

How have I lived without him in my life?

Without this?

"I'm close..." Shay gasps. "*Please...*"

"He's begging," Eden points out.

"Please what?" D'Angelo draws his finger below Shay's balls to his taint, pressing hard.

"Please let me come."

D'Angelo and I nod at each other, before removing our hands from Shay at exactly the same moment.

Shay wails, as his orgasm is denied.

His dick twitches like it's trying to come but can't.

"Did you really think that we'd let you come already?" D'Angelo drawls.

Eden edges his finger down to my clit circling it, and my heart speeds up. Pleasure is winding through me.

Seeing Shay's desperation to come, D'Angelo's dominance, and feeling Eden's hands on me, I'm as close to coming as Shay is.

D'Angelo draws his finger up and down Shay's cock in maddeningly light touches that make Shay whimper. "Your cock is mine. *You're mine.* And you'll never, *ever*, come by anybody's hand but ours again."

"Y-y-yours," Shay whispers, tears of frustration in his

eyes, but still struggling to speak. His gaze slides between D'Angelo and me. "Both of yours. Forever."

I almost come on the spot.

"Good boy." D'Angelo twirls his finger around the head of Shay's cock at the same time as Eden dips his finger into my pussy.

Shay and I both jump.

"Please, I need...I can't." Shay throws his head side to side. "I need—"

"Is this about what you need?" D'Angelo says coolly, removing his hands completely from Shay's cock. "Or about what I decide to give you?"

Shay sobs in desperation, but I can see how his pupils are dilated.

He's fucking turned on, but then, so am I.

Shay's muscles are tense and straining. Sweat slides down his chest.

"W-what you...y-y-you..." He can't seem to go on, gasping.

"Color?" D'Angelo asks.

"Green. But f-f-fuck, I n-n-need...please, it's too m-m-much...I'm going to come..."

"You're not, until I give you permission." D'Angelo straightens, before leaning over Shay and pressing their bodies together in a way that makes Shay shudder. Then he pushes Shay's sweaty hair out of his eyes gently, searching out his gaze as he kisses him. "Because you want to please us. You want to be our good pet, don't you?"

Shay nods, dazed.

Finally, D'Angelo smiles, before he glances around at me.

I can't hold back the moan at the way that Eden's thick finger is working in and out of my pussy in the perfect way, while he sucks at my neck.

D'Angelo looks amused. "Are you two distracted? Boring you, are we?"

Eden arches his brow. "We should tease them at the same time."

D'Angelo tilts his head. "Good plan."

He glances down at Shay's painfully hard dick. A tear runs down Shay's cheek, and D'Angelo licks it away.

Fuck, that's hot.

D'Angelo stands and steps to the side.

My gaze meets Shay's for a fleeting moment, before Eden is pushing me at the waist. Suddenly, I realize what Eden's plan is, as he bends me over the table.

I'm seriously on board.

Eden eases his fingers out of my pussy. I hear the rip of a condom, then I feel his cock nudging at my pussy, teasing back and forth.

I struggle not to squirm, as in turn, I grip Shay's cock at the base and begin to lick up and down it.

Shay makes a choked sound.

All the muscles in his body tense.

He's not going to be able to last long.

But then, I'm not going to either.

I slide Shay's cock into my mouth, suckling the head.

"Fuck, f-f-fuck, please, please, please." Shay's chanting *please* now in his desperation. "I need…"

Eden thrusts into me in one long steady thrust. His confidence to do this in front of other men impresses me.

Yet he pushes into me like we're the only two people in the world.

This can't be easy for him, but he still has the courage to join in.

I encourage him by pushing back to meet his thrusts, and he speeds up.

It's mind-blowing being caught between these twins.

When I raise off Shay's dick to stave off his orgasm yet again, I notice that D'Angelo is stroking himself.

Now, that doesn't feel fair.

I raise my hand and wave it in his direction in encouragement.

D'Angelo edges closer to me, and I grasp his large, velvety shaft, loving the feel of him in my palm.

I float then in the sensation between these three men, fucked by one, sucking another, and jerking a third off.

Yet I'm the one that connects the three men. I feel worshiped by them…loved.

Ecstasy is winding through me. I can't hold it back, even if Shay has astounding levels of self-control.

I don't.

My orgasm hits me like a tsunami

It's unexpected and mind-blowing.

I shudder, clawing my fingers into Shay's hips. I hurriedly pull off Shay, panting and gasping.

"Come, cucciolo." D'Angelo's voice is strained.

Shay's reaction is immediate.

He howls as he convulses. Unable to move much in his

bonds, he still struggles. He comes more powerfully than I've seen a guy come before, longer too.

It looks intense enough to be walking the line between pleasure and pain.

Finally, he slumps in his ropes. His chest is rising and falling.

D'Angelo moves his hand to join mine around his own cock now, directing it first to run over my lips and then toward Shay's balls. "I'm going to mark you now."

See? He may share us but D'Angelo's possessive.

"You all please me." D'Angelo's voice is shaking. "You're perfect. *So fucking good for me.*"

When he comes, pearly liquid sprays across Shay's balls, catching my chin and mouth at the same time, marking us both.

Shay gives me a sated, contented smile like he couldn't be happier.

"Robyn..." Eden's hips stutter.

Then he's coming as well, stroking his hand up and down my spine.

It's overwhelming, when I'm already oversensitive and feeling so many emotions.

Incredible.

I've never felt anything like this.

Tonight, none of us have held back.

I understand why Shay wanted to share this with me. I'm honored that he did.

Plus, when can I be the one tied to the table and teased?

I kiss Shay's hip, as Eden eases out of me. "You were amazing, Shay. I loved that."

"You did?" It looks like it's difficult for Shay to speak but he's beaming.

"I did." I wrinkle up my nose. "But I'm going to get a cloth to clean you up. Then we can have something to eat and drink from this midnight feast that Eden made and we can cuddle up in the lounge, before we go to sleep."

"I'll give you a quick massage," D'Angelo offers, "to make sure that your muscles don't ache too much tomorrow. I can also run you a hot bath before bed. Let's get you untied."

Eden moves to drop the condom in the trash.

All of a sudden, the tinny sound of The Strokes' "You Only Live Once", rings through the kitchen.

I kiss Shay's stomach. "If this is your post sex music, it hasn't got quite the right vibe."

"It's my phone." Shay is suddenly more alert.

His concern, which is dragging him out of subspace, pulls at my heartstrings, when he's still in such a vulnerable position.

"I'll answer it." D'Angelo pats him on the hip, reassuringly. "Where is it?"

"On the counter I think."

"I'm here." Eden walks back to duck beside Shay's head, taking his bound hands between his. "Would you like me to put that tablecloth over you now like a blanket?"

Shay laughs. "So, now I'm allowed it…?"

I lean over and kiss him. "Anything you want."

"Only you."

D'Angelo snatches Shay's phone off the counter and answers it. "Shay's phone. He's a little tied up right now, so if you could leave a message…"

Shay laughs, and I slam my hand over his mouth.

I turn to glare at D'Angelo, only to pale, when I realize how still he's become.

He's looking horrified.

"Coach, why are you calling so late?" D'Angelo croaks.

It's Dad…?

Shit, shit, shit.

Instinctively, I cross my hands over my pussy.

I know that Dad can't see me through the phone but I have the weird feeling that he'll somehow know that he's talking to a naked D'Angelo, while Eden and I are equally naked, and Shay is covered in cum and bound to the kitchen table.

Can you ban parents from calling you during sexy times?

"Why is he calling *my brother* so late?" Eden demands.

His expression is hard and protective.

I want to know that as well.

Dad has truly been on Shay's case this week, but after his last game, he should have eased off.

I rest my hand protectively on Shay's chest.

D'Angelo arches his brow at me, and I shake my head.

The last thing that I want to do right now is talk to Dad, especially in the happy afterglow of one of the best orgasms of my life.

I want to go into the lounge, snuggle under a blanket with Shay, and be fed a blueberry muffin by Eden.

D'Angelo's expression clouds. "So, you rang round each of us, until one of us answered because you're trying to get hold of your daughter…? Well, she's not answering your messages because she's asleep. In bed. She does need to do that occasionally. None of us can respond to you at all hours of the night and day. So, I'm tired and am going to…"

He winces like he's being yelled at.

It was a valiant effort. But what if this is important?

I sigh, holding out my hand for the phone.

D'Angelo stalks over and hands it to me.

I hold the phone up to my ear. "Hey, Dad."

"Sleeping Beauty awakes," Dad growls. "That was fast."

"I have three Prince Charmings to do the waking. What's the problem? Why do we need to talk at this hour?"

"I wanted to talk earlier, but you didn't reply to my messages."

"We were celebrating." I shift from foot to foot, as unease swirls in my stomach. "It's been a tough couple of weeks, and I needed a break from being glued to my phone."

"You're PR Director," Dad barks. "You need to know how much the story has blown up about that Melanie interview and then the victory in the game. From tomorrow, you've got to be on top of it. It's going crazy."

Suddenly alert, I nod. "I promise that I will. It is good press, right?"

"You should know that there's damn well no such thing." Dad sounds weary. "You'll be going on your first road trip with the Bay Rebels in a week. I need you to be prepared before that happens about the danger of this bullshit intense press interest."

"What's he saying?" D'Angelo mouths.

"Road trip," I whisper.

D'Angelo blinks, as confused as I am.

In a hockey season, you play some games at home and some away on road trips.

Why is that dangerous?

I've been looking forward to it.

Yet I can't help glancing between these three men who I love: the twins, who've carved out new places for themselves in my heart, and D'Angelo, who simply possesses my heart.

I'll do whatever it takes to protect them.

"I don't understand, Dad." My knuckles whiten around my phone. "Why are the away games going to be a problem? Plus, why couldn't this have waited until tomorrow?"

There's a long silence, and I don't think that he'll answer.

Then he replies, "If I left it until tomorrow, when I've come down from the high of watching that damn interview and game on repeat, then I know myself. I'd find reasons not to tell you this, and I need to. I've had a lot of time to think in the last few months. Hell, the truth is that *you* and those assholes who I know are listening, tied up or otherwise, have *made* me think about things. The way that I took out my anger on the ice ruined your childhood and that's having consequences even now."

"It is." I keep my voice steady. "To Cody as well."

"I screwed up after your mom's death. I hold my hands up to that. I barely remember that first year. It was a haze. I know that I didn't treat Cody right. Sometimes, I still don't. It's hard to see him as a man and not the boy who I raised. The problem right now is that I never thought there'd be this much press and social media scrutiny, as well as wild speculation, focused on the team or I wouldn't have dragged you back into this. But then, you're the one who was meant to be stopping scandals, remember?"

My eyes burn with tears. "I'm sorry. I tried."

"I'm not scolding you." Dad's voice hardens. "I'm explaining. After this last incident, all of our pasts will be looked into. Simply because Melanie is locked up, doesn't mean that the press or anyone else will leave us alone. And this road trip…hell, the shit is going to hit the fan. I can't protect you. Every dark family secret will be exposed."

I become ashen.

Terror grips me.

D'Angelo sweeps toward me, wrapping me in his arms. "We're here with you, principessa. Whatever it is, we've got you."

We've survived this opening to the season.

We've defeated Melanie.

And we've conquered the demons from our pasts.

Now, together we need to face this pucking road trip.

Want to know what happens to Robyn and her men on the hockey road trip?
Continue the Bay Rebels adventure in PUCKING ROAD TRIP by clicking HERE!

https://rosemaryajohns.com
MERCHANDISE AND SIGNED BOOKS
Go to: http://www.rosemaryajohnsbooks.com

Thanks for reading **SECRETLY PUCKING**! If you enjoyed reading this book, **please consider leaving a review on Amazon.** Your support is really important to us authors. Plus, I love hearing from my readers!
Thanks, you're awesome!
Rosemary A Johns

CLICK NOW to sign up to Rosemary A Johns' Rebel Newsletter and receive these special perks: promotions, exclusive teasers and art about the Bay Rebels and Pack Bonds worlds, and hot releases before anyone else.

PUCKING ROAD TRIP

WHAT TO READ NEXT: PUCKING ROAD TRIP BAY REBELS!

Three NHL hockey players. One second chance. And a PR nightmare.

Word to the wise, never go on a road trip with your forbidden lovers. Especially when they lose everything, if they don't win the season. Doubly, when you're the coach's daughter.

Why did I? Because I'm their live-in PR.

I'm also madly in love with these men who have bodies like gods. And they're obsessed with me.

The tall, dark, and grumpy captain. The star forward with spellbinding gray eyes and golden retriever energy. And his tattooed, protective PA twin.

Forced to share a tour bus and hotel rooms, the tension is as explosive off the ice as on it. Will we survive, however, when a dangerous secret from our past catches up with us?

On this pucking road trip, I may not be able to wear my men's jerseys to games but I'm desperate to be forever theirs.

PUCKING ROAD TRIP is a why choose hockey romance by USA Today bestselling author, Rosemary A Johns.

TROPES:
- Pro Hockey Romance
- Why Choose
- Forced Proximity
- Second Chance
- Found Family
- Men obsessed
- Grumpy/Sunshine
- Forbidden romance
- Road Trip

PUCK & HER BLADES ICE HOCKEY ROMANCE

YOUR NEXT WHY CHOOSE ICE HOCKEY ROMANCE WITH AN OMEGAVERSE TWIST, PUCK AND HER BLADES!

Something is really wrong.

This is more than stress catching up with me or sweating in this hockey mascot suit. More than going down with the flu.

Is this my first heat, hitting me unexpectedly?

But how's this possible?

Please, *please*, don't let this be happening now, during such an important game, when I've made a promise not to distract my Alphas.

I have to leave.

"Cygnus, I need a break," I call to the beautiful male Omega, not caring about breaking the number one rule not to talk in the suit.

He nods.

Right now, nothing matters but getting out of the arena, before I wreck this game.

Thank fuck I'm wearing a pheromone blocker, or it wouldn't only be the game that would be in danger. With thousands of Alphas surrounding me, and still being officially unbonded, it'd be dangerous for me as well.

The Beta bodyguards are looking at me, uncertainly.

Since I'm hidden inside the costume, no one else can tell what's going on yet.

Then my pussy gushes with wetness, and I know that it's too late.

My first heat is here. There's nothing that I can do to stop it.

No...

Cygnus turns to look at me, alarmed.

His pretty violet eyes widen in alarm. "What's wrong, treasure?"

I stagger forward, stumbling into the boards with a loud clatter. The glass shakes.

Asher, the star Beta player, misses his step himself at the sound. His gaze catches on mine.

Cygnus is desperately trying to pull me back upright, before I crumple to the ground.

Asher can make this shot.

He can win the game.

To my shock, instead he abandons the puck and changes his direction on the ice. He nods his head at Jackson and Zev, our two Alphas, who turn to glance over at me as well.

Then all three players abandon the most important game of their lives and skate across the rink toward me.

The crowd is in uproar.

My mind is fuzzy. I'm raked with tremors. I can't think.

I can hear the coach's furious yelling.

The Blades are throwing the game for me.

They've lost.

We're all dead.

Then my eyes flutter closed, and everything fades to black...

KEEP READING PUCK AND HER BLADES HERE!

ABOUT THE AUTHOR

ROSEMARY A JOHNS is a USA Today bestselling and award-winning romance, omegaverse, and fantasy romance author. She writes sexy shifters and immortals, swoonworthy book boyfriends, and addictive romance.

Winner of the Silver Award in the National Wishing Shelf Book Awards. Finalist in the IAN Book of the Year Awards. Winner in the Best Indie Book of the Year Awards. Runner-up in the Best Fantasy Book of the Year, Reality Bites Book Awards. Honorable Mention in the Readers' Favorite Book Awards. Shortlisted in the International Rubery Book Awards.

Rosemary is also a traditionally published short story writer. She studied history at Oxford University and ran her own theater company. She's always been a rebel…

Thanks for leaving a review. You're awesome!

Want to read more and stay up to date on Rosemary's newest releases? **Sign up for her *VIP* Rebel Newsletter and get FREE novellas!**

Have you read Rosemary A Johns' Contemporary Romance?
Elite
One Secret Rule
Darling Madness
Being Pucked, Bay Rebels
<u>**Secretly Pucking, Bay Rebels**</u>
Pucking Road Trip, Bay Rebels
Rebel & Her Knights
Ember & Her Marshals
Angel & Her Champions
Jewel & Her Kings
Puck & Her Blades
Mercy & Her Devils
Candy & Her Saints

Have you read all the series in the Rebel Verse by Rosemary A Johns?

Rebel Demons
Rebel Academy
Rebel Gods
Rebel Werewolves
Rebel: House of Fae
Rebel Angels

Shadowmates
Rebel Vampires
Rebel Legends

Have you read all the series in the Oxford Verse?

Biting Mr. Darcy
Hexing Merlin
A Familiar Murder
A Familiar Curse
A Familiar Hex
A Familiar Brew
A Familiar Ghost
A Familiar Spell
A Familiar Yule
A Familiar Bride

Read More from Rosemary A Johns
Website
Merchandise
Facebook
Instagram
TikTok
Bookbub
Twitter: @RosemaryAJohns

Become a Rebel here today by joining Rosemary's Rebels Group on Facebook!

APPENDIX ONE: BAY REBELS MEMBERS

PLAYERS
Jude D'Angelo, Captain, Center
Shay Prince, Right Wing
Grayson, Left Wing
Atlas, Right Defenseman
Lucas, Left Defenseman
Zach, Goaltender

COACHES
Austin McKenna, Head Coach
Colton, Assistant Coach
Goalie Coach
Strength and Conditioning Coach

TEAM SUPPORT AND OPERATIONS/MANAGEMENT
Robyn McKenna, Austin's daughter, PR Director
Eden Prince, Shay's twin, D'Angelo's PA

Operations Manager, Felix
Finance Manager, Silas Anderson
Senior Board Member, William Bronwyn
Equipment Manager

MEDICAL SUPPORT

Cody McKenna, Austin's son, Director of Physical Therapy
Noah Anderson, Team Nurse
Team Doctor
Sports Therapist
Nutritionist
Psychologist
Massage Therapist
Mental Skills Coach

APPENDIX TWO: FRIENDS, FAMILY, OR ENEMIES

Doctor Michael Gaines, Cody's husband, Doctor at Freedom Heart Hospital

Neve, owner of Merchant's Inn

Tom, bartender in Merchant's Inn

Blythe, Shay's ex-Domme

Melanie Helt, journalist at Peninsula Daily News

Wilder Talon, Robyn's ex-husband, player at Pittsburgh Penguins

Maria, D'Angelo's sister

Bruno, D'Angelo's brother

Mr. and Mrs. Prince, Shay and Eden's adoptive parents

Maddan, rival defenseman

Garcia, D'Angelo's friend and PI